Once Upon A
Mulberry
Field

A NOVEL

To Yenny,

C. L. Hoàng

Chúc Mừng Chị,

C. L. Hoàng

WSP
Willow Stream Publishing
San Diego

Once Upon A Mulberry Field
by C. L. Hoàng

Published in the United States by Willow Stream Publishing
willowstreampublishing@gmail.com

ISBN (paperback): 978-0-9899756-7-4
ISBN (e-book): 978-0-9899756-8-1

Library of Congress Control Number: 2013950346

Cover design: Derek Murphy
Interior layout: Nick Zelinger

First Edition

In loving memory of my parents
who lived through it all with untold courage and grace

Mulberry fields forever
　Where the blue sea once was . . .
A new season of upheaval
　Has cloaked my heart in sorrow

—Nguyễn Du, Vietnamese poet (1766–1820)

Preface

One of my favorite authors is Jack London. It has been said that while growing up in a portside neighborhood of West Oakland, California, in the late 1800s, the future writer would hang around a local saloon called Heinold's First and Last Chance, listening to sailors and journeymen recount their adventures. Those eavesdropped yarns left a lasting impression on young Jack and later inspired him to an adventurous life of his own. Many of the tales found their way into the great novels that would propel him to worldwide fame.

Few of us are born to such glorious destiny. But we all remember our own First and Last Chance, that special place in our childhood – at the knee of a grandparent, at the family's dining table, or in the classroom—where we first came to learn about life through fascinating stories of love, courage, and occasionally, sorrow. Stories that would stay with us the rest of our days and influence our lives in more ways than we could have imagined.

My early memories of my childhood in Sài-Gòn during the Việt-Nam War were filled with tales of a different kind: the real-life stories of struggle and survival and, more often than not, of death and destruction. The tentacles of war had touched virtually every family in our homeland. It was a reality from which no one could hide, not even children.

When I came to America in the mid-1970s at the end of the war, those memories were buried under the day-to-day demands of a new life and lay dormant for the next three decades. Until, as a nostalgia project for my dad, who was up in years and ailing, I began to scour the Internet for old photographs and writings about our former hometown—Sài-Gòn in the 1950s, '60s and early '70s. Before I knew it, a bygone world had reopened its door and pulled me in.

As my father and I reminisced about that forgotten place and time we had once shared and the people, events, and stories that had defined it for us, it occurred to me that I should write down those recollections. First, as a legacy of family history for upcoming generations. And second, as my way of bearing witness to the period of upheaval that had seen our family transplanted to a new continent.

To ensure historical accuracy, I would do in-depth research on the documented Việt-Nam War before putting pen to paper. Little did I suspect that in the process I would open another door. Through various websites and published memoirs by American veterans who had served in Việt-Nam and through my conversations with some of them, I caught a revealing glimpse into their experiences. These voices of truth, lost in the political cacophony of the time, all contributed to an oral history that should be heard—and preserved, for the veterans' families and for those still in search of answers.

It was my wish to bring together those two very distinct yet complementary accounts of the war: the personal stories of the native people who had suffered through it, and the life-changing ordeal for the participants from a distant land. But instead of compiling a collection of disparate anecdotes, I felt it better to weave them into a single, coherent narrative around a cast of fictional characters. And despite the background of turmoil and violence, I knew from the outset I did not want to write a "war book." In my heart, *Once upon a Mulberry Field* is first and foremost a love story—an ode to the old and the new homelands, and a celebration of the human spirit and the redemptive power of love. In an attempt to be objective and to view things from a perspective different from the one I had known growing up, I chose to recount the events through the voice of an American soldier. Needless to say, it was an eye-opening experience.

As I'm putting the finishing touches on this six-year labor of love, my thoughts drift to the fallen victims of the Việt-Nam War and to the millions of others whose lives were affected by it, or for that matter, by any armed conflict. This book is dedicated to all of them.

San Diego, California
December 2013
C. L. Hoàng

PART I

"What Beck'ning Ghost"*

San Diego, California
September 1999

*Alexander Pope (1688-1744)

Chapter One

It's a given. Most of us don't get to choose the timing of our own demise.

But if presented with the option when such time nears, would we step up, seize our last remaining privilege, and decide how graceful our final bow will be?

On this brilliant afternoon of the last summer of the millennium, I feel exhilarated and free, having reached my decision on this ponderous matter.

Life at Whispering Palms Senior Community carries on as before—a steady succession of leisure routines occasionally interrupted by nonevents. Laughter streams into the men's locker room from the swimming pool. I can hear bodies thrashing about in the water, followed by the patter of wet footsteps chasing one another down to the whirlpool, then the swooshing of the hot bath swirling on. Another day in paradise, as members of the mission-style clubhouse often remark with contented smiles, in between nodding off on lounge chairs in the hot, dry breeze of Southern California.

A shadow moves past my locker toward the exit. Glancing up, I rush after the old man before he stumbles, stark naked and dripping wet, into the harsh sunlight.

"Al, buddy," I say, grasping his elbow.

"But I showered," he protests.

"Your swim trunks. You need to put them on."

He looks bewildered for a moment before a blush shows under his tanned wrinkles.

I let go of his elbow, and he lumbers back to his locker. Poor Al, never quite the same since his wife died last year. After he is properly suited, we traipse out to the whirlpool in silence.

Long, airy corridors under red-tiled roofs encircle the pool court-yard. Above them rises the decorative bell tower, almost as tall as the swaying palms that give the neighborhood its name. Not a wisp of cloud threatens the sparkling sky, and aside from the mournful cries of a dove, time hangs still. Such an idyllic setting. A tranquil harbor for old ships, albeit one that can't keep out the undertows of life.

"Well, looky here!" A girlish voice greets us as we tiptoe into the bubbling bath. "Hello, Al. Hi, Doc. Where've you been?" My neighbor Margaret slides over, leaning against the man seated next to her. He stretches his arm around her ample shoulders and makes room, causing mini-waves of steamy water to bounce off my chest.

"This is my boyfriend, Buster."

The balding man half rises and reaches out with his big hand. A scar several inches long runs down the middle of his heavy chest. He must be a visitor; I haven't seen him around before.

"Buster didn't believe me when I said I live next door to Marcus Welby, M.D. See, hon? Isn't he Robert Young in person? And just as sweet, too. I'm sure he wouldn't mind if you chatted with him sometime about your bypass." Margaret smiles at me. "Would you, Doc?"

I smile back, shaking my head. Once a doctor, never a retired doctor. Nowhere is this truer than in a community like ours, where the "active adult" residents periodically drop out of commission, sometimes for good, due to any combination of ailments. Also true is the two-to-one ratio by which the ladies routinely outlast their counterparts, which makes single gents at Whispering Palms even more popular than in their heydays.

"Three months already since they fixed him up," Margaret chirps. "And he's doing better every day. Lots of TLC, my Buster needs." There is tenderness in Margaret's little-girl voice as she snuggles closer to the stocky man. For a moment, they remind me of sweet young loves in high school. Here, away from teenage grandchildren and the need to project an exemplary air of propriety, the elderly couples are free to act as young as their hearts feel.

"Been out of town again, Doc?" She tilts her head coquettishly in my direction.

"Until today," I say. "I went backpacking in the Sierra. Beautiful up there this time of year. It was like going home for me."

It was a trip home. After taking leave of my doctor last week, I rushed back to my house with one intention: to gather my camping gear, get the hell out of there, and escape to the mountains—my secluded mountains. That was also what Dr. Graham recommended as we shook hands on my way out of his office.

"You should take some time and get away, think about what I proposed. Surgery can take care of most of the mass in your left lung. Then we'll follow up with radiation. Maybe a little chemo to wrap up."

He caught me off guard when he placed his free hand on my shoulder. "You recognize, of course, that we won't know for certain until we operate. But it looks promising. Keep me apprised of your decision. Good day, Dr. Connors."

For a full week I climbed rocks, hiked in the sun, pitched my tent, and cooked freeze-dried meals. When tired, I stopped by a stream to read or daydream. But I made my choice that first night in the mountains while I rested my sore back and stared out the screened roof of my tent at the shimmering skies above. Staring back were my wife's eyes from years ago, hollow from exhaustion yet still questioning, as she'd slowly but steadily lost ground in her battle with breast cancer. Had it all been worthwhile, the disfiguring surgery followed by rounds of chemotherapy that had left her retching her guts out, sobbing from depression? Not once had she complained, but toward the end it was all too clear she'd been hanging on solely for my sake. In the gray daybreak that highlighted the jagged peaks looming all around, I sat up in my one-man tent and realized, clear-eyed and with a surprising sense of detachment, that I didn't have a single person in this wide world to hang tough for.

Margaret's voice rises over the rumbling hot bath as she playfully wags her finger at me, "Dottie tried to call you, but your answering machine wasn't on, mister." Bless her heart. No one keeps abreast of the goings-on the way Margaret does, even now with her busy social calendar.

"I must've forgotten to set it. Was it something urgent, did she say?"

I sometimes wonder if I am doing a disservice to the single ladies at Whispering Palms, including Dottie, my neighbor on the other side, by responding to their frequent pleas for assistance. Their lonely struggles with the aggravations of daily existence must be disconcerting, I reckon, from a stopped-up sink to a dead car battery or a stuck closet door. Far worse, however, are the times they're startled awake at night, alone in bed, dead convinced that some prowlers are scratching at their back doors or that their own thumping hearts are under imminent attack. But loneliness is a devious intruder with multiple disguises they'd do best to confront on their own. Often, though, their phone calls for help are mere pretenses to invite me over for coffee and homemade pie on their patios overlooking the communal green, yet they still send me home later with a steamy casserole as a token of their appreciation for my "trouble." Margaret was as guilty as the rest until she began dating her new boyfriend recently.

"Someone's been wanting to get hold of you, Doc. All week long." There's an inquisitive note in Margaret's voice she does not bother to conceal. "*A man.*"

Her excitement is understandable, given that my wife and I led a quiet life, which has grown even quieter for me after she passed. I no longer claim any living relations, at least none who stays in touch, and the few couples we knew have drifted away since her death.

"He left word for you, with Dottie," Margaret says. Then, with a discreet glance in Al's direction, she whispers, "Is everything okay, Doc?"

"Must be the IRS catching up with me." I wink at my well-meaning neighbor and wade toward the steps. "If you'll excuse me now, lady and gentlemen. Time to get back into the swing of things."

A man? Someone from Doctor Graham's office?

———◯

Dottie looks pleased when she opens her door and finds me standing in the shade of her covered patio. "My, my. To what do I owe this nice surprise?"

She points me to a wicker chair on the patio before disappearing inside to bring us back some iced tea. Health-conscious thin, fastidiously coiffed and made up, she moves with the brisk efficiency of a former doctor's office nurse. We exchange pleasantries, then I bring up the main reason for my visit.

"I saw Margaret earlier. She mentioned I missed some mysterious visitor?"

"Indeed you did." Dottie leans in closer and lowers her voice. "He must have stopped by every day while you were gone—kept circling the place and knocking on your door. I also caught him peeking inside your windows. Your car was gone, but I called to alert you anyway."

"And I had my answering machine turned off. Sorry, Dottie."

She reaches and pats my arm. "We neighbors have to watch out for each other, you know. Especially Margaret staying out with her boyfriend all hours . . ." She falls quiet, seeming to pursue a private thought.

I drink my iced tea and wait.

"Ah, yes. Your friend. Sometimes he'd stop back later in the day. I was very concerned, so I kept an eye on him the best I could. I was all set to call nine-one-one. In case."

"What did he look like?"

"He was a big man. Six feet or taller, quite robust looking. I imagined he'd have no trouble kicking in your door if he chose to. Short-cropped silver hair. A catch in his step—more like a limp, actually. I was an absolute ball of nerves."

The warm Santa Ana winds have died down and the sun has dipped behind the hills, the dwindling twilight now a balmy evening.

Her eyes bright with excitement, Dottie continues. "And Doc, he came knocking on my door yesterday! I got a good look at him. There was a ruggedness about him, but he sure was easy on the eye, if I dare say so myself. And what a smile. A charmer." Her hand moves to her heart. "He said he'd noticed me watching, and he apologized if he had caused me concern."

Dottie leans back in her chair and sighs wistfully, while I rack my brains to recall any acquaintance who may fit that description.

"He asked when you would be back. I was so rattled I could barely get a sentence out. Then he reached in his pocket and handed me an envelope."

She disappears into the house, soon reemerging with a letter. She gives it to me with an apologetic frown. "Your friend was out of here before I could glean more information for you. I'm sorry, Doc. He got me all flustered."

It's an ivory-colored envelope with the name of a nationwide hotel chain printed in gold letters in the upper left-hand corner. In the center, my name is scrawled in blue ink in strong handwriting. Sealed, the envelope feels light, almost empty.

"You did fine, Dottie," I say. "Thank you so much."

She beams, and as I rise to leave she places a hand on my arm.

"Hang on. You probably don't have time to cook, just getting back today and all. I have some fresh lasagna I want to send home with you."

The handwriting on the envelope looks bold and masculine but otherwise unfamiliar. Seeing no markings indicative of its content's importance or urgency, I decide it can wait until later, and so I toss it in the tray by my chair the minute I get home. There it remains for the rest of the evening while I sample Dottie's home cooking and unpack. It's ten o'clock when I finally plop down in the chair, shoes still on and teeth unbrushed, thinking how wonderful it will be to sleep in my soft bed again. Then, out of the corner of my eye, I spot the letter.

Exhausted, but now well fed and caught up, I feel my curiosity piqued. A stranger took the trouble to seek me out. Every single day for a week, according to Dottie. Must have been for something important, at least to him.

Reluctantly, I pick up the envelope, tear it open, and pull out a single sheet of paper folded in thirds. Putting on my reading glasses, I unfold the flimsy note and adjust its distance until the few lines of scribbling come into focus before my tired eyes.

When I next blink, the note is lying face up on the carpeted floor, the writing on it no longer legible at this new distance. How or when it has slipped through my fingers I do not know, as I'm only aware of a floating sensation in my head accompanied by a pounding in my eardrums. Then, the skin on my neck and shoulders starts to crawl with goose bumps that quickly spread down my arms like icy breaths.

Dropping my head back against the headrest, I shut my eyes and breathe deeply.

As the shockwaves gradually ebb, the short message replays itself in my mind, word by stunning word, and its extraordinary content begins to sink in.

Chapter Two

Every once in a while, you experience a rough night like this:

In the dead of night you rise from deep sleep, not jolted awake by a terrifying nightmare, but rather emerging softly from the mist of your dreams. Straddling the fault line between reality and the subconscious world, you wander space and time, reconnecting with people and places of your past. When you least suspect it, a magical door opens on a treacherous landing that lures you down a trail best left unexplored—one that trespasses on secret dead ends strewn with pieces of your own broken heart and shattered dreams from days gone by. Trapped in this time warp, an unwitting prisoner of the past, you find yourself sinking in the quicksand of nostalgia and regret, reliving heartaches and disenchantments of younger years.

I am wading through this waking nightmare as I bend to pick up the innocuous-looking letter from the floor. With just a few written words, the bottle has been shattered and the genie set free, and with it, years of suppression and denial. Old memories shut away for decades are tumbling forth faster than I can catch my breath. His handwriting has looked unfamiliar because we ceased corresponding ages ago. Yet I can still recall his voice, even his rare laughter, as if we had parted ways only yesterday. And burned forever in my mind is a clear picture of his face, surrounded by other young faces. Some more grubby or weary than others, but all still glowing with youthful vitality and innocence.

It was another lifetime. Another country.

Sunday, Aug 22, 1999

Hello kiddo,

Surprise! I finally got hold of your contact info.

Just so happens I'm in town this week, so I thought I'd take my chances and look you up in person. Lousy timing as always: no one answered the phone or the door.

Acquaintance from Việt-Nam would like to speak with you. If/when you get this, call me at the hotel and we'll make arrangements to swing by again.

Hope to hear from you soon.

Dean Hunter

It's not unlike Dean Hunter to be laconic in his message, which reads more like a riddle to me. Yet his cryptic intimation has torn open a forbidden past, one I have attempted—clearly in vain—to put behind me.

An acquaintance from Việt-Nam.

Can it possibly be *her*?

It's been thirty years or more since I've seen either of them. Funny how the passage of time burnishes certain memories while dulling others, and not necessarily in accordance with our wishes. As diligently as I have strived to keep that compartment of my life clasped shut, my subconscious mind sometimes escapes and tiptoes back. In my half-awakened dreams she returns, frozen in time, looking the same as she did that afternoon, forever captive to her grief.

This lovely ghost I struggled all these years to bury—has she now returned among the living?

PART II

"The Dogs of War"*

Biên-Hoà, South Việt-Nam
July 1967 – July 1968

*William Shakespeare (1564-1616)

Chapter Three

I met Dean Hunter only days after arriving in Việt-Nam in late July 1967.

Fresh out of medical school and having just completed my internship at a hospital in San Diego, California, I'd been commissioned into the US Air Force in exchange for an earlier deferment. My assignment was a one-year tour of duty as general medical officer at Biên-Hoà Air Force Base in South Việt-Nam. As was true with most young draftees, it was my first trip overseas. And what a journey it turned out to be, carrying me halfway around the world to this sultry land about which I knew nothing except its foreign-sounding name and the war footage shown nightly on television.

On this particular afternoon, I found myself in the 3rd Tactical Wing Dispensary getting oriented by Captain Bob Olsen, a flight surgeon and the rotating MOD (medical officer of the day), who also happened to be my hooch mate. There had been spectacular thundershowers almost every hour since midday—typical July weather in monsoon season, with an average monthly rainfall of twelve inches. With one hundred percent humidity, the temperature around a hundred degrees Fahrenheit, and the dispensary only partially air-conditioned, I had my first introduction to jungle warfare.

Bob, a gregarious type from the Midwest who looked like a rawboned lineman with the World Champion Green Bay Packers, wiped the sweat off his sandy eyebrows with the back of his hand and grinned sympathetically at me. "Don't worry. You'll get used to it soon enough. I arrived in April, the start of the season, and already

I'm paying no mind to the rain. It's wet all the time. Soon, you don't know any different."

It had been a rare quiet day. After the regular rush of morning sick calls, things had settled down. So far we'd had no in-flight emergencies and only one non-critical work-related injury. On days like this, the 3rd Tac Dispensary at Biên-Hoà seemed just like dispensaries on air force bases in the continental United States. We weren't operating a field hospital on the front line, like the one in nearby Long-Bình Army Base, nor were we saddled with the responsibility of a casualty staging unit (CSU) to assist in out-country medical airlifts. The latter fell to our sister base to the south, Tân-Sơn-Nhất AFB, on the outskirt of Sài-Gòn, the capital. The reason was simple. With a skeleton staff, we already had our hands full trying to meet the needs of our own base's personnel of several thousand strong and growing. Since 1965, Biên-Hoà had developed into the busiest airport in the world, commercial or military, bar none.

"You'll learn fast to speak in acronyms, too," Bob went on. "Some will catch on naturally, but most are plain ridiculous. Takes more time to figure out what they stand for. They're a lingo all their own." Chuckling, he added, "That, on top of sounding out those impossible Vietnamese names you have no clue how to pronounce."

We were going over the various tables of organization and equipment, or TOE, when the telephone rang. Bob picked it up. A rapid exchange ensued, which concluded when he bounded from his chair.

"You betcha. We'll be right there," he said and hung up.

"Tweety," he hollered to our cohort in the back room before proceeding to give me a quick rundown. An Army helicopter was coming in for a crash landing. Hard hit by enemy fire while returning from a routine ash-and-trash supply run, the crew had radioed in a Mayday.

Bob gathered his tool bag. "Operations asked me to assist. Their own flight surgeon is away on a mission. Why don't you come down to the flight line with us?"

Tweety was a twenty-year-old medic who looked no older than a high school kid, short in stature but built like an armored personnel carrier, whose chipper disposition and last name Finch earned him the nickname.

Tweety came barreling down the hallway. "Yes, sir?"

"Get a 'cracker box' ready and grab one of your buddies," Bob told him. "We're going out to the Bird Cage." Then, addressing me: "Bring your flak vest and steel pot for protection in case of an explosion."

⌒

As soon as the two medics had hopped in the back of the cracker box, a three-quarter-ton truck fixed up as military ambulance, Bob Olsen grasped the steering wheel, brow furrowed and jaw firmly set. I jumped in the front seat next to him.

"We'll take the perimeter road," he said. "It's longer but faster."

Biên-Hoà Air Base was spread out over a vast dust bowl, with the small city by the same name encroaching on its southern border and the Đồng-Nai River to the west. From a minor airfield left behind by the French, it had grown considerably in recent years but still retained a distinct transitory feel, as if the powers that be had expected a short war and a quick exit. Built around a nucleus of dilapidated buildings in the French colonial architectural style was a huge military camp— a sprawling hodge-podge of canvas tents, wooden hooches, Quonset huts, and trailers, thrown in among two-story barracks, hangars, and concrete revetments. Protected by sandbag bunkers all along their foundation lines, these ad hoc structures were interconnected through a maze of crisscrossing dirt roads. The single runway, Runway 27, had undergone a complete upgrade from temporary pierced-steel planking to permanent concrete paving. It now stretched ten thousand feet to accommodate jet landings.

"This road wraps around the base to the Army side," Bob shouted over the background din as our cracker box bounced away from the dispensary complex. "We're heading straight to their helipad. The Bird Cage."

The airbase was home to USAF squadrons of various functions including fighters, air commandos, forward air controllers, as well as rescue parajumpers. It also housed a US Army battalion of assault helicopters and multiple units of the Vietnamese Air Force. In addition, it served as one of the most important logistical airports in South Việt-Nam and controlled heavy traffic of cargo transports and troop carriers in and out of the country. Day and night, aircraft of every description lined up over the windy runway for takeoff or landing, deftly performing a perilous ballet in the air, where one mistake could result in fiery disaster.

This madness in the sky was matched by feverish activity on the ground. The roads always seemed clogged with heavy-tonnage trucks rumbling through congestions of jeeps, buses, bulldozers, and ambulances. Adding to the chaos, base personnel and civilian contractors were constantly on the run, weaving their bicycles and motor scooters through the gnarled traffic like ants on a hill. Meanwhile, the rolling thunder of bombs reverberated in rice paddies and jungles just beyond the safe confines of the base, an incessant reminder of the reason we were here: a full-blown war was raging out there at all hours of the day.

"This can get nasty," Bob bellowed against the strong wind. "They've activated Local Base Rescue. Pedro 75 is airborne and ready." Sensing I was lost, he elaborated. "It's the Air Force rescue helicopter. A Kaman Huskie with fire suppression kit. It's escorting the wounded bird in as we speak."

We'd barely passed a French "pillbox" on the roadside, a fortified circular bunker topped with a metal turret, when Bob hung a sharp right. The cracker box flew past the first L-shaped revetments at the Bird Cage and screeched to a stop on the sideline of the short helipad runway. We all jumped out and raced for cover behind a stack of sand-filled canisters, where another group had already gathered. Everybody was craning to watch the spectacle unfolding over the far end of the runway, a safe distance away from all the parked birds.

An Army Huey, in this instance a "slick," or troop-carrying chopper with no machine guns mounted on the outside, was gyrating dangerously in a slow, unsteady descent. Even from where we stood, it was obvious the twin blades of its main rotor had sustained serious damage from enemy artillery, causing the helicopter to shake violently as if it might shatter into pieces at any moment. Above it, the ungainly-looking Huskie with its double tail sections hovered at the ready. The laminated blades of its tandem rotors slashed the air in counter circles, creating a powerful downwash that would smother the flames in case of fire.

"Holy cow," Tweety uttered, pointing at a smokelike tail that trailed down to the ground. "The slick's bleeding fuel. Charlie must've busted a hole in its belly."

JP4 jet fuel was highly flammable and could ignite instantly if the wind blew it up into the hot exhaust. The fire suppression kit had already been lowered from the Huskie. The two airmen from the LBR team, dressed in shiny fire suits, had laid down a blanket of fire-retardant foam on the ground where the wounded bird was trying to land. Base fire trucks had also arrived on the scene and stationed themselves around the hot spot, ready to intervene.

A group of soldiers was silhouetted in the open cargo door on each side of the wobbling aircraft, seemingly frozen so as not to upset its balance.

Bob whispered in my ear, "They normally ride the skids and un-ass the ship before it even touches ground. But that might cause it to topple in this case."

We all held our breaths as the helicopter hovered a few feet above ground, suspended in time. Suddenly it dropped to the landing pad with a loud thud, took a couple of rough bounces, and nosed forward through the splattering foam. Having lost momentum from the impact, the Huey shuddered like a dying beast before slowing to a full upright stop on its skids.

The crowd gave a collective cheer of relief.

In one big blur of motion, the transported troops in tiger-stripe uniforms hopped off the carrier and dashed away from the danger zone. The regular crew of two in green fatigues, their flight helmets still strapped on, yanked the cockpit doors open and helped the pilot and copilot down before they all scurried to safety. Right on cue, the firemen swooped in with hoses, blanketing the area with fresh foam.

Bob tapped my shoulder. "Let's go."

We ran out to meet the incomers halfway and directed them toward the company's dispensary. Bob recognized a face among the helicopter riders.

"What the hell. Dean Hunter. You all right?"

The guy was about the same age as Bob, who at thirty was deemed an "old man" in this war fought by youngsters. Tall and powerfully built, a steel pot on his head and a flak vest over his jungle fatigues, he looked like a regular Army guy but was toting a medicine bag instead of an M-16.

He gave Bob a nod. "I'm fine. Make sure you check out the crew chief right away. The kid took a round in his helmet. I have to look my guys over, too. Let's catch up when we're done."

He rounded up the tiger-stripe uniforms, all six of them, and together they disappeared into the back room of the dispensary.

———

In the front room, Sp4c. "Rusty" McCormick kept staring at the broken helmet in his lap while running his fingers through his short red hair. "Fucking unbelievable," he mumbled over and over, more to himself than to anyone in particular.

Bob smiled sympathetically but at last had to place his hands on Rusty's shoulders to settle him down. "Can't swab this cut unless you hold still a minute, dear boy," he told Rusty.

The young crew chief had cheated death and literally gotten away with a bloody scratch. He'd been hunkered down in the portside gun well of the chopper when a bullet from the ground pierced the thin aluminum fuselage, tore through the back firewall into the cargo compartment, ricocheted off the ceiling, and hit him smack in the head. It struck his helmet on the right side, smashed the earpiece, then exited to the front, leaving a trail of blood across his right temple.

"It was like my head exploded." Rusty shuddered. "I grabbed my brain-bucket. There was blood all over my hand. 'I'm a fucking goner,' was what I thought."

But as he recovered from the initial shock and scrambled back into position, Rusty said he realized with utter amazement that he had somehow escaped death.

"Hot damn. Talk about a close shave." He blew out a long breath, his shaky hand grazing the red stubble below his right temple.

After applying a bandage over the superficial wound, Bob dismissed him with a gentle slap on the back. "You lucky son of a gun. Your tetanus shots are up to date, so you don't even need a booster." He laughed. "Go easy on the celebration tonight. You don't want to wake up with a monster headache in the morning. And check in with your surgeon tomorrow, okay?"

The only other patient needing attention was the copilot, also called the "peter pilot," a nickname for rookies still in training. A peter pilot was customarily teamed up with a more seasoned veteran who retained command of the aircraft. Sour-faced 1st Lieutenant Barron Ashford Jr. appeared not to share the jovial mood of his captain commander, who stood next to him at the exam table, an arm draped around his shoulders, wracked with laughter.

"Two months in country, Ashford, and you already got your ass shot into the record book," hollered the captain. "Attaboy, Junior."

Beside me, the snickering gunner explained in a hushed tone. The frustrated lieutenant had been plagued with a dubious reputation. Though generally considered a decent pilot with good "air sense," he'd always seemed to attract special wrath from the enemy. If any ship took a hit during company sorties, it would undoubtedly be Ashford's, no matter which commander he happened to fly with at the time.

Earlier that day, Barron Ashford and his assigned crew had run ash-and-trash to a Special Forces A-team camp in War Zone C, west of Biên-Hoà. Riding with them was Army Captain Dean Hunter, who was charged to bring back some ailing CIDG troops from the camp. Despite having no escort gunship to protect their lift chopper, the outgoing trip had been uneventful, and they'd landed without incident. The copilot had expressed hope that the return flight would turn out just as smooth, a rare experience for him—an entire mission without a single hit on his ship. But that was not to be.

As the Huey with its full load of human cargo lifted off from the camp and crossed into the "dead man's zone," that dangerous airspace above treetops but still within range of Charlie's artillery, it was greeted with a barrage of small-arms fire. Its twin rotor blades were struck and damaged on the spot, and soon the helicopter trailed smoke, or actually fuel in this case. It was no small miracle it remained airborne and managed to limp back to the Bird Cage. The crew was obviously elated to have squeaked through unmolested, but Barron Ashford Jr. looked none too pleased to be anointed the new "Magnet Ass" of his company.

Bob did well in keeping his composure. "Say, what have we here, Lieutenant?"

He lifted the young man's left arm, which hung bare at his side. Ashford had removed his flak jacket and the "chicken plate," a piece of protective armor for the pilot's upper body, and had freed his arm from his flight suit. Shattered metal and Plexiglas had sliced through the suit's fire-retardant fabric, and the arm was bruised with shrapnel wounds and spattered with dried blood.

"You're another lucky guy." Bob nodded thoughtfully. "No deep punctures here, just lots of frags to extract. But first we have to take an x-ray to find them all. Good thing the cuts are small. They won't require stitches." With a conspiratorial wink, as if he'd read Barron's mind, he added, "Don't worry. We'll get you back in the air in no time."

That almost brought a smile to the sulky young face.

Turning to me, Bob motioned with his chin toward the back room. "This will take a while. No reason for everyone to wait around. Why don't you check in with Dr. Hunter, see if he can use a hand with his men?"

I stuck my head inside the door to the back room just as Dean Hunter was finishing examining his last CIDG man. The rest of them waited outside in the hallway, languishing on the floor next to their rifles. They were a weary-looking bunch, short and slight of build, almost like teenage boys, but wiry, with skin so dark they wouldn't need face paint for camouflage. Their tiger-stripe outfits could have stood a wash many battles ago, and floppy boonie hats with the same stripe pattern shielded their bloodshot eyes. These men were the first native armed forces I'd come across since my arrival.

"Captain Hunter? I'm Lieutenant Connors. Roger Connors, GMO with 3rd Tac."

No reply. I went on. "I was wondering if you need help, but I see you're almost done."

Dean glanced up, motioned me to an empty chair, then returned to his patient, who was getting dressed. He gave the man short instructions in his native tongue then walked him to the door, pulling it shut after he was gone.

"You a newbie with Bob Olsen?" Dean asked, offering me his hand.

"Three days and counting." I stood and accepted his iron grip. "You speak Vietnamese?"

"The best way to communicate with them," Dean said. "But that wasn't Vietnamese. It's Khmer, or Cambodian." Catching the expression on my face, he clarified, "CIDG, Civilian Irregular Defense Group, is bankrolled by the States. Special Forces recruit them from various minority groups, Cambodians among those. We train and organize them to help in remote areas outside government control."

Since they weren't part of the conventional army, Dean explained, they couldn't be admitted to regular military hospitals. He and another US Army doctor were specifically assigned to care for the CIDG in III Corps out of the Provincial Hospital in Biên-Hoà.

He fixed me with a steady gaze. "Not to change the subject, but you mind taking a look at my upper back? I think I got hit in my left shoulder."

"Holy crap." I rushed to his side. "Why didn't you mention it right away?"

He raised his hand. "Slow down. It's no biggie."

In his hurry to examine the men in his charge for critical wounds, Dean hadn't bothered to remove his own flak vest or steel pot. I admonished him to sit still while I peeled off this extra gear. As his vest came off, a small shiny lump fell to the ground with a metallic clink. He reached down to retrieve it, then held it up to me between two fingers.

"Here it is, Lieutenant. Your very first war memento."

The bullet had punched through the ballistic nylon layer of his jacket, drilling a perfect hole in it before lodging itself against the inner plate. He remembered being jolted by a sharp pain on his left shoulder right after Rusty had taken that ricocheted shot in his helmet. The same missile must have continued on its exit path from the helmet and struck Dean, who was crouched nearby with his back to Rusty. Even after bouncing off multiple obstacles, the slug still carried enough momentum to dent the metal plate and break his skin at the point of impact.

"Never go anywhere without protective gear," advised Dean while I dressed his wound. "It's saved my ass on several occasions."

Then he scoffed at the irony. "My boys had no gear, yet nobody got scraped. They're all sick as dogs, but they must be immune to VC fire."

The instant I finished, Dean leapt to his feet and in one swiping motion gathered all his stuff.

"I must get them to the hospital before dark, or we'll risk another ambush. Did they tell you? Around here, the night belongs to Charlie."

The Provincial Hospital, I learned, was a small clinic constructed by the French at the turn of the century. Located off base within the city of Biên-Hoà, it had recently been expanded through USAID funds to include a basic surgical suite. A humanitarian group of Australian physicians and nurses operated the civilian wing, which was always overcrowded, while Dean and his Army colleague, both with the 5th Special Forces Group, ran the paramilitary ward to provide medical service to CIDG troops in III Corps. More often than not, these two independent but undermanned teams would cooperate and work side by side as one cohesive unit.

As Dean and I headed back to the front room of the dispensary, followed by the straggling men in tiger-stripe uniforms, I noticed a lingering limp in his step.

"Did you hurt your foot, Captain?"

He shrugged. "It's nothing. I sprained my ankle in a bad jump a couple of months ago and didn't stay off my feet long enough for it to heal properly. But it feels fine now."

Bob Olsen was finishing up with Ashford when we walked in. Without taking his eyes from his task or slowing down, Bob caught Dean up on the progress of a civic project they were both involved in. Even as a wide-eyed rookie observing and learning, I recognized that the two of them made a special team. Maybe one day I, too, could become part of that team.

There were but a few precious minutes of daylight to spare, since nightfall in the tropics arrives abruptly, as if an invisible hand suddenly reaches for a switch in the sky and turns out all the light at once. At 1900 hours it would be coal-dark on the dirt roads off base, making them dangerous to navigate no matter how short a distance.

Dean promptly waved us good-bye, then hurried his men to a Red Cross ambulance parked outside Operations. At the far end of the helipad, the maintenance crew had cleaned up the mess and towed the damaged chopper to the repair hangar. There was no trace left of the disaster that had almost happened. Things had returned to "normal," whatever that meant.

Back to SOP—Standard Operating Procedure—as Bob Olsen would say.

⌒

"Congrats, Woody." Bob gave 2nd Lieutenant Anthony Woodward a hearty slap on the back. "Can't get rid of you, can we? But don't make a habit of it now, you hear?"

"Enjoy the steaks and booze, Doc." The "Hun" pilot, as indicated by the colorful insignias on his flight suit, appeared more than a little inebriated as he grappled for Bob's hand, seized the wrong one, and pumped it with exuberance. "It's a fucking dogfight, but we shall outlast it," he yelled in Bob's ear over the general hubbub before staggering on to a nearby table.

After our shift, Bob and I had decided to stop at the officers' club and unwind from the frantic afternoon, only to find the place packed with pilots and crews from one of the Tactical Fighter Squadrons. It seemed as if we'd stepped into a regular bar stateside on New Year's Eve. The crowded room was thumping with loud music from the corner jukebox, and dense cigarette smoke had transformed the normally drab setting into the familiar watering hole in everyone's neighborhood back home. In the middle of the room, a large tub filled with ice was regularly re-stocked with cans of beer and soda pop. By the counter, which was loaded with a rich assortment of wine and liquor bottles, famished revelers waited in line for their sizzling steaks. The crowd consumed food and alcohol with lusty relish, whooping and hollering their wild approval.

"I'm parched as a camel," Bob shouted. "What d'you drink?"

"A Falstaff, please. What was that all about, with Woody?"

Bob grabbed my beer and a Pabst Blue Ribbon for himself, and I followed him to a small table in a corner. "This," he said, opening the can with his "church key" before passing it to me, "is Woody's Glad-To-Be-Alive party. It's an Air Force tradition, among pilots. It completely slipped my mind that it was tonight."

According to Bob, a jet fighter pilot, in the unfortunate event his machine was hit and brought down by anti-aircraft artillery, had no choice but to "punch out," ejecting himself from the aircraft and parachuting into enemy territory. This, of course, would expose him to extreme danger. He could be shot out of the air or captured within minutes of landing unless immediately rescued by friendlies on the scene. Should he beat the odds and return safely to home base, as Woody had, the entire squadron would turn out to fete the lucky survivor.

"See those Army guys over there?" Bob nodded to a group of four helicopter men seated at the table with Woody, who again raised his glass—a fresh one, no doubt—for another drunken toast. "They're tonight's guests of honor, the gunship crew that went back and plucked him out of harm's way. Saved his life."

"They're a breed apart, aren't they, these jet jocks?" I'd heard wild rumors of their warrior's machismo and propensity for a good time.

"They've got the worst of it," Bob replied before taking a long draft from his PBR can. Glancing again at Woody's table, which erupted from time to time in uproarious laughter, he went on. "Most of them fly solo, often seven days a week. When they crash and burn, God forbid, it's almost certain death or captivity. I'm not sure which is worse." He turned to me. "Know what their standing joke is?"

I shook my head.

"Live fast, die young, and make a good-looking corpse." Bob looked away. "And it ain't pure bravado, either."

We fell quiet amid all the commotion. "Yellow Submarine" was playing, a favorite of the buzzed crowd, who spontaneously broke into a rollicking chorus with the Fab Four.

Bob winked at me. "What a day for you, eh? Better get used to it. Par for the course around here." He took another swig. "What d'you make of Dean Hunter?"

"He's one dedicated doctor, from what I saw," I tried to sound neutral despite my curiosity.

"He's a man of action who loves what he's doing," said Bob. "Maybe a little too much."

He went on to explain that they'd met earlier through their involvement with the Medical Civic Action Program, MEDCAP for short, which provided medical aid to the civilian population. Biên-Hoà had been a sleepy hamlet under the French, but with the war, refugees uprooted from the countryside had flooded into town and created a health-care crisis for the tiny Provincial Hospital. When they heard about it, Bob and his colleagues had organized groups of weekend volunteers to come to the assistance of the Australian medical team and the two US Army doctors at the hospital. A fast friendship had formed between him and Dean through this shared endeavor.

Bob drew one last draft and emptied his can. "Most people don't know this," he said. "Dean won't talk about it, but he's a full-fledged Green Beret. A graduate from the JFK School of Special Warfare in Fort Bragg, North Carolina. As a doctor, he wasn't obligated to undergo this hardcore training. But he went whole hog for it before he volunteered for Việt-Nam. Without coercion, mind you. Unlike other guys."

Touché. I shifted discreetly in my seat.

Himself a man to follow his own heart, Bob told me he appreciated the free spirit he encountered in his new friend. As an Army brat who'd grown up hero-worshipping his father, a much-decorated WWII veteran, Dean had devoted himself from an early age to the pursuit of two seemingly incompatible ideals: that of a true combat soldier in his father's mold, and the role of a healer tending to the wounded and the suffering. The latter, Bob surmised, was Dean's way of paying tribute to the selfless medics in WWII, who had more than once saved the life of his wounded father at the risk of their own. From these boyhood aspirations of heroism and compassion would emerge the future Army doctor with the green beret.

"But this choice of lifestyle exacts its own price, as you might guess," Bob said pensively. "It might very well have cost him a chance at happiness."

I drank up the last of my beer, waiting.

"Ever heard of the 'John Deere' letter?" Bob asked.

"'Dear John,' you mean?"

"Here in country, the guys call it the John Deere letter. As in John Deere tractors, since the poor recipient must feel like he's been crushed by one. A little military humor for you." Bob's voice softened. "It's more commonplace than people would suspect. Some wives and girlfriends back home simply can't cope with their men going off to war. The separation, the uncertainty, loneliness, and anguish . . . it's all too much for them, so one day they just up and walk away."

I hesitated. "Is Dean married?"

"Girlfriend only. She wrote him less than a month after he arrived in Việt-Nam."

Bob caught my reaction and nodded. "Yup. His very own John Deere."

My thoughts flashed to Debbie, my girlfriend. We'd agreed to wait until I finished my professional training to get married. Then unexpectedly came the "doctor draft" due to a severe shortage of medical personnel to care for nearly a half-million US servicemen on active duty in South Việt-Nam. So once more we'd postponed our wedding plans until I returned. We'd still be under thirty, both of us, with bright futures ahead. But sitting here at this late hour with an empty can of beer in my hand, one year suddenly seemed a long way off.

"The Aussie nurses at the hospital are real sweet on him," Bob said with a half smile. "In fact, our guy has caught the eyes of more women than you can shake a stick at. But after the girlfriend's unceremonious brush-off, he remains a resolute loner. Burying himself in work. So they invented a nickname to tease him."

"Nickname?"

Bob got up and stretched. "Fits him to a tee, sadly enough."

Thus, with my first taste and smell of war that sweltering summer of 1967, began my acquaintance with Dean "the Lonely" Hunter.

Chapter Four

Barring any emergencies, there wasn't much activity at the 3rd Tac Dispensary on a late afternoon. Bob would leave word with Tweety on our whereabouts, then take me down to the flight line to watch, in his words, "the best free show in town."

"This place is incredible," he'd remind me every time. "It's like a live air show, only better. You get front-row seats to all the action."

Growing up as an only child in the small town of Little Falls, Minnesota, Bob had discovered his ideal hero in The Lone Eagle, known to the world as the great Charles Lindbergh. Many a time after class, he had trekked the two miles from school to the historic farmhouse south of town where the famous aviator used to spend his early summers. There, he would sneak onto the porch overlooking the Mississippi and imagine himself, like young Lindy decades before him, gawking in awe at a biplane barnstorming over the treetops. Through his reminiscence of those innocent days, I learned of my hooch mate's lifelong passion for aviation.

Bob could easily hang out at the flight line for hours on end, pointing out every single type of aircraft that whizzed by, naming its manufacturer and exact model number, and rattling off a long list of impressive specs—much like a teenage hotrodder around speed cars. The main object of his admiration was a bevy of sleek jet fighters in perpetual motion on Runway 27.

"*That* is one superb fighting machine," Bob shouted in my ear as an F-100 Super Sabre, or "Hun," took off in a thunder. "The world's first supersonic jet, by several months over the Soviet MiG-19. It held the world records in speed, altitude, and distance. The Thunderbirds couldn't have picked a more impressive demo engine."

Squinting at the fast-disappearing aircraft, he shook his head in amazement. "D'you know it can be fitted with 'special stores' as needed? The old bird is actually suited for nuclear warfare. I can't wait to ride in the two-seater model. Hopefully soon."

Tugging at my sleeve, he pointed to another smart-looking ship that had just landed. "Man, are you in for a treat. Take a good look at the F-102 Delta Dagger, nicknamed the 'Deuce.' Note its distinctive delta wing shape, like a giant bat, as opposed to the Hun's more traditional swept-wing design." Turning to make certain I had the right airplane in view, he continued. "We have only six of these birds standing alert here at Biên-Hoà. They can be airborne and combat ready in five minutes, day or night. *Five* minutes, my friend."

Once in a while, our base played host to unexpected visitors, like the time a US Navy F-4 Phantom jet with stuck landing gear due to damage from enemy fire was forced to touch down on its belly. As a rule, such a wounded bird was not to return to its home carrier for fear of endangering the whole ship. Again, Bob and I were on hand to assist in the Local Base Rescue effort, successfully conducted with a Huskie helicopter and on-base fire trucks. Bob lingered afterward to chat with the pilot and came away thoroughly impressed.

"That was a Mach-2 aircraft just landed on our runway. Twice the speed of sound with more than double the bomb load of the Hun. Dollars to doughnuts it'll be our warhorse of the future." Then, his eyes shining bright, "You saw the pilot's G-suit? We're talking space age here, kiddo."

As engrossed as Bob was with all the technological wizardry that defined modern military aviation, his real fascination lay with the pilots who flew these experimental wonder-machines. Serving as one of the flight surgeons under the base medical commander, he was responsible for the pilots' safety and well-being and had the authority to revise their flying status when necessary. In this capacity, he had come to know them on a personal basis and was regularly invited to parties at their squadron headquarters. He also made it a point to partake in their "fini-flight" celebrations on the flight line.

This ritual took place upon a pilot's completion of his final mission in Việt-Nam. It signified his imminent return to The World— The Land of the Big PX, of air-conditioning and indoor plumbing. Climbing down from the cockpit for the last time in country, the fortunate pilot would be swarmed by cheering comrades who doused him with cold water before presenting him with a bottle of champagne. Bob would drop in to shake hands with the happy short-timer and congratulate him on heading home.

"How come you never tried out for flight school?" I asked Bob one late evening as we were stretched out on our cots, listening to the steady rain and the nondescript music on Armed Forces Radio, about to drift asleep. "You were born to fly, man."

"Not good enough eyesight," he mumbled at first. Then a moment later, I heard his voice again in the dark. "Truth is, it meant a lot to my old man that I follow in his footsteps and become a doctor. So I did." He chuckled softly. "But after med school I rebelled and joined the Air Force, did my residency in aerospace medicine, and became a flight surgeon. Instead of a family physician like Dad. *Uff-da!*"

I laughed. "You do get to fly, though, being a flight surgeon?"

"Not as a pilot, obviously," he said. "But I've flown on all kinds of aircraft, rotaries as well as props and jets. We're required to log in minimum flying time each month. Most pilot guys are cool, and if you ask them they'll be happy to show you how to fly their machine. Some even let you have stick time and get hands-on, as long as it's a two-seater."

While admiring the jets for their sleek beauty and raw performance, Bob saved his affection for the older and slower propeller airplanes, of which there were many squadrons on base. This wasn't so much because he got to fly on them more frequently as due to the high regard he held for the crews. To him, those pilots were among the true unsung heroes of the war.

"Take the single-engine A-1 Skyraider, for instance," Bob explained to me one day. "This old fighter can swoop in real low and inflict more damage with better accuracy than high-flying high-speed jets. Then there's the O-1 Bird Dog observation plane, a little high-wing job that routinely defies ground fire to direct the big strikers to their targets. And let's don't forget the Ranch Hand commandos. D'you realize how low and slow they must fly those thick-bellied Providers when they're out spraying defoliant over enemy territory? It takes skill and guts to carry out all those dangerous missions day in and day out, and survive."

"You really dig this stuff, don't you?" I remarked. "Biên-Hoà seems a natural fit for you."

He didn't reply immediately. When he did, his voice lacked its usual hint of laughter.

"I've always loved flying since I was knee-high to a grasshopper. There's no denying it. As for Biên-Hoà, like it or lump it, we've still got a job to do here. And I for one am going to focus on the things that interest me, not on all the nonsense I can't control."

Looking past me, he went on. "You and me, we're very fortunate we're noncombatants. The lucky dogs 'in the rear with the gear,' as they say. But even so, nobody can hide from the war, and it sure as hell can trip you up. If you let it."

Bob was no doubt alluding to the scenes that played out every day on the flight line, a fact that should have made it easier to ignore them after a while, but it didn't. In late summer 1967, new troops continued to arrive in country at a clipped pace through Biên-Hoà AFB. Most were flown in on Boeing 707s operated by commercial airlines such

as Continental or Pan Am or by military contractors like World
Airways or Flying Tigers. The rest were transported by the Air Force's
C-141 Starlifters, which were reconfigured upon landing for medical
evacuation flights back to CONUS. It was a remarkable sight to watch
those imposing jets drop out of the sky in a precipitous descent onto
the runway—a tricky maneuver to dodge snipers' fire from the jungle
surrounding the base.

Caught in the glaring sunlight, the new arrivals, in rumpled
khakis or dress greens or blues, staggered down the ladder, looking
jet-lagged and disoriented. They were herded to a processing center
inside a shed right off the tarmac, filing past a long line of boisterous
veterans headed the opposite way. The latter, their worn uniforms
decorated with all kinds of colorful insignias, had trouble containing
their euphoria as they waited to board the same plane. The sweet
moment they'd dreamed about throughout their one-year tours was
finally here, and they were aching to be whisked away on that "Freedom
Bird" and returned to their loved ones at home. "Fresh meat, suckers,"
they hollered with glee and pumped their fists at the newcomers, who
glanced back nervously. But among that exuberant crowd flying home,
a keen observer might also spot a few soldiers, unusually subdued,
whose eyes bore the saddest vacant look.

"Those poor kids," Bob whispered to me once. "They've seen more
combat than their rattled nerves could stand. That haunted look in
their eyes? We call it the 'thousand-yard stare.' They've got a bumpy
road ahead of them. Even with help."

A more disturbing sight that never failed to jolt me no matter how
often I'd stumbled on it was the unloading of body bags. Strapped
down on cargo pallets, the olive-drab rubberized bags were delivered
by propeller transports straight from the front, a small yellow tag of
personal data dangling from each one. In the hazy heat waves, the
stench of death rose from the bags and blended with the powerful
smells of jet fuel and exhaust fumes to create an indelible impression.

A convoy of cracker boxes—their red lights flashing, unnecessarily it seemed—met the sinister cargo at the flight line and hauled it off to the morgue. Inside, civilian contractors set out at once to embalm the corpses to stave off further ravaging by the tropical heat. The prepared bodies would later go back to the flight line, this time in stacks of tightly sealed metal caskets to be loaded onto a C-130 Hercules or C-7 Caribou for homebound destinations. Even when hidden from sight, death remained on the prowl, never more than a few steps away from us.

At the base, we sometimes could tell when the fighting was getting intense out in the field. Beside an increase in sorties for the fighter bombers, a palpable tension would build in the air that eventually erupted in an awesome spectacle over the skies of Biên-Hoà. It would begin with a distant thumping that grew louder and more ominous by the minute until it was almost directly overhead, drawing one's attention skyward. There, ascending across the blue expanse, was a giant snakelike formation of over a hundred helicopters—troop-carrying slicks escorted by gunships, in staggered rows of two—as they lifted an Airborne battalion to battle. It was an extraordinary sight, and for me, one of the most unforgettable images of the Việt-Nam War. As I stared up in awe, I could almost make out the faces of the young troops being taken to the front. It startled me to realize that many of them, barely a year removed from high school, would never reach drinking age. They were the marked ones, the ones who'd be returned to the base a few hours or a few days hence, concealed in tagged body bags.

"Old man" Bob had proved dead accurate in his assessment. The broodings engendered day after day by these baleful observations, if allowed to fester in one's mind for any length of time, could drive one to the brink of madness. So most of us elected to channel our free time and energy into worthwhile causes like MEDCAP, or toward entertaining endeavors of our own, the way my hooch mate made himself an aficionado of military aviation. When it came to self-preservation, no pursuit could be deemed frivolous if it managed to steer one's obsession from the senseless realities of war, even for a moment.

One Sunday morning, I found my way to the "library" in hunt of the latest James Michener epic novels, which were perfect to fill the long evening hours before bedtime. The library was located in a stuffy trailer in the main complex, which also housed the post office, movie theater, chapel, and different clubhouses. It served as a trade-in center where airmen could exchange their used paperbacks for unread titles. It also held a limited supply of records and reel-to-reel tapes that people were allowed to make copies of if they had a tape recorder. In fact, Bob periodically took advantage of the facility to supplement his own music collection with missing songs from his favorite artists—Peter, Paul and Mary, and Bob Dylan, among others.

When I got back to the hooch, Bob was sitting on his cot amid a mess of half-opened packages and scattered old magazines and newspapers.

"Another care package from home?" I asked. "Just like the good old college days, eh?"

No response. I glanced over and saw a letter in his hands and a stunned expression on his face. He gave me a blank stare, then muttered a hoarse whisper. "It's from Nancy."

An awful thought raced through my mind and made my heart sink. It couldn't be happening. Not to Bob. Not one of those "John Deere" letters.

From earlier chats, I understood he had waited until after medical school to marry his long-time sweetheart. Following an intimate wedding in their hometown, he and Nancy had moved to Brooks AFB outside San Antonio, Texas, where he did his three years of residency in aerospace medicine. In spring 1967, Bob finished the training and received his flight surgeon wings, along with his orders for a one-year tour in Việt-Nam. He used the thirty-day leave before reporting for duty to help Nancy move back to Minnesota.

It must have been tough on the couple. Bob spent much of his free time in Biên-Hoà writing letters or recording taped messages to his wife. Except during our busiest spells, he seldom forgot to sign up for a time slot to call her on the MARS (Military Affiliate Radio System). This ingenious communications system employed short-wave carriers to patch a phone line in Việt-Nam to one in the US and allowed our service people to talk with their families back home for five minutes per scheduled call. Despite that stringent time limit and the slight inconvenience imposed by Citizens' Band protocol—only one party could speak at a time, ending his or her turn with a punctuating "over"—this free service was a popular morale booster, a true lifeline that kept us connected to The World. Nobody even seemed to mind the lack of privacy, with the operator staying on the line to flip the receive-transmit switch after each "over."

I dared not ask another question, holding Bob's stare in awkward silence.

His face suddenly broke into the brightest smile. He leapt to his feet, charged toward me, and clutched me in a bear hug, shouting some gibberish that took me a moment to register. "Guess what, Roger? I'm going to be a daddy. A *daddy*, you hear? This is out of this world! Best birthday gift I ever got!"

Then just as abruptly, he set me down and started pacing, head in hands in disbelief. As his words tumbled out in an excited flood, I did my best to piece together the story.

It seemed Nancy had waited for Bob's upcoming birthday to spring the happy news on him. They'd been trying for a number of years with negative results, including one devastating early miscarriage. This time she'd decided to keep mum, at least until the pregnancy had progressed beyond the critical first trimester, so as not to raise false hopes and resurrect the painful memories that still haunted them.

"Congratulations to both of you." I shook his hand, relieved and grateful there was fairness in this world after all. "That's tremendous news. How far along is she?"

"Just over five months. A bit longer than I've been here." He grinned from ear to ear. "She managed to keep it from me all this time—can you believe it? Even my parents didn't breathe a word to me. Ah, naughty girl, my Nancy. It must've been killing her, though, all this secretive business."

"You're all alone over here. She just wanted to make certain for your sake," I reassured him. "She doing fine? Everything all right so far?"

Bob reached into the pile of wrapping paper on his bed and pulled out an elegant silver picture frame, which he proudly showed to me. It was a portrait photo of an attractive young woman with shoulder-length blond hair, violet-blue eyes, and an engaging smile, in a pink floral dress that complemented the healthy blush on her cheeks. I whistled my admiration. "She's a stunner. What on earth did you do to deserve her, you lucky devil?"

Bob laughed and ran his fingers tenderly across the framed glass. "It's my girl all right. Soon to be the mother of my child." He raised the picture closer to his face. "This was taken last month, for my birthday. There's a glow about her already. I can tell."

Then he turned to me with furrowed eyebrows. "She's due around Christmastime. If I postpone my R&R, we may be able to hook up in Hawaii by end of January." He hesitated before completing his thought. "Aren't you taking yours about that time, too? I'd sure hate to be gone the same week, seeing how short-handed we are."

All service people in Việt-Nam looked with great anticipation to the halfway point in their tour, when they were granted a week of Rest and Recreation at an out-country destination of their choice. The list of exotic locales included Thailand, Malaysia, Hong Kong, Japan, Australia, and Hawaii. Married personnel could also put in a request for their spouses to join them on their R&R. Most couples chose Hawaii because of its convenient location and its "at-home" setting.

I dismissed his concern with a wave of hand. "Not a problem from my end. I haven't firmed up any plans yet. You go ahead and make yours, and I'll schedule around them." I then reminded him with a wink, "Don't sweat it, Poppa. You have much bigger worries now."

"This calls for some serious celebrating," Bob announced, setting the photo on his footlocker. "But before we head down to the club, let's have a quick listen to this."

He placed a 45-rpm single on the phonograph next to the picture frame. It was an old RCA tabletop he'd been carrying around since his high school days—for sentimental reasons, he said. His late mother had redeemed it with her books of S&H Green Stamps as a surprise gift to him. To my amazement, the ancient widget kept cranking out beautiful music, albeit a little scratchy in its old days.

As the melodic sound filled our hooch, I shook my head in disbelief. "Haven't heard this in ages. It goes back a few years, old man."

Bob smiled. "'In the Still of the Night.' It's our song. Nancy and I slow-danced to it at our senior prom. That's when I knew she would wait for me."

"To Nancy and your little bundle of joy," I made an impromptu toast, raising an imaginary glass. As the big man looked up with gleaming eyes, I nodded at him and smiled. "And to my hooch mate and buddy. A future All-Star dad."

Chapter Five

All my life I'd believed I was born an average person destined for a simple existence, with not a seed of heroism or adventure in my heart. Nor had I come equipped with a lion's share of talent or driving ambition, the kind that would have set me apart from other residents in my hometown of Lone Pine, California. Truth be told, as a child I had always considered myself a country boy, or more romantically, a "nature boy." That shouldn't have surprised anyone, least of all my parents—God rest their souls—since I had arrived in this world cradled in the long shadow of Mount Whitney, as native a creature of the Eastern Sierra as a black bear cub or a baby mule deer.

From an early age, I learned my way around various nooks and crags in the local mountains and high desert, partly by picking up trail skills from my father and other grownups and partly through my own observation and experimentation. By the first summer in high school, I had developed a habit of disappearing for days into the wilderness with just a camping pack on my back. My time had come to sample the freedom and privacy teenagers so crave, and I found mine amid some of the most breathtaking scenery on earth. My favorite hero, the naturalist John Muir, figured prominently in my young adulthood, as I vowed to follow his credo to "climb the mountains and get their good tidings."

That same year, my parents were working hard to resurrect their slumping bed-and-breakfast operation. Out of desperation, they struck on the idea of putting my newfound hobby to use. In the summer of my sixteenth birthday, I began to serve as the nature guide to seasonal guests at Moon Meadows. My job was to take them hiking to Whitney Portal just outside of town or, for the more ambitious, into the wilderness beyond. This extra service proved a boon to our family business and helped turn things around.

It never entered my mind to live anywhere but in the foothills of the Snowy Mountain Range, where my earliest memories were of the same serrated peaks captured by the camera lens of Ansel Adams. My parents and I recognized early on that unlike my older brother Jerry, who showed ample evidence of business acumen and discipline, I wasn't cut out to follow their footsteps in the tourism trade. Thus freed up from family expectations, I had total flexibility in pondering options for my future. Because of my fascination with the natural wonders around us, it didn't seem overreaching to branch into the life sciences, and it became clear by the time I left for college that medicine was to be my calling.

In retrospect, it was proof of my immaturity to assume the future could be charted on a clear, straight path. What dream could be simpler than to spend my life as a country doctor in a mountain hamlet? Besides, I had a supportive partner who shared my outlook on life and my vision of the future and wanted to be part of it. She aligned her plans with mine, and we enrolled at UCLA in the fall of 1959, myself majoring in pre-med and she in nursing.

Debbie Knowles was the girlfriend most mothers would wish for their sons. Pretty and radiant though not the beauty-queen type, congenial in a gentle, unassuming way, smart but down-to-earth, and best of all, discreetly traditional in her values. My mother was thrilled when Debbie and I became close friends in high school, and she did everything in her power to nudge us toward a more serious relationship. She shouldn't have had to try so hard, seeing how compatible we were and how we enjoyed each other's company. So, blame it on the moon, a premonition, or my lack of readiness, but it wasn't until our senior year that my mother's wish at last came true. I finally asked Debbie to go steady.

"I knew all along that's what *I* wanted," she'd later confide in me, her arms wrapped around my neck. "But, boy oh boy, was it ever nerve-wracking waiting for you to come to your senses."

As I labored through the long years in medical school, Debbie finished her nursing degree and returned home to Owens Valley. She found work at the small local hospital in Bishop while waiting for me to conclude all my training, at which time we planned to get married. Then, with Debbie's assistance, I could open my private practice in our hometown, and we'd settle into the pastoral lifestyle we both yearned for.

If only life could be that simple. But in 1966, halfway through my last year in medical school, a letter arrived from the draft board detailing my two options. By enlisting "voluntarily" with the service branch of my choice, I would receive a reserve commission and a deferment until summer 1967, when I was due to complete my internship. Should I decline, I could be drafted any day but without either benefit and for a longer service time. The choice was easy. I promptly signed up with the US Air Force—where there should be the least chance of seeing combat, or so friends in the know had whispered in my ear.

Until that time, I had never even heard of Việt-Nam. In my narrow view of the world, abroad simply covered Canada and Mexico, while overseas meant Western Europe, Japan, or South Korea. In truth, my study schedule hardly allowed me time to eat or sleep, much less follow the news. However, I couldn't entirely escape widespread rumors of a war brewing inside a former French colony—a skinny piece of land with a funny name, squeezed between India and Red China. The US had taken much interest in it lately for reasons related to the Cold War and our fight against the spread of communism. But to me it might as well have been Antarctica, so removed was I from anything nonmedical.

With my draft order, I was roused, once and for all, from my blissful ignorance.

The only people of Asian descent I'd known were my childhood buddy, Dick Hayashi, and to a lesser extent, his family. Short and chubby, with a mob of unruly black hair and narrow eyes squinting behind thick glasses, Dick had the sweetest disposition of all the kids in my class. Always smiling, he was nonetheless quiet and preferred to listen in on other kids' conversations than participate. As I also tended to be somewhat reticent then, we gravitated toward each other, spending time at each other's house doing homework or just hanging out. His parents and older sisters always treated me with friendly courtesy, but they seemed even more quiet as they moved noiselessly about their small house like shadows from the past. Only later, when Dick and I had grown to trust each other enough to share our secrets, did I begin to understand this enigmatic trait of his family, which I'd wrongly attributed to their culture.

In the process, I learned of Manzanar.

This pretty word means *apple orchard* in Spanish. But the wasteland that still bore this name was an orchard no longer. A stone's throw north of downtown Lone Pine, Manzanar appeared even more forsaken than the gold-mine towns that still littered the Old West. A handful of wooden barracks were all that remained, scattered across a desert landscape that looked incapable of sustaining life.

Yet during World War II, more than ten thousand Americans of Japanese ancestry, under suspicion of disloyalty, were uprooted from their homes and relocated to an internment camp built on that very site, the first of ten such camps around the nation. Among the early prisoners were the Hayashis, who arrived from Los Angeles in May 1942. My friend Dick, a two-year-old toddler at the time, was blessed with no recollection of those traumatic years. His parents and older sisters, on the other hand, could not erase the painful memories from their minds even decades later. After the war, with no home to return to, the family had decided to stay in the Owens Valley and start over from nothing. Not a word of bitterness ever passed their lips in my presence, but their dark eyes, I sometimes imagined, still spoke volumes of this heartrending betrayal.

Although Dick and I had parted ways since high school, each pursuing his own dreams, my thoughts harked back to him and his family as I pondered my impending departure to Việt-Nam. Our earlier acquaintance had inevitably colored what sketchy notions I had of Asia with a shade of grief and despair. The three weeks of combined officer training and medical service orientation I attended at the Lackland and Sheppard AFBs in Texas in early summer 1967 only served to reinforce this bleak impression. Through training films and photographs, Việt-Nam emerged in its total misery. A strip of tropical land laid bare from centuries of colonial exploitation by the Chinese, the French, and the Japanese, mired in poverty and ravaged by civil war, about to be submerged in the rising red tide of communism.

Until the USA, leader of the free world, stepped in to help.

Thus, it was with a clear sense of purpose tempered by vague apprehension that I said good-bye to my loved ones and headed to Việt-Nam in July 1967. Stuck in my mind through the seventeen-hour flight to Biên-Hoà was a catchy tune I'd heard over the radio on my last night with Debbie: Scott McKenzie's new hit single, "Be Sure to Wear Flowers in Your Hair." The hippie movement was in full bloom. One could almost smell change in the air. But not once did it enter my mind on that summer evening that an entire way of life was indeed passing.

Biên-Hoà AFB, 5 Aug 1967, 2100 hrs

Dear Debbie,

My first hello to you from Việt-Nam, and I'm still learning to get all the name spellings correct. How've you been, sweetie? Seems like weeks since I last saw you, though it was only a few days ago. I am missing you something awful already.

Now, where to start? There are a million things I want to share with you, but I'm still processing them myself, so just bear with me. First off, Biên-Hoà is a small town only 19 miles northeast of Sài-Gòn, the capital. Its name means "peaceful borders" in Vietnamese. Maybe true in some distant past, but the place is anything but peaceful these days. For starters, we've built a huge base here, the busiest airport in the world, I was told, all carved out of a gigantic dust bowl. You wouldn't believe how dusty and windy it is around here. Comparable to Owens Valley in the worst days of summer. Same with the heat. The one big difference, though, is the humidity. We're registering 100% humidity during the monsoon season, which is now and the next four months. It pours every day, sometimes hard and fast for thirty minutes or so, other times on and off all day long, turning the red dust into mud. Can you imagine, 100°F with 100% humidity? That's why I had to wait till bedtime to write you. It's simply too steamy in here during the day. And guess what, it's still raining as I write.

I share a cozy 8'x20' "hooch" with a mate. Real nice fellow from Minnesota named Bob Olsen. Not sure how to describe our hooch, except that it looks to me like a chicken house. The lower half is wood, the upper half some type of screen to allow air circulation while keeping the bugs out. There are louvered windows we can crank open in sunny weather to let in more breeze (or hot air), and a corrugated tin roof that makes even the lightest rain shower sound like pea-sized hail. Not the best amenities, for sure. But hey, we're at war after all, and I'm not complaining.

There's a Vietnamese woman who comes in every day to clean the place for us. She makes the beds, does the laundry, and polishes our shoes. All for $4.25 a month, which converts into 500 đồng for her, handsome wages by local standards, according to Bob. She's our "mama-san," a nickname first used by American GIs in Japan for a maid or service provider. But her actual name is Bà Bảy, which means "Mrs. Seven." You know why? As tiny as she appears, Bà Bảy is the mother hen to a brood of seven, or so she claims. At least as best I can make out her broken English.

She sometimes brings her youngest with her, a cute little boy of five. He's the most inquisitive little squirt I've seen. If I happen to be in the hooch when he and his mommy arrive, he'll fall in step right behind me wherever I go, staring, giggling, and not bashful about touching my arms either. A hairy foreigner! I must be quite a novelty to the tyke. Bà Bảy calls him Cu Bóng, or "Little Cue Ball," for his bald head. You should've seen his eyes open wide like saucers when I gave him a pack of gum the other day. Which reminds me. If it's not too much to ask, would you drop a small toy in the next package you might be sending me? A toy car, a fire truck, or GI Joe, anything like that would do. I bet Cu Bóng has never owned a toy in his young life, and you'd make him so happy by sending one for him.

Well, sweetheart, the night is getting on, and you must be bored silly with my ramblings. You understand, though, I want to share this experience with you as I go along. It's such a different world over here, Debbie, and not a pretty one either, as I'm already finding out in a few short days. Anyway, my dear, when you take your lunch break every day at noon (that's 3 a.m. my time), walk over to our favorite park by the lake and enjoy a peaceful moment in the gazebo overlooking the water. That's where I want to visit you, in my dreams.

Love, R.C.

In those early days, I didn't fully grasp how worried my family was for me. Back when I was still safely sequestered behind the walls of medical school with my nose to the books, they'd been following with growing concern the latest developments in Indochina. With the superpowers getting more involved by the day, amid political unrest in the US, everyone could feel this international conflict was fast reaching critical mass. The relentless reporting of war casualties only heightened the tension.

Once I had departed for Việt-Nam, my family, like countless others all across America, waited in suspense for news of their loved one overseas. My mom kept every single letter I sent from Biên-Hoà so she could reread it during those busy spells when I couldn't find time to write. Years later, long after we turned our backs and ran from that nightmare, she'd present me with an unexpected gift when she handed me back the complete set of my wartime mail, neatly secured in a bundle. Her words at the time were, "Don't be in a hurry to dispose of these letters, son. They're a journal of your past. Who knows, you just might want to revisit it some day."

My mother wasn't the only one to feel this way. Debbie, too, had preserved the few pieces of mail she'd received from me during that tumultuous year.

Biên-Hoà AFB, 7 Aug 1967, 2030 hrs

Hi, Mom and Dad,
    A nice big hug from your son, finally! Sorry I couldn't write sooner, but it really has been a whirlwind so far. Both of you and

Jer must also have had your hands full at Moon Meadows, this being the peak season and all. Please make sure you hire plenty of extra help so you don't get all worn out by the end of summer.

Now let me set your minds at ease, one more time. I've been assigned as a general medical officer at a secure airbase in the rear, so don't worry yourselves sick over me going out on patrol in the bush, because I'm NOT. Our clinic here is not very large, as we only handle sick calls and minor injuries, with rare overnight stays. Major cases are stabilized then immediately med-evac'ed by chopper to larger field hospitals in Sài-Gòn, Long-Bình or Cam-Ranh. Don't get me wrong. We're still shorthanded in providing 24-hour care to the on-base personnel of several thousand, and six-day workweeks are the norm, in addition to pulling calls. During hectic times when the shifts all run together, we live on black coffee and APC tablets for aches and pains so we can keep going, same as the pilots and ground crews around here.

On Sundays, many of us participate in various civic projects to offer much-needed medical service to the local population, which is constantly swelling with refugees from the countryside. These poor souls live in such squalor you can't imagine, and every bit of help goes a long way in improving their lot. We've written to pharmaceuticals back home to solicit donations of antibiotics, pain relievers, vitamins, and whatever else they can spare, and they've all responded with an outpouring of generous support.

One final note on this subject: if you guys have stuff you want to get rid of, anything at all—old clothes, shoes, toys, blankets, sleeping bags, canned foods etc—pack it all up and ship it to me. We'll put it to humanitarian use, down to the very last item. That's how immense the need is among these destitute peasants. The following will show you what I'm talking about:

Most of our guys detest C-rations, which they deride as "dog food left over from WWII." Among their least favorite items in the C-rat boxes is the tropical chocolate bar, nicknamed the "John Wayne Bar" because it's made extra hard so that it won't melt in the heat. It's regularly discarded without so much as a thought, but now we're starting to collect every bar we can get our hands on. It's for the kids in local orphanages, since we hear they fight over it for what little sweetness it does contain. So you see, Mom and Dad, you could really help promote our cause by spreading the word when you get a chance, in church or at town hall meetings, if you feel so inclined. Tell the folks at home: don't toss anything out. Send it our way and it'll be used to assist some unfortunate person over here, in one small way or another.

Still on the subject of food. Gosh, Mom, I'm absolutely starved for your home-fried pork chops with real mashed potatoes and fluffy biscuits, corn on the cob with gobs of butter, and a generous side of green beans. I even dreamed about all this the other night, which scares me. How will I survive a whole year without your scrumptious home-cooked meals?

You know what else I dreamed of? Our mountains and meadows, and the pine forests and snowmelt streams in late spring. I woke up one recent morning smelling the heady fragrance of damp pine needles drying out in the sun, thinking for one ecstatic second I was back on the trail again. Speaking of smells, we have the foulest air around here, for lack of a sewage system. The outhouses are built atop recycled 55-gallon drums that serve as collecting tanks, and once a day a crew is assigned to remove those drums with their precious contents and replace them with empty new ones. The old tanks are then doused in diesel fuel and set ablaze, and the designated "honey-dippers" must stir and mix that burning mess until it's rendered to ashes. Such crappy detail, poor kids! The billowing black smoke from the fire permeates the air day and night, and I've got a sneaking suspicion this distinctive odor of Biên-Hoà AFB will stick in my memory for as long as I live.

It's getting late, I really should get some shut-eye. Once again, please stop worrying about me. Except for the lack of "civilized" comfort, I feel very safe and secure on base.

Mom, do take good care of that bum shoulder of yours. And Dad, please see to it that she does. Say hi to old Jer for me. Tell him I'll write him soon. If you're sending foodstuff, make sure it's wrapped tightly in foil paper to keep the ants out.

Love, your son R.C.

Chapter Six

"Say, how about a short excursion to the Pearl of the Orient?" Bob asked me a couple of weeks after I'd met Dean Hunter. It had been a quiet afternoon at the dispensary, which gave us a rare chance to catch up with paperwork.

Raising my head from my desk, I tossed him a questioning look.

"That's what the French used to call old Sài-Gòn," he clarified. "Must have been some truth to it, at least before the war. I was told some famous English writers visited the city back in those days and really enjoyed their stays."

"Oh yes. I started Graham Greene's book on Việt-Nam before I left home," I told Bob. "*The Quiet American*, I think it was. Never got around to finishing it, but it's still in my bag. Anyhow, what's in Sài-Gòn that needs tending to?"

It turned out Bob wanted to follow up on one of his charges, a wounded parajumper he had ordered airlifted to 3rd Field Hospital just outside the capital shortly before my arrival.

"Want to come?" he asked. "You can tour the facility, meet some people we work closely with, like the folks in the 9th Medical Lab. Then we can catch a taxi into town and kill an hour or two playing tourists. It'll be my second trip there."

Generally speaking, Sài-Gòn, like other big cities in the country, was off-limits to American military personnel, except on official duty. But Bob and I would have a legitimate excuse to be in town, and hopefully a rare opportunity to combine business with pleasure. Though only a short hop on Quốc-Lộ Một (National Highway One) from Biên-Hoà, the hospital was customarily reached by choppers, due to security reasons. It was located right outside the gate of Tân-Sơn-Nhất AFB, which also doubled as the civilian airport to the capital.

"3rd Field is a showpiece to the VIPs," Bob explained further. "Clean and modern, and air-conditioned, of course. The nurses wear traditional white, but visitors like us are allowed in civvies to be more comfortable."

We decided to make the trip that same Saturday to give ourselves more time afterward for sightseeing, such as it was, since there was no volunteer project planned for that weekend. As a newbie, I looked forward to my first chance to get off base and see a bit more of the country.

Early Saturday, we hitched a ride on an Army helicopter sent to pick up visiting dignitaries at Tân-Sơn-Nhất that morning.

On the flight over, Bob filled me in on the case at hand: twenty-year-old Airman Oliver Perez, known to his mates in the 38th Air Rescue and Recovery Squadron as Jolly Olly for his sunny temperament. His was an impressive tale of courage and dedication.

Jolly Olly had been part of a rescue team of two Huskie choppers, call sign "Pedro," dispatched on a med-evac mission in the jungles east of Biên-Hoà. Deep in the bowels of the triple-canopy forest, an infantry company had stumbled into an ambush and was pounded by enemy troops that vastly outnumbered them.

With no clearings in sight, Army Dustoff helicopters had been unable to land to retrieve the dead and wounded. In came the Air Force Huskies, which hovered over the dense canopy while their crews lowered a pair of Stokes litters through the trees. On the ground, a wounded soldier was hastily strapped into each litter before it was winched back up into the aircraft. The choppers immediately took off for the nearest field hospital, then returned for the next retrieval. This tedious process bogged down in the absence of well-trained medics on the ground, which threatened to jeopardize the entire operation. Jolly Olly requested permission to go in.

Intense enemy fire zinged past the daring PJ as he rode the "jungle penetrator," a long hoist with spring-loaded legs that extended into seats, into the inferno below. After touching ground, he moved quickly to coordinate and speed up the rescue by assisting casualties onto the Stokes litters or the flimsy seats on the penetrator. Thanks to his expertise, many more wounded were safely evacuated than would have been.

Jolly Olly held out until nightfall, when darkness put a halt to the operation and he was ordered to return to his aircraft on the final lift. Only then did his crewmates realize he had sustained multiple gunshot wounds, one from a tracer round that scorched a lower leg of his fatigues. Back at the base, upon assessing his serious condition and doing all he could to stabilize it, Bob had him airlifted to 3rd Field Hospital for further treatment.

"It's incredible what the human body is capable of, once we decide to step up to the plate," Bob remarked. "Had he not been ordered to quit when he did, Jolly Olly would've pushed right on until he dropped from losing too much blood. He sure did his Maroon Berets proud. It's no bullcrap they call themselves 'men of steel.'" As I pondered the airman's heroic deeds, Bob finished his thought. "Bragging rights aside, what he did truly exemplified their motto, 'That others may live.' One serious badass, our young fellow."

At that moment, a familiar-looking scene began to unfold on the ground below. Through a shimmering haze of heat, exhaust fumes, and billowing black smoke emerged another hotbed of nonstop activity and blurry motion, not too different from what I'd grown accustomed to at our home base. Over the din that reached up to greet us, the crew announced our descent to Tân-Sơn-Nhất, the second-busiest airport in the world behind Biên-Hoà.

From the air, Bob pointed out the front entrance to the base, and across the street from it, a sprawling complex of two-story structures that resembled oversized metal boxes. A colorful display of international flags flew on the main structure's rooftop.

"There it is. The headquarters of the Free World Military Assistance Command in Việt-Nam, MACV for short, or 'Pentagon East,'" Bob said. "Few people know it also houses the 7th Air Force headquarters. I've never been inside, but that's who we report to."

A short distance up the road, I made out an impressive compound of white-stucco buildings with red-tiled roofs. Covered walkways meandered among the buildings between patches of green grass that shone brightly in the sun. It was amazing to discover such an oasis of calm in the heart of chaos.

"Let me guess," I said, motioning to the immaculate compound. "3rd Field Hospital?"

Bob nodded, then pointed with his chin at a discreet villa across the road from the hospital. "Check this out. From up here, you can practically peek inside the private residence of the Big Chief." Anticipating my question, he went on. "Yessiree. The One and Only. Westy, aka General William C. Westmoreland."

In a swirl of dust, the Army Huey touched down on the helipad at 3rd Field. Bob and I hopped out and ran toward the nearest walkway, waving good-bye to the crew as their helicopter immediately took to the air to make room for another to land.

⌐‿⌐

To save time, Bob suggested we split up and go our separate ways during our visit. After introducing me to some hospital staff who offered to show me around, he disappeared into the convalescing ward to find Jolly Olly. We agreed to meet up in the lobby after we were done.

By noontime, I found my way back to the lobby, overwhelmed by what little I'd glimpsed of the monumental work being carried out at the hospital. The appearance of serenity I had admired in the courtyard belied the crisis and urgency that prevailed the moment one stepped through the door. Among the echoing corridors of the wards, one was assailed by the uneasy feeling of Death on the lurk.

"Look who I bumped into." I heard Bob's voice behind me and turned to see him walking up the hallway in the company of a tall man in casual street clothes. When the man said hello with a firm handshake, I recognized a well-scrubbed, clean-shaven Dean Hunter. Clad in Levi's and short sleeves, Dean looked fit and relaxed—quite the dashing young doctor, with an added edge of Old West ruggedness about him.

"Nice seeing you again, Captain," I said. "You coming or going?"

"Just dropped off some blood work at the 9th Lab," Dean answered with a friendly wink. "I'm cleared for the rest of the day. How you doing, kiddo? Over your shell shock yet?"

"Dean was nice enough to offer to be our tour guide in the city," Bob said. "He's been there on several occasions and knows his way around. Right, Captain?"

"Actually, I'm meeting a friend in downtown Sài-Gòn. He's the tour guide, as a member of the press. But I can get us downtown, if you guys care to hang out together."

We got a Jeep ride to the busy airport terminal next door, where Dean flagged down one of the blue-and-yellow taxicabs, a French-made Renault 4CV that looked like a Volkswagen Beetle from the last war, only tinier. As we piled into this sorry relic of an automobile, Bob said, "Jolly Olly's doing fantastic. Right on schedule for recovery."

During the bumpy ride downtown, I received a crash course on the recent history of Sài-Gòn, courtesy of Dean Hunter. Not too long ago, this quaint capital city in the tropics had been extolled as the "Paris of the East" for its low-key urban charm. Then along came the war. It put Sài-Gòn on the world map and transformed it overnight into an international metropolis, military complex, and giant refugee camp all rolled into one. The result was a city of stark contrasts: between Old World elegance and the commercialism of new money; the high, fast living of the privileged few and the squalor among the masses; a humble colonial past and a volatile, dangerous present.

Originally planned for a citizenry of fewer than a million, Sài-Gòn had seen its population explode in recent years to upwards of three million people in 1967. Many were refugees who had fled the fighting in the countryside for a safe haven within the city limits. In fact, just outside the airport, we crossed over a muddy canal whose banks were covered with decrepit shanties under tin roofs, a squatters' colony like countless others around the capital.

Traveling less than five miles from Tân-Sơn-Nhất to downtown took us more than half an hour, so horrendous was midday traffic. With no air conditioner, the cab's windows were rolled down, and I gawked in disbelief at the chaotic hodgepodge that ensnared us. Up and down the narrow street, a few US Army trucks and European-made cars were hopelessly snagged in a sea of bicycles, motorbikes, pedicabs ("cyclos"), and three-wheel jitneys ("Lambrettas"). Except for the more bulky vehicles, all managed to weave and swerve and surge forward like giant schools of fish, though not as quietly. In a cacophony of screaming voices and honking horns, everyone fought for their right-of-way with little assistance from scarce traffic lights. A blue curtain of exhaust fumes hung heavy in the afternoon heat, tickling my throat and burning my eyes.

The street was lined on both sides with private residences that confronted first-time visitors with a startling mix of old and new. Next to venerable French villas that had seen better days behind their wrought-iron gates stood five-story concrete boxes with mini-balconies and open rooftops. New constructions sprouted on every corner, and it seemed just a matter of time before they'd supplant the lovely old dwellings. As we got farther inside the city, the French colonial-style houses became more stately and widely spaced, with an occasional small park squeezed in between. The road appeared much improved with fewer potholes and lighter traffic. Policemen dressed in all-white uniforms, hence their nickname "white mice," directed traffic from raised platforms in the centers of intersections.

As our taxicab finally picked up speed, Dean leaned forward in his seat.

"We've arrived in the heart of the city," he announced, tapping the Vietnamese driver on the shoulder, signaling for him to slow down. "Coming up on your right is the Presidential Palace, which looks more like a glorified bomb shelter. See the park in front of it?" He motioned to our left. "Look through the trees. You can make out the new US Embassy complex just beyond the park. A fortress itself."

Bob and I fidgeted uncomfortably in our crammed seats as we craned to follow Dean's nimble finger. He paused briefly to get his bearings before speaking to the smiling driver in the native tongue. The cab hung a sharp left onto a wide, tree-lined boulevard, speeding away from the imposing iron gate of the palace in the direction of the embassy.

Dean resumed his rapid-fire tour guide's spiel. "Gentlemen, we're about to head down the most famous street of Sài-Gòn, perhaps of all Indochina. Rue Catinat, if you prefer its former French name. Or Tự-Do, which means 'freedom,' as it's known nowadays to the locals."

As if on cue, the ever-smiling driver took an abrupt right turn, leaving the embassy complex in his rearview mirror.

Anchored at one end, where we had just turned, by Notre Dame Cathedral and the central post office, two landmarks dating from the late nineteenth century, Tự-Do was a short avenue stretching several blocks down to the west bank of the Sài-Gòn River. Its spacious sidewalks, shielded by tall trees from the blazing sun, provided a pleasant promenade past elegant boutiques and restaurants, luxury hotels, and sidewalk cafés. The atmosphere was charming and intimate, reminiscent of old Europe since the buildings were French colonial from the turn of the century, no more than five or six stories tall. However, there were indications that the times had caught up with the street. Whole sections toward the park overlooking the river had been stripped of their shade trees and lined with seedy nightclubs and massage parlors under garish neon signs.

The taxicab pulled up to the entrance of a stylish-looking hotel at a main street corner bordering on a square. It wasn't a formal entrance, strictly speaking, but rather a large and airy veranda, raised several steps above pavement level and fronted by grand arches that opened onto the sidewalks. The veranda appeared to wrap around the entire block. Emblazoned in bold black letters across the white awnings that shaded its periphery was the establishment's name, "Hôtel Continental Palace." In the center of the adjacent square stood a massive building with an ornate, half-domed façade.

Dean caught my wandering gaze. "That's the old opera house, recently renovated to serve as home to the elected national assembly. We're going to Continental, the oldest hotel in Việt-Nam, open since 1880. Arguably the best known, also."

We crawled out of the cab, climbed the steps, and escaped into the cool shade on the veranda, which turned out to be a terrace bar-restaurant. Quiet electric fans hung from vaulted ceilings, circulating a fresh breeze throughout the terrace. Bob whistled. "White tablecloths. And white-shirted waiters. Fancy schmantzy place, Captain Hunter."

Someone got up from a nearby table and approached our group. Dean recognized his buddy, greeting him with a slap on the shoulder and a handshake. When they turned back to Bob and me for introductions, my jaw dropped.

"Dick? Dick Hayashi?" I stammered, not trusting my own eyes.

"Well, well. Small world," Dean said as Dick led us back to his table, which faced out to Lam-Sơn Square. The bar was obviously a popular hangout since all the tables looked occupied—by Westerners, mainly.

"First things first," Dick said, putting up his hand to hold back my questions. "You guys must be dying of thirst after that taxi ride. If it's your first time here, let me suggest Algerian red wine, or the local beer. Tiger Beer, it's called, or *Ba Mười Ba*, which means 'thirty-three' in Vietnamese."

We all opted for a cold Tiger Beer, named for its curious logo that depicted the outline of a tiger's head above the enigmatic number 33. After the waiter in starched-collar shirt brought the bottles and glasses, Dick turned to me and smiled. "Okay, then."

He had scarcely changed. Still not quite the ladies' man he'd often fantasized growing into, being rather short and stocky, with uncooperative black hair and squinty eyes that smiled behind thick glasses, he seemed to have remained that gentle, down-to-earth kid of our high school years. It had been a good while since I'd last seen Dick, right before we headed off to different colleges. Funny how quickly we'd drifted apart and lost touch, faster than I would've imagined, considering what close pals we'd been growing up. Last I heard, he was working on becoming a published author.

"I'm an 'obligated volunteer,' thanks to the doctor draft. That's why I'm here," I told Dick, trying to soft-pedal it so I wouldn't offend Dean or Bob. "What's your excuse?"

"Until I publish the next Great American Novel, there are bills to pay, unfortunately." Dick still had that same easy laugh I'd known so well. "I've been a correspondent for AP in Sài-Gòn for over a year now. Dean and I met while I was doing a piece on Special Forces."

The Associated Press, like NBC News, maintained an office in the taller Eden Building across Tự-Do Street from the four-story Hôtel Continental Palace. Dick said he'd been extremely lucky to have found a small apartment in the same building on the ground floor, having inherited it from his predecessor as part of the package deal with his job offer.

"Couldn't be a better location," he said with a thumbs-up. "This area around old Rue Catinat is a happening place. The epicenter for everything. News, rumors, espionage, nightlife. There's a good reason it's been dubbed 'Radio Catinat,' going back to Graham Greene's days in the early fifties. You just keep your ear to the ground. And stay tuned."

From the "Continental Shelf" where we sat sipping ice-cold Tiger Beers, watching sparrows fly in from the street through white-washed arches, Dick pointed out some major landmarks of downtown Sài-Gòn from a reporter's perspective. Since the Joint US Public Affairs Office, or JUSPAO, held their daily war briefings at the Rex Hotel, one block up on Lê-Lợi Street past the giant Marines Statues nobody liked, all the news organizations had congregated in this neighborhood. Time magazine ran an office on the second floor of the Continental, while across Lam-Sơn Square, ABC and CBS News operated their Sài-Gòn bureaus from the tallest high-rise in the city, the ten-story art nouveau Hôtel Caravelle. Both UPI and Reuters headquarters were a leisurely stroll away. And camped out at their regular tables on the Shelf were French journalists with the Agence France-Presse (AFP) or the Parisian dailies *Le Figaro* and *Le Monde*, looking very much at home in their former colony.

It turned out Dick was a big fan of Graham Greene's novel *The Quiet American* because of its immediate relevancy to Việt-Nam. Even before he arrived in country, it had provided him with a mental map of downtown Sài-Gòn. "It felt almost eerie when I first got here. A strong sense of déjà vu, you know, very *Twilight Zone*," he explained.

"Then I remembered the core action in the book took place right in this area. Pyle and Fowler met each other here at the Shelf. Phượng went for her mid-morning 'elevenses' at the 'milk bar' at Givral's, that small café in blue and white across the way. And of course, the explosion. It was set off just steps from our table, on Lam-Sơn Square, or Place Garnier in the story."

I smiled as I remembered how Dick had always loved a good read.

He went on. "It was all so realistic in the book. Such excellent writing. A true master. Do you know some cynics still insist that in real life Mr. Greene himself might have been the greatest 'spook' in town, back in the day?"

"But how do you cover the war from inside the city? If you don't mind my asking." Bob spoke up for the first time, twirling the beer bottle in his fingers.

Dick shot him a glance, shrugged. "I can only speak for myself. As a rule, I try to verify whatever news is broadcast on Radio Catinat, including casualty stats from the 'Five o'clock Follies.' That's what we call the daily briefings at JUSPAO. I head out where the action is to see for myself. As often as the boss lets me."

He explained that accredited journalists were accorded full cooperation and assistance by the military to go almost anywhere in Việt-Nam to report on the war. In fact, their travel priority on military transports was on a par with that of a colonel.

"We all bought jungle fatigues from the surplus pile when we first arrived. To wear out in the bush, was the idea." Dick laughed again. "I sure got my money's worth, but not everybody did. Have you guys noticed how my esteemed colleagues prefer to go out on the town in safari suits instead? Take a good look around you. Those green garbs are all the rage, custom-made by local tailors to a perfect fit, with cool sleeve pockets and everything. Now, picture me in them rags. Ain't it a riot?"

He paused to light a Pall Mall—the first time I'd ever seen him smoke—then turned to Bob.

"I get what you're saying. I sometimes wonder the same thing. Many of the fellows here are content to hang around the city, report on the rumor mill, and regurgitate the bulletin news from official briefings." He took a long drag before continuing. "The closest they ever get to any real fighting is the rooftop bar at the Rex after sundown."

Dick told us about a popular pastime of foreign correspondents in Sài-Gòn. Nightly, when the searing heat of the day had subsided, they'd frequent the outdoor lounges on the top floor of the Caravelle or the Hôtel Majestic, another old haunt of Graham Greene's at the end of Tự-Do Street, overlooking the river. Occasionally, a lucky few might receive an invitation to that most exclusive club in town, the Officers' Club on the rooftop of the Rex BOQ, also known as the Generals' Hotel. From high above the city, with a refilled cocktail in hand, they'd stare out over the black river and watch the war unfold live on the outskirts of the capital. Illumination flares, red and green tracers, and napalm bombs lit up the horizon in an ongoing pyrotechnic sideshow, complete with audio effects. Those sights and sounds of live combat, even from a safe distance, had inspired many eloquent reports on the state of the war without subjecting their resourceful authors to any imminent danger.

"That, guys," said Dick in conclusion, "is the Sài-Gòn my fellow journalists have come to love. A big stage of sorts. All very kitschy and surreal."

He stubbed out his cigarette and smiled at Bob and me. "Not to change subjects, but I promised Dean I'd take him to a favorite hangout of mine a few blocks from here. You're both welcome to join us. It's a hole in the wall, but unlike anything you've seen before."

I turned and deferred to Bob. He glanced at his watch, then nodded. "If you're sure you don't mind. Our ride back is not until 2000 hours."

Chapter Seven

"How the hell did you all manage to squeeze into that little taxi?" Dick laughed as he slipped behind the wheel of the Peugeot 404 he'd borrowed from his office. "It's true *everything* here is miniature. You get used to it."

On our way from downtown, I recognized again the red-brick cathedral with its twin towers and the glass-and-wrought-iron central post office designed by famed architect Gustave Eiffel. Shortly after we sped by the US Embassy on our right-hand side, a sprawling mass of six-story buildings, Dick hung a left and drove down a busy street alongside the Presidential Palace garden, which extended over two entire blocks. Immediately past the garden stood a large, open complex with a fair amount of traffic at its gate.

"That's the Cercle Sportif, playground to Sài-Gòn's elite," Dick said. "Its membership roster reads like the city's Who's Who. French plantation owners, wealthy Vietnamese businessmen, politicians, generals, you name it. Very chic country club. But we ain't going there."

He broke away from the thoroughfare and took the next left onto a shady drive that cut through an English-garden park with towering exotic trees. On either side of the road ran a trail wide enough to accommodate single-file horseback riders on a leisurely outing. The surprising scene seemed a throwback to the genteel colonial days under the French.

"Tao-Đàn Park, a gem snuggled away in the middle of the city," Dick announced. "The French-sponsored equestrian club, the Cercle

Hippique, is in the park. Nearby is the National Music Conservatory. Charming old neighborhood, this is."

We emerged from the park onto a quiet tree-lined avenue and drove through an upper-class residential area with ivy-walled villas behind closed gates. As if reading my mind, Dick pulled over to the curb and parked.

"Here's the scoop on this place." He turned and fixed us with his gaze, his hands clasped in front of him. "It's an exclusive club, members-only. You guys are my guests, so do me proud." Then half-jokingly, "I want to hang on to my membership. It's invitation only."

According to Dick, the club was owned and managed by Madame Yvonne, a black *métisse* whose father had served in the French Foreign Legion in Indochina at the onset of WWII. She and her older American-contractor husband operated the club out of their home, a discreet villa just steps from where we had parked. In the tradition of the social *salons* of Paris in its heyday—at least that seemed Madame Yvonne's aspiration—the club provided a private, pleasant setting in which contributing members could gather, socialize, and unwind from the stresses of life. The original patrons had been business associates of her husband's, but as word spread, her list of invited-only *habitués* had expanded to include people from various walks of life, predominantly American. To assist her in ensuring that all her guests received personal attention and enjoyed a good time during their visit, Madame Yvonne employed a bevy of hand-groomed Vietnamese hostesses who delighted guests with their fluent English and graceful manners.

"Absolutely no hanky-panky allowed," Dick stressed. "This ain't like those snack bars on Tự-Do Street. Everything's on the up-and-up."

"What the hell kind of a place is she trying to run? The 21 Club in Manhattan?" Dean grumbled, winking at me.

Dick shrugged. "Just telling you, men. Hostesses here are just hostesses. Many of them are married, as are most of the guests. Feel free to invite any of the ladies to join you at the table for conversation or a dance. Just make sure you refill and pay for her drinks and yours. I'll take care of the cover charge." Eyeing Bob's wedding band, he quickly added, "But if you'd rather be left alone with your drink, nobody will bother you. Guaranteed."

We got out of the car. Dick led us up the sidewalk to the solid iron gate that stood guard under an arbor of orange hibiscus flowers. Nodding and smiling at us, he reached for the little bell above the mailbox.

———

In subsequent years, how often I caught myself wandering back in time, lured by a siren song from the past, reliving over and over that first afternoon *chez* Madame Yvonne. It was an altogether different world we crossed into the minute the double gate clanked shut behind us. In silence, we followed the young girl in black silk trousers and white shirt along a stone-and-grass walkway, between two high walls covered in tropical vines. Inside, we could hear indistinct voices mixed with laughter, the merry clinking of glasses, and floating in the air, a soft strand of orchestral music, "Moon River." The walkway opened onto a lush lawn with flowering shrubs and small trees decorated with strings of Christmas lights. Scattered across the lawn were round tables draped in white cloth, occupied by small groups of two or three. On the grass, an oblivious couple was dancing slowly to the easy-listening music over hidden speakers. The atmosphere felt intimate and welcoming, as if we'd arrived at a summer-evening wedding reception back home.

"*Salut, salut*, Ree-Shaar," someone greeted Dick with effusion, pronouncing his formal first name with a thick French accent that rolled the R's in a guttural purr. "How are you doing, *mon chéri*? It has been much too long."

A tall, thin black woman in a blue evening gown glided toward us with arms open wide. She and Dick hugged and exchanged kisses on both cheeks. Even with makeup, she couldn't have been older than thirty, with slanted wide eyes and pronounced cheekbones that reminded me of a famous Italian movie actress. A round of introductions ensued and Madame Yvonne, all honey and sugar, played the impeccable hostess to the hilt.

"*Bienvenus*, doctors. Any friends of Richard's are friends of ours. Please make yourselves at home. Let me rearrange some tables together for you, right over here, in the cool shade." She smiled broadly at Dick and continued in her lilting voice, "I shall let Vivienne know you're here, *mon chou. Tout de suite.*"

We were seated at three small tables pushed together under a trellis of bougainvillea the color of fire engines. The other guests, all Westerners and men of different ages dressed in casual street clothes, looked up in curiosity and raised their glasses or waved at us with friendly smiles. The women in their company, who listened to them with keen interest, looked Vietnamese. Most of them donned the graceful traditional *áo dài*, form-fitting gowns made of beautiful silk or brocade, over flowing trousers in black or white silk. A few were attired in western-style evening gowns, but nowhere to be seen were the miniskirts that ruled the sidewalks on Tự-Do Street. The women sat erect in their chairs, hands folded in their laps and heads tilted to pay full attention to what the men had to say, nodding and laughing at appropriate times.

Over Henri Mancini's orchestra and muffled voices from nearby tables, I heard the happy twitter of birds in the trees for the first time since arriving in country. The warm breeze was suffused with the sweet fragrance of jasmine in bloom and felt like a caress on my face. What a welcome change of pace from the reigning madness at Biên-Hoà AFB, I thought with relish and leaned back in my chair, eyes half-closed, as the tension in my neck and shoulders began to seep away.

"Hello, Dick," a raspy voice pulled me back from my reverie. "How are you, darling?"

A young woman in a gorgeous *áo dài* was leaning over the back of Dick's chair, her long, tapered fingers resting on his shoulders.

He jumped up, took both her hands in his, and gave her quick pecks on the cheeks. "Everyone. This is Vivienne," said Dick, a warm smile in his voice.

Straightening, she looked a tad taller than him—rather unusual for a Vietnamese woman, even in high heels—with permed black hair and a friendly, open face. As Dick introduced us, we stood and shook hands with her. Her hand was small and soft, but resolute, neither nervous nor timid. Vivienne asked us what we'd like to drink, and we all ordered the local Tiger Beer whose crisp taste we had just discovered at the Continental Shelf.

"I invite a couple friends to join us?" she inquired casually as she was about to walk away. Dick turned to us, his eyebrows raised in anticipation.

Dean stared ahead without a word, while Bob blushed, shook his head, and mumbled, "No, thanks." I smiled and told Vivienne, "There's no rush, thank you. We'll get up and stretch our legs in a while." Behind her back, Dick rolled his eyes at us in obvious disappointment.

Vivienne soon returned with our refreshments, an iced tea for herself, and sat next to Dick. She carried out her hostess duties with aplomb and good humor, speaking excellent English and proving quite adept at the art of small talk to put her guests at ease. The moment she sensed us relaxed and ready to open up, she turned into a sympathetic listener. Although not exactly what you'd call a classic beauty, she was all poise and charm. It wasn't long before Bob showed her his wallet picture of Nancy and told her all about their baby on the way.

Someone must have put on a new record, as I recognized Andy Williams' baritone crooning "Days of Wine and Roses" in the background. Meanwhile, Vivienne had leaned closer to Dick and discreetly looped her arm around his. I couldn't help but notice how relaxed and content he appeared, and I was happy for him, recalling how self-conscious he used to be around the fair sex in high school. It struck me that perhaps the two would appreciate a moment alone.

"I'd like to wash my hands, if I may," I chimed in at the next lull in the conversation, hoping Dean and Bob would pick up on my signal.

"*Toilette* is inside the house. Past lounge and turn right," Vivienne said. "I show you." She started to get up.

"No, no, you stay, please," I said. "I'll find it." I motioned to my two colleagues but neither one budged, blind as bats to my suggestion. Finally, I excused myself and headed for the house.

Through double French doors, I stepped into a spacious living area decorated like a clubroom for big gatherings, with couches, chairs, and cocktail tables around the shiny tile floor. Propped against a long wood-paneled wall, a small black-and-white TV was tuned to channel 11, the Sài-Gòn station for American TV broadcast on AFVN. There wasn't a soul in the lounge. Aside from a couple of busy bartenders at the counter in the corner, everyone else was outdoors enjoying the beautiful landscaped garden, which was on display through the floor-to-ceiling glass windows flanking the French doors.

I found the bathroom as directed and went in. It was immaculate and beyond luxurious compared to the showers and outhouses at the base. I took my time and gave myself a mini-bath, splashing warm water over my face and my arms, indulging in the delight of indoor plumbing. A brand-new me emerged from the bathroom.

"Doctor Connors. Did you find everything you needed?" Mme Yvonne got up hastily from a couch inside the big lounge, where she had been speaking in hushed tones with somebody, and hurried over to my side.

I had the awkward impression of having trespassed on a private scene. Despite a ready smile, Mme Yvonne wasn't able to conceal her uneasiness and preoccupation. Behind her, on the couch, a distraught-looking woman turned away from us to dab her eyes, her face half-hidden by a cascade of long black hair.

It was an uncomfortable moment. I felt caught off guard, at a loss for words. After a few seconds of silent hesitation, Mme Yvonne took me by the elbow and nudged me toward the door, out of earshot, where she confided her delicate situation in a whisper. "I am truly sorry you had to witness this. There's a new hostess who just started with us this afternoon, and she's having a tough time with it." The puzzled look on my face prompted her to continue. "Well, it's rather complicated. She's married, and her husband doesn't yet know she works here. Now she's not sure she's doing the right thing."

Holding a hand to her forehead, Mme Yvonne sighed. "She's a sweet girl. I'd do anything to help her, but this is not going to work out. She will not even venture outside in the garden."

In retrospect, I've always wondered what came over me in that instant, but I did what must have seemed the most natural thing at the time. I asked Mme Yvonne, "Do you think I can help? Would she agree to sit and have a drink with me in here? You're welcome to stay and join us. That way she won't feel so nervous, all alone with me."

She stared at me, surprised by my offer. Then she gave me a hug. "*Vous êtes un ange*—what an angel. You really would do that? Bless your heart. That just might work."

"What's her name?" I inquired, which reminded her of an unfinished business.

"*Mon Dieu*," she exclaimed. "I haven't had a chance to choose a working name for her. All the other girls have theirs. It makes it easier for our guests, you see. Her Vietnamese name is Liên. L-I-E-N."

"Sounds like Lee Anne, if you say it fast," I remarked.

Mme Yvonne concurred enthusiastically, "Lee Anne. That's it. Very pretty name. I'm sure she will like it. Give me a few minutes to speak with her alone."

When Mme Yvonne returned, she was all smiles, once again her composed and gracious self. "Thank you for doing this," she said. "We owe you big. Let's give this a try, shall we?"

I followed her back inside the lounge. The woman stood by the sofa waiting for us, her face still angled away. Someone had cranked down the volume on the TV set.

"Doctor Connors," Mme Yvonne said. "This is Lee Anne."

She turned toward me with an apprehensive half smile, and bowed slightly. I was struck by how young and innocent she looked, almost like a college student, with her unadorned long hair reaching down to the middle of her back. The *áo dài* she wore was lovely, although not quite as elaborate or dazzling as the ones I had admired earlier in the garden, and it embraced her small form exquisitely. There was still a trace of puzzlement in those long brown eyes the shape of bamboo leaves, but I sensed she was struggling with all her might to put her best face forward.

We all sat at a table, with Mme Yvonne between Lee Anne and me. Her perfect posture notwithstanding, the young woman was obviously nervous, almost scared. She barely looked at me, kept fiddling with the front flap of her gown. I noticed a gold band on her finger. To make conversation, I asked her some simple questions, repeating or rephrasing them as necessary so she could understand. She replied in her hesitant, formal English—the kind taught in academic surroundings. I found her accent charming, her voice soft and pleasant, albeit with a tremor in it that made me think of a frightened bird.

"You can relax. It's not a job interview." I regretted the joke at once, as she blushed deeply and became more flustered. Mme Yvonne asked if they could offer me something to drink, then the two women wandered off together toward the counter.

Lee Anne brought me a glass of icy lemonade and another for herself.

"This is on the house, Doctor," said Mme Yvonne, clearly relieved to have averted a personnel crisis. "Now, if you'll excuse me, I need to go check on my other guests." She flashed an encouraging smile at her newest employee. "I know I can count on Lee Anne to take excellent care of you. *À tout à l'heure*—till later."

The young woman's eyes opened wide with a flicker of panic, but already Mme Yvonne had ambled away. I waited until Lee Anne had retaken her seat, with Mme Yvonne's empty chair still between us. "I'm sorry. I wasn't making fun of you earlier."

She blushed again, shaking her head politely.

"I'd be more than glad to help you practice your English, if you'll allow me," I proposed. "But you must promise in return you'll be patient when you teach me a few Vietnamese words later. Agreed?"

She looked up with a shy smile and uttered a simple, "Thank you."

"How about we take turns asking and answering questions? Just pretend it's Conversational English hour, in school. I'll go first, if you prefer."

I scooted over to the empty chair between us. "May I sit here?"

She nodded in response, this time with a bigger smile.

We spent the remainder of the afternoon getting to know each other. Given its rough start, I was pleased at how smoothly our "classroom" session proceeded, because once she began to loosen up, Lee Anne allowed herself to really get into our little game. It turned out my initial hunch was spot-on. She was indeed a part-time third-year student, majoring in English as a foreign language at the University of Sài-Gòn.

"The department is very poor," she said. "We study to read and write English, but we have no audio labo—laboratory. We have to look in dictionary how to pronounce new word. Also, we do not practice to speak English enough." Her voice dropped. "Nobody to practice. So this is helpful to me. Thank you very much."

I asked what had influenced her choice of study. She fell quiet momentarily, then gave me a quick glance. "It is long story. I am afraid you bored with it."

"I've all the time in the world, if you care to share it," I assured her.

She rearranged her *áo dài*, discreetly pulling the back flap out in front and folding it over her white silk trousers. "My parents were born and raised in the North," she started hesitantly, searching for the correct words, her beautiful eyes peering through an invisible curtain before her. "After World War II, their generation fought against French for independence. Then communists took over, and they forced tota—totalitarian regime. They said 'social reforms,' but they spread terror and suffering. Shed so much blood, of their own people." Her voice quivered, and she paused to compose herself.

"Lee Anne. You don't have to talk about this now," I said gently.

She swallowed, tried to smile. "I am okay . . . I like to finish story."

Drawing a deep breath, she went on. "In 1954, French lost battle at Điện-Biên-Phủ. Geneva Accords divided Việt-Nam in two: communist in the North, and free country in the South. I was eight years old, my brother only five. Our parents decided to not live with communists. They packed everything in bags and wrapped my brother and me in warm clothes. We ran and walked during the night to seaport Hải-Phòng. It was one of few migration centers. We hoped to get help to move to free South."

Her eyes glistened. Her breathing grew faster. "Of course, communists did everything to stop people to leave. They chased after us and fired guns. My father and my brother were shot. We dropped and lost all our bags, but we arrived finally in Hải-Phòng."

Tears rolled down her cheeks as I sat transfixed by the surprise revelations.

"We were checked into refugee camp tended by very young and very helpful *Bác-sĩ Mỹ*—American doctor. But it was too late for my baby brother. He died there. Lost too much blood and wound was infected very bad. But good doctor was able to save my father's life."

Lee Anne stopped and turned away to dry her eyes. I thought it best to leave it up to her whether to continue.

After a moment, she cleared her throat before resuming her fascinating story. "When my father recovered, the kind doctor helped our family get on next US ship for Sài-Gòn. We were among one million people evacuated that year under Operation Passage-to-Freedom conducted by US Navy. Many of us received care from doctor and his friends, and we were grateful to all of them. I begged my father please write down his name. I promised myself to try to contact doctor when I grew up, to thank him. His name was Dr. Thomas Anthony Dooley, medical officer in US Navy."

She looked up at me with a sad smile. "You maybe heard of him. He is no longer with us. I learned later that he died very young, from cancer, in 1961. Only thirty-four years old. What do you say—only the good die young?"

I nodded in silence. Lee Anne seemed lost in thought for a moment, then collected herself and continued. "In high school, I found a Vietnamese translation of the book he wrote about his experience in Hải-Phòng. It made me cry, and I told myself that one day I will learn English very well so I can read the original. His book is called *Deliver Us from Evil*. I have now read the English version. Many times."

She suddenly appeared self-conscious, rushing to conclude, "That is very long explanation why I chose to study English. I am sorry I talk too much."

"Please don't be," I hastened to set her mind at ease. "I'm honored you decided to share your remarkable story with me. Thank you."

Then I tried to lighten the mood. "Now it's only fair I fulfill my end of the bargain. You relax, enjoy your lemonade, while I tell you a little about my hometown and my family."

I proceeded to describe Lone Pine with its diverse scenery of mountains, meadows, and deserts, as well as my parents' bed-and-breakfast along the lonely highway.

"Moon Meadows," she whispered dreamily. "What a romantic name for a—hiding-out? It must be beautiful there." Like a child full of wonder, it gave her obvious pleasure to let her imagination transport her to new horizons.

On a roll, I confided to her the long-term plans that Debbie and I had made together, namely to hang out our own shingle in the shadow of Mount Whitney upon my return from Việt-Nam.

"So exciting," Lee Anne exclaimed, genuinely appreciative of our good fortune. "I am sure you will be very successful and happy." Drawing her thin shoulders closer together, she retreated once again behind a resigned smile. "It is wonderful you can make plans for future. You are very lucky. I am glad for both of you."

Fingering her bare wedding band, she admitted that life had been anything but predictable for her and her husband, a junior officer in the Army of the Republic of Việt-Nam. He was away from home most of the time, constantly on rotation from one battlefront to the next, with a rare couple of days off in between assignments. To make ends meet, they stayed with her parents in their tiny one-bedroom house, and still couldn't afford to start a family of their own. She continued to help her mother around the house while enrolling in night classes at the university, in the hope of one day assuming a larger share of responsibility for the family. Without warning, the day had arrived sooner than she'd anticipated.

"My father had stroke two months ago," she explained. "He is better but cannot go back to work for long time." She smoothed some loose strands of long black hair and swept them back over her shoulder. I felt her soft exhale. Then she spoke, as if to herself, or maybe to some-one who wasn't there. "He is only low-level function—functionary, but we depend on his pay beside my husband's. With no pay, plus medical expenses, I had to find work. Any work."

She wore light makeup, and only then did I notice how pale her face was when she wasn't blushing, with a hint of darkness under her eyes.

She straightened as if pushing back against an invisible weight over her shoulders. "But I believe if you are good person, things will be okay for you. Honestly, it is truth," she said with conviction. "Mme Yvonne is an old friend of us, but we lost contact long time ago. Until I saw her again last week at Bến-Thành Market downtown, and she invited me to come work for her. Then today I meet you here, and you are so kind. How can I thank you?" She choked up. I felt like reaching for her hand to comfort her but thought better of it for fear of embarrassing her.

"I think somebody looks for you," she whispered, alarmed by an interruption at the French doors behind me. I turned and saw Bob standing at their threshold. Mme Yvonne had probably updated our group on my situation since they'd left me on my own in the lounge all afternoon, until now. I'd lost track of time, and it must have been getting late. We would need to hit the road soon if we didn't want to miss our helicopter ride at Tân-Sơn-Nhất. I signaled to Bob for one additional minute. He gave me the thumbs-up before disappearing back outside.

"You go already?" Lee Anne asked.

"Yes, I'd better. Listen. It's been so nice to meet you. I hope things continue to improve for you and your family." I hesitated before adding, "Mme Yvonne seems like a very nice lady, and this place appears . . . pretty safe, you know. Truthfully, I don't think you need to worry about anything, working here."

She looked down at the floor, a rosy glow on her cheeks. "I see you again?"

"I certainly hope so. I just don't know when," I replied, flattered that she would even ask. "But the next time we're back in town, I'll pop in and say hi. You owe me still. You didn't get a chance to teach me any Vietnamese words today, remember?"

We got up. I wasn't quite sure what to do next, so we simply stood there looking at each other. Then she gave me a polite half bow, which I promptly returned.

"Good-bye, Lee Anne. Take good care," I said, as she leaned to pick up our empty glasses.

"Awfully quiet over there," Dean said to me. "Penny for your thoughts?"

Dick was driving us back to Tân-Sơn-Nhất. We had all thanked him for introducing us to his favorite hangout, which had been a big hit with everyone, including hard-to-impress Dean. That in itself was prize enough for Dick, to whom, I suspected, Mme Yvonne's private club had become a home away from home. As the conversation carried on, I'd lapsed into silence.

"I'm trying to grasp what a struggle it must be for the people here just to survive from day to day," I answered Dean. "Colonialism, endless wars, a total wreck of an economy, not to mention the change-over from old society to new. Talk about having the deck stacked against you." I told the story of Lee Anne and her family with their problems.

"I'd like to think that's why we're here—to lend them a hand," Dean said. "And I hope we're providing them with the right kind of help that will leave them stronger and capable of fending for themselves, down the road." Looking out the car window, he went on with his personal assessment. "It's a daunting task, though, this business of nation-building. It requires a great deal of patience and total commitment on our part, the US of A. Which explains why some folks back home are ambivalent about it, if not downright against it."

We all fell quiet after that, each wrapped in his own thoughts for the remainder of the trip. At the airport, Dick pulled over to the curb and we jumped out.

"Hey, listen," he said, as he shook hands with us and gave me a bump on the shoulder. "Anytime you guys have business in the city and need a place to crash, you're welcome to use my pad. It's no Hôtel Caravelle but it ain't too shabby, and just a step from everything. *Mi casa es su casa*. All right, boys?"

"Where do you live?" I yelled as he turned to go.

Dick swung around, tapping his forehead. "I never took you guys to my place, did I? It's real easy to find, on the ground floor inside the Passage Eden building. You can use the entrance on Nguyễn-Huệ Boulevard, the one facing the Rex Hotel. Here's the complete address." He scribbled it on a crumpled piece of paper and handed it to me.

"Now, another important detail," he added with a grin. "Down the street from the entrance, toward the gingerbread City Hall, there's a gourmet shop that carries loads of wines and food imports from France and Algeria. The owner is a ropy old Corsican fellow and a good buddy of mine. He's got my spare key. In case I'm out of town you can still drop in, introduce yourselves, and get the key from him. And while you're in the store, charge whatever you want to my tab."

"You may regret that," I warned Dick as I gave him a slap on the back. "It's great to see you again, man. Hang loose, until next time."

I was happy to reconnect with my old friend, but even more thrilled to discover he was still the same kid I'd grown up with, kind-hearted and generous to a fault.

In the heart of the foreign capital that summer evening, it suddenly felt like the good old days again.

Chapter Eight

As it turned out, Dick, Dean, and I saw quite a bit of one another over the next two months, from mid-August through October 1967. There were enough official matters for Dean and me to tend to at 3rd Field Hospital, which justified our helicopter-hopping to Tân-Sơn-Nhất every few weekends, between our MEDCAP activities around Biên-Hoà. We'd coordinate to fly those trips together and to meet Dick at the Continental Shelf in downtown Sài-Gòn after business.

For the most part, Bob would opt out of those weekend excursions, preferring to spend the time writing letters or recording taped messages for Nancy and their unborn child. "I want the baby to start learning my voice when Nance listens to the tapes," he told me. Despite the great distance between them, the happy couple was caught up in the same flurry of preparations that typically absorb first-time expecting parents: picking out names, selecting paint colors for the nursery, discussing a bigger house, school choices, and finances; in short, mapping out the future for the three of them. Besides the mail, Bob also reserved five-minute slots at the MARS station to call home on weekends, and thus he was more than happy to delegate the medical follow-ups at 3rd Field to me.

While in the city, Dean and I regularly returned to Mme Yvonne's place, in the beginning still as Dick's guests, but subsequently as full-fledged members on our own. Our official invitation to join the club had been extended by the proprietress herself, who dubbed the three of us *Les Trois Mousquetaires*—The Three Musketeers. With sufficient notice from Dean and me, resourceful Dick usually managed to arrange for our favorite hostesses when we arrived *chez* Mme Yvonne.

From the outset, I'd been aware of the special friendship between Dick and Vivienne. They seemed like a perfect match, both being very considerate and down-to-earth people. The surprise, instead, was with Dean "the Lonely" Hunter, who didn't appear to reject outright, as I'd thought he would, the cozy setup those two had devised for his benefit. In his tacit way he might even have welcomed it, worn down by his loneliness perhaps, although it was never easy to tell with Dean. At any rate, the situation with him started this way.

In that same lounge where I had first met Lee Anne, in the corner by the French doors stood an upright piano. It was an old Baldwin Acrosonic Console purchased for Mme Yvonne by her American husband. I hadn't seen anyone sitting at it, let alone playing it, until one Sunday afternoon when a flash thundershower sent everyone scampering into the lounge—a crowd of about thirty, all annoyed at being disrupted from their outdoor picnic and crammed into a closed-up space with no entertainment, since there was nothing on TV at that hour but the news. Then suddenly, out of this restless chaos of voices and footsteps, rose the scintillating sound of piano. Somebody had sat down at the instrument and brought it to life, playing the nostalgic "Autumn Leaves" with beautiful aplomb. The noise died down as a quick-thinking hostess switched off the TV, and the crowd gathered in admiring silence around the pianist.

She was an elflike creature with an urchin haircut evocative of a young Audrey Hepburn. One of the few hostesses in Western attire, she looked poised and elegant in a knee-length dress the bright color of canaries. As we watched her tapered fingers glide effortlessly over the keys, it was evident she had received more training than just casual lessons. For a solid half-hour, she mesmerized us with a remarkable repertoire from memory: excerpts from well-known pieces by Roger Williams and Burt Bacharach, melodies from popular Vietnamese and French songs (according to Vivienne, standing next to me), and lastly, short extracts from a pair of classical works for a resounding finish. As the audience erupted in cheers and applause, I whispered to Vivienne, "Who's she? I don't think I've seen her before."

"You know last tune she played?" Vivienne whispered back in her raspy voice.

"Beethoven's 'Für Elise'? She did an outstanding job with it."

"It is her signature. She always ends with it," Vivienne said. "Mme Yvonne is smart lady, she used title for her name. So that was Elise playing piano. It is good name, yeah? She started here a month before Lee Anne."

I lowered my voice even more. "Don't stare. But I think Dean is very impressed with her." Out of the corner of my eye, I couldn't have helped noticing how entranced Dean had been throughout the impromptu concert. His gaze hadn't left Elise's face for a moment.

"You think?" said Vivienne with a cryptic smile. "I was hoping."

I had no inkling what she was alluding to until later when she and Lee Anne returned to our table with trays of refreshments, accompanied by none other than Elise herself. We all stood and congratulated the talented pianist on her masterful performance. Up close, she seemed even younger and prettier than I'd realized, yet there was no hint of the shyness or naïveté that her tender youth and delicate appearance might have implied. She was at ease and gracious without being forward, and spoke good English, albeit with a distinct French accent like Mme Yvonne's. True to form, Dean was less than effusive during that initial encounter with Elise. However, his inquisitive eyes didn't try to elude hers, a small but perhaps telling sign that didn't escape Dick.

Later that afternoon Dean had to leave early, and after dropping him off at Tân-Sơn-Nhất, Dick and I grabbed one last drink together in the smoky airport lounge.

"He likes Elise all right," Dick declared, sounding mighty pleased with himself. "What say you, Roge? Any chance they'll hit it off?"

"Aha," I said. "Someone decided to play matchmaker, I see."

It turned out the idea had been germinating in Vivienne's head for some time. Having learned from her boyfriend of Dean's self-imposed celibacy, she'd taken it upon herself to arrange an introduction, but the opportunity hadn't presented itself until that rainy Sunday afternoon.

"Why Elise?" I asked, still unconvinced of Dean's positive response. "Yes. She's obviously very attractive and talented, and nice as all get out—"

"But—what?" Dick retorted. "I don't recall our guy objecting to any of that."

"You know what I mean," I said. "It's not like he hasn't been around attractive women before. *Au contraire*. What made you guys think it would be any different with Elise?"

That was when Dick shared her story with me, but not before swearing me to confidentiality. "I couldn't have written more compelling fiction if I tried," was his opening comment.

⟋⟍⟋⟍

Elise came from a prominent family in Huế, the former imperial capital under the Nguyễn dynasty. She had royal blood in her veins, since her mother was a *Công Tôn-Nữ*, a great-granddaughter of an emperor from the waning years of the nineteenth century. Among Elise's blue-blood cousins were Bảo-Đại, the last emperor of Việt-Nam, and Madame Nhu, the "Dragon Lady" of South Việt-Nam's political scene in the early 1960s.

"She's as close to a real-life princess as I'll ever know," Dick mused.

Like Audrey Hepburn in *Roman Holiday*, I thought, still taken by their resemblance.

Elise's father himself belonged to an elite family in the ancient capital. The grandson of a senior mandarin at the imperial court, he had achieved high status in the city as a well-to-do businessman. The key to his success was his family's long-standing association with the

French colonial administration. Educated for a number of years in Paris, he remained a staunch admirer of French culture who wished for his offspring to follow in his privileged footsteps.

And so, when Elise turned fourteen, he made the difficult decision over protest from his worried wife to send their daughter to stay with relatives in Sài-Gòn. This was to afford her the finest education money could buy. She enrolled at the prestigious Lycée Français de Jeunes Filles, the French high school for the city's upper-class young ladies, which was later renamed after famed physicist Marie Curie. It was never a secret that Elise's father harbored high hopes and ambitions for his precocious daughter. After high school, she was expected to sit for and pass with flying colors the selective entrance exam to the National Music Conservatory next to Tao-Đàn Park. There, according to her father's plan, she would hone her skills and fully develop her budding talent as a concert pianist.

"How often does life unfold according to some blueprint?" Dick asked rhetorically, maybe harking back to the tumultuous early history of his own family. I nodded in sympathy as I mulled over my personal circumstances, the unexpected events that had conspired to drop me here at the heart of a brutal conflict I wanted no part of.

In Elise's situation, her tidy life took a sharp turn during her last year in high school. Destiny came knocking at her door in the seductive form of a tall, handsome music teacher from the south of France. He was single, dapper, and deadly charming, the quintessential French lover. She was a lonely young woman away from home with a sweet romantic bent like many of her peers, also his favorite and most talented student. The inevitable happened. The two became caught up in a torrid and reckless love affair that erupted in a damaging scandal. Overnight, Elise was summoned back home to Huế, where she stayed through Noël of that year, grounded until things cooled off, or so her parents had hoped. To be allowed back to school after the holidays, she promised she would sever all contact with the music teacher.

That, predictably, wouldn't come to pass. By then, facing considerations of his young career, the French teacher had sobered up and tried to break off the illicit relationship, but Elise had hopelessly fallen for her former mentor and couldn't keep away from him. In a last desperate move to squash the scandal, the school transferred the teacher to Lycée Yersin, a small institute in Đà-Lạt, a tiny resort town in the highlands two hundred miles northeast of Sài-Gòn.

Over the murmur of the air conditioner in the airport lounge, Dick let out a long breath. "What one wouldn't do for love. Or infatuation. Whatever you choose to call it." I sat in stunned silence, waiting for him to continue.

Elise somehow managed to track down her former teacher. In a brazen act of revolt against the traditional value system within which she'd been nurtured her entire life, she dropped out of school, stole out of Sài-Gòn with a small suitcase, and trailed him to Đà-Lạt—an amazing feat for a privileged young girl who'd never traveled anywhere on her own. Against all odds and counsel, in spite of themselves, they resumed their doomed affair for a brief time until the young teacher panicked anew and put in for an immediate transfer out of the country.

Dick shook his head. "That was the end of the road for Elise. She dragged herself back to Sài-Gòn, broken-hearted and covered in disgrace. Next came a bout with acute depression, followed by a failed attempt at suicide. But all that mess was just a precursor to bigger storms ahead for the poor child."

When she was released from the hospital, Elise learned she'd been expelled from her school. The whole episode had tainted its heretofore sterling reputation, and she was deemed unfit to return. Worse yet, the scandal had become gossip fodder among the upper social strata in both capitals, Huế and Sài-Gòn. Angered and humiliated by the dishonor she'd heaped on the family, Elise's father disowned her despite tearful pleas from her distraught mother and grandmother. To compound her problems, the relatives who'd provided her room and board asked Elise to move out after her father cut off her financial support.

"This all took place a year and a half ago," Dick clarified. "Since then she has subsisted on meager income from various odd jobs, combined with what little help her mother could sneak to her behind her father's back. An acquaintance hooked her up with Mme Yvonne, and this gig may well be the best thing that's happened to her in a while."

"It's mind-boggling to think what she's been through already, at her age," I said. "I hope she doesn't give up on the piano, no matter what. Some serious talent there." Then I squinted at him. "And how did you unearth all this history, Mr. Reporter?"

"I rely on my excellent source. Vivienne." Dick chuckled. "She tries to look out for the new girls—Elise, Lee Anne, and a few others. Takes them under her wing, so to speak. There's great sympathy and rapport between them, you know. It's not like it's everybody's first choice to work at Mme Yvonne's. Yet it's a dire necessity for all of them."

"And the Lonely Hunter fits how, in this big picture?" I asked.

"That's the reason I've shared Elise's story with you, man." He shook his head in mock chagrin. "Don't you see? They've both loved and lost before. Paid a huge personal price for it, actually. That understanding alone can bring them together, not to mention they'd make a great-looking couple. They seem clearly cut out for each other."

"You may have a point there," I conceded. "Wouldn't it be poetic justice if it works out between them? My fingers are crossed."

We fell silent, staring out the tinted glass window onto the busy tarmac. Then I pursued the open opportunity and asked him, for the first time, "And how's it going with you and Vivienne?"

Dick shrugged without saying a word. Then, just as I was giving up, he spoke. "Would you find it ironic if I told you I actually know much less about her than I do about Elise or Lee Anne, or even Mme Yvonne?"

He struck a match and lit a Pall Mall. "Nasty habit I've picked up," he acknowledged, even without my chiding him about it. "But hell. At eleven cents a pack at the PX, it's about the only vice I can afford anymore." His eyes looked tired behind the thick glasses. "What can I tell you, man? I've never been one to figure out women."

"I thought you guys got along famously," I ventured.

"As what? Best buddies?" He snickered at the idea. "Sure we do."

He hesitated, then appeared to want the burden off his chest once and for all. "It's true we get along swell, Vivienne and I," he said. "It's no act on her part either, that much I'm certain of. That's what's so damn frustrating about the whole thing."

I could only imagine how heavy it must have weighed on his mind, since he'd never been comfortable broaching such personal subjects before, going back to our high school days.

"Oh hell, Roge," he continued, his eyes avoiding mine. "You know damn well I want more of a relationship with her. And you're right. Don't need to remind you I never had much success in this department. But this time, it matters to me. I *really* do like her."

"And you've told her, I presume?"

"Never had even a shadow of a chance. Problem is, she refuses to discuss anything of a private nature. This may sound crazy to you, but I don't know squat about her. All we have is the moments we share when we're together. No past. No future." Glancing back at me, he flashed an ironic smile. "She likes me, yet I can't ask her anything about herself."

"Take this from me, for what it's worth," I said to him as nicely as I could. "She'll open up to you when she's ready. Remember back when we were kids, how long it took before you even mentioned about Manzanar and what happened to your family? It's no different here. She may be dragging around some baggage she's not yet prepared to deal with." I then reminded him of the incredible hardships already endured by both Elise and Lee Anne despite their youth. "But they all have their own ways of coping. Not everyone's willing and ready to sit down and pour out her life story to you. Give it time."

Dick sighed. "Let's hope you're right." Then, completely out of left field, he asked, "So what's going on with you and Lee Anne?"

———⟶◦

The very question, formulated in a dozen different ways, had been lying in wait in the back of my mind, all set to pounce when I least expected—during a cold shower, or in my half-awake state in the wee hours of the morning, or worst, while I was penning my weekly letter to Debbie. The frequency with which the question reared its head increased as the months rolled by and I found more opportunities to spend Sunday afternoons at Mme Yvonne's.

Yet none of that changed my pat answer.

"We're good friends," I told Dick, doing my best to sound casual. "It's fun helping with her English." Then I slammed the door on the subject, to both him and myself. "You're certainly aware she's married, yes? You're the reporter, Hayashi."

That shut him up, but the words had a hollow ring even to my ear.

There was no denying I enjoyed our get togethers in Mme Yvonne's beautiful garden. It felt as though we were among old friends there, with the same regular crowd gathered on most weekends and people spontaneously pairing up with their favorite partners. The pleasant routine lent a touch of normalcy, even elegance, to a world gone berserk. Something fun and exciting to look forward to, far away from the devastations of war.

But seldom had I dared to pause and give further thought to the situation. Until one rainy night before bedtime, when I realized with a knot in my stomach just how much I longed to be with Lee Anne, alone. No longer to be ignored was this crazy yearning I had to peel away the layers and discover for myself every lovely secret about her.

For her part, she'd grown more confident in her job as a hostess and appeared to be making the most of this unique chance to practice her English. But I felt that the social stigma attached to such a job, within the traditional culture of Việt-Nam, remained her major concern. It must have wreaked much pain and anguish on her, not to mention the shame and guilt of having to conceal the truth from her own family.

"I have not told them what I really do for work," she admitted one day when we were alone at our table under the bougainvillea. "They will be shocked. This is not, how you say, respect—respectable job, you understand. Especially for wife of Army officer."

"So what did you tell them?" I asked.

"I said I was secretary at USAID office nearby," she replied, her cheeks turning red. "They were happy for me because it was a job I wanted. But you need to know someone in there to get interview, and I did not know anybody. So I came here instead."

"You did what you had to do. No one can fault you for that," I said, looking into her eyes. "I can appreciate your family's concern for you; that's why I'm glad you're working here for Mme Yvonne. No matter what anyone else may think, this is a decent job in a well-protected and safe environment. You know that's true. You've done nothing to be ashamed of."

We talked more about her family, then in a moment of openness I asked, "So how did you meet your husband?"

Lee Anne reflected for a minute. "He is five years older than me," she finally said. "His parents and mine came from same small town in the North." She looked down at her folded hands. "My parents believe it is important for a good marriage that families know each other. Even more important during times of war."

I decided to push my luck. "Had you known him for a long time?"

"We had met, but I was too young. He and his family waited until I finished high school to ask my parents for my hand." She fidgeted in her chair. "I know you do not understand, but that is how things are arranged in our society. He is from good family, and very nice and responsible man, also officer in the Army. Everyone says I am lucky." Then wistfully, she added, "It is not safe to be single woman in wartime. Very dangerous."

I fought off an impulse to reach over and take her in my arms.

Sad but true, children have a way of growing up fast in trying times—a simple rule of survival. In Lee Anne's case, she had transitioned straight from childhood into womanhood without the benefit of a regular adolescence with its playful rites of passage. For her, no such things as a sweet-sixteen birthday, or prom night, or even a clumsy first kiss in high school. Overnight, she'd gone from innocent school girl to wife, and now, ready or not, to co-bread winner.

There was still so much more I wanted to learn about her, but for the time being it felt as if I'd trespassed enough into her private life. For my own peace of mind, however, I ventured one final brazen question: "Are you happy?"

She gave me a puzzled look but didn't seem offended. "My husband's father had died, so after the wedding we went to live with his mother," she said, sweeping her long silky hair back over her shoulders. "My mother-in-law treated me like her own daughter. But she became ill and passed away last year. After that we moved in with my parents, so I am back at home again." Then, with an embarrassed smile, "Now you know my life story. Very boring, yes? Nothing exciting like *Gone with the Wind*."

I thought it better not to press the issue, and played along. "You've read the book? It's an American classic. I can see how you might relate to the story. Different time and place, but similar circumstances."

"I only saw the movie. It was marvelous," she gushed. "I am looking for the book in English, not a Vietnamese translation. It is hard to find in used bookstores, but it is on my list to read. Also *Doctor Zhivago*."

As I watched her pretty face grow animated with such innocent joy and enthusiasm despite all the deprivations and challenges in her life, I thought what a shame it was that the child in her heart must grow up someday.

"Lee Anne. Would you go downtown with me sometime?" I proposed on the spur of the moment. "We can go for a Coke or a milkshake. Or maybe a hot cup of Vietnamese or French espresso. Anything you wish."

"I don't know if I can leave here." She sounded surprised, unsure.

"Let me handle the arrangements with Mme Yvonne. Come on. It'll be fun."

She didn't promise, but in the bright afternoon sunlight, her eyes smiled back at me.

Just then, over the speakers, Ol' Blue Eyes started a new serenade, "The Way You Look Tonight." I turned to her. "May I have this dance?"

"I don't know how to dance. It is truth." There was panic in her voice, in her eyes.

"Not to worry. I'll lead. You just follow. It's like taking a walk in the park, together."

I stood, leaned down toward her chair, waiting.

She hesitated, looked up at me, then stood slowly.

I reached and took her hand, so small and soft in mine—for the very first time.

Chapter Nine

The fall of 1967 began with a flurry of new activities at Biên-Hoà AFB. The sweltering month of August marked the arrival of two brand-new aircraft making their experimental debut in the Southeast Asia theater. Both in time would prove formidable weapons of war, one for the Air Force and the other for the Army, but they were as diverse birds as might be found in the actual feathered kingdom.

The Cessna A-37 Dragonfly was a new subsonic jet fighter slotted to replace the venerable Douglas A-1 Skyraider in close air support and counterinsurgency missions. Lighter and more nimble than the F-100, it carried as much ordnance as the latter while trading supersonic speed for greater maneuverability and pinpoint target accuracy.

"You've got to watch it perform its Viking takeoff," Bob told me, nodding his head emphatically. "A vertical zoom right off the ground. *Un*-believable. It's a stunning feat, matched by no other prop or jet. I'm afraid my Skyraiders have finally seen their day."

Under Operation Combat Dragon, the USAF had deployed to Biên-Hoà a squadron of air commandos whose task was to evaluate the effectiveness and survivability of the A-37 in combat missions, a classic example of trial by fire. This resulted in an increase in workload and overtime for the staff at the 3rd Tac Dispensary. On the upside, among the newcomers, Bob had run across a long-standing acquaintance from his hometown in Minnesota.

"Joel Bronstad. Or little Joey, I used to call him," he said, chuckling at the memory of more innocent times. "His big brother Jimmy and I were best pals in high school. Where did the time go?" He looked over at me, then casually suggested, "One of these weekends when you're free, maybe we can get together with Joey for a drink or some-thing. One hell of a nice kid. And now, one of the best pilots around. So I've heard."

I mumbled a noncommittal, "We'll see." If I were honest with myself, I wasn't too keen on missing any weekend jaunt to Sài-Gòn unless it was unavoidable.

Bob let it drop, and nothing more came of it.

Meanwhile, the Army side of the base was abuzz with the recent delivery of a dozen Bell AH-1G Cobra assault helicopters, accompa-nied by a New Equipment Training Team of fifty officers, enlisted men, and civilian technicians. Nicknamed the Snake, the new super gunship boasted a slim fuselage, a wide-bladed rotor, tandem cockpits, stub wings with "store" stations, and an under-nose turret. Zipping along at twice the speed of the traditional Huey UH-1B, the Snake also proved more elusive to enemy fire, thanks to its narrow airframe. As such, it was expected to deliver superior air support to ground troops even in the absence of USAF involvement.

In the true spirit of Tri-Service Care, which mandated that all medical care from the Army, Navy, and Air Force be coordinated as one single task force, we regularly lent a hand to our buddies in the Army Medical Corps who were overworked even before the arrival of the Cobra NETT. In return, their choppers and pilots were available to us to assist in medical evacuations or routine transport. In fact, many of my memorable trips to Tân-Sơn-Nhất were aboard one of their Hueys.

As fall came into full swing, albeit without noticeable change in the weather, everyone on base logged in long hours, with six- or seven-day workweeks. With fresh troops and new military equipment arriving daily, sometimes twice a day, we all felt tension building in the air—electric, positive tension in anticipation of a breakthrough. This pervasive excitement found its way into a letter I wrote during that period to my older brother Jerry.

⌐‿‿‿‿⌐

Biên-Hoà AFB, 10 Oct 1967, 1800 hrs

Hey big guy,

How's life at Moon Meadows? Are you guys coming up for air, now that the travel season has wound down? You all realize, of course, I'm really envious of you since this happens to be my favorite time of year in the Eastern Sierra, when the summer heat finally subsides and the last remaining tourists have vacated the area. But you better hurry and enjoy these next few weeks of peace and leisure before the first snow on Mammoth Mountain sends them skiers stampeding back your way.

I'd give anything to be home right now, to go backpacking in the high country or squeeze in the last fishing of the season with you, Jer, doing all the simple things we love but always take for granted. If you think of it later, would you hand Mom a few postcards from the rack by the front desk to include in my next care package? They sure capture our spectacular scenery well, and I'd like to glance at them now and then before lights-out. Then maybe, just maybe, I can make it back there in my dreams. A poor substitute for the real thing, I reckon, but better than nothing. While you're at it, can you throw in a healthy supply of Yard Guard, too? It's there on the counter behind the postcards, if memory serves. The bugs over here are horrible, they devour you alive! Unfortunately, our screen doors and windows aren't enough to keep them out. And last time I checked, our BX was completely out of insect spray. Not a single can left.

We've been swamped for the past couple months. Lots of classified activity going on that we're not at liberty to discuss. Suffice it to say everybody's been working overtime, and will be for the foreseeable future. I'm on a 12-hour shift today, with two more hours to go. Thank goodness things have slowed down from the madness earlier this afternoon. Gives me a chance to catch a breath, and at least get started on this letter I kept telling Mom I'd write you. Sorry for the delay, brother.

Half-hour ago before sitting down at my desk, I walked to the front of the dispensary to stretch my legs. Day or night, there's always some exciting action above the runway that we can observe right from our doorstep. It's the best diversion to help clear my head after a long day, and I take full advantage of it as opportunities arise. Tonight was no exception. I got to watch a scene that still leaves me in awe every time I chance upon it.

It was the beautiful sight of a Boeing CH-47 Chinook helicopter, darkly outlined against the sunset sky, sling-loading a battle-damaged gunship back to home base for repair. You'd have a better appreciation of it than me, since you're a lot more mechanical-minded. But even I can tell this chopper is a flying wonder. Nicknamed "Shit Hooks" by the crews who care for it, it can haul any type of cargo from the hooks under its belly: Howitzers, trucks, choppers, jet fighters, etc. Anything up to 25,000 lbs, no sweat. Can you imagine the monster blast it generates with its tandem rotors during takeoff or landing with such a mega-load? These hurricane-force winds can knock a careless airman off his feet and send him rolling across the tarmac like tumbleweed. I once witnessed it with my own eyes.

What boggles the mind is that the Chinook is but one of many wonder machines in our modern arsenal. In fact, advanced weapons of every kind are rolling out our factory doors on a regular basis, right into this battlefield, where they undergo the most rigorous testing to help improve them further. With such superior technology at the disposition of our well-trained and disciplined troops, does anyone doubt we can wrap up this nasty business in a timely fashion? And no, I'm not working in Psywar. It's all personal opinion.

Enough of that. I just have one more favor to ask you. Can you possibly order through our book club new copies of Gone with the Wind and Doctor Zhivago? Maybe Farewell to Arms and The Grapes of Wrath, too. Don't worry. I'm not going literary on you in my old age. No time for me to even browse the Stars and Stripes or the Air Force Times, much less repeat my American Lit class. I just thought they'd make a nice gift for a Vietnamese friend who's very serious about studying our language and culture.

Thanks for your help, big guy. My love to Mom and Dad. Please let them and Debbie know I'm behind on my letters because of our busy schedule, but I'm doing well and thinking of them often. I'll write them as soon as things let up. Just patience, please.

Take care, Jer. Now go enjoy your late summer before it's gone.

Happy hiking, camping, fishing, etc., R.C.

As with the rest of my letters, no matter to whom they were addressed, this one would make the rounds to everyone in my family including Debbie, who had always been accepted as one of us. It was then set aside, with all my other mail from Việt-Nam, in my mom's special collection. Neatly bundled in chronological order, these hand-written pages were stashed away in a round tin box, then turned over to me several years after my homecoming.

"Hang on to these, son," my mother told me at the time. "We all go back in search of our pasts eventually. These old records come in handy when you're ready for your own trip down memory lane." She was right, of course.

As it happened, the more hectic our schedule at the base, the greater my anticipation of the weekend trips to Sài-Gòn. They became the highlight of my weeks, to which I looked forward with increased excitement, especially after my decision to invite Lee Anne for an afternoon downtown.

One Sunday in Mme Yvonne's garden, as we were waiting for our hostesses to return with the beverages, I consulted with Dick on how best to approach Mme Yvonne.

"You sure you want to do this?" he asked me point blank, staring me straight in the eyes.

I inferred from his reaction that he knew of my engagement to Debbie. But Dick had never been one to sit in judgment of others, so I nodded firmly, convinced of my pure intentions.

He crossed his arms in front of him. "You understand why Mme Yvonne can't allow the girls to come and go as they please just because some customer asks them out. It would defeat the very purpose of her club."

The disappointment must have registered plainly on my face.

He blew out some air, leaned back in his chair as if to gather his thoughts before speaking again. "I suppose you could pay up front for the drinks you'd normally order. That would take care of business as far as the club goes. It'd make it easier to convince Mme Yvonne to make an exception. Worth a shot. She can always say no."

The following weekend, we tested out his plan.

While Dick was having his tête-à-tête with Mme Yvonne on my behalf, Elise, who along with Vivienne and Dean had been let in on our little scheme, approached me.

"Will Dick drive you two downtown?"

"I wouldn't dream of disrupting his afternoon with Vivienne," I said. "He's doing me a big favor as it is. We'll get a taxicab."

Elise nodded. "That's easy. The National Music Conservatory is only a block from here, on your right. There are taxicabs waiting in front at all hours." She turned to Lee Anne, who was smiling nervously. "You make sure the driver doesn't cheat Roger."

Dick strutted over at that moment, a triumphant smile on his face. "It's all cleared," he announced, rubbing his hands together. "The one request she has is that you kids be discreet when you leave. She doesn't want to set a precedent for everybody else."

Elise's hand shot up. "I can help with that. Let me know when you are ready. I will start playing the piano."

Elise was immensely popular with the regular crowd at Mme Yvonne's, a valuable asset for the club. When she sat down to play, people gathered around to listen and cheer.

I smiled. "How about now? So you all can get back to business as usual."

"À votre service, monsieur." She leaned forward in a half-bow, took Dean's hand and pulled him from his chair. "Get ready." She winked at us as she and Dean linked arms and headed for the house.

Soon the keyboard roused to life, its sparkling music streaming from the lounge into sunlight. The boisterous crowd in the garden fell silent, then one couple after another got up from their tables and started indoors.

I nodded at Lee Anne. "Shall we? Now?"

We hurried past the lounge to the front gate. I recognized the buoyant piece Elise was playing, "Never on Sunday" at faster tempo than usual. The bouncy tune had people on their feet, clapping and stomping, so nobody noticed us slip by. This is like playing hooky, I thought, glancing over at Lee Anne who probably shared the same idea, her cheeks flushed pink and her eyes twinkling with mischief. I felt the familiar butterflies in my stomach—that intoxicating mix of guilt, trepidation, and exhilaration, the palpable sense of the forbidden. Like school kids sneaking away from homeroom in search of a thrill, we tiptoed through the wrought-iron gate onto the street, hand in hand.

Dick had provided some options for where to go downtown. "The main pastime, of course, is people-watching," he had declared with the self-assurance of an old hand. "The Shelf is a great spot for that, but it's all foreign correspondents, and you won't find a table after two o'clock anyway. La Pagode nearby also has a nice *café terrasse*, but mainly for locals, so you'll stick out like a sore thumb. Forget Givral as well. It's the favorite haunt of spoiled brats from rich families in the city. That leaves Brodard as your best bet."

Located at the corner of Tự-Do and Nguyễn-Thiệp Streets, one block up from the Hôtel Continental Palace, Brodard was a cozy, intimate restaurant-ice cream parlor popular with both Vietnamese and Western crowds.

"Delicious espressos and French pastries. You can also order light meals or sandwiches, with a milkshake or ice cream for dessert," Dick had said, giving me the spiel. "Make sure you get a table on the second floor where you can look out the big windows at Rue Catinat below, in both directions. That's one fine view you don't want to miss."

Armed with insider knowledge, I felt confident enough to suggest to Lee Anne we try the place. The taxi driver dropped us off in front of the restaurant, and it was our good fortune to walk in at the same time a table for two became available upstairs. We were seated next to the expansive glass wall that opened onto the street scene below. The place exuded casual elegance. Its quiet air conditioner felt like heaven, which might account for the never-ebbing crowd inside. Excellent choice, Dick, I thought, as the waiter handed us the menus.

"Have you been here before?" I asked Lee Anne. She hadn't said much since we came in.

She simply shook her head, her face hidden behind the menu.

"Is something the matter?" I reached and gently brushed aside the carte.

She avoided my eyes. Still, I could glimpse the shadow in hers.

"What's wrong, Lee Anne?" I asked softly. "Please tell me."

She composed herself before returning my gaze, then struggled to explain in a faint voice, "I have heard this is a very nice place. But it is so expensive."

"You're my guest," I said, smiling. "This is on me."

"That is not what I mean." She shook her head again, her eyes opening wide, pleading for understanding. "A meal on the menu costs more than one week's pay for my husband. How can I sit here and enjoy while he makes sacrifices for our family? It is not right. I—I don't belong in this place."

I reached across the table, covered her nervous hand with mine. "I'm sorry. I didn't realize. We don't have to stay here if you're not comfortable. Would you rather leave?"

She hesitated. "Are you sure that is okay? You made effort so we can spend the afternoon downtown. I don't want to . . ."

Then an idea appeared to strike her, and she gave me a timid smile. "Can I show you *my* Sài-Gòn? Very simple, nothing fancy. But I promise we will not get lost."

I smiled back, surprised. "It's more than I dare ask. I wouldn't miss it for the world." I stood and helped her with her chair.

From Brodard we strolled over to Lê-Lợi Street, another wide avenue downtown, away from the ritzy hotels and posh restaurants on Tự-Do. Beyond the fountained traffic circle in front of the Rex Hotel, the bustling sidewalks became crowded with peddlers' stalls of all kinds, like a teeming flea market.

"Most important thing first," Lee Anne said, taking her tour guide duty seriously. "I want you to try a drink we all love. *Nước mía*, or fresh sugarcane juice mixed with mandarin orange juice. Best thing for you in this heat."

My heart quickened at her suggestion, but I managed a smile so as not to offend her. Repeatedly, we'd been cautioned against consuming native foods and beverages lest we succumbed to "Uncle Hồ's Revenge," a debilitating form of gastroenteritis.

What the hell, I thought. Live big. Enjoy the adventure. Hopefully, Kaopectate and Lomotil would combat any nuisance later.

We rounded a street corner and arrived at a large juice stand with a long line of thirsty, noisy patrons in front. A weathered awning displayed "Nước Mía Viễn-Đông" in faded red letters. Lee Anne left me waiting on the sidewalk and got in line. She emerged minutes later with two big glasses filled with a golden, frothy liquid.

"Viễn-Đông is very well known," she said, offering me an ice-cold glass. "It has been here for years. Its name means 'Far East.' I am happy I can show you this tradition of real Sài-Gòn."

She smiled shyly and raised her glass. "To my wonderful friend, Roger, who has been very kind to me. I have not said it enough times, but thank you again with all my heart."

I'd never seen her more carefree or radiant than that afternoon, standing on the sidewalk among the crowd, relishing her favorite fruit drink. In the sunlight, her long hair shimmered like black silk against the exquisite lavender of her *áo dài*. It was an unforgettable sight, a soothing and welcome vision in the jungle heat of the capital.

I drank my cold juice in one gulp—greedily, insatiably. It was delectable and went down smooth and easy, leaving a frothy mustache that I licked off in one big smack, much to Lee Anne's delight.

"Where to next—boss?" I asked.

She laughed. "Sài-Gòn Zoo and Botanical Garden?"

Squinting into the bright sunlight, I declared, "I'll follow you to the ends of the earth."

———

The Municipal Zoo and Botanical Garden were situated at the other end of Đại-Lộ Thống-Nhất (Reunification Boulevard), a spacious, tree-lined avenue that originated from the imposing gates of the Presidential Palace and ran past the back of Notre Dame Cathedral and the sprawling US Embassy. It was a ten-minute taxi ride from downtown.

Lee Anne insisted on paying for the tickets, and we went in through the turnstiles. After the crazy hubbub of downtown, we suddenly found ourselves in an oasis of peace and serenity. Behind the green copper gate, along the broad main walk stood a couple of stately buildings that appeared to belong to a time past.

"The French founded the zoo and garden in late 1800s, short time after they conquered Việt-Nam," Lee Anne said. "The buildings were added later, in 1920s."

On our left was the National Museum, a handsome multitiered structure that rose above the trees like an octagonal pagoda. Its architecture, according to my lovely guide, had been inspired by the Summer Palace in Peking. To our right, atop a wide stone staircase adorned with dragon sculptures, an ancient-looking temple beckoned to the faithful.

"That is the Temple of Remembrance, dedicated to our earliest ancestors, the eighteen Kings Hùng," Lee Anne explained. "Its design was copied from imperial mausoleums in the old capital Huế. Maybe Elise can tell us which one."

The air was suffused with burning incense, and from the bowels of the temple emanated the deep echo of a gong. We climbed the steps to the terrace fronting the main entrance and sat on a stone bench. Neither of us spoke for a while.

"It's heavenly in here. Do you come often?" I whispered.

"As a kid, I came with my parents on special days." She smiled at the memory. "We brought fruit and flowers for the ancestors' altar, burned incense, and prayed for their blessings. But I could never sit still through the praying. I was itching to get to the zoo next."

"Why did you stop coming?"

"The war," came her answer, soft as a sigh. "It upset everything, and made life difficult for all. My parents were always busy coping. Then I was a kid no more."

"We must thank Mme Yvonne for allowing us to be kids again," I said cheerfully. "If only for an afternoon."

"I need to thank her for a lot more." Lee Anne's gaze followed a pair of sparrows in a tree nearby. "She really saved us. Without her job, I don't know what would happen to my family."

"You mentioned she's an old acquaintance?"

Lee Anne looked hesitant. "We have known each other since childhood. But it is a long and boring story for you."

"Don't you know by now I never get bored listening to your stories?"

"If you like, we can walk down to the lily pond," she proposed. "I will tell you on the way."

We stood and headed down the steps.

Like the sound of a stream in the distance, a soft breeze rustled the stands of century-old poinciana trees, sprinkling the pathway with bright red flowers.

"Mme Yvonne is a remarkable woman with a heart of gold," began Lee Anne.

From what Lee Anne told me that day, I later researched the time period in question and was able to reconstruct some historical context to Mme Yvonne's amazing story.

Nobody knew exactly where her father had come from. Some French colony in the heart of the "Dark Continent," Africa, was her mother's best recollection. To escape the abject poverty of his homeland, he joined the multinational French Foreign Legion at a young age and wandered to far-flung corners of the French Colonial Empire. In 1939, at the onset of WWII, he was stationed with the 5th Regiment in Indochina.

In Việt-Nam at that time, the Foreign Legion's reputation had been seriously tarnished by the unethical and violent conduct of many bad apples among its rank and file. Widely circulated were horror stories of rape and pillaging committed by out-of-control members of the Legion, mostly in the countryside. A tragic consequence was the escalating number of fatherless children whose mixed-blood features clearly told of the brutality befallen their mothers. The mere presence of these kids was a prickly reminder of the country's collective shame under foreign occupation, and thus they were considered dregs of society, to be relegated to its fringes. Those with dark skin like Mme Yvonne bore the brunt of the injustice.

Mme Yvonne, however, always maintained that her family history was an exception rather than the sad norm. She claimed her *Légionnaire* father had actually married her mother and the two had lived together during his sojourn in Việt-Nam. When he left Indochina in 1940 to join the Free French Movement in North Africa to fight the Germans, he'd promised his Vietnamese wife, pregnant with their baby, that he would come back for them after the war. He never did.

"She told me as a child she looked for her father's return every day," Lee Anne said, her voice filled with empathy. "Other kids made fun of her, but she never gave up hope, even now."

In 1954, when Lee Anne's family came south and settled on the outskirts of Sài-Gòn, young Mme Yvonne and her mother had recently moved into the same neighborhood. Her mother was employed as a kitchen aid at a French catholic boarding school in the capital, Le Couvent des Oiseaux ('The Convent of the Birds), and barely scraped together a living for the two of them. Every morning the young child, known to neighbors simply as Nhỏ Đen (Little Black Girl), tagged along with her mother as she left for work, returning home by her side only after dark. At the school, Nhỏ Đen helped out in the kitchen, and mother and daughter were allowed to partake of the food left over when the school cafeteria closed. The little girl received no formal education to speak of, though she learned to read and write in Vietnamese from her mother, along with a few greetings in French for her papa, should he ever come back.

Since it was obvious she was an abandoned *con lai* (half-caste), most kids in the area wanted nothing to do with Little Black Girl, except to pick on her. Though five years younger, Lee Anne, herself a new kid on the block and lonely, felt sorry for the young outcast and befriended her. A close bond developed between the girls, who grew to be like sisters to each other.

"We were both so grateful to have a friend who listened to our troubles," Lee Anne said pensively. "My brother had died one year earlier and I was missing him so much, while she was crying every night, praying for her father's return. At least now we could confide in each other and cry together."

Their young friendship lasted over a year until Yvonne's mother died unexpectedly after a brief illness untreated due to lack of money. Overnight, Little Black Girl found herself alone in the world with nowhere to turn, at the worst possible time. There were rumblings of a new war on the horizon.

Lee Anne bowed her head. "My parents wished they could take her in. But we, too, had big problems, and my father already struggled to support us. So we stood by helpless. It was awful."

In the end, the kind-hearted nuns at Le Couvent offered Nhỏ Đen food and shelter in exchange for part-time help in the kitchen, to be increased to full-time when she grew older. It was their hope to allow her to take over her mother's position.

"The morning before she left for the school, we hugged and cried and never wanted to let go," Lee Anne said. "Then the sisters came to pick her up, and out of our lives she was gone. I never got to play with her again. Our family moved a few more times, and I lost contact with her." She glanced up at me with a gentle smile. "Until we bumped into each other by luck at Bến-Thành Market, two months ago. Even after twelve years and a lot of change, we recognized each other immediately. Our hearts knew."

We had arrived at the lily pond—a picturesque, timeless setting right out of a Monet painting. Along the edge, wispy willows leaned out over the water, their graceful branches bowing low in deep sorrow. A mother duck navigated her young between the broad, flat leaves of the lilies, deftly paddling around the gold koi fish lurking beneath the surface. Overhead, a canopy of dense foliage provided welcome shade, while all around us carefree birds joined the last few cicadas in a late summer chorus.

A low stone bridge arched over the pond, beckoning. We strolled to the middle.

No longer able to contain my curiosity, I prodded Lee Anne. "Did you find out what happened with Mme Yvonne in the intervening years?"

Her black eyes shone, sparkling pebbles of ebony. "Ah, that is the most exciting part of the story. You like to hear the rest now, I guess?"

I rolled my eyes in response, which made her giggle.

According to Lee Anne, it didn't take long for the good nuns at Le Couvent des Oiseaux to realize their young charge was no average orphan. Blessed with a sharp, inquisitive mind and cheerful personality, it was clear Nhỏ Đen had the potential to go further in life than the school kitchen. After discussion, the sisters agreed to try an experiment. They dressed her in an old school uniform outgrown by a former *couventine*—white shirt tucked inside a navy blue skirt—and placed her in a class several grades behind her age. She was seated alone in the back so as not to distract her younger classmates.

Nhỏ Đen, whose new baptized name was Yvonne, went on to exceed all expectations. Buoyed by an unquenchable thirst for learning and a single-minded determination to rise above her circumstances, she excelled and quickly made up lost ground, progressing through the grades faster than anticipated. This she accomplished while still working many hours in the kitchen to hold up her end of the bargain.

Six years after the nuns took her in, Yvonne graduated from high school with the finest education her mother could ever have dreamed for her.

Lee Anne nodded in admiration. "It is unbelievable, what she achieved. And that was just the beginning."

A survivor, young Yvonne sensed winds of change blowing. The French, though still present in Việt-Nam after Điện-Biên-Phủ, were relinquishing their lead role in this former colony to the newly arrived Americans. Armed with her academic knowledge of English and a foresight beyond her years, she sought employment with the USAID office in Sài-Gòn, one of the first locals to do so. The year was 1962.

"It began a whole new life for her," Lee Anne said. "Nhỏ Đen does not exist anymore—except in her heart, because she keeps believing her father will one day come back for her."

Through her job at USAID, Yvonne met a nice, decent man—a government contractor from Atlanta, Georgia, who was running away from his own grief and loneliness after his wife of many years died. He was impressed with Yvonne's charm and education, but it was her kind heart that captured him. There was but one inconvenient detail, a twenty-year gap between their ages. In time, however, his sincere affection won her over.

Lee Anne breathed a happy sigh. "At last she has somebody who loves her and wants to spend the rest of his life with her. I am so happy for Yvonne. She deserves every good thing. She and Mr. Bill have been happily married for three years already."

⌒‿⌒

In the center of the bridge, I rested my elbows on the low railing, wishing the sweet voice that so enthralled my imagination would go on forever. Fancy that. My very own Thousand-and-One Nights dream weaver, I told myself with a quiet chuckle. Only we were standing in a public park in the center of Sài-Gòn in broad daylight.

"What a wonderful story," I said. "And such a storybook ending. I've a feeling you're a die-hard romantic. One of the few remaining."

"I think we are all romantics at heart," she replied, looking out over the glimmering water. "Who does not wish for love and romance? Or a happy ending. Or peace. But for many of us reality is messy and cruel, and not at all our choice." A sad smile trembled on her lips. "I see my husband maybe two days a month, and each time I am afraid it could be the last."

Surprised by her frankness, I couldn't think of something proper to say, even as I ached to reach out and comfort her. For a moment, she seemed lost in thought, standing motionless and lonely on the stone bridge, her *áo dài* fluttering around her like ribbons of light. I leaned against the railing, still speechless, my eyes trained on the enchanting picture before me.

Nothing stirred. We both froze in contemplation.

A cool breeze wafted by. Lee Anne shuddered as if awakened from a dream. With one hand she brushed back her hair from her face, pointing with the other to the lilies on the water. "How beautiful they are," she murmured.

They were of a variety of colors—most in shades of white or pink, with a few reds or blues in their midst—rising pristine and luminous from the mossy water. A delicate fragrance permeated the air, sweet, but softer than jasmine.

"So beautiful," she repeated.

Yes, just like you, I thought, and turned away—my chest about to burst.

"These are really lotus flowers, not water lilies," she said. "They look alike, but the lotus flower has larger petals and a big seedpod at its center."

I kept my voice casual. "Your Vietnamese name, Liên, doesn't it mean 'lotus flower'?"

Her eyes widened. "How do you know?"

"I have my sources." Never good at playing coy, however, I quickly relented. "I made a mental note of your name the first time we met, and asked Bà Bảy when I got back to base. She's the Mama-san who cleans our hooch. All this time, I meant to ask you, but—" *whenever I'm with you, everything else slips my mind.*

She seemed pleased, blushing lightly. "In Vietnamese customs, parents give their children meaningful names that express their highest hopes for the little ones. The lotus flower is the symbol of purity—something that grows out of the mud, yet so beautiful and unspoiled. It also represents spiritual growth, in Buddhism." She blinked and lowered her gaze. "I have not lived up to my name . . ."

I interrupted. "I'm sure you have. Don't be so hard on yourself."

She glanced up in grateful silence, then looked away.

The day was winding down. The sun had slipped off its peak and the air felt lighter, fresher. I straightened. "I hate to be a party pooper, but I'd best get you back to Mme Yvonne's. I've really enjoyed our afternoon together. It was the most wonderful time I've had in quite a while." Taking in the scenic surroundings for the last time, I nodded. "Never in a million years could I have found this delightful spot on my own. I shall always remember it. Like this."

Her face lit up with a radiant smile, and she bowed her head graciously.

"How do you say 'thank you' in Vietnamese? The correct pronunciation?"

"*Cám ơn,*" she enunciated each syllable, all the while shaking her head as if to say, "There is no need."

I stepped toward her, bent down until my face was inches from hers. Looking in her eyes, I took both her hands in mine. "*Cám ơn,* Liên." In the cool dampness over the lily pond, I felt her rushed breath on my face, mingled with the lovely scent of the lotus.

⌒⌒

It was after 2100 hours when I made it back to Biên-Hoà AFB.

My head still spinning with all the sights, sounds, and smells from the day's special outing, I threaded my way through rows of hooches toward my own. For the umpteenth time, I relived in my mind the entire afternoon, moment by sweet moment.

I almost passed our hooch, failing to recognize it as it was drowned in silent darkness. This was unusual since Bob always stayed up until lights-out at 2200 hours, scribbling love notes to Nancy and listening to his music.

His favorite record of late was "Puff, the Magic Dragon" by Peter, Paul and Mary, which he played at all hours while singing along. A loyal fan of the popular folk-music group, Bob loved that song even more now as he looked forward to singing it to his baby.

"It's a real cute children's song," he once remarked. "I've told Nancy it'll make a sweet lullaby when the baby fusses at night." Then he laughed out loud. "Ya sure. Just not the way Daddy butchers it. We all know how atrocious that is."

The song title had also been borrowed to nickname the fabulous AC-47 gunship, call sign "Spooky," to which Biên-Hoà had had the distinction of being the birthplace. Basically a WWII Skytrain transport made over, the AC-47 had been equipped to deliver crippling firepower from the air. At night, when its mini-guns all blasted at once at six thousand rounds per minute, the visual effect was that of a cone of fire pouring down from the sky on the enemy, like a dragon's breath. Meanwhile, the guns' thunder reverberated through the open cargo bay and intensified the eerie illusion for observers on the ground. By chance, one such awestruck eyewitness in the early days happened to be a reporter from the *Stars and Stripes*. His subsequent write-up in the *Stars* was so descriptive it instantly earned the new gunship its nickname Puff the Magic Dragon, Spooky for short, and made it a legend among our fighting men.

As a proud member of the Air Force, Bob was taken lock, stock, and barrel by the newborn legend and by the song itself, whose lyrics were modified by the AC-47 crews to better suit their story of war. I once asked him, half-jokingly, if he'd consider naming a son of his "Puff." That had him in stitches, though he never did give a categorical negative.

I stepped inside the hooch, fumbled to turn on the light, and almost jumped when I saw Bob sitting on the edge of his cot—head hung low, fists pressed hard against his temples, his thick body slumped forward, leaning inertly on bent knees.

Puzzled and somewhat alarmed, I strode over and laid a hand on his shoulder.

He slowly sat up, a dazed look on his face. His eyes were bloodshot.

"They just had a baby," he uttered in a hoarse voice. "Right before he shipped out."

"Who you talking about?"

"Joey and his wife." Bob buried his face in his hands, fighting to suppress a doleful groan. "Joey Bronstad. My buddy's kid brother."

As I stood, stunned, the story came dribbling out, bit by painful bit.

Earlier that afternoon, Bob had been pulling call at the dispensary when Joey dropped in for a visit. It was shortly before his fragged sortie in the evening, and he seemed especially agitated. Gripped with inexplicable anxiety all day long, Joey was looking for a "Sky Doc"—flight surgeon—to consult with.

"How many hours have you flown this month already?" Bob asked him.

It wasn't unusual that overexposure to combat could result in frazzled nerves. As a preventative measure, fighter pilots were limited to ninety flight hours per month. Beyond that, they were required to check in with their flight surgeon, who could then clear them for another thirty hours upon satisfactory examination. It was well known that the flyboys in Operation Combat Dragon had been pushing hard lately.

But Joey had barely reached his hours' limit. Nothing excessive as yet.

"You're exhausted," Bob suggested to him nonetheless. "I understand you guys don't like to be grounded, but I can order a simple crew rest. It's only for eight hours."

Joey politely declined. He had no intentions of letting his buddies down or having someone pull a double shift to fill in for him. He just needed to talk.

Though Bob could have forced the issue, he chose to let it pass. "I get that it's a matter of pride to them," he explained. "No pilot ever takes kindly to being grounded. So instead, I just invited him to stay and shoot the breeze, hoping it would help calm his nerves."

They'd spent time catching up, the most they had since Joey's arrival on base. The young pilot had shown Bob a wallet picture of his wife with their infant son.

"Beautiful baby boy." Bob grabbed his head at the recollection, his voice breaking. "Just one month old when his proud daddy shipped out."

To Bob's relief, the visit had seemed to do Joey good. He had appeared calmer when it came time for him to go. "Stop by again when you get back," Bob had told him as they shook hands. "I'll prescribe something for a good night's sleep. You'll be good as new in the morning."

Bob squeezed his eyes shut, exhaled, momentarily speechless.

"That was the last I saw of him," he finally whispered, his eyes still closed. "He's gone, Roge. Shot down over 'Parrot's Beak.'"

I sank down on the cot next to Bob.

After some time, he resumed. "It was confirmed he didn't eject. There was no Mayday on the Guard Frequency." While I remained dumbstruck, he droned on. "His buddies went back and combed the area. No sign. No signal whatever. They had to call it off for the night and wait until morning, for the wreckage—and his body. What's left of it."

I put my arm around Bob's shoulders, which heaved with each gasp. The big guy was breaking up.

"I should have grounded him." He let out a sob. "He came to *me*, Roger. He had a sense something bad was going to happen. Yet he went anyway."

There was nothing I could say, so I just held him tight by the shoulders and let the storm blow over. Afterward, Bob was drained, his body sagging with grief. I helped him stretch out on his cot, struggling a bit with his long limbs and bulky frame.

"You need to get some rest, my friend," I said. "Let me fetch you some Sparine."

No sooner had he ingested the medication than he lapsed into a restless slumber.

I turned out the light, slipped into my own bed. In the dark, Bob tossed and turned, grinding his teeth and mumbling unintelligibly. Although I was fearful to go there, my thoughts drifted to this fallen soldier I hadn't taken the time to meet, and to the young wife and infant son he had left behind. When I finally dozed off, in the small hours of the new day, my pillow was soft with moistness.

All through my fitful sleep, jumbled images flashed on my mind's screen in a dizzying go-round, like a broken newsreel: Lee Anne's smile; the frosty glass of sugarcane juice; Bob's bloodshot eyes; the mother duck and her brood on the lotus pond; Joey's jet blowing up in the night sky; Debbie's gentle face . . .

In my fretful torpor, I even dreamed I heard the roaring thunder of Yosemite's waterfalls in early summer, only to awaken, bewildered, to the ominous rumble from a B-52 bomber in the distance. Rolling flat on my back, I peeked groggily at the tin roof above—and remembered, with a jolt, the events of the past twenty-four hours.

Unable to return to sleep, I awaited sunrise.

Chapter Ten

As we approached Thanksgiving 1967 and the southwest monsoon season began to wind down, Charlie stepped up his hostilities against Biên-Hoà AFB. From the jungle outside the base's periphery, the stealthy enemy routinely nagged at us with every type of launch weapons available at his disposal, from crude anti-tank recoilless rifles and rocket-propelled grenades to more damaging long-range mortars. But in recent days, the danger had increased exponentially with the advent of Soviet- or ChiCom-made 122-mm rockets. Even when launched from miles away, these powerful missiles still wreaked horrific devastation at impact. Known to be capable of punching through twenty-five layers of sandbags over four layers of steel planks, they could blow up all but the most fortified bunkers, leaving behind ghastly footprints six feet wide by three feet deep. It would look as if Death had swooped down from the sky and pulverized everything in its path. In an all-out campaign of terror, the Việt-Cộng would soon launch the same lethal weapons against innocent civilians in Sài-Gòn and other big cities in South Việt-Nam.

It was like some crazy mind game, the way the attacks on the base played out. "Like a thief in the night" they came, after lights-out, between 2230 and 2330 hours, hence the nickname "Eleven-o-clock Charlie" given to the perpetrators. At that late hour many of our young servicemen, out of boredom as much as curiosity, would tune to Radio Hà-Nội to check out the enemy's propaganda. Sugar-coated like a poison pill, it was delivered in the soft, sexy voice of "Hà-Nội Hannah," who began her nightly broadcast with a seductive, "How are you, GI Joe?" By and large, American soldiers laughed and poked fun at her propaganda tirades and scare tactics but enjoyed her music program, which played antiwar songs banned on Armed Forces Radio. Often enough, though, she succeeded in rattling nerves by tauntingly announcing on the air the names, units, and hometowns of Americans killed in recent combat. Such information could be obtained from open sources like the AP or UPI wire services, or even in the *Stars and Stripes*, but was generally suppressed on the Armed Forces Vietnam Network.

As if to back up Hà-Nội Hannah's threats, Eleven-o-clock Charlie would mount his attack during her broadcast, triggering the air-raid siren in the process. Shrill enough to wake the dead, the sudden alarm shattered the evening stillness to warn that radar had picked up incomings and we had less than seven seconds to dash for cover at the nearest bunker. Then all hell broke loose. Klaxon horns went off inside the barracks and lifted everyone out of bed. Floodlights flashed on and off as the PA blared out emergency instructions. Pilots raced to report to the flight line in anticipation of taking to the air, while the rest of us scrambled like mad to the closest shelter.

The rockets dropped from the night sky, four or five on average per raid. They were clearly "walked in" across the base for maximum damage. We could hear their frightening whistles as they landed closer and closer, sometimes exploding almost right on top of us. It was the sound of Death stomping the ground in search of unsuspecting victims. There wasn't much one could do except—as Tweety, our medic, put it—"pucker up and wait." But thanks to the sheer vastness of the base and the inaccurate aim of enemy artillery, most attacks had caused only material damages so far. On the few unfortunate occasions when our living quarters took a direct hit, the consequence had proved horrendous in fatalities and severe injuries.

Attending to the resulting mayhem seemed at times an exercise in futility and frustration. Our dispensary wasn't equipped to handle serious combat injuries, so we quickly learned the rule of triage. All wounds above the shoulders must be routed to the 24th Evacuation Hospital, the only neuro-surgical trauma center in Việt-Nam and the busiest in the world. Everything else went to either the 93rd Evacuation Hospital or the 3rd Field Hospital at Tân-Sơn-Nhất. Both the 24th and the 93rd were located on the huge Army base at nearby Long-Bình, up the road from Biên-Hoà AFB.

Some of the hardest moments for me as a physician were spent holding the hands of the severely wounded to try to comfort and sustain them with moral support, for that was all I had to offer. Together we would await the Dustoff helicopters for their medical airlift, which sometimes arrived too late. That feeling of utter helplessness was a bleak memory I could never erase.

With this new danger now hanging over our heads came the sober realization that a safe rear zone where one could run and hide no longer existed. Prepared or not, we were all serving on one massive front line across the entire theater. This grim reality, when experienced firsthand through the nerve-shattering rocket attacks, was enough to unhinge grown men and send them home emotional wrecks. Here again, our Tweety had his unique, insightful way of sizing up the situation. Without batting an eye, he once quipped that even a trip to the out house to use the "honey bucket" became a memorable event when punctuated by incomings. At the time we all chortled, but little did anyone appreciate how spot-on he was. For in the end, war stamped its indelible imprint on every facet of our lives.

One evening around a fortnight before Christmas, Dean Hunter appeared unexpectedly at the dispensary as we were getting ready to call it a day.

"We need to talk about this weekend," he said, motioning at me while shaking hands with Bob and the flight surgeon who was coming on the evening shift. Just then the phone rang and interrupted our greetings. Bob reached for it and answered what turned out to be a very brief call. When he hung up, concern was written all over his face.

"Reverse call from Senator Goldwater," he said. "I've got to take this one. They're routing it to the back office." With that, he disappeared to the back of the building.

Senator Barry Goldwater, an avid amateur radio "ham," was well known and loved by the troops in Việt-Nam for his staunch support of them and their families. From the ham shack at his half-acre hilltop home in Paradise Valley, Arizona, he operated one of many Military Affiliate Radio Stations stateside with the help of a small army of volunteers. Around the clock, they monitored and intercepted radio signals originated by service people in Việt-Nam, then patched them over to domestic phone lines to connect the callers with their families in the States. His station, call sign AFA7UGA, was the most prominent MARS located outside of a military base. Due to overwhelming demand for this free service, all calls were limited to five minutes and had to originate from Việt-Nam. Reverse calls from the States, as a rule, weren't permitted, with extremely rare exceptions in case of emergencies.

In the front office we exchanged nervous looks, as we all couldn't help but wonder the same thing. The conversation died down, and together we awaited Bob's return in silence.

Suddenly, there was shouting coming from the back, followed by a commotion, like someone or something heavy bouncing off the floor. Everybody sprang to his feet, ready to storm in and kick down the door at further signs of alarm. Next, we heard Bob pound on the desk, his muffled voice booming through the shut door. Another long minute passed before the door flung open, and Bob came barreling out. As we watched, befuddled, he charged past us toward his desk and began rooting through it.

He finally straightened and turned to face us, the found packet in his raised hand. A big grin flashed across his sweaty face as he winked at us and spoke in the softest, sweetest voice he could muster, "Why don't you pick one up and smoke it sometime?" Before any of us could react, Bob stretched both arms overhead in a triumphant touchdown sign and roared, "It's a boy, fellows. Nancy and I just had a baby boy. Come on, now. Have a cigar on us."

The whole room erupted in wild cheers and applause as we swarmed around him to pump his hand and accept a Muriel Magnum. Over the joyous ruckus, I could hear Tweety's voice piping up. "Sir. That was the hottest Edie Adams impersonation this side of the Pacific. You surely could stand in for her in the commercial." The men howled and stomped their feet in approval. Dean, standing back alongside me, wiped his brow with his hand. "For a minute there, I thought it might be something disastrous," he whispered. "Lucky SOB. I'm real happy for him. For them both."

According to Bob, Nancy had gone into labor the day before and had to grind and push her way through a twelve-hour marathon session to give birth to a healthy baby boy. "Twenty-one inches, nine pounds six ounces, with a hefty set of lungs and an appetite to match," announced the proud new daddy. "Biggest surprise of all, he turned out a carrot top."

"Have you all picked out a name?" someone shouted from the gathered group.

"Ricky, short for Eric—Eric Alexander Olsen," answered Bob.

"How fitting. A hearty welcome to Eric the Red, everyone," came the quick repartee amid a new round of happy laughter and applause.

Prior to the big event, and without Bob's knowledge, his family had arranged with AFA7UGA for a one-time exception to place a reverse call to him following the baby's delivery. Due to weather disturbances, however, the frequency had been down all day until this evening. When the call at last came through, it gave Bob a jolt—literally. The earlier commotion, he readily admitted, was from him jumping with excitement when told the news.

"Let's go celebrate at the club," I suggested to Bob and Dean once the party had cleared out except for the small evening staff and things had settled back to normal. Bob grabbed handfuls of Muriel Magnums and stuffed them in his pockets on our way out.

It was a good move on his part since the officers' club was packed that night with pilots, many of whom happened to be his friends. While I went to get our drinks, Bob made the rounds of the tables to share his great news and hand out the stogies.

"We may be stuck in here awhile, kiddo," Dean told me when I returned. "Let's hope you and I won't have to carry him out tonight." He pointed with his chin at Bob, who was getting toasted uproariously as he stopped at every table.

"You mentioned something about this weekend?" I reminded Dean.

"Have you heard from Dick since our last trip to Sài-Gòn?"

I shook my head.

"Me neither," Dean said. "It's odd. He usually calls to touch base before the weekend so he can make arrangements at Mme Yvonne's. Not a word this time. I couldn't find him, either." He turned to me. "You still want to stop by her place this Sunday, without Dick? Maybe the girls will have heard from him by then."

"I'm game."

With that settled, Dean changed the subject. "I'm going on R&R for five days, starting next Monday. Hong Kong. Anything in particular you want me to check out?"

"Nothing, thanks." No sooner had the answer slipped out than I changed my mind. "On second thought, if you have time to kill, see if you can't find me a stuffed toy dragon. I hear dragons are popular there."

"Whatever floats your boat," Dean deadpanned. "Any favorite color?" It was so like him not to bother following up with any prying question. Not even a sarcastic rib.

I laughed. "It's for Eric. I'd like to give it to Bob before he leaves to meet Nancy in Hawaii next month." Dean didn't seem to get it, so I gave him a nudge with my elbow. "Puff, the Magic Dragon? Bob's into it, big time. A fire-red dragon would be perfect for Ricky. Daddy's sure to get a kick out of it. Trust me. And speaking of the devil . . ."

Bob dropped into the chair next to ours, exhausted but all smiles from his victory lap. Draped over his arm was a collection of scarves in assorted colors: red, blue, yellow, purple. "Gifts to Ricky from the flyboys, right off their necks," he explained, showing them off with pride. "These three are from Thunderbird platoons, and this purple one from our Ranch Hand Commandos. I'm starting a collection of pilot scarves for my boy. Pretty cool, eh?" Besides serving to distinguish one unit from another, these scarves were worn by pilots to prevent hot shell casings from the crew chief's machine gun, positioned directly behind their seats, from slipping inside their shirt collars and burning their necks and backs.

Never had we seen Bob in a more exalted mood. His blue eyes were all fire and crinkled up around the corners from a broad smile that wouldn't quit, and his voice had gone gruff from all the cheering and celebrating. Yet I had no doubt that he still could, and would, carry on well into this special night.

"I see you've shared a few toasts already," I remarked, shoving another Diesel and Juice in his hand. "One more won't kill you."

We raised our glasses.

"Here's to little Ricky," I proposed. "May our boy be blessed with a wonderful life. But most important, may he grow up to be as great a guy as his old man."

As we clinked glasses in honor of his firstborn son, Bob's face was aglow with sweat, tears, and his ecstatic smile. That singular image of my hooch mate overwhelmed with the joy and pride of new fatherhood remained etched in my mind as among my happiest and most cherished memories from Việt-Nam.

Generally speaking, the weather in Sài-Gòn is at its most pleasant around Christmastime, cooler and dryer than any other time of the year. Such was the case when Dean and I arrived at Mme Yvonne's that Sunday afternoon, feeling a bit odd without our regular companion, Dick.

The place looked positively festive. Blinking stars and angels hung from low branches around the garden, and tinsel garlands sparkled among string lights over the green shrubbery. The holiday music playing over outdoor speakers was more playful than traditional: "Little Miss Dynamite" Brenda Lee, with Bobby Helms (of "Jingle Bell Rock" fame), and the Beach Boys, among others. The radiant hostesses all wore their best attire, and many had draped a colorful sweater across their shoulders, more for a touch of seasonal fashion than necessity.

With all her girls busy, Mme Yvonne herself greeted us with open arms as we strolled in. "Welcome back, *mes amis*," she exclaimed, giving us big hugs. "I'm so glad to wish you *joyeux Noël* in person. What did you do with my other *mousquetaire*?"

"We think he might be out of town," I said as she led us to the last open table in the garden. "I take it you haven't heard from Dick either?"

"Not since the last time all three of you came by. Now, what can I bring you to drink, dears? I'll let the girls know you're here, as soon as they become free."

She took our drink orders then scurried away. Dean and I settled back and checked out the scene. The place was buzzing with pre-holiday excitement, more lively than at any time before. With just over a week until Christmas, it was obvious nobody cared to stay holed up alone in his hotel room ten thousand miles away from home. Even if Dick had let the ladies know to expect us, I doubted we'd have been allowed to monopolize their time for long.

"Hello, Dean, Roger." Vivienne appeared with a small tray. "Mme Yvonne asked me to bring you your drinks, but I cannot stay. It's crazy here today. But Lee Anne and Elise will be free soon." She looked impeccably groomed as always, though somewhat subdued.

"Don't worry about us," I assured her. "We'll be here awhile. You take care of business first, okay? We'll catch up later."

She set our glasses down, started to turn away, then stopped. "Have you heard from Dick?"

I shook my head, trying to disguise my fast-growing concern. Of all people, I was hoping Vivienne would be the one to shed light on Dick's whereabouts, yet she seemed as much in the dark as the rest of us. I felt she was going to say something else, but she bit her lower lip and rushed off.

Dean and I were finishing our first drinks when Lee Anne and Elise, all smiles and giggles, swooped down at our table. They seemed glad to finally be able to get off their feet. For both, this was their first holiday season working at Mme Yvonne's, and as fun and exhilarating as it was, the two friends were clearly not used to the frenzied pace. Lee Anne caught me staring and smiled, her cheeks blushing the color of lotus. I was hoping to have a few minutes alone with her, but she could not stay long, having to hurry off to cover for Vivienne, who also looked in sore need of a break herself.

"Are you holding up all right?" I asked Vivienne after she sat down. She nodded, forcing a smile. It must have been a rough day since I'd never seen Vivienne, heretofore the consummate hostess, so quiet. Thoughtful Elise went to fetch her an iced tea, then we left her to relax and enjoy her much-deserved break.

On the grass, a few couples slow-danced to the soft music now being played. When Nat King Cole's smoky baritone launched his beautiful "Christmas Song," Dean surprised us all by pulling Elise up from her seat to join the dancers. I was impressed how sure-footed and graceful Mr. Rough-and-Tumble turned out to be as he swayed a delighted-looking Elise in his arms. What a handsome couple they made, I couldn't help notice again as I watched them dance under the tinsel garlands.

"You have few minutes, Roger?" Vivienne's voice interrupted my reverie. "I like to know what you think about something. In private, if okay." There was a note of urgency in her tone.

"But of course, Vivienne. Where can we go to talk?"

"There's office inside," she replied. "I asked Mme Yvonne to use it during break. It's quiet there, and nobody will bother. Are you free, now?"

"I'm all yours." We stood, and I followed her into the house.

Vivienne led me through the lounge, down the hallway, and past the bathroom on the right to a closed door opposite it. On this second door hung a small plate marked *Văn-phòng* (Office). She knocked, listened, then opened it.

We stepped into a small, cluttered room furnished with a large wooden desk, a metal file cabinet, and a pair of chairs. Behind the desk, a sliding glass door looked out onto a covered patio decorated with potted bamboo trees, hanging baskets of orchids, and a miniature mountain scene. A hidden Zen-like sanctuary.

She pulled the floor-length curtain halfway shut to dim the natural light in the office. We sat, she behind the desk and I on the other side. Her face was half turned away, but I could still make out her shaded profile against the sunlit glass door. In this incongruous setting, with deliberate words that instantly captured my attention, Vivienne poured out her heart to me.

"You will not understand everything I am going to tell you," she started hesitantly. "But still I must tell story. So please be patient, and have open mind.

"You and Dick were close friends when you were young, but did you really know how alone and different he felt, growing up? I think he did not talk to you about it. We Asians keep things close to heart, and it took him long time to even tell me. As young kid, Dick always smiled, even when his feelings were hurt. It was simple way to protect himself. He was clumsy, helpless, and big mean kids called him 'Fat Sumo Boy' and 'Yellow Devil' around school playground. Also, maybe you know, his family was sent to camp during last war. Bad memory followed them like ghost. So he always felt like outsider, he said, always worked very hard to get in, but no luck. It is why he came to Việt-Nam. New start, new chance."

Vivienne's voice had grown soft and reflective, and I strained to catch her every word.

"Him and Mme Yvonne became friends first time they met. She also had very tough life at young age, so she understood and treated him like brother. Both have been kind and helpful to me because they know I have troubles, too. I feel so lucky we are best friends. The three of us share same hope that life will be better for us. We think everyone deserves chance to be happy. But between us three, I am only one who hide my past, and it bothers Dick a lot."

She paused, as if to reflect on how best to proceed. I had an inkling that what was to follow might help unravel the mystery of Dick's disappearance.

With a deep exhale, Vivienne dropped her head and shoulders, as if shedding all pretense along with her erect posture. She shifted in her chair, turning farther away so I found myself staring at the back of her neck.

"I am youngest of five children, with four big brothers," she began anew, sounding drained and more gravelly than ever. "I came as big surprise to my parents, at late and not convenient stage in their lives. Some of their grandkids, my nieces and nephews, are older than me. But after first shock, they welcomed and loved me with all their hearts, especially my mother. She always wanted little girl, you see, even if Vietnamese culture favors boys."

Listening to Vivienne sharing about her life for the first time, I wondered what it had to do with Dick gone missing. But I dared not make a noise and break her train of thought.

"As the baby and only child at home, I was very close to my mother. She took me with her everywhere. I was always excited to go do things with her. She was whole world to me: my mother, my teacher, my best friend, and I could not love her more. She taught me everything she knew about making happy home. My best memories of childhood were hours we spent together in kitchen or at sewing table. By high school, I already made clothes for myself and my nieces and nephews, to save money.

"Things were tough for us, like for everyone in country. At least we had roof over our heads and enough food from one day to next. You can say I lived normal life for young girl growing up in Việt-Nam. With only one problem."

I sat still while Vivienne fidgeted with the front flap of her *áo dài*. Her hands finally folded in her lap, and her whole body seemed to tense up.

"A girl—I am *not*," she said in a hoarse whisper. "Not really."

I caught every word she said, but somehow the message didn't register. My mind drew a blank, refusing to understand. I must have misheard, for sure. Or at least misinterpreted what I thought I'd heard. What on earth was she talking about?

For a long, awkward moment, neither of us stirred. Then Vivienne sat up straight in her chair, her face still angled away from me. She cleared her throat, as if waiting for my reaction. Hearing none, she ventured ahead, her voice uncertain, full of weariness.

"It is my dirty secret, Roger. The reason I try very hard to hide my past," she said. "Yes. I am female, but only in mind and heart, because I was born in male's body. Very cruel joke from nature. I do not wish it even on worst enemy."

She stopped, allowing her words to sink in. As my mind grappled feverishly with the blunt revelation, pieces of the puzzle, for the first time, started to fall into place: her deeper voice and taller stature; her meticulous makeup; her dazzling but none too revealing attire. What other clues had I overlooked? I wondered in disbelief.

"Until now, nobody knew except my family," Vivienne went on, as if reading my mind. "Of course my mother already knew since I was little, just watching me play. I was not rough and noisy like my older brothers at same age. Very shy, she remembers, and spoke softly and always tried to please. She remembers I liked to play house with my nieces, not kick soccer ball with boys. And I loved to put on all her things—her clothes, her makeup, her rings.

"But you know, it did not upset my parents as you maybe think, for one special reason. Before I was born, people envied my parents for having four sons, my brothers. It is considered rare blessing, very lucky. They call it *Tứ Quý*, or 'the precious four.' On other hand, a group of five boys—like my brothers *and* me—is called *Ngũ Quỷ*, or 'the five devils.' People believe odd number breaks harmony and brings bad luck to family. So, to take jinx away, my parents let me do what was natural to me. My mother even dressed me like a girl when I was little. It was happiest times of my life, when I was allowed to be my mother's daughter. But they lasted just few years, until school age. Then I was forced to change, to be like other boys."

Vivienne leaned back against her chair and lapsed into silence, apparently caught up in the past. For my part, I had hardly taken a breath or formulated a coherent thought while listening to her, so stunned was I by this turn of events. It all seemed like a strange dream that kept evolving.

"School was rough experience for me," she finally continued, her raspy monotone an echo from some faraway place. "People say they want to be different, or special. But they really mean to be like everybody, only better. Believe me. Different is no good. I was treated bad all those years because I was different. I was 'girlie' boy. Kids made fun, gave me very hard time because how I looked and talked, how I walked and carried my books. Everything I did, they laughed, like funny joke. Do you know how cruel some children are? Sometimes I still wake up from same nightmares, things that happened to me in schoolyard. But all of us find ways to live our lives, deal with private problems. And I learned to live with mine. Because there were bigger worries every day. Like food, and place to stay. And most of all, war."

Vivienne let out a deep sigh, head bowed and shoulders bent under an invisible weight.

"War," she repeated. "It changed everything. Before last year in high school, I faced big, scary trouble. I was one of oldest boys in class, by two years. So I would be drafted into military after school finished. Now, one thing you must know: I can never be a soldier. Not even lousy one. I get sick in stomach when I see blood. Few special times when my mother prepared live chicken or fresh fish for cooking, I ran and hid far away from kitchen. So everyone in my family asked same question: How can I be trained to defend myself by shooting at enemy soldier? My answer: he will kill me first."

It began to dawn on me, the burden of Vivienne's secret. The nagging pain and loneliness. The terror of life-threatening ramifications. How had she managed to hang on when there was no future in sight? My heart aching with empathy, I inched forward in my seat, but she kept going, her voice tense, her breathing strenuous.

"As time got near, I panicked and decided I must do only thing possible. I must take new identity, someone that cannot be drafted. So the summer before my last year in high school, my mother helped me to change how I looked. Everything: hair, clothes, makeup. Now

I looked like what I should be: young woman. To keep secret, I dropped out of school that year and went to stay with my aunt and uncle. They have no children and live on other side of town. Timing was good because more and more refugees of war arrived in city every day. Police did not know everybody coming and going in neighborhoods.

"But still I must be careful. Very tough penalties for avoiding draft, to punish cowards like me. If police caught me, they sent me to frontline as *Lao-công Chiến-trường*—battlefield labor. Same as death sentence. So I stayed home most of day and took English classes at night school near my aunt's house. I wanted to learn English really good, because everything changed fast with Americans arriving. If I am lucky and find work with them, maybe it is start of new life for me. Americans are strangers, my secret will be safe. At least I hoped."

Vivienne paused, her shoulders dropping and rising with ragged breaths. It was a moment before she resumed, in a calmer but tired voice.

"A year later, I saw ad in newspaper to be hostess at private club just opened. It was how I met Mme Yvonne. Did she guess my real identity? She never asked, but she hired me. I became first employee, two years ago in August. I cannot explain how thankful I am that she gave me a chance."

⌣⟶⌣

The sunlight through the half-curtained glass door had turned a deeper hue, as it was getting late in the afternoon. Vivienne sat perfectly still, a statue of despondency. She must be exhausted from the whole ordeal, and I wondered if I shouldn't respect her silence. At the same time, I had the impression she was expecting some comment from me, though I hardly knew where to begin, so jumbled were my thoughts and my emotions.

"Did you share your story with Dick?" I asked. It seemed a superfluous question, to buy myself some time. This no doubt had to be the cause of Dick's vanishing act.

A long minute passed before she answered. "I did not have chance. Everything happened so fast. He was gone before I knew."

My jaw dropped. "You mean—he has no idea? What happened, then?"

Vivienne slowly turned toward me. Her face looked pained and jaded, dried tracks of tears messing up her otherwise impeccable makeup. There was something absurd and tragic about it.

"Last time all of you were here, Dick came to me when I was alone in the lounge," she said. "He took my hand, pushed something in it, but said nothing. Then he stood back and watched me, like waiting for answer."

She had to pause, apparently fighting for control.

"It was small box with diamond ring in it." Vivienne sobbed, burying her face in her hands, overwhelmed.

It was a good thing I was sitting, for my head took a spin at this latest revelation. Oh, Dick, I muttered under my breath, not believing what I'd just heard. My heart instinctively went out to him and Vivienne, even as my brain scrambled to make sense. Their situation had grown beyond complicated. I almost got up and rushed over to Vivienne to wrap my arm around her shoulders, then thought better of it, not certain how either of us would react under the circumstances.

Her tears finally subsided as I stayed glued like a dummy to my chair.

"Dick gave me great honor by asking me," Vivienne said, her voice still shaking. "It is most special gift anyone can give me—the real me, inside. But of course it is not possible."

My stomach was in such knots it felt almost painful. "What did you tell him?"

"I was so shocked when he gave me the ring I must sit down," she went on, as if not hearing me. "You know I really care for him, and I am very touched by his love. But it can never happen like he wants. How can I stop it now? I panicked, but no time to think. It was my fault because I did not tell him shameful truth. Then suddenly idea came from nowhere, and I said I could not accept offer because I was engaged to be married."

I gasped. "You said *what*?"

Vivienne turned to me with imploring eyes. "I believed in my heart I did what was best for him. But the look on his face, it was so painful, I realized I made terrible mistake. But before I could explain, he turned his back and ran out."

I vaguely recalled how somber Dick's mood had been that evening as he drove Dean and me to Tân-Sơn-Nhất Airport. We had simply attributed it to his recent workload. Later, when we got off at curbside, he'd shot me a curious glance as if about to say something, then apparently changed his mind and waved us off without a word. That was the last we'd seen of Dick.

Vivienne lowered her gaze. Her voice grew more earnest, with a hint of despair.

"I know I hurt him terrible, and he does not want to see me again. So I need to ask you big favor, Roger. Because you are his closest friend. If you see Dick alone, please explain for me. Tell him my story. Tell him I am ashamed of everything I did, and I am very sorry I hurt him. I understand he cannot forgive. But I will always care for him. It is truth."

My heart ached for her and for my childhood friend. Even as my mind still grappled with their unique situation, I understood her sense of loss and her immense sadness. What illusive happiness she and Dick had enjoyed together over the past months had been shattered beyond repair. Gone indeed were a fleeting chance at love and romance and the fantasy of a future together, through no one's fault but the impossible circumstances.

Before my eyes I saw only a friend in great pain, and it troubled me that I could do so little to help.

"Vivienne," I called out softly to her. "You need to know that nothing changes between us, you and me. We'll always be friends. I've no idea what happened to Dick or where he is now, but you have my word that I shall find him and give him your message."

She nodded in forlorn silence.

"Hey, kiddo." I tried to catch her eyes.

She finally looked up at me.

The words came naturally, to my surprise. "For what it's worth: you're one heck of a lady, in my book."

I thought I detected the faintest trace of a smile through her tears.

Chapter Eleven

Biên-Hoà AFB, 2 Jan 1968, 2100 hrs

Hi, Mom and Dad,

Happy New Year and a big hug to everyone!

Thank you so much for your holiday care package. I also received goodies from Debbie, Aunt Millie, and even Mrs. Anderson, my history teacher in high school. That was so sweet of her. You must thank her for me the next time you see her in church. I'll write Debbie and Aunt Millie later to thank them, too. I ended up with all kinds of nuts, cookies, and chocolates, not to mention your fruitcake, all of which I shared with our staff at the dispensary after setting some aside for the kids at the orphanages. Thanks for wrapping everything in foil paper; that kept the ants out this time.

We enjoyed a relatively quiet Christmas on base despite cease-fire violations elsewhere by the Việt-Cộng, which were ex-pected. Somehow we also managed to miss all the whirlwind VIP tours this holiday season. AFVN News reported that President Johnson made an impromptu stop at Cam-Ranh Bay, north of here, on 23 Dec, upon returning from his visits to Australia and Thailand. Then right on his heels arrived Bob Hope and his USO troupe for their annual Christmas Tour, with stops in Sài-Gòn, Long-Bình, Cam-Ranh, Đà-Nẵng, and at several remote outposts where the morale could use some boosting. I understand they put on a fantastic show with celebrity guests like Raquel Welch, Barbara McNair, and even the new Miss World. Some lucky guys who got to go to the one in nearby Long-Bình joked that they'd volunteered for Việt-Nam just to get tickets to Mr.

Hope's Christmas Special. But you folks at home really had the best seats anywhere, watching it on TV from your own couches.

On Christmas Eve Sunday, a bunch of us escorted Santa Claus (our MEDCAP leader) to an orphanage run by Buddhist nuns outside a hamlet on the Đồng-Nai River. We went by jeeps but traveled the last portion of the trip in leaky sampans, since the hamlet sits on a small island in the river. It was a bit hairy, I must admit, but we wanted to take advantage of the cease-fire to make our visit, and we were hoping, naïvely perhaps, that Charlie would observe it, too. To our relief, he did, at least where we went. I wish you could have seen the joy in those kids' eyes when they received, probably for the first time in their lives, armfuls of new clothes and gifts of toys and sweets. It really made it worthwhile. It also encouraged the kids to cooperate in the physical checkup that followed. So I want to thank you—Mom, Dad, and everybody at home who donated to our charitable cause and made it such a success.

We had a wonderful dinner on Christmas Day. Each of us got a small folded bulletin as we sat down to eat, which looked like a nice traditional Christmas card on the cover. Printed on the inside were a Christmas prayer, a message from our commander, General Westmoreland, along with the elaborate holiday menu. I bet you'd like to know what was on the menu, wouldn't you, Mom? Keep in mind that none of it could compare to your home cooking, of course, but for a bunch of single guys away from home, it was pretty decent fare. Here goes, off the top of my head: shrimp cocktail, turkey with cornbread dressing and cranberry sauce, mashed potatoes, glazed sweet potatoes and mixed vegetables, then for dessert, fruit cake, mincemeat pie, pumpkin pie with cream, fresh fruits, nuts, and candies. And yep, we sampled it all. So much for moderation. But let me tell you, there's no greater euphoria than a satisfied stomach. It makes everything else almost bearable.

Just this morning I received your mail with all the Polaroid photos taken on Christmas Day. Now, Dad, congratulations on that brilliant idea, getting the Land Camera for Mom for Christmas. Anybody I talked to who knew anything about instant cameras loved it. And no wonder. The colors came out beautiful. My favorite snapshots are of Dad replacing a string of burned-out lights on the Christmas tree in the Moon Meadows lounge, of Mom preparing the big dinner in the kitchen, and of Jer dozing off in the chair after being well fed (so what else is new). It seemed like nothing had changed, and I was right there with you guys. But then I got homesick when I saw the picture Mom took from the parking lot of the snow-covered Eastern Sierra. With the day temperatures hovering in the 80s here, even during this coolest month of the year, I'm truly a long ways away from my favorite winter land.

Good news is I'm coming up on the halfway point in my tour. Just over six months to go, but then time has a way of stretching out interminably here in Việt-Nam. It seems an eternity ago when I first stepped off the C-141 onto the red soil of Biên-Hoà, yet it was only last summer. I'm not complaining, just making an observation. I also get you didn't want to trouble me with all the goings-on stateside, but I'm not totally unaware of the unrest at home, especially the brouhaha of Stop-the-Draft Week, followed by the big antiwar march on Washington D.C. in October. In my gut, though, I still believe we're doing the right thing helping the poor folks who live here, and I'm happy to take part in it.

Anyway, Mom and Dad, this national debate may rage on for months to come, if not years. In the meantime it's fast approaching lights-out here, so I'll need to sign off for now. Please give everybody my love and a big hug from me. Goodnight, all, and sleep tight.

Love, your son R.C.

It turned out I wasn't the only one about to reach a significant milestone in his tour. One evening in mid-January, about a week before his scheduled R&R rendezvous with his wife in Hawaii, Bob Olsen asked me to take a short drive with him after work.

"Where to?" My curiosity was piqued since this wasn't part of our regular routine.

"Not far," he said. "Just to the other side of the base. Away from all this madness."

A half-hour before sunset, we hopped in a jeep and Bob drove to the open area on the north side, far enough removed from the noise and bustle of the runway and the Army heliport. Once there, he switched off the engine, and we could hear the rumblings of nonstop activities behind us in the smoky distance. He reached into the back seat, fished out a small poster, handed it to me. "Tweety gave me this earlier today."

It was a curious pinup poster with a curvaceous female figure on it, covered by little squares numbered from 100 to 1, with the lowest numbers lodged in strategic spots.

"Ever seen a short-timers calendar before?" Bob asked. "One hundred squares for your last hundred days until DEROS. You mark each day off as you start counting down toward flight date home." He looked at me. "I'm officially a short-timer, starting today—square 100."

I grabbed his strong hand and shook it. "Hot damn. Congratulations."

And then the news hit me like a tropical blast in the face. Another three months, and my hooch mate would be going home. "You and Nancy must be excited. Soon a new phase in your lives, with Ricky along for the joy ride this time."

Bob pointed at a promontory outside the base to the northwest. "See that pagoda atop the hill there? So tranquil and blissful—a slice of heaven on this scorched earth, wouldn't you say?" He scoffed. "Uh-uh. It's actually under VC control. They have spotters up there around the clock calling in every aircraft movement on base. Never forget, pal. Nothing's quite as it seems."

He turned back to me with a thoughtful smile. "What's the first thing you can't wait to do when you get back? Ever thought about it?"

I laughed. "More than I care to admit. I suppose I'd want to vanish into the John Muir Wilderness for about a month, all by my lonesome. Never thought I'd miss it so much. The scenery there is beyond spectacular. Streams and lakes, and meadows and canyons as far as the eye can see. Normally it's not advisable to go it alone in those mountains, but I'll want to get away by myself, at least for a while at the outset." I winked at him. "And then you must come out to visit, so I can hike your ass all over the Sierra. We may even go camping up on Mount Whitney, if you're in half-decent shape."

He gave me a slap on the back. "Only if you come visit us in Minnesota first. Bring Debbie with you, of course. The girls can hang out with Ricky and spoil the little guy all they want or go do fun stuff together. You and I, we'll take my boat out on the lake and catch us some walleyes for dinner. Nance has a damn good beer batter she uses to cook the fish. It'll make a scrumptious meal with homemade biscuits and gobs of buttercup squash and sweet corn on the cob. Oh, and you'll have to save room for her rhubarb pie for dessert. She won't let you leave until you've sampled it." Then his eyes lit up at a passing thought. "You had a Hamm's beer before? Remember the cute commercial?"

"Ah, yes. The Hamm's Beer Bear." I smiled and started humming. "Tom, tom, tom. From the land of sky blue waters . . ." Bob joined in and we bellowed out the rest of the jingle together, drumming our thighs with open hands as we went, bursting out in laughter upon finishing.

"Catchy little cartoon," I said. "But it hasn't yet persuaded me to taste-test a Hamm's."

"Truth be told, it's nothing out of this world," Bob replied good-heartedly. "It's popular with the younger crowd on a budget 'cause it's one of the cheapest brands around. But it's a specialty from the Land of Ten Thousand Lakes, and I've been craving it like crazy. We'll make sure you imbibe plenty of it when you come."

Caught up in the warm, fuzzy thoughts, we lapsed into contented silence.

Then I asked him about any family plans or career moves he might be contemplating for the future. He became pensive.

"Well, there are long-term goals and there are short-term goals," he finally said. "In the long haul, I'd love to get a shot at the new astronaut-scientist program NASA has been promoting for over two years now. Hopefully, I'd have a leg up on other candidates with my pilot training. But on the practical side, the lengthy selection and training process would take another heavy toll on the family. I'll have to think long and hard about it. As for nearer-term projections . . ."

He hesitated, shot me a curious glance then went on. "I get that you're here not entirely of your own accord, so there's a chance we may not see things quite the same way. But you asked, and I'll be straight with you." He redirected his gaze at the serene-looking pagoda in the dying sunlight atop the hill. "I'm a simple man with simple ideals and an uncomplicated view of the world. It's my personal feeling that we have a moral obligation to assist the people in this country so they can be left alone by the Việt-Cộng, who are armed to the teeth with Soviet and Chinese weaponry. The only thing these helpless folks have ever wanted is to be allowed to eke out a peaceful living on their ancestral land. But what chance would they stand without our help, when even their places of worship are desecrated and hijacked by the commies and turned into rocket-launching pads?"

There was a reflective pause, then Bob told me. He was seriously thinking of volunteering for a second tour. "But of course I'll need to discuss it with Nance, and together we'll decide," he said. "The past year has been so tough on her already. And now, with Ricky . . ."

"You're not bringing this up with her next week in Hawaii, are you?" I asked.

"Fuck, no," he shot back. "We'll spend every minute catching up and enjoying each other. You know, we've never been apart this long before. I really miss her."

Darkness was fast falling around us, as if some celestial curtains were being drawn across the scarlet sky. Bob started up the jeep. "Time to get back," he said.

"Hungry for our world-famous grub at the old club?" I asked.

"My dinner will be mostly liquid." Bob laughed, swinging the jeep around toward the main complex. "Word leaked out about my short-timer's status, and some of the flyboys insisted on helping me celebrate tonight. To give me my ribbon." Anticipating my question, he explained, "You know how their lives are fraught with danger and traditions. This is just another example of those traditions that bond them for the rest of their days. Remember the famous words, 'We few, we happy few, we band of brothers'? Hell, it's the only Shakespeare you'll ever catch me quoting, but it pretty much sums up the spirit."

As the guest of honor of the evening, Bob would be presented with a bottle of Seagram's V.O. that he was to finish by his last day in country. The ritual also dictated he be given the trademark black-and-gold ribbon draped around the bottle's neck to loop through the top buttonhole of his shirt. Every day from then on, a tiny bit would be clipped from the ribbon until all of it was gone on his departure date.

"I suppose the tradition is a good reminder to newbies of a happy milestone they can all look forward to," Bob said. "Also a testament to the spirit of survival in all of us. At any rate, it does well to promote the *esprit de corps*, besides being a blast." He gave me an elbow nudge. "Come join our little funfest tonight? In your hooch mate's honor?"

"I'll swing by later," I replied. "It's always fun to see you shit-faced. But first I've got to take care of some paperwork. Can you drop me off at the office?"

As the jeep pulled up in front of the dispensary, I turned toward him. "For your information, Captain, you and I aren't that far apart in our thinking regarding the war. We can discuss this at greater length later. But thanks for speaking your mind tonight." He nodded, and I hopped out.

"Don't be too far gone before I get there," I yelled out after him, as jeep and driver roared off in a swirl of choking red dust.

———

It didn't take me long to wrap up my unfinished business in the office. I was set to turn off the light on my way out when the phone rang. It was Dean Hunter, gone since Christmas.

"Well, hells bells," I said. "Welcome back from exotic Hong Kong. Where are you?"

"In the Provincial Hospital, finishing up my last round for the night," he answered. "They were swamped while I was gone. We're just now catching up."

"So how was the trip? I want a full report."

"Was nice," he muttered in his typical understated way. "The kids who went with me were quite impressed with the service on our chartered Pan-Am. You know, sexy blond, round-eyed attendants passing out sweet smiles with warm washcloths for your face and hands. A welcome touch of civilization."

"How was the Fragrant Harbor itself? Did the city live up to your expectations?"

"It's like Manhattan in the tropics, with one difference: you can see row upon row of laundry flapping in the wind on the skyscrapers' balconies. It's colorful, actually. Wonder why they chose not to show that in *Love Is a Many-Splendored Thing.*"

I laughed. "Of course you wandered up the windy hill in search of Jennifer Jones?"

"We stayed on one," he said. "A plush hotel on a hill of Kowloon. It was mind-boggling to imagine Việt-Nam less than three hours away from all that commercial prosperity. I'll tell you more about it, next time we meet. Did you happen to look in the lower left drawer of your desk?"

I did as instructed and pulled out a shopping bag with bold red Chinese characters printed on it. Inside, I found an adorable stuffed animal that looked half-dinosaur half-dragon, in red and yellow velvet, with a funny crunched-up face no little kid could resist.

"You found Puff," I exclaimed. "Not particularly spooky-looking. But it'll do."

"You don't want to scare the poor child, do you?" Dean chuckled. "Anyway, that was the best I could do. I stopped by a while ago on the way back from our milk run, but you weren't around. I didn't want to leave the bag out on your desk in case Bob might see it."

"Thanks a bunch, Dean-man. I owe you one."

"There's something else," Dean hastened to add. "I talked to Hayashi early in the week."

"Dick! Really? Where? Was he in town? Everything okay with him?"

"Hold your horses, kiddo," Dean said. "He called me. We had a brief chat on the phone."

It turned out Dick had returned to Sài-Gòn only for a couple of days, to check in with his boss at the AP Bureau and to take care of his overdue bills. He'd been traveling around with a buddy of his, a young Japanese photojournalist of great renown, Kyoichi Sawada at competitor UPI, whose work had garnered him a Pulitzer Prize the year before. Together, they'd been roaming the northern region of South Việt-Nam to track a string of bloody skirmishes known as the Border Battles, shooting pictures and gathering stories wherever the action led them.

"He tried to get hold of you but couldn't," Dean said. "He's already headed back north to 'Eye' Corps, to try to sneak into the US Marine Combat Base at Khe Sanh, just below the DMZ. Big news story, he claimed. A set-piece showdown in the making."

"Sounds dangerous. How was he doing, could you tell?" I wanted to be careful not to let on too much of what I knew of Dick's personal plight. Vivienne had mentioned that Mme Yvonne and I were the only people apprised of the situation.

"Not too bad, I think," Dean said. "Though I did sense some fatigue and sadness in his voice. Perhaps from having witnessed so much war in the past two months." Then, softly, as if to himself, "That'd sure take away your laughter for a while."

I know what else is preying on his mind. That, too, would kill his laughter. "When's he back in town again? Did he say?" I asked.

"He didn't know. Which reminds me. He asked us for a favor. To look in on his apartment every once in a while when we're in Sài-Gòn. Just to make sure everything's cool."

"Easy enough," I said. "I can do that this Sunday when I'm in the city. You coming?"

He hesitated. "Not sure yet. Let me get back with you in a day or two."

I started telling him about the short-timers party for Bob when it suddenly dawned on me. "Say, aren't you going 'short' real soon, yourself?" I asked Dean. "Come on over and celebrate with us. The fighter boys would love to pick on another victim besides Bob."

He laughed. "Too late, kiddo. I already signed up for a second tour before I went on R&R. My congratulations to Captain Bob. But right now, I just need to flake out and hit the sack."

After we hung up, I hurried to the officers' club, my mind still preoccupied by our conversation. With one of my best friends immersing himself in nonstop combat reporting and the other two either having decided or still considering to extend their tours of duty, the end of this war must still be far off, contrary to my naïve belief up until now.

In the distance, illumination flares slithered down the black sky like snakes of fire, lighting up the horizon for invisible bombers. But even squinting, I could barely make out the hillock where the little pagoda stood, much less the temple itself. In the flickering yellow light of flares, the landscape seemed eerily murky and laden with unsuspected danger, as imponderable as one's own future. For the first time since my arrival in Việt-Nam, I felt nagged by uncertainty— even by something akin to foreboding.

As raucous laughter greeted me at the club's door, I snapped myself out of it.

Chapter Twelve

Sunday arrived in a blink of an eye.

The weekend had been shaping up into a rather unusual one. First, Dean had telephoned on Friday afternoon to beg off our trip to Sài-Gòn. He'd been called out on emergency to an A-team camp in the Plain of Reeds near the Cambodian border and didn't expect to be back for at least a few days. This meant for the first time I'd have to rely entirely on myself getting around the capital without a navigator.

"Sure you won't get lost?" he teased.

"Absolutely. Every time we went, I watched and learned."

We were only a couple of weeks away from *Tết*, the Vietnamese New Year's according to the lunar calendar. I decided to put Dean's knowledge of the native language to the test.

"How do I say Happy New Year in Vietnamese?"

"You sure picked a winner with that one." He laughed. "It's *Chúc Mừng Năm Mới*. It's a mouthful all right, but you have till Sunday to practice to impress the ladies. Good luck, kiddo."

Bob, on the other hand, was worried now that I'd be left to my own devices in the big city. "Stay extra alert," he cautioned me again early Sunday morning, as I watched him pack for his Hawaii trip the following day. "Ever notice how most cafés and restaurants in Sài-Gòn have steel gratings on their windows? It's to protect their patrons against Việt-Cộng's underground agents. These thugs are known to scoot by on motorcycles and toss satchel charges or grenades into the crowds. You think they care if innocent bystanders are blown up? It's precisely their goal. To spread terror and chaos."

In response to my wide-eyed reaction, he shrugged. "If they use cold-blooded tactics like that against their own people, what won't they do to you and me? Beware of the so-called Dragon Lady while you're out and about on the capital's streets. She's rumored to ride around the city on the back of a Honda scooter, looking for careless Americans and shooting them point-blank with a .45. Some say she's a man disguised in *áo dài* to slip past security checkpoints."

He stopped in the middle of packing and looked up. "You know you're like a brother to me, right?" he said in earnest. "So I must say something to you, just this once. Okay?"

I nodded hesitantly. He sounded much more serious than usual.

"I'm a square," Bob went on, "and I'm going to call it as I see it. Why on earth are you taking such unnecessary risks hopping to Sài-Gòn every chance you get? It's not only your personal safety. It's also your relationship with Debbie you're jeopardizing. For Christ's sake, Connors. Why play with fire?"

I was completely blindsided by his uncharacteristic outburst, and my face must have turned crimson red as I felt the blood rushing to it. I scoffed in silent disbelief. *So this is what I get in exchange for sharing my fun escapades with him all this time. A sanctimonious lecture.*

"You shouldn't have bothered. It's really none of your business," was the retort I hurled back at Bob as I brushed past him on my way out the door. He raised his hands as if pleading for calm and reason, then thought better of it and let me by without another word.

Bob's butting in left me fuming, so much so I barely touched my breakfast at the officers' club. How dare he, I kept muttering to myself over a plate of cold scrambled eggs. How dare he touch a sore spot I had attempted in vain to ignore and go right to the heart of a sensitive matter that had kept me up many lonely nights. Underneath the angry protest, however, I felt the real question lurking, the one that struck fear in me: Had I been a fool, burying my head in the sand when the truth was always there, plain as day for all to witness?

It had been my intent this morning to surprise Bob with my special gift for Ricky—Puff, the stuffed toy dragon—immediately after breakfast, so he could pack it in his luggage and take it to Nancy in Hawaii. I'd been having fun imagining his reaction when he opened the gift bag. No doubt another priceless moment we'd enjoy reminiscing over, long after the war. But with the current state of things, it might be wiser to postpone it until my return later this evening, to let both of us cool off first.

With a twinge of guilt, I caught my own thoughts racing ahead to the pleasant afternoon in the city. I hadn't seen Lee Anne since before Christmas, and there was no denying how long and drab the days had been. Bob's admonition had stoked the secret anguish in my heart without in the least dampening my desire to be with her. True, it had forced me for a minute to confront my private struggle. But like a moth that goes darting into the bright flame, my mind briskly swept aside such heavy ponderings to dwell instead on the long-awaited rendezvous with even greater anticipation—consequences be damned.

For who could predict anything in this volatile environment?

Tomorrow and the time for judgment might never come.

"I am glad you came. I have a surprise to tell you."

Lee Anne gave me an excited smile as she set a glass of chilled Tiger Beer on the table and sat down next to me. She was wearing a yellow-silk *áo dài* with sequined flowers sprinkled all the way down its front flap and a headband made of the same pretty material.

"You look stunning today," I said, flattered that she seemed genuinely happy to see me. "That beautiful gown looks like a dream on you."

A light blush rose to her cheeks. "It is my *áo dài* for Tết. I am wearing it first time today because I thought you might like it if you came. These are my favorite flowers. Chrysan—chrysanthemums.

They bloom this time of year." Then she added with innocent pride, "My first new gown in a long time. Thanks to this job."

Hesitantly she placed her hand on the table, and for an instant I thought she might reach and hold mine. But instead, she pushed a small red envelope across to me.

"It is New Year's custom to hand out *lì-xì*, or lucky money," she explained. "It will bring you good luck through the year. Happy New Year to you, Roger. I hope you receive a lot of money, good health, and happiness in the Year of the Monkey."

I accepted the *lì-xì* envelope then reached for her hand, warm and tender in mine. She made no objection. "*Cám ơn*, Liên. *Chúc Mừng Năm Mới* to you and your family."

It took her a second to process my atrocious pronunciation. Then her eyes opened wide, and she chuckled with delight. "You said it perfectly, and it is not easy. I should teach you some new phrases while you are—how do you say—on a roll? And thank you for your kind wishes."

Leaning in closer so no one could overhear, she revealed her surprise for me. "If you prefer to leave here after finishing your drink, I will be glad to take you downtown and show you *Chợ Hoa Xuân*, our spring flower market. It is a beautiful sight, with just ten days before Tết."

"Take me wherever you please," I whispered back. "I'm in your hands. But before we go, I need to speak with Vivienne. How's she been doing?"

"She has not been the same lately," Lee Anne said. I wondered how much she knew of the situation with Dick. "We are all worried about her. You may find her in the lounge. I saw her in there getting drinks for her guests." Then, discreetly, she waved me off. "I will wait for you right here."

The lounge appeared all spruced up for the traditional weeklong celebration of Tết: a fresh coat of paint all around; lucky-red banners imprinted with golden Chinese characters brightening the walls;

potted plants overloaded with miniature orange fruits in every corner (these were kumquat, as I later learned); and atop the coffee table in the center of the room, a huge antique oriental vase with branches of spring blossoms stuck in it. Mme Yvonne had obviously made all these thoughtful preparations to invite her foreign guests to partake in this most important of her people's holidays.

Standing at the bar in the far corner, Vivienne was arranging her drinks onto a tray. She happened to look up as I crossed the doorway, and we spotted each other at the same time. I rushed over to her. She seemed flustered by my unannounced visit but managed to set the tray down on the counter and greet me with a brave smile.

"Roger. Long time no see," she said jovially, for the benefit of the nearby bartenders. But her sleepless eyes betrayed the turmoil that must have been raging in her heart. In them, I thought I glimpsed, like afternoon shadows passing over a window, a mix of apprehension, shame, despair, and even a glimmer of hope. We walked over to the coffee table, out of earshot.

"You look awfully thin, Vivienne," I said. "Are you okay?"

She nodded without looking at me. "Have you seen him? Is he— with you?"

Her voice was weak and breathy, almost shaking with trepidation.

I gave her every bit of news I had on Dick. "He probably needs some time and distance to get over what happened, is my guess," I said in conclusion. "At least he's keeping active, maybe even a little too much. But it sounds like he's managing, somehow." I waited briefly. "The question is, are you, Vivienne? Frankly, I'm not too worried about Dick. He's a veteran survivor. He'll find ways to cope. But I'm worried about you. Please, you've got to take care of yourself."

"So good news he's okay." She heaved a long sigh. "It's only thing that matters. I was afraid he did something crazy." She slumped down on the couch, looking worn out from the stress.

I sat on the edge, next to her. "I know I'll catch up with him again. Sooner or later," I said. "I'll be sure and explain everything to him then, as you asked. You can count on it."

We sat in silence for a minute before I took leave.

"It's unlikely I'll see you again before Tết. So *Chúc Mừng Năm Mới* to you and your family, Vivienne." I put on a cheerful face for her. "Things will turn out much better next year, just you wait and see. Meanwhile, I want you to promise me one thing. That you will pamper yourself over the holiday and gain back some lost weight. Okay, young lady?"

She answered with a sad smile as we stood, then followed me with her eyes as I was leaving. At the door, I turned once more and gave her a thumbs-up and a grin of encouragement. She waved back, a forlorn figure so out of place against the cheerful backdrop of blossoming sprigs. Suddenly overcome with emotions, I hurried to rejoin Lee Anne.

"*Alors, mon pote* Richard, when is he coming back, *hein*?" asked the gregarious Corsican owner of the convenient store as I handed him back the spare key to Dick's apartment. His expression indicated he hadn't expected such a quick turnaround on it.

"Hard to say," I said. "You have a nice store here, so *I'll* be back soon, to shop. *Merci bien.*"

Lee Anne and I stepped out of the little food bazaar, which was chock full of edible goods imported from exotic locales all over the world, but mainly from Europe, North Africa, and the Middle East. Anything a discerning stomach might fancy, from coffee, wine, and liquor to cheese, bread, pasta, and sausages, all available in a bewildering assortment. The place looked and smelled like a gourmet's paradise.

Earlier, we had flagged down a taxicab in front of the National Conservatory and told the driver to drop us off at the entrance to Passage Eden across from the Rex Hotel. From there, we strolled to the food store at the street corner. I introduced myself as a friend of

Dick and asked the storeowner for the spare key to his place—exactly per Dick's instructions. The man shot an appreciative glance at Lee Anne before handing me the key with a complicit wink. I could feel my face and neck redden at his unmistakable innuendo, and the burning thought of it lingered in my mind. Fortunately, the embarrassing episode escaped Lee Anne's notice, as she was busy checking out the deli with the awed look of a first-time shopper.

Expecting the customary mess encountered in most bachelor pads, I asked Lee Anne to wait in the hallway while I took a quick peek inside Dick's apartment. It was a modest studio with a window overlooking the sidewalk, not particularly bright or spacious, furnished with the stylish simplicity of a Japanese home. And surprisingly tidy: no dishes piled up in the sink, not a single piece of dirty clothing on the floor, and the double bed neatly made and ready for sleep. My face felt flushed anew at the sight of the inviting bed as a frisson of desire raced through my body. If only . . . I shook the frivolous notion out of my head, picked up the mail slipped under the door, and placed it in the in-box atop the desk by the window. After making sure the window was secured, I locked the place up and returned the key on our way out.

"Mission accomplished," I told Lee Anne, rubbing my hands in relief. "Thanks for letting me take care of that for Dick. And now, on to the main program. You lead the way."

"We are close to the flower market," she said, pointing ahead in the direction of the river. "It is on this same street—Nguyễn-Huệ, or Rue Charner in the old days—just on the other side of Lê-Lợi Street. It has been a Tết tradition for as long as I remember, and it only opens for a short time. From two weeks before Tết until New Year's Eve. Come. Let us walk."

We had barely crossed Lê-Lợi Street behind the giant Marines Statues when I beheld, out in the center of Nguyễn-Huệ Boulevard, on the sunny median island, a mirage of explosive colors—a tropical garden floating serenely amid swirling traffic. The visual effect was startling.

"Wait until we get inside the market," Lee Anne giggled, reading my reaction. "You will forget everything else except New Year's celebration. When I was a kid, every year we children would get so excited when the flower market opened. It was the sign that Tết was near, which meant no school for two whole weeks, and lots of candies and *lì-xì* money from the grownups." She smiled at the memory. "We knew nothing about our parents' financial worries. It was all innocent fun to us."

We gingerly picked our path through oncoming traffic, half running, half dodging, and laughing all the way to the oasis in the middle of the boulevard. Greeting us was a kaleidoscope of colors and motion, sounds and smells, all enhanced by the intense afternoon heat. I recognized but a few of the flowers that proliferated along the narrow walkway, some in decorative pots, the rest in fresh bouquets: mums, daisies, marigolds, sunflowers, lilies, orchids, and many exotic unknowns, in countless varieties and shades. Competing with the flowers were miniature kumquat and tangerine trees loaded with luscious fruits the size of golf balls, ornamental plants sculpted in the shapes of mythical birds or rare animals, skeletal branches of spring buds stuck in antique vases, not to mention a vast selection of bonsai in porcelain planters.

I whistled. "I'd buy them all. I wouldn't know what to choose. Are you finding something you like?"

She was admiring a green shoot of daffodil in a small ceramic bowl, with half-opened white-and-yellow buds on it. "This is *hoa thủy-tiên*—water fairy—which grows from a bulb," she explained. "There is an art, almost lost to us young kids, in how to prepare the bulb for planting so that it blooms exactly on the First Day of Tết, or New Year's Day. My father practiced it for years and had amazing success. But he cannot this year, after the stroke. I will get this for him before we go."

I followed her to the next stall, which displayed long stems of fresh-cut gladiolas. "Tết is a sacred time for us," she continued. "The whole family gathers to remember our ancestors and pay respect to their memory. Every home sets up an altar for the ancestors during the holidays. My mother loves to use these *glaïeul*, the red ones especially, to decorate ours. The French brought these new plants to Việt-Nam a century ago. It's funny that they have become very popular but we still call them by their French name only."

She bent down to pick up a bouquet of elongated spikes of white flowers that reminded me of Mexican tuberoses. "These, Roger, are called *hoa huệ*. In Buddhist families like mine, we place offerings of these on Buddha's altar. Look how pure, how lovely they are. And very nice fragrance, even sweeter at nighttime. Like lotus flowers, they symbolize spirituality."

Dodging around long strips of red firecrackers that dangled across the stall entrance, she spoke as if making a mental note to herself. "I also need to buy a couple of these strings for my father. He always went out and got them himself in years past." Then turning to me, "Have you ever heard firecrackers this size explode? They scare me half to death, like real gunfire." She laughed. "They must be loud enough to chase away evil spirits. The past few years, for security reasons, we are allowed to set them off only on New Year's Eve and on the First Day of Tết, during the cease-fire. That's plenty for me."

She was excited and happy, flitting like a butterfly from one stall to the next, touching and admiring everything in sight. Watching her, I imagined the wide-eyed little girl who had held her mother's hand during annual trips to the flower market in preparation for Tết and for a lifetime of familial duties. Just like that, her turn had now come. To play grownup herself.

I nudged her gently. "Say, Lee Anne. I didn't give you any *lì-xì* money. So let me pay for whatever flowers you're purchasing here. It's only fair."

She put up a fight but relented in the end, when I threatened to return her little red envelope otherwise. I helped her pick out a beautiful bouquet of red gladiolas and one of white tuberoses. "The water fairy and firecrackers can wait until later," she decided at the last minute. "I don't want to carry too much back to Mme Yvonne's."

It was just as well, since I barely had enough change left for taxi fares later. My run-in with Bob this morning had so upset me I'd neglected to exchange my Military Payment Certificates for more local currency, or Đồng, before leaving. I was lucky to find enough of it in my pocket.

While I was paying for the flowers, the vendor's daughter, a sprightly teenage girl with a ponytail and a cheerful smile, mentioned something to Lee Anne that made her blush as she accepted the long bouquets in her arms and muttered "Cám ơn" to both of them.

"What was that all about?" I asked on our way out.

"Nothing important, really," she said, brushing me off at first.

Then encountering my prodding stare, she gave in, with fresh color on her cheeks. "The silly girl said I looked like a queen. But it was really my new áo dài she was talking about, because in the old days yellow silk was reserved for the emperor and his wives only."

I swung around, did a double take on her. "You do look like a queen, actually. A beauty queen, holding the bouquets in your arms like that. May I take a picture of you, Miss Sài-Gòn?"

I wasn't toting a camera so I made a frame with my fingers and focused it on Lee Anne, who stood radiant in the sunlight among a sea of spring flowers with the colonial hôtel de ville (city hall) in the background. My mental camera snapped away at this lovely sight, trying to sear it forever in my memory. In that moment of clear-eyed focus, the realization struck, stark and sobering, though hardly a total surprise. Welcomed or not, a big change was taking root in my heart that would no doubt alter my life and the lives of those closest to me, in ways and with consequences nobody could yet foresee.

It was dark by the time I got back on base, around 2000 hours.

Earlier, after returning Lee Anne to Mme Yvonne's, I'd decided to heed Bob's warning and head back to Tân-Sơn-Nhất for the next chopper ride with the sun still high above the capital's skyline. Besides, my newfound perspective and all its tangled ramifications had been brewing in my mind, driving me to complete distraction.

I winced at the prospect of soon facing Bob, recalling with embarrassment my stubborn reaction to his well-founded concern this morning. Time to own up like a man, I told myself in resignation. After doing a mea culpa, which clearly was in order, maybe I should sit down and seek counsel with him on my conundrum, since ignoring the issue hadn't made it go away—quite the contrary. I felt certain he'd be the last person to hold a grudge, that I could count on him to lend me a sympathetic ear and to be forthright and sensible in his advice. As most people who knew him would agree, there was no better friend, in good times or bad, than Bob Olsen.

Remembering the toy dragon in my desk drawer at the office, I made a beeline for the dispensary as soon as we touched ground. The cute stuffed animal was for little Ricky, of course, but I couldn't wait to watch Bob's expression when I pulled Puff the Magic Dragon out of the shopping bag. That alone must be worth Dean's trip to Hong Kong to find the darned thing. The thought made me smile as I arrived at 3rd Tac Dispensary.

Bob and I shared a double front office seldom occupied by the skeleton evening staff except in rare instances of emergency overflow. It was a surprise, then, when I walked in and found all the lights on, with nobody inside.

Something else felt out of kilter.

Bob had thumbtacked a map of Việt-Nam to the wall behind his chair as a clever tool to break the ice when a new pilot stopped in.

Invariably, the flyboy would be drawn to the map to point out with pride all the target locations he'd flown. Before long, the men would be trading war stories like long-lost comrades. It was a creative gimmick by Bob to set his high-strung patients at ease, and it worked every single time. Next to the map was a hook where he would normally hang his stethoscope.

Both map and stethoscope had disappeared from the wall.

Likewise, the adjoining side wall looked oddly bare. Previously displayed on that wall in all its red, white, and blue glory was a Minnesota Twins 1965 American League Champions Pennant, another popular conversation piece for "Doctor Bob" and his patients. Tweety and I had long since learned to block out Bob's endless recounting of that dream season of the Twins and his heated debates with his patients about the national pastime. For payback, we'd cooked up a good prank to play on him. At the first chance, one of us planned to lure him out of the office while the other seized his prized possession from the wall and concealed it. In its place, we would unfurl a 1965 World Series Pennant of the Los Angeles Dodgers, who had conquered the Twins in seven games in claiming that year's championship. So far, however, we hadn't had any opportunity to carry out our devious scheme.

But the pennant was no longer there for the taking. Staring at me now was a blank wall.

Slowly, my uncomprehending gaze drifted down to the top of Bob's desk, kitty-corner from mine. It looked uncommonly tidy, with nothing on it. Gone was the disparate clutter he'd never seemed to have the time to clear out: small piles of unfinished paperwork; stashes of dog-eared medical journals; months-old issues of *Air Force Times* or *Stripes and Stars*; all scattered willy-nilly across the top, weighed down by well-worn editions of the *Physicians' Desk Reference* and his own weathered steel pot. Someone must have come in earlier and cleaned up the mess. The desk now appeared empty and unoccupied.

There were voices and footsteps approaching from the back of the building. I turned around as Tweety and two other medics trudged through the door.

"I'm glad somebody's around," I said. "Are we switching to new quarters? Looks like Captain Olsen has already cleaned out his desk. Did he say how soon I need to move my junk?"

One could have heard a pin drop.

I looked up to see Tweety staring back at me. Our eyes locked. An icy, tingling sensation crept up my back. We were all frozen. Trapped in the surreal moment.

Then, in slow motion, I watched Tweety pull out the chair from behind my desk and slide it toward me. Over the thumping in my eardrums, his voice reached through—a muffled echo from a distance. "Lieutenant Connors. Please have a seat, sir."

———

I knew. The instant I caught the look in Tweety's eyes, I knew.

My body sank down in the chair, all the wind knocked out of it. I closed my eyes, my head spinning, a churning queasiness in the pit of my stomach. It was so hot and stuffy in the office that I practically gasped for air.

A window, I screamed in silence. We need a goddamn window in here.

"How did it happen?" The words squeaked out like a growl from my parched throat.

"I am so sorry, Lieutenant . . ."

"What the fuck happened?" I gripped my chair arms, my body steeling itself.

In a voice strained to control his own emotions, the young medic proceeded to take me through the whole chain of events. Reluctantly. With palpable, halting pain.

Stuck in the waking nightmare, in shock and disoriented, I stumbled to follow.

———

Earlier, Bob had planned an easy Sunday to run some last-minute errands at the BX then finish packing for his trip. And so he hadn't signed up for MEDCAP, the first time in a long time he would miss the weekend jaunt with the Civic Action volunteer team. Ironically for him, today's was supposed to be a fun-filled, event-packed outing, the culmination of months of hard work and preparation by the Dollars-for-Scholars Committee, of which he was a founding member.

Having observed firsthand the atrocious conditions at the local schools, the Civic Action team had decided to expand its involvement beyond the mere provision of medical care to the poor. A new program was initiated that aimed at improving the classroom environment for indigent children and doing whatever possible to promote learning. The civil engineers on base, the Red Horse Squadron, contributed time, labor, and recycled material to shore up the schools' crumbling infra-structures. Meanwhile, a base-wide drive was launched to raise funds and collect donations of books and school supplies. It received an overwhelming response from airmen as well as their friends and families stateside. As the project rolled forward, a committee was put in place, the Dollars-for-Scholars Committee, whose charter was to coordinate the overall effort and to select the recipients for a limited number of scholarships.

On this day, after months of wrestling with detailed logistics, the committee was ready for their inaugural trip off base. They couldn't have picked a more propitious time, ten days out from the end of the Year of the Goat. They'd be making the rounds of schools in the surrounding rural area, bearing gifts of school supplies, which like everything else in this part of the world were in severe shortage:

slate tablets, chalk, pens, notebooks, pull-down maps, globes, and more. There would be ribbon-cutting festivities to dedicate rebuilt and expanded facilities, followed by a picnic, then the much-heralded presentation of scholarships.

"I was pissed I couldn't go with them," Tweety said wistfully. Besides Bob and me, he also hadn't signed up for this weekend's function, having to wait on base for a MARS phone patch to call home. It was his parents' silver anniversary today. Shaking his head at the fortuitous coincidence, he mumbled, "Who's to argue? Just wasn't meant to be."

Something else wasn't meant to happen this morning. Captain Silverman of the base Dental Corps, our Civic Action leader, woke up with a virulent case of FUO (fever of unknown origin): fever, shakes, nausea, diarrhea, the whole nine yards. Around the time I stormed out of the hooch after my heated exchange with Bob, Captain Silverman had just concluded that he, too, would have to scratch his day's plans and remain in bed. That meant our regular team of eight would miss half its members, not the least its leading representative, on this most ceremonious occasion. It appeared a cancellation and reschedule were in the offing.

After a flurry of phone calls, however, Bob let himself be persuaded at the eleventh hour to stand in for Captain Silverman, because "the show must go on." There had been such anticipation on the part of schoolteachers and their young pupils that a last-minute postponement of the events would have caused huge disappointment. For the deprived children, who had so looked forward to receiving their gifts, the affair was to be their early celebration of Tết. Nobody had the heart to deny them that simple joy, if it could at all be helped.

His loose ends almost tied up, Bob gallantly agreed to lead the team on the road. His only stipulation was that everyone was to "haul ass" so they wouldn't run further behind with this late change. Finally, around 0830 hours, the five volunteers climbed aboard an Army Huey nicknamed Patches, after the numerous pockmarks scored on its body by Charlie's gunfire. From the Thunderbirds' helipad, Tweety waved them off, feeling the full letdown of one left behind.

"I would've been right there with them, if I didn't have to wait at the MARS station," he explained again, almost apologetically, holding his head in his hands. "Just wasn't meant to be." His two medic buddies had slipped out some time ago, leaving us alone in my office.

Even in my daze, I could hear Tweety's rapid breathing. Slumped over in a chair opposite mine, he seemed to be staring at some invisible screen on the floor, watching in fixated horror as the movie replayed once again. His weary voice droned on.

"Shortly after they left, my phone patch came through. It was late for my folks in Nevada, but they were tickled I'd called to wish them happy anniversary. No sooner had we hung up than I was put through to another line holding for me, this one internal and urgent.

"It was my buddy Tommy at the Bird Cage, who knew I'd been waiting at the station. He sounded completely flipped out. I had to yell at him to slow down so I could read him. 'Patches,' he shouted in my earpiece. 'Patches went down. Search-and-Rescue's on the scene right this minute.' I dropped the phone, hustled like hell back to the Cage."

Tweety's voice broke, and he paused. His hand shook as it went to pinch the bridge of his nose. I sat motionless, sweat streaming down my face and my back.

"When I arrived, all out of breath, SAR had just checked in. I overheard their confirmation on the radio with my own ears: Patches had crashed and burned. Of the crew of four and the five passengers— not one single survivor. The rice paddy was strewn with blood-stained debris and school supplies, they said."

There was a gasp, more like a sob being choked back. I looked up. Through the tears, we stared at each other. No words came.

It was a while before Tweety resumed his account.

"You know how the chopper would normally dance in and out of the palm trees along the Đồng-Nai River, for cover? Eyewitnesses on the ground reported that Patches wasn't rock-and-rolling like that. Instead, it was flying low and straight, full-throttle forward, which made it an easy target for AAA. Overconfidence or pilots' error? Or were they so rushed for time they just cut corners? Nobody knows. No matter now. SAR determined that a .51-caliber from the jungle below had raked the ship and dropped it from the sky just minutes after takeoff. Unfortunately for all aboard, Patches' luck had finally run out."

I kept staring at Tweety. My brain frozen, incapable of grasping the facts. They sounded much too simplistic, too arbitrary, to even make sense. Might it all have been a horrible mixup, that it wasn't Patches' smoking carcass in the rice field after all?

And then the big picture hit me full blast, unlocking my brain and sending it in a tailspin of agonizing questions. In the chaotic aftermath, had the children and their teachers been forgotten and left waiting in the schoolyards for the gift bearers who never showed? And Nancy. My heart squeezed. Had someone been able to contact her before she'd already left for Hawaii? Dear God. Please let there be families or friends by her side when she got the news. Not all alone, stranded at some airport away from home or waiting in a honeymoon suite on Waikiki.

I shut my eyes, but the images kept dancing before them: my hooch mate's big smile; the wallet picture of his newborn son, whom he'd longed to cradle in his arms; Puff's scrunched-up mug, which I never had a chance to surprise him with; our whirlwind excursions to Sài-Gòn . . .

A lifetime of friendship and memories, crammed into a few short months.

But for my own selfish agenda, I, too, should have been aboard that chopper today.

My chest felt so tight that it might explode at any moment.

"The medical commander was looking for you in the afternoon." Tweety's voice reached through the fog and dragged me back into the present. "Graves Registration Service needed assistance to gather Captain Olsen's personal effects so they can be packed up and shipped home to his family. A couple buddies and me volunteered to help, in your absence. We're just now done clearing out the hooch and his office." He hesitated. "I hope you don't mind, Lieutenant. It all had to be done ASAP."

I nodded, started to get up, but my knees went wobbly and I had to stay put for a minute.

Tweety was already on his feet. As I slogged past him, I stopped and placed my hand on his shoulder. Our eyes said what we couldn't: we'd both lost a friend and a brother today. No words could express the true depth of our grief. He turned away, choking back the emotions.

"A memorial service is being planned for later this week." He fought to keep his voice even. "Details will be communicated as they become available. I'll keep you informed, sir."

I gave his shoulder a tug then lumbered through the door into the warm night. Somehow, I found my way back to the hooch.

It looked deserted. Bob's side of it had been stripped bare—as if it had never been occupied. A pall settled over the room, heavy and forbidding. Had I not been so exhausted, I probably would have tried to crash somewhere else for the night. But it was approaching lights-out, and my body had already hit the wall a long time ago, hurting all over. I collapsed on my cot.

Something made a crinkling noise as my head hit the pillow. I reached down behind my head and pulled out a wrinkled sheet of paper. A hand-written note. I sat back up and moved under the overhead light bulb.

Roger,

What do you know. I'm heading out with the MEDCAP team after all. Long story for later. Just want to say I'm sorry about this morning. I was out of line. You do what you need to do. But be alert and watchful while in the city, that's all. Hopefully we'll have time tonight for a cheeky few at the OC before I hit the road in the morning. See you then, pal. Remember: We few, we happy few, we band of brothers. We are. Bob.

Bobby. Bobby. You and your Shakespeare. I couldn't help smiling, even through the tears. It was just like him to not leave things hanging. Set them right whenever you can, 'cause you never know, he'd always maintained. How tragically prophetic.

We never had our chance for a proper send-off as you'd wished. So whatever unknown road you're traveling on now, here's to you, big guy. Now and always. My buddy. My brother.

Chapter Thirteen

The next week unwound like a bad dream that wouldn't quit, shrouded in thick mental fog.

I was going through the motions, not seeing or hearing much of what went on around me. My days were colored by a pervasive sense of numbness and detachment as I tried my damnedest to tend to business as usual. My nights, on the other hand, seemed hopelessly engulfed in grief, the relentless kind that fed on itself and kept sleep at bay.

Since day one in country, my schedule had been structured with Bob figuring prominently in it, in some way or another. Aside from us sharing the same hooch and office, he'd also played the roles of superior, mentor, and best pal to me. We'd spend the bulk of the day by each other's side: from the moment we awoke to the rousing "Gooood Morning, Việt-Nam" from the Dawn Busters gang on AFVN Radio; through the busy workday at the dispensary, punctuated with occasional emergencies on the flight line; to the wind-down evening hours at the club, when we joined the rowdy crowd around the TV set to watch Bobbie Keith, the Weather Girl, perform her nightly gags in miniskirt or bikini and to raise a glass to her at the end of the show as she bid us good-night, "weatherwise and otherwise."

Now, with my sidekick suddenly vanished, I found myself cast adrift without bearings. A hollow, unsettled feeling—as if a part of me had gone AWOL—would dog me for the remainder of my tour.

In the aftermath of the tragedy, I remember going out of my way to avoid any conversations that might bring up Nancy and baby Ricky. Having seen their pictures proudly displayed atop his footlocker and listened to the dreams Bob had built for all of them for when he returned home, I felt I'd known them on some personal level. It broke my heart to think how lonely and deprived their lives would now be without him. All those plans for their future—up in smoke on one single afternoon. And there wasn't a damned thing anyone could have said or done to stay the heavy hand of fate. This sense of powerlessness drove me out of my mind, so I turned away and ran to hide. Never once did I seek to confirm that somebody here had managed to reach Nancy on that fateful day before she'd left for Hawaii. The alternative scenario, too horrendous to even contemplate, was best left unknown.

The sole token I wished to hang on to, as a reminder of my hooch mate in Việt-Nam, was Puff the toy dragon. Even then, the little stuffed animal was promptly stowed away at the bottom of my suitcase as I struggled to move past the pain and to regain some semblance of normalcy in my daily life. This would prove a tougher and longer process than I'd suspected, with no letup in sight, especially in the days leading up to the memorial service.

The service was planned for Friday afternoon. Quite a number of base personnel, both Air Force and Army, had indicated their intentions to attend. Since the makeshift chapel might be too cramped for the turnout, it was decided to hold the service on the large empty lot behind the Bird Cage. Dean Hunter made a point of swinging by the dispensary that afternoon so he and I could go together. He had already stopped in earlier in the week, as soon as he'd heard the news upon returning from the Plain of Reeds. I'd had the miserable task of filling in the details for him, as Tweety had done for me on Sunday night. When I was through, we'd sat in my office and shared our grief in silence. For Dean also, Bob's untimely death had been too great a loss for words.

I don't have clear recollection of the entire service, only mental snapshots here and there. A lot of people showed up. Some had just come off their work shifts, others on their return from the day's sorties. All the ranking officers, including the base commander, were present. Even a small contingent of South Vietnamese pilots recently assigned to Biên-Hoà to take over the old A-1 Skyraiders, or "Spad," came to pay their respect.

Lined up side by side on the red dirt were the fallen soldiers' boots and helmets, recovered from the crash site. Directly in front of those, in a straight row, stood the nine M-16s turned upside down with bayonets stuck in the ground. It was a simple sight, like white crosses in a cemetery, yet overwhelming in its stark symbolism.

I couldn't hear most of the eulogy delivered by the nervous chaplain, who seemed unaccustomed to a crowd this size, except his closing statement, a quote from some unknown source. "To most people, the sky is the limit. To those who love aviation, the sky is home." That's Bob through and through, I said to myself.

Then Captain Silverman stepped forward, picked up the helmets, and placed them over the rifle stocks, one by one. Behind us, the bugler played Taps. We saluted our departed comrades for the last time. No gun salvo. No waving flag. Just the haunting lullaby at sunset, with red dirt swirling in the wind—and silent tears of farewell.

My memory flashed back to something Bob had pointed out to us on a recent MEDCAP trip. It was the memorial statue at the entrance to the Nghĩa-trang Quân-đội (National Military Cemetery), situated off of National Highway One on the south side of Biên-Hoà. Bob, who'd visited there before, had suggested we stop off at the site for a break and a close-up peek at the statue. The stone sculpture depicted a South Vietnamese soldier sitting on a rock, his backpack still strapped on his shoulders and his M-1 carbine laid across his lap. His helmet was untied and pushed up above the forehead, and he was staring off into the distance, eternally lost in thought.

"The statue is called Thương Tiếc, pardon my pronunciation," Bob had explained at the time. "It means remembrance, or mourning. Something to that effect. The subject is said to be commemorating his fallen comrades. When unveiled a year ago, it created quite a sensation. It's only grown more famous since."

Indeed, the unknown soldier's face and countenance conveyed an impression of weariness and deep melancholy so realistic that we had all felt touched by it. Little had anyone suspected that the impromptu side trip had been a presage of things to come.

As the assembly dispersed after the service, Dean and I wandered out onto the open field, away from the Cage's wooden structures. The sun slipped over the horizon, a shimmering disk veiled in tails of amber clouds. A breeze lingered on my face, warm and dry. Monsoon season was still a couple of months away, thank goodness.

Suddenly I felt drained, weighed down by immense sadness and regret, like the pensive statue at the National Cemetery. I flopped down on the bare red soil, leaning back on my arms. Dean sat down beside me. Almost in unison, we exhaled.

Squinting into the sunset, I broke the silence. "Should've been me on that chopper. But all I could think that morning was to get to Sài-Gòn as early as possible—"

"Don't even go there," Dean interrupted. "It changes nothing. Only drives you straight over the edge, is all. There's no rhyme or reason in who lives or dies, and nobody gets to pick his time to go. One thing we know for sure—Bob was a good, decent man. True to his heart till the bitter end, doing what he wanted. Let's leave it at that."

It was the most we had exchanged all week.

A single pair of wild ducks crossed the twilight sky without a sound. It occurred to me we'd rarely seen or heard any feathered creatures in this area. Where had all the songbirds gone?

Darkness was rising fast all around us. Just like that, it was nighttime. The inscrutable night of the tropics. Dean pushed himself up off the ground, and I followed. We were about to turn and head back when I felt his arm around my shoulders.

"I miss him, too, kiddo," he said quietly, his eyes gleaming in the twinkling light of flares.

Chapter Fourteen

S tartled awake from deep sleep, I sprang up in bed.

For one foggy moment, I forgot where I was, even as the siren continued to shatter the night. Then my bleary eyes caught sight of the dim alarm clock atop the footlocker. 0300 hours. Biên-Hoà time. My brain engaged. *Incomings!* The survival instinct kicked in. Seven seconds. I had seven seconds to get to the nearest bunker. Barely time to grab my clothes and boots, throw on my flak jacket, and cover my head with a steel pot—all of which had been laid out within reach in case of an attack like this—then un-ass the hooch.

Outside reigned the usual chaos. Floodlights flashed on and off; klaxon horns blared, lifting sleepers from their beds; PA speakers shouted emergency instructions; and groggy airmen scrambled to their assigned posts or the closest shelters as fast as they could. A scene that had become part of our nocturnal landscape. On this night, however, Eleven-o-clock Charlie had thrown in a new twist by postponing his regular rocket launch until 3:00 a.m.—in the middle of the Tết cease-fire, no less.

The previous night, January 29–30, 1968, the local New Year's Eve or *Giao-Thừa* had turned out uneventful, with the exception of sporadic bursts of firecrackers around the city of Biên-Hoà. It was almost impossible to distinguish them from the staccato of machine guns fired off in celebration at nearby ARVN III Corps Headquarters. I had thought of Lee Anne and wondered if her husband had made it home on their most sacred night of the year. Despite an official thirty-six-hour truce, the Army of the Republic of Việt-Nam had kept on full alert a minimum strength of fifty percent in all its units. Meanwhile, to our relief, Charlie hadn't bothered us since the start of the ceasefire at 1800 hours on Monday the 29th. But then, all through January 30th, the First Day of Tết, reports had trickled in that confirmed bloody infractions up country as well as enemy movement in our own neck of the woods.

And now this.

Inside the jammed bunker near the hooches, we fell flat on the ground and buried our heads under our arms for protection. God save us all should our simple refuge (sand bags over pierced-steel planks) suffer a direct hit. Those Soviet or ChiCom-produced 122-mm rockets were horrific weapons capable of blasting most on-base structures to smithereens. Like Death pouncing from the night sky, the fin-stabilized six-foot missiles zoomed toward their doomed targets with a ghastly whistle that rose to a full-throated roar before all hell let loose in a deafening explosion at impact.

We lay squirming in the dark, listening to the rockets being "walked" across the base and praying they'd march past our shelter and never find us. On any regular night, Charlie would lob from five to ten rockets into the base then quickly vanish into the jungle before our choppers had time to get airborne and retaliate. As conditioned as we'd grown to these nocturnal visits, we still had little control over the feeling of dread and suspense that gripped us each time the blasted siren went off. It was precisely VC's intention, with their deadly game of cat-and-mouse, to wear our nerves ragged and test our resolve and patience to the limit.

On this early morning of January 31st, however, something was terribly amiss. For ten minutes mortars and rockets slammed down on us with unrelenting ferocity, shaking the ground nonstop as if we were being carpet-bombed. Under the most intense heavy-artillery blitz we had experienced to date—close to two hundred hits total, with one third by rockets—ten minutes seemed like an eternity of hell.

And then, it suddenly stopped. My ears still buzzing and my body aching from all the concussions, I strained for any signal in the eerie silence. In the smoky darkness, I could almost hear the question on everybody's mind. Had the furor blown over, or were we simply stuck in the eye of the storm? Finally, the all-clear signal rang out to a collective groan of relief. Our stupefied bodies stirred back to life. We'd made it through yet another rocket attack—this one, by far, the most vicious in recent memory.

Men crawled up on their hands and knees, gathered their personal effects and stumbled out of the bunker, too weary to talk. Stuck in a corner, I was waiting to exit when I heard someone moaning. It had been so dark inside the bunker that one couldn't even tell who had dropped on the floor next to one.

"Somebody here? You okay?" I called in the direction of the noise.

The moaning grew louder, then degenerated into a whimper.

I felt my way toward it, inching closer until my hand touched a human form lying in the dirt. The man was curled up in a tight ball, his knees to his chest.

"Are you hurt?" I inquired, getting no answer. There hadn't been any big explosions in our proximity, but with so much shrapnel flying around during the attack, I wouldn't have been surprised if he had sustained some injury before reaching the shelter.

"I'm a doctor," I said. "I'm going to roll you over and check you out, okay?"

I gently turned him on his back and untangled his twisted limbs. He shook like a leaf, whining meekly as I ran my hands over his body to feel for signs of trauma. Down his upper legs, I detected dampness. A quick smell test revealed it wasn't blood, but urine. Apparently, the poor fellow had been scared out of his mind and lost control of his bladder. A greenhorn, most likely. For some men, their first taste of war—or, in military parlance, the first time they "saw the elephant"— might prove too nerve-wracking, an experience for which no training could have prepared them sufficiently. As I helped him sit up, the man clung to me and began sobbing like a child, still unable to speak.

Just then a vehicle, its brights full on, screeched to a halt at the entrance to the bunker, now mostly vacated. In the reflected light, I looked down at my distraught patient and stared into wide-open eyes filled with tears and the utmost terror—the eyes of First Lieutenant Paul Nilsen.

We'd met when Bob had taken him around the dispensary and introduced him to the rest of us, soon after his arrival on the day after New Year's. A young general medical officer about my age, with hair the color of corn silk, bright blue eyes, and the fresh complexion of a Sunday choirboy, hence his instant nickname "The Kid." Lieutenant Nilsen, like my former hooch mate, hailed from the American heartland. Decorah, Iowa, in his case. Like many of us, he had volunteered for a reserve commission in the Air Force in exchange for a deferment until completion of his two-year residency in pediatrics. Or so he'd thought.

It must have been a blow when, halfway through the first year, he'd received his orders to report for active duty. Due to a shortage of doctors, the USAF had found it necessary to assign him immediately to fill an urgent requirement from Biên-Hoà for a new GMO. Unlike most of us, who just went with the flow, he'd hired a lawyer and appealed the decision, but to no avail. He arrived in Việt-Nam a very unhappy camper. The cause for his great reluctance soon became obvious. Being of a gentle and sensitive disposition, and from a religious background, he was appalled as well as terrified by the whole war scene and felt utterly out of place at Biên-Hoà. In a sad way, he reminded me of Vivienne. How many like them, I wondered, hopelessly trapped yet vulnerable and ill-equipped for survival in this crucible of war?

"It's all right. It's over now," I assured him. "It appears you're not hurt, but we'll get you to the dispensary to make sure." I threw my arm around his sweat-drenched back and leaned in to support his trembling body.

"Anyone in here? You all okay?" a familiar voice shouted from the entryway as a flashlight beam painted a bright circle around the bunker.

"Tweety, over here," I yelled toward the looming shadow, motioning the young medic over. As was their routine, he and his fellow medics had jumped into their cracker boxes at the first all-clear to start their search-and-rescue throughout the base.

After they assisted the badly shaken officer into the ambulance, I pulled Tweety aside. "He's in shock. I want him kept overnight for observation." I grasped his forearm. "He'll need a change of clothes. In the meantime throw a blanket over him, you hear?"

"Aye aye, sir. You're not riding back with us?"

"Just need to gather my stuff. You guys go on ahead. I'll walk."

"You sure, sir?" Tweety directed my gaze toward Runway 27. Only then did I notice the commotion out there. A "Hun" jet had caught on fire in the middle of the runway and had started to cook off ammo, shooting bright sparks and tongues of flames in all directions. Not far from it, the burned carcass of an AC-47 gunship, better known as Puff the Magic Dragon, smoldered, apparently struck down by mortars during an aborted takeoff. The eastern sky lit up with yellow flares and streams of red and green tracers. All around us, the night air crackled with the rapid firing of automatic weapons and the urgent *thwacks* of assault helicopters in action.

Bewildered, I turned to the young medic.

"Enemy sappers have snuck on base, sir," he explained. "Sons-of-bitches managed to shut down the runway, as you see. The east perimeter was breached during the rocket attack. Now they're taking it directly to us, *on the ground*. We're in danger of getting overrun, sir."

Thus, without much preamble, we found ourselves plunged headlong into the fire maelstrom known in the annals of the Việt-Nam War as the 1968 Tết Offensive.

For all of us at Biên-Hoà AFB, it was an unforgettable night. A night of terror and death, of dauntless fighting and dogged survival, like none other we had lived through. It was a night of bravery for many, heroism for a few. In more ways than one, it was our night of truth.

The sprawling airbase, inside its ten-mile perimeter, was home to twenty-five hundred unarmed Air Force personnel. The responsibility for their protection rested entirely with the 3rd Security Police Squadron, the so-called Sky Cops. In the wee morning hours on that final day of January 1968, the three hundred men of the 3rd SPS along with one hundred augmentees of various job skills were suddenly thrust, without crew-serviced weapons or armored vehicles, in a deadly struggle for their lives—as well as all ours.

We were under attack, and severely overmatched, by two North Vietnamese infantry battalions with heavy artillery and death-defying sappers. Under the cover of darkness and a barrage of rockets, mortars, and Bangalore tornadoes, the enemy punched through the perimeter fence line off the approach end of Runway 27, despite it being rigged with mines and concertina wire. From this vantage point, they set up machine guns and cut off access to the runway, effectively shutting down our air support. They appeared on the verge to overrun the base and pull off the big coup—the demolition of hundreds of millions of dollars' worth of aircraft.

That was until they crashed into a pivotal obstacle standing in their path: Bunker Hill 10, a concrete remnant from the French colonial days, defended by a small but tenacious contingent of security police. The enemy hurled everything they had at the bunker, yet the valiant SP hung on until ground reinforcements arrived and the Army gunship helicopters—Hueys and Cobras with their nighttime Firefly teams—had a chance to take to the air. A backup Spooky AC-47 was diverted from its off-base course to join the rescue.

The battle raged all night into the next day. A handful of North Vietnamese Army sappers managed to infiltrate the airbase and destroy several birds, but the bulk of enemy troops were stopped in their tracks outside Bunker Hill 10. Elsewhere, a storage tank at the Petroleum, Oil & Lubricants Dump had been hit and burned brightly in the night, casting a ghastly glow against the black sky. The fiery scene reminded me of the movie *Gone with the Wind*, a favorite of Lee Anne's, and my thoughts flashed to her briefly.

Before dawn, just when the tide began turning in our favor, the buildings were shaken to their foundations by mammoth shockwaves both underground and in the air. Tweety, back from another search-and-rescue run around the base, burst into the dispensary with his latest update.

"Charlie just blew up the Long-Bình ammo depot," he announced breathlessly. "Holy cow. Never seen anything like it in my life. Looked like an A-bomb went off."

He said he had first glimpsed a blinding flash of light in the distance, followed by a giant mushroom cloud rolling soundlessly into the sky. A second or two later, the thunderous clap had caused him to almost drive off the road. It was reported later that the concussion had been felt miles away at the US Embassy in Sài-Gòn. A few choppers hovering in the depot's vicinity almost got blown out of the air by the resulting windblast.

In bits and pieces, we learned that Biên-Hoà AFB was one of many targets under attack by the NVA in egregious violation of the holiday cease-fire. All major cities and townships across South Việt-Nam including the cultural and political capitals, Huế and Sài-Gòn, had come under communist assault, as had many American military bases. To support his primary objective of capturing Sài-Gòn, Charlie had pulled out all the stops against the capital's first line of defense, namely the Army complex at Long-Bình and the airbases at Biên-Hoà and Tân-Sơn-Nhất. It was a gutsy move, the scope and intensity of which caught everyone completely off guard.

The dispensary was swamped with casualties throughout the night. Serious injuries required hospitalization, but all med-evac operations had been suspended since the nearest hospitals at Long-Bình and

Tân-Sơn-Nhất remained inaccessible due to the developing situation. In the end, it boiled down to a desperate waiting game for the wounded, with life and death in the balance. Like my colleagues, I forced myself to stop worrying about things beyond our control and to focus on the tasks at hand. Even at full staff, we were critically short-handed and welcomed any help from able-bodied personnel, medical or not.

Toward daybreak, the stream of patients started to taper off. But before I could step out for a bathroom break, a Security Alert Team jeep, an M-60 machine gun riding atop its hood and a big coffee urn dangling from its rear, roared up to the front entrance in a swirl of dust. Out jumped two security policemen lugging the limp body of a comrade. Mired in mud, gunpowder, and dried blood, the men still had on their blue helmets with white stripes. Captain John Morgan, my new superior and a USAF flight surgeon, called my name as he rushed to lend the men a hand.

We carried the wounded staff sergeant into a small room in the back. The shorter SP was near hysterics as he tried to recap what had taken place earlier. His SAT of four—the sergeant, also the team leader, a grenade launcher, a rifleman, and himself, the M-60 gunner—had been dispatched to the east perimeter as part of the reinforcements for Bunker Hill 10. They left their jeep to set up positions in a ditch north of the bunker, where the enemy was breaching through. More backups arrived shortly after, and together they held the invaders at bay through the night. During the entire time, the sergeant stayed on the horn with Central Security Control, shouting his reports over the din of live combat.

"Wasn't until sunrise when we had a brief lull that I realized I ain't hearing his voice no more," the gunner said. Glancing over his shoulder, he had discovered the sergeant slumped over the radio, apparently struck in the back by a fragment from Charlie's B-40 rockets. Armed with his M-60 and covered by friendly fire, he and the rifleman had scrambled to drag their sergeant back to the jeep and at once set out for help.

"I had my arm around his back. It was soaked with blood," he went on, looking at us with wild eyes. "Please, Doc. Help him, please. Can you get him evac'ed right away?"

We eased the wounded man down on the cot. Even before Captain Morgan knelt down to check his carotid pulse, I knew it was too late. His eyes were half open, but lifeless, showing the white underside—the eyes of a dead man. Captain Morgan straightened the sergeant's limbs, ran a hand over his eyes and closed them, then slowly got up. His face betrayed little emotion except for the clenched jaw muscles.

He turned to the two SPs and pronounced quietly, "I'm so sorry. He's gone."

A hush fell over the room. The haggard policemen stared at each other as if wondering what to do next. They seemed stunned by the swiftness and simplicity of death, probably never before this up close for either one. I felt them struggling to grapple with their sudden loss.

Finally, the gunner spoke up on both their behalf, his companion too dumbfounded for words. "Sir, may we stay here with Sarge? Till the chaplain arrives?"

Captain Morgan nodded. As we turned to leave, I caught a glint off the sergeant's inert hand. A gold wedding band was on his finger. My chest swelled with emotions, as in my mind I saw his eyes again, half peeking just moments earlier. I wondered what loving images of his family had flashed in front of them, in the final instant before darkness fell.

Hastening to close the door behind us, I reminded myself I had yet to look in on Paul Nilsen.

As if on a timer, daylight switched on full bright around 0700 hours, robbing the assailants of their last shred of night cover. Then, to everyone's immense relief, more reinforcements turned up as Armored

Cavalry assault vehicles rumbled through the base's front gate and Army slicks swooped in and unloaded paratroopers from the 101st Airborne. Teaming up with the 3rd SPS, the newcomers worked through the morning to expel the enemy from the base and eradicate remaining stragglers, including snipers hidden in the water tower outside the gate.

By early afternoon, the smoke of gunfire began to clear and the dust finally settled over Biên-Hoà, revealing close to one hundred and fifty bodies of enemy soldiers abandoned over the east perimeter. The majority of the dead looked quite young, even for Vietnamese, probably in their early to mid-teens. Subsequent tests of their blood samples indicated they'd been high on opium-laced wine, no doubt given before the battle to help overcome their fear and spur them to fight to the death. In the somber aftermath, their child-sized bodies were picked up by a bulldozer and interred in a common grave at the end of the runway, covered in lime.

By contrast, it seemed a miracle that we'd suffered only a handful of fatalities, injuries notwithstanding. This impression was strengthened as the day unfolded and we came to appreciate the gravity of the overall situation. The night before, as rockets rained down on Biên-Hoà, Việt-Cộng sappers in black pajamas and red armbands had breached the outer wall of the US Embassy in Sài-Gòn and gained access to the inside grounds. For six tense hours, they laid siege to the Chancery building until American troops landed by helicopter on the roof and took them out. Elsewhere in the capital, VC also mounted an attack on General Westmoreland's MACV headquarters at Tân-Sơn-Nhất and even made a run at the Presidential Palace in the city center. Although all of those suicidal missions ultimately failed, they nonetheless shocked the world with their sheer audacity.

But even as the firestorm was contained around military bases and airports a mere twelve hours after its initial eruption, fierce fighting raged on inside cities and population centers. It was later discovered that communist guerillas had slipped past security checkpoints disguised as civilians traveling to town to visit their families during Tết. Once blended with the citizenry on the inside, they were almost impossible to dislodge and eliminate without also endangering the population at large. Under such circumstances, the South Vietnamese Army and the Allies were forced to engage the enemy in house-to-house combat that would drag on for days or weeks, reducing much of the contested sites to smoldering rubble. For a while at the base, we could see the flames and smoke from burning buildings in downtown Biên-Hoà, just blocks away.

As news and updates streamed in through the day, my concern grew for the security and safety of my Vietnamese friends in Sài-Gòn. There were reports of heavy casualties and damages from Charlie's mortars and rockets—the same lethal weapons aimed at us on base, now trained at innocent civilians in populated areas. Equally disturbing were details of atrocities committed by the Revolutionary Army on its own people. The barbaric cruelty the Việt-Cộng routinely dispensed with their brand of social and political "justice" was meant to strike fear into people's hearts, to warn them against cooperating with the South Vietnamese government and the Allies. During the Tết Offensive, VC more than lived up to their ghoulish reputation, leaving behind a long trail of gory evidence that would take months to unearth.

Captain Morgan couldn't help notice my increased restlessness. Attributing it to fatigue, he finally suggested I take a break and catch some shut-eye. "I'd keep my gear on if I were you, and sleep in the bunker. Just in case," he said matter-of-factly before returning to his patient.

I took him up on the offer, but decided to head back to my hooch. You can flee, but you can never hide, I told myself in resignation. After the past fifteen hours, all I wanted was to crash in my own bed, come hell or high water. Or even rockets.

But as exhausted as I felt, the anxiety about my friends' unknown fates kept me awake, staring at the tin roof above my cot. What a way to usher in their New Year. Then again, what a crazy way to live. Always on the hustle to stay one step ahead of danger. It gnawed at me that I could do nothing to help them during these perilous times but pray for their and their families' safety. Turning away from such dark broodings, I rolled over on my side and looked at Bob's empty cot across the way.

"Some fireworks you ducked out on, big guy," I said, speaking to him for the first time since last week's memorial service. "Lucky you. No more breaking your neck scrambling for shelter in the middle of the night. I'm glad you're in a safe place now, my friend."

Somehow, I could glean no joy or comfort from the thought.

Chapter Fifteen

Biên-Hoà AFB, 4 Feb 1968, 2100 hrs

Dear Debbie,

How are you and the family doing? You all must have been following the news on TV, so I'll cut to the chase. But I've no idea how soon this letter will get to you. Our mail service has been interrupted since Tết, probably backlogged at Tân-Sơn-Nhất or in San Francisco APO due to recent events.

I'm doing fine, knock on wood, except for a little sleep deficit since early morning Jan 31st. You've no doubt seen some footage of the fighting on the news, so suffice it to say it was rough going here for a while. For many of us in the rear, it was by far the most intense combat exposure to date, but with luck and teamwork we pulled through in flying colors. The "Battle of Biên-Hoà" lasted over twelve hours, though at no time were we at serious risk of losing control of the base. But even in the aftermath, with other active fronts still counting on us for air support, life remains a long way from its pre-Tết routine. The pilots have been pulling twenty-hour shifts, while ground crews and medical staff are working around the clock. My scheduled R&R trip to Penang, Malaysia, was cancelled. No big deal. It surely can wait.

Due to demand for combat personnel, everyone including cooks and company clerks now has the chance to apply their basic infantry training and fill in as helicopter door-gunners or Security Police augmentees. So guess what, dear heart. No more hot meals in the mess halls. Just plain old C-rats for one and all, which aren't really all that bad. It's about time us brats get a taste of what it's like living out in the weeds.

As you might have heard the President say in his recent press conference, and notwithstanding the near-panic reaction from some in the media, our enemy has been dealt a major setback in their latest gamble. It may take some time to clean up the mess, but by all accounts the worst of the Tết Offensive is already behind us. Hopefully we can return to standard operating procedure before long.

Unfortunately, the same can't be said for the local folks who got caught in the crossfire. Many did perish, used as human shields by the Việt-Cộng, while a great many more were forced to abandon their homes and flee for their lives. Remember Bà Bảy, the Mama-san who cleans our hooches? She showed up for work today with her five-year-old boy in tow, the first time I'd seen them since before Tết. Came to find out that their little shack in the village had been burned down by VC during their retreat, and she and her brood of seven are now taking shelter with relatives in a thatched-roof house on the outskirts of town. No tears. No pity party. Just a sad, resigned smile, as if their misfortune had simply been an act of nature, a part of life. I gave her a few extra Đồng for her work and my C-rat lunch to Cu Bóng because the boy looked famished. Besides, I lost my appetite after hearing what had happened to them.

Know something else, Deb? I've wanted real bad to dream about you taking your lunch break in the park near your office, or the two of us hiking the trails over Mammoth Lakes like we used to, but every time I close my eyes lately, it's been either dead sleep with no dreams, or a lot of tossing and turning with jumbled images of war churning round in my head. Seems a lifetime ago when life was simple and unambiguous and sleep came easy— until I got lost in a time warp in this tropical Twilight Zone. You

*can tell, can't you, it's my fatigue-induced neurosis talking now.
So please ignore all this rambling.*

*I better wrap it up here and catch some rest while I can, before
any emergency arises. Take real good care of yourself, Deb, and
don't worry about me. I promise to be extra cautious and not play
hero for the sake of it. My love and big hugs to everyone,*

Love, R.C.

I came to realize it served no helpful purpose to share every detail of
my life in Việt-Nam with Debbie or my family. What good would it
do them to know that since his failed attempt to seize the airbase,
Charlie had kept on badgering us night after night with killer rockets?
Or that death and destruction had become as commonplace around
here as at the frontline? Gradually over the remainder of my tour, my
letters home grew shorter as well as less frequent even as life on base
continued to evolve at accelerated pace.

With increased rocket attacks, the Red Horse squadrons of civil
engineers were engaged full time in demolition and rebuild projects.
The morning after an attack, they rolled up in bulldozers and with
disconcerting efficiency proceeded to raze the damaged structures and
fill in the craters in the ground, converting the eyesores into parking
lots. Concurrently, on a nearby site, civilian contractors from RMK-
BRJ raced against the clock in their ochre-colored trucks and oversized
equipment to erect new barracks and hooches. It was indeed a rare
occurrence that we'd awaken to the same landscape from one morning
to the next.

Meanwhile, a rumor circulated that had many short-timers up in
arms. It was said that due to recent developments coupled with spiking
air traffic at the AFBs, all Freedom Flights had been suspended

indefinitely and all service personnel in country would be extended an extra three months. Since my DEROS was still half a year away, I didn't want to get my family all in knots over this possibility, so I never breathed a word of it to them.

Likewise, I decided to keep mum about my hooch mate's death. It would have struck too close to home for my folks and needlessly added to their worries. Besides, the pain of it was still raw and I couldn't yet bring myself to discuss it with anyone. The best thing to do, I thought, was to bear up and let time work its healing magic, a little each day.

But weighing most heavily on my mind was the fact I was totally in the dark regarding the safety of my friends in Sài-Gòn. In addition to grim updates of continued fighting inside the city, a sense of foreboding kept nagging at me, even in my sleep. In my dreams, I'd see the girls—Lee Anne, Vivienne, and Elise, with Mme Yvonne sometimes—swept along a river of refugees fleeing on foot from danger and death, the horizon on fire behind them. They stampeded toward us, faces etched with terror and arms extended in silent screams for help. As fierce enemy fire cut them off from us and the flames began to engulf them, I would spring awake in a cold sweat. The same scene of horror with varying details haunted my nights in the weeks after Tết, crowding out the last sweet memories from home.

In many ways, this short, eventful period precipitated a sharp break with the past, shattering the status quo once and for all. I felt the war heading into a new, critical phase and that life in country would never be the same again. With a mix of puzzlement and nostalgia, I realized that a part of my old self had slipped away, lost forever. Should I be fortunate enough to return home safely one day, I'd go back a different man, a stranger, perhaps, even to my loving family.

That hardly seemed an appropriate subject to write home about. And so I never did.

One afternoon about a week after Tết, Dean Hunter popped in at the dispensary toward the end of my shift. I felt a wave of relief when I looked up and recognized his familiar face, albeit with a days-old beard and bleary eyes.

I hurried to him. "You look like hell, old man. But it's sure great to see you."

"Have time for a swig?" he asked.

"I sure can use one."

We strode to the officers' club, ordered a couple of bottles of the local brew *Ba Mươi Ba* ("33"). They had run out of American beers days ago, and with backed-up traffic on the runway, it was anyone's guess when the next supply might come in. But Dean and I had developed a taste for the local drink anyway, and after plopping down in our seats, we kicked back and took nice long drafts of it in silent contentment.

"Glad to see you in one piece," I finally said. "Been rough for you, too?"

"Not near as bad as for you guys, from what I heard. We were damn lucky Charlie didn't get a chance to start in on the hospital that night. Our CAV guys rolled in first, saved our butts in the nick of time." He paused, emptied his bottle. "Next day, my buddy and I got called out to a camp at the Black Lady Mountain in Tây-Ninh. Big fucking mess out there. Heavy casualties." A long exhale. "Haven't slept much since. We just got back this afternoon."

Then with a wink, he changed the topic.

"Bet you don't know yet. We're going to be next-door neighbors, kiddo."

It turned out that Dean and the officers of the 145th Combat Aviation Battalion (the Huey pilots), with whom he'd been bunking at their rented two-story BOQ in downtown Biên-Hoà, were moving back on base for better security.

"It was a close call this time," he explained. "We were fortunate to have escaped unscathed. But we ain't betting our lives on luck no more."

"Swell. Makes it easier to coordinate our next trip to Sài-Gòn."

There was no immediate response.

"You realize it'll be a while before we're allowed back in the city," he said at last. "There are still pockets of intense fighting, the knock-down, drag-out, house-to-house kind that may go on for weeks. The government has imposed a curfew to restrict movement around the capital." He concluded with a shrug, "We'll have to wait on that next trip."

"Any idea how our friends are managing?"

"Last time we were there, I wrote down Mme Yvonne's phone number," he said. "So I called to check. She and Mr. Bill are doing okay, but the business is closed for the time being. She hasn't heard from any of the girls since before Tết. None of them has phone service at home, and nobody in their right mind ventures outside these days." Noting my disappointment, he added, "Nothing we can do. I'll keep you posted, as soon as I hear anything."

I heaved a long breath, suddenly feeling drained. "What about Dick? Any news of him?"

Dean got up and motioned at my empty bottle. "Another one?"

I nodded. In the corner, a group of pilots conversed in hushed tones over their own pile of dead soldiers, probably unwinding after a long mission day. Someone stood and dropped his dime in the jukebox, and the wistful sound of Simon & Garfunkel's "Homeward Bound" drifted up over the cigarette smoke. The voices fell quiet.

"I can't figure the guy out," Dean remarked upon returning from the bar with two opened bottles. "He must have a death wish or something."

According to Dean, Dick and some other journalists had ignored warnings of deteriorating conditions and squeezed their way into the USMC combat base at Khe Sanh, a remote outpost up country, near the DMZ. Rumors of an imminent showdown had lured them to this forsaken spot, which controlled access to the strategic Hồ-Chí-Minh Trail. On January 21st, ten days before Tết, their suspicions bore out when three NVA infantry divisions with thirty thousand soldiers supported by tanks, heavy artillery, and sapper units launched a full-scale siege of Khe Sanh, defended by six thousand combined troops from the USMC and the ARVN. It was the onset of what would become the longest, bloodiest, and most controversial battle of the war.

"The only road access, Route 9, was completely cut off," Dean said. "The airstrip is pounded day and night by rockets, so nothing can land or take off." He blew out a rush of air. "They're all trapped in there, the dead and the living. No telling for how long."

I emptied my new bottle in one long draft. That was enough news for one day.

"You wait and see," Dean went on. "Both campaigns, Khe Sanh and the Tết Offensive, will be the last straws that break Charlie's back. But that'll come at a price to us as well." His voice took on an urgent note. "It's a dangerous time, kiddo. Don't play foolhardy like Dick. I'll let you know when we can get to Sài-Gòn again."

I nodded thank-you but my heart was troubled by the possibility, more distinct than ever, that I might never see some of my friends again, particularly Lee Anne. Who would have imagined? In a matter of weeks, the war had caught up with every one of us, gripping us tight in its claws of death and violence, touching our lives in ways most personal and unexpected.

Dean gave my shoulder a gentle tug. "Come on. Let's get you some fresh air."

We got up and left, as the final strands of "Homeward Bound" dissolved in the lazy-blue haze of cigarette smoke.

⁓

"What say you—we get you a new hooch mate, Connors?" Captain Morgan asked me one morning, his head of prematurely gray hair bent over the paperwork backlog on his desk.

Caught off guard, I offered no comment.

He looked up. "Paul Nilsen. Remember him? His hooch mate DEROS'ed around the time Bob was—" He stopped short, cleared his throat, then continued. "Anyway, I figure it may help him to have someone around to talk to. Since you rescued him that night, and there's a spare cot in your hooch . . ."

"It's a two-man hooch," I said. "I've no problem with that."

The Kid moved in that same evening. We hadn't run into each other much since the night he was taken to the dispensary, and at first he appeared self-conscious and kept to himself. But I took an instant liking to him. There was an innocent kindness about him, very Boy Scout-like. Watching him unpack his personal effects and carefully lay out some family pictures atop his footlocker—like a college freshman, first time away from home—I couldn't resist teasing him. "I'll try and keep my mess from spilling over to your side. But if not, you're just going to have to excuse me." He looked uncertain, then smiled.

I gathered from other colleagues that Paul had proved a decent GMO after all. Once recovered from the shell shock of that first night of Tết, he had gradually adjusted to our volatile situation, gaining greater confidence with each passing day as he continued to work with the sick and the wounded on base. In a twist of irony, his gentle, nurturing nature—having overcome the initial turmoil—seemed to have found its niche here in the war zone of Biên-Hoà AFB. Though far from thrilled to be in country, he now at least had a purpose.

It had been quiet in the hooch since Bob was gone, but now there was life again: the sound of voices and laughter, and sweet, sentimental music from Paul's record collection. Just as Bob had been stuck on "Puff, the Magic Dragon," Paul had a short list of favorites he kept playing over and over, especially Tom Jones' "Green, Green Grass of Home." Sometimes he'd hum along with the melody, eyes half closed in deep reverie.

"You must be sick and tired of this number by now," he said with a sheepish grin when he saw me looking. "Yeah, it's kind of hokey. But it makes me feel good inside."

I asked what he missed most from home.

"I'm no big-city boy, you know," he answered. "It's the simple things in our backyard that I really miss. In 'Little Switzerland,' where I'm from, we're blessed with beautiful scenery. I wish I had some photos to show you: rolling woodlands as far as the eye can see, shiny white bluffs all along the Upper Iowa River, and of course, lilacs—lilacs everywhere in springtime. It's truly God's Country." He turned away, embarrassed by this sudden gush of emotions. His voice was softer, more sober, when he resumed his thought. "It's those images I try to bring up in my mind each time we hit the ground inside the bunker." Glancing back at me, he added, for the first time, "Thank you, Roger. For what you did for me that night."

Not long after Paul became my hooch mate, on-base activities returned to SOP—kind of. To our collective relief, since C-rats had long grown stale on everybody, the mess halls once again served hot chow. Even more exciting was the rumor that good old American brews might soon make a comeback at the clubs.

"Don't get me wrong. I'm grateful for all the good news, but you know what I'd give my left arm for right about now?" Paul admitted to me one day, before dinner. "A nice, juicy steak of prime championship beef. Mm-mmm." He chuckled at my surprised reaction. "What can I say? I'm a meat-and-potatoes kind of guy. Every year at the local fair auction, my dad and some neighbors would split a side of blue-ribbon beef from the 4-H Club. They'll have some set aside for me when I come home, and let me tell you, it'll be well worth the wait. Yes, siree."

I smiled at him. "Sure sounds like something I'd be thinking about inside the bunker."

Seeing how well he had adapted to the daily happenings, I made a point of showing him around on our free time, as Bob had done for me earlier. It also helped to distract me while I waited to hear back from Dean with news of our friends.

For various reasons, sundown was usually an eventful time of day. Many memorial services were held at that hour, sometimes capped off by a Missing Man Flyby in honor of fallen pilots. It was remarkably stirring to behold the sight of four aircraft flying over in V-formation, with the leader—the Missing Man—suddenly pulling up and away into the clouds. In case of helicopters, the aircraft approached from the south, then the Missing Man banked left and flew off into the sunset. The first time we came upon such a flyover and I explained its symbolism to Paul, he stood and gave an awkward salute, following the airplanes with moist eyes until they disappeared from view.

Another evening, we spotted a big black bird with long, glider-like wingspan spiraling up into the crimson sky, much like a raven riding one last thermal at the end of a summer day.

"What in the world is *that*?" Paul wondered out loud, squinting at the unusual spectacle.

"That, buddy, you never saw—or weren't supposed to have seen. It's a rare U-2 spy plane out on nightly recon somewhere up north."

I shared what I'd learned earlier from Bob. Nicknamed Dragon Lady, the specialized aircraft was shrouded in secrecy and flown by CIA operators instead of USAF pilots. Reputed to attain an incredible altitude of seventy thousand feet, it floated beyond the reach of Soviet fighters and missiles and outside the detection range of radar. Although no official ever confirmed it, most of us were aware that Biên-Hoà AFB actually housed a pair of these rare birds.

"No U-2 is allowed to operate on foreign soil, supposedly," I told Paul. "Now that you're in possession of national top secrets, you realize they'll have to kill us both, don't you?"

He looked thoroughly impressed.

As darkness erased the last vestige of daylight from the sky, the horizons continued to retain a deep red glow. "How long is it before the sun completely sets around here?" Paul, who had seldom ventured out late on his own, marveled at the phenomenon one evening.

"A long time," I replied. "It's no sunset you're watching, over there in the distance. It's the bombs exploding, courtesy of our Flying Fortress B-52. That goes on all night long." I placed my hands on his shoulders. "Hold still for a minute. Feel the rumblings in the ground?"

Paul nodded. "All night long, huh?" he repeated pensively.

It was a good thing we got out rather than hang around the club after dinner and discuss the politics of war. Since late February when Walter Cronkite wrapped up his visit to Việt-Nam before going on the air to declare the war "a stalemate," more and more journalists also felt compelled to offer their own editorial opinions on the matter. It was great irony that at the same time Hà-Nội was ordering a general retreat from their Tết Offensive debacle, American media seemed to have given up on a victorious outcome for our side. While the communists paid a dear price for their failed aggression, which would leave their military reeling for the next two years, they scored a publicity coup with members of the American press, who in large part deemed Tết, at a minimum, a psychological defeat for the Allies. Picking up on this dismissive pessimism in one newspaper clip after another with our mail from home, many of us in country were driven bonkers with frustration.

"One patient at a time, that's *my* argument in this debate," I kept reminding Paul and myself. "As long as we're here, let's just do our job as best we can. Enough hand-wringing, already."

For his part, Paul showed little inclination to opine on the subject, opting instead to keep his nose to the daily grindstone.

One evening in early March, as he and I were closing shop, getting ready for our routine excursion around the base, the telephone rang. It was Dean, calling from his office at the Biên-Hoà Provincial Hospital. My pulse quickened.

"Can you get away this Sunday?" Dean asked. "We're going to 3rd Field—to see Dick."

Chapter Sixteen

"There wasn't a whole lot more than what I already told you on the phone," Dean said.

It was Sunday morning. We were on our way to Tân-Sơn-Nhất AFB by Army helicopter.

"Dick called on Thursday afternoon and told me he was in 3rd Field Recovery Ward," Dean repeated patiently. "After we hung up, I called you and Mme Yvonne. She'll be waiting for us at the civilian terminal so we can all head to the hospital together. Just not sure how long we'll visit with him. He sounded groggy and could barely talk." He put up a hand to stop my question. "I have no information on his condition. We'll find out together."

It had been many weeks and much upheaval since I had last seen Mme Yvonne, just days before Tết. I instantly recognized her tall, thin silhouette among the crowd of local passengers, and we rushed toward each other to exchange hugs, somewhat surprised by the surge of pent-up emotions. She had on a simple floral dress, with a large handbag slung over her shoulder. Her face revealed signs of stress, though she managed to greet us with a broad smile.

"*Bonjour, mes amis. Comment allez-vous?*" she said. "It's wonderful to see you both again. It's been much too long." Her eyes filled with apprehension. "Please tell me straight, was Dick seriously injured?"

"Let's go find out." Dean wrapped a comforting arm around her shoulders as we headed out.

At 3rd Field Hospital, a short jeep ride from the main gate, Mme Yvonne and I waited in nervous silence outside the front office while

Dean went in to make inquiries. He soon emerged waving a visitor's badge, which he handed to Mme Yvonne.

"We can go in now," he declared. "Right this way."

After we crossed the front lobby, he led us down a tiled hallway that opened on both sides to well-lit rooms occupied by smiling, chatty young men—all recovering, many of them likely to be sent home soon to their loved ones. As we traipsed past the recovery ward with no hint of slowing down, I shot Dean a quizzical glance.

"Don't worry. I was told our friend is doing well enough to receive visitors," Dean assured us. "But the recovery ward is one hundred percent full, as you just saw, so they gave him a bed just around the corner, inside the Death Ward."

"The Death Ward?" Mme Yvonne stopped in her tracks.

Dean hastened to her side. "Sorry. Bad choice of words. It's where they keep the 'expectants'—" He let out a sharp breath, running a hand through his crew cut. "Another atrocious term. I meant the worst casualties, who aren't expected to make it but are carefully monitored for any hopeful signs." Then, in a softer voice, "Just want to give you the heads-up before we go in, 'cause it ain't pretty in there."

We rounded the corner, tiptoed down another hallway and into a long, dark room toward the middle. It was lined with two rows of beds that held immobile bodies draped in bloodied white bandages and hooked up to IV poles and an assortment of monitoring equipment. Except for the whirr and hum of the machines, occasionally interspersed with delirious mumblings or muffled groans, the place was uncannily quiet. A pall hung over it, the smell of preying death—heavy, suffocating.

"There's our man," Dean whispered, pointing toward the far side of the room at a bed by a second door that exited into the next hallway. Dick was propped up against a stack of thin white pillows. Dressed in a blue hospital gown, he sat motionless as if lost in deep contemplation, his eyes wide open but apparently not seeing.

As we moved closer, he looked up. I was relieved to detect recognition in his eyes. Mme Yvonne hurried to the bedside, bent down and hugged him around the shoulders—very gingerly, so as not to disturb the wide tapes wrapped around his torso. Aside from appearing haggard and unshaven, he wasn't hooked up to any accessories, which was a good sign.

"Hello, stranger," Dean and I said at the same time. Dick nodded, still speechless.

"I brought you some flowers, *chéri*." From her shoulder bag, Mme Yvonne retrieved a little vase of yellow roses and set it on the small stand by the head of the bed, next to a telephone. "I'll give them a drink of water before we leave. So, how are you, darling?" Her eyes welled up even before his answer, and she turned away to dab them with a handkerchief. I'd never seen her this emotional. It was rather odd and unsettling.

Dick shook his head slowly, his fists gripping the sheets tight.

"He'd just landed a deal with Newsweek. His first big break." Those were the first words out of Dick's mouth.

Mme Yvonne glanced at Dean and me, concern written all over her face. I felt no less confused, but thankfully, Dean came to our rescue. "Hey, buddy," he said, leaning over Dick. "How about we find a wheelchair and get you outside to catch some rays. Think you can handle that?" Then, motioning to me, "Can you check with the charge nurse?"

After scrambling to gather what we needed, Dean and I helped Dick out of his bed and into a wheelchair, ever so carefully since he was cringing in pain.

Dean pushed the chair out in the hallway, and Mme Yvonne and I couldn't be happier to escape from the chill inside the Death Ward.

Without talking, we followed a warm, gentle breeze to a bright veranda that overlooked an inner courtyard.

It was splendid out—always summer in Việt-Nam, someone had noted—as we came upon an oasis of flowering shrubs and trees, complete with a babbling fountain in the center where birds frolicked. Hard to imagine it was just a month ago when blood and guts had spilled freely across the street from this idyllic spot, during Charlie's suicidal assault on the airbase and MACV headquarters.

Dean parked the wheelchair in a shady spot on the veranda, then plopped down on the tiled floor next to it. I followed suit, on the other side of the chair. Mme Yvonne sat down on the edge of a small stool I'd carried out for her, at an angle from Dick so she wouldn't obstruct his view.

"Sorry, guys," Dick finally broke the silence. "I'd just gotten off the phone with the bureau and my head was still spinning when you all walked in." He closed his eyes momentarily, taking a slow, deep breath. "A friend of mine had gone missing for a week. Only this morning did they learn what happened to him."

He turned to Mme Yvonne with a wistful smile. "It's always struck me how easy it is to form new friendships here in Việt-Nam. Seems like people understand there's precious little time to be squandered, so they just cut the crap and try harder to be civil to each other."

As anxious as we were to find out about Dick's condition, we sensed that he needed to talk. Discreetly, Dean signaled to Mme Yvonne and me not to interrupt.

Dick went on. "I met this new friend in Khe Sanh, a young freelance photographer by the name of Bob Ellison. Only twenty-three years old, fresh out of college and in country for just a few weeks, but as fearless as they come. Half the time I couldn't keep up with him, since he loved to accompany the Marines on patrols, risking life and limb in the hunt for that unique angle for his story. The day I was injured and getting med-evac'ed, he hopped on the same plane so he could take his film back to Sài-Gòn and have it developed. My last memory of young Ellison was his sunburned face hovering over mine as he squatted next to my stretcher and whispered jokes in my ear, trying to distract me from the pain while I drifted in and out of consciousness.

"I later learned that Bob did indeed develop his photos and show them to *Newsweek*. They were impressed enough to purchase the entire portfolio for publication in the upcoming issue. It was a tremendous coup to pull off for a young unknown like him.

"Then without a trace, he up and disappeared. Just gone, nobody knew where." Dick ran his tongue over his parched lips. Save for a chopper slashing away at the warm air in its descent to the helipad a few buildings over, all was tranquil. No one stirred.

He began anew. "Turned out Bob had tried to sneak back into Khe Sanh on another C-123. Somebody remembered seeing him lugging a case of beer and a box of cigars onto the aircraft. A little surprise for his Marine buddies at the base, he'd said at the time." Dick's voice grew weary, almost doleful. "The kid never made it. His plane was shot down on approach to Khe Sanh and crashed into a hillside, killing all forty-nine people aboard. This happened last week, but they only discovered today he'd boarded the plane as a last-minute add-on, which explained why his name never showed on the manifest."

Exhausted, he fell silent, his gaze fixated on the birds playing in the fountain. Mme Yvonne coughed in her handkerchief. None of us spoke.

"We're so sorry for your loss, Dick," I said at last. "But how are you recuperating? What happened to you?"

He scoffed. "Nothing heroic, for sure. But fortunately, no serious damage."

Massaging his temples with his fingers, he seemed lost in recollection. A minute passed before he resumed his narration in a tired monotone.

"It was clear from the get-go Charlie intended to make Khe Sanh the American Điện-Biên-Phủ. And man, did they bring it to us. You all know I don't scare easy, but for a while there I wasn't sure I'd crawl out of that hellhole alive.

"We were completely surrounded by NVA regulars who outnumbered our boys five to one. They just popped up overnight, out of caves and tunnels in nearby mountains. Armed with Soviet and Chi-Com big guns, they rained living hell on us around the clock. One day sticks out in my mind. Over thirteen hundred incomings pounded the base in a span of eight hours, followed by repeated onslaughts on the ground. Remember the old Korean War documentaries that showed wave after wave of Red Chinese lunging forward, as if nothing in hell could stop their advance? This was just like that. But thanks to our flyboys who risked their lives to bring close air support, the Marines managed to withstand the ferocious attack, even to give back some.

"Route 9 was blocked, so we got resupplied exclusively by air, mainly through paradrops since anti-aircraft fire was too intense for the birds to land. Also the dreadful weather restricted airfield access to only the most skilled and brave of pilots. Here in Sài Gòn it's clear and dry at this time of year, but up north at Khe Sanh we were severely hampered by the winter monsoon that blew in from the South China Sea. Low clouds and dense fog socked in the entire area for most of the day, rarely lifting above two thousand feet."

Dick closed his eyes, his breathing heavy and ragged. I was concerned, but he kept going, his gruff voice droning on as if dictating his report.

"To survive, we dug deep into the red mud. Miles and miles of narrow trenches, up to six feet deep, crisscrossed the entire base camp like a giant ant farm. This underground trenchway connected the company command to all the platoons and bunkers on base, and we lived inside it because most structures above ground had been leveled by VC artillery. Who would've thought, right? Trench warfare in this day and age . . . as though the Great War had never ended.

"In fact, I about got buried alive in one of them ditches. Bunch of us had just dived into it when a new round of shelling started. A rocket hit and caused it to cave in on us. It killed a couple of US Marines and ARVN soldiers on the spot. Could've just as easily delivered me from my troubles. Instead, I escaped with a handful of frags up and down my right side and a pair of broken ribs. The fellows rushed me to Charlie Med where the surgeon removed all the metal from my body, filled the holes with Merthiolate, and closed them up as best he could. I wasn't handling the pain well, so he doped me up with a morphine injection, a tetanus shot, and IV fluid with Penicillin G for good measure. Next morning, during a lull, they evac'ed me out. That's a story in itself, for another time—how we made it in one piece.

"Here at 3rd Field, the staff has been very accommodating. I even get the luxury of a private telephone so I can stay in touch with the bureau and do a little work while recuperating. All in all, I've been fortunate, deserving or not."

I waited until he paused, then asked if he wanted to get back in bed and rest. His eyes looked red and bleary, and his hand was twitching slightly.

"Not yet, thanks," he said. "I've got two more weeks in here to rest all I want. Right now, I'd just like to hear how everyone's been doing this past month."

Dean and I took turns giving him a quick rundown on what had transpired at Biên-Hoà during Tết, both in town and at the AFB. He waited a moment after we'd finished, then inquired in a tone almost too casual, without turning to Mme Yvonne, "And how are my lady friends holding up?"

Seconds passed before Mme Yvonne muttered, "We're doing fine, Dick." Her voice sounded weak, almost frightened, and she fidgeted closer to the edge of the stool. "Don't you worry about us, *mon cher.* Just concentrate on getting well."

"Thanks for coming today. I assume everything's under control for you and Mr. Bill?" Dick persisted. "What about Lee Anne? Please tell me all her family is safe and sound. And my little princess, Elise, is she managing on her own through all this mess?"

"*Oui, oui.* We're all doing as well as can be expected these days, although Elise happens to be out of town at the moment." I could hear panic rising in Mme Yvonne's voice, as her breathing became faster. "Please. Do try and get some rest now, darling. We can finish catching up later, when you're back on your feet again. *D'accord*?"

She stood, clutched at her shoulder bag, and looked helplessly at Dean and me. "Gentlemen. Shall we get going and let Dick have his 'poc' time? I'm sure he's ready for it by now."

"Aren't you going to tell me what's going on with Vivienne?" Dick interjected quietly, still staring straight ahead.

I felt my back muscles tense as Mme Yvonne dropped back down on the small stool, her handkerchief tightly scrunched in her fist. "Please, let's don't do this now, Richard. This is not the time or place . . . It's not why I came . . ." Her voice broke into muffled sobs.

"What's the matter, Yvonne?" Dick's voice rose higher, now quavering with alarm.

Like an idiot, I realized all too late something was deadly wrong. My heart jumped.

"Why are you making me do this?" Mme Yvonne was crying now, her face buried in her hands. "I don't know how to say it, my friends. I'm afraid I have terrible news . . . Vivienne, she . . . she's no longer with us."

Mme Yvonne let slip a heartbreaking wail. "*Elle est morte.* Our little Vivienne is *dead.*"

It was a good thing I was already sitting on the ground next to Dick's wheelchair. My head was suddenly swimming as if from seasickness, and things went dark before my eyes. The only sound I heard was the fury of my own heartbeat and, somewhere in the distance, the gay twitter of birds.

It seemed a long time before I heard Dick's voice again. It was all breath, strained with bewilderment and pain. "What happened?"

I leaned back on my hands—arms shaking, ready to buckle—and gazed up at the blurry blue sky. Dean had gotten up and moved to stand behind Mme Yvonne, his arm bracing her back.

"Do you remember she lived with her aunt and uncle in Chợ-Lớn, the big Chinatown?" Mme Yvonne said in between sobs. "It's where some of the fiercest fighting took place during Tết. I don't have all the details, but it was confirmed she was among the many victims in their neighborhood." She placed a trembling hand on Dick's shoulder. "When you're well again, if you wish, we can pay visit to her aunt and uncle together, you and me. I'm so, so sorry, Dick."

We remained speechless—for how long, I wasn't sure.

Then, slowly, Dick turned his face away from us. "We didn't even say good-bye, last time I saw her. I was being a real jerk, so angry with her, you know." His voice crumbled to a hoarse whisper. "Didn't even have the decency to congratulate her on her engagement news."

I pulled myself together and knelt in front of his wheelchair. "Hey, bud. Listen to me. There's something I've got to tell you about Vivienne. I promised her I would."

In my narrow field of vision, I caught a glimpse of Mme Yvonne's face. Her expression was one of utter astonishment and panic. She put up her hand as if trying to stop me, but then gave up and covered her mouth. Her eyes, however, made one last plea with me not to complicate things further. Poor Dean, being out of the loop, shifted his doubtful gaze back and forth between us.

"It was all a big misunderstanding, you see," I told Dick, wondering myself how I was going to pull this off. "Shortly after you'd gone MIA on us, Vivienne came to see me and explained everything. She asked that when I had a chance to talk to you, would I please relay it to you on her behalf. So you need to hear this, my friend.

"There was no engagement. It was just a fabrication on the spur of the moment, a knee-jerk reaction. You're the only one she cared about, and that's the truth she wanted you to know. But you startled her so with your sudden proposal, she grasped at the first delay tactic she could think up on the spot—and what a lousy one it was. But in its crazy way, it worked. It put the issue to rest, though it also hurt you both deeply."

Dick sat so still I wasn't sure if anything I'd said even registered.

"It was an enormous decision for her, and she panicked," I repeated softly. "She told me she'd give anything to take back what she had said, because of all the pain it caused you. But Dick, I got it straight from her— there was never anyone for Vivienne but you."

Silently, Dick closed his eyes, shutting out the world. From his lips escaped a long, soft sigh. A lament of unspeakable sorrow.

I placed a hand on his knee, and soon I felt Mme Yvonne's hand, damp with tears, on top of mine.

After we'd put Dick back in bed and taken our leave, the three of us trudged to the front lobby. Outside the main entrance, Mme Yvonne slipped down onto a bench and gave way to her emotions, her shoulders heaving with unrestrained anguish. Dean and I sat on either side of her and waited in silence.

Eventually the storm subsided. She gathered herself, looked up at us with puffy red eyes.

"I did not mean to bring that up today," she said. "He must have sensed something and just kept pressing until I had no choice. I am really sorry, my friends."

I patted her hand. "It had to come out at some point. There's never a good time."

She gazed down at the ground, her handkerchief balled up in her hand. "Actually, I did not tell the whole truth. Last week, when I still had not heard from Vivienne, I became worried and ventured out to pay her aunt and uncle a visit. That's when I learned of her death, even *how* she had died. But I could not bring myself to tell Dick all the details. Not in his current condition." Sensing how anxious we were to hear the complete account, she turned to me for clarification first. "Is Dean aware of Vivienne's background?"

"No," I said, glancing at Dean, who looked understandably lost. "But I'll fill him in later. I doubt it matters much anymore—all the secrets."

Mme Yvonne's hands moved to her chest as if to help steady her nerves. "It's a tragic story. There's not a day I don't cry thinking about it. The district in Chợ-Lớn where she lived with her aunt and uncle was swarmed by the Việt-Cộng right from the start. They seized control of it for two days before the South Vietnamese Army fought back and reclaimed it. During that time, an informant accused Vivienne of collaborating with the Americans, no doubt based on local gossip about her job. So the men in black PJs came and dragged her away in broad daylight along with many other 'enemies of the people': government officials of the South, military members on Tết leave, intellectuals, business owners, and so on. You know, the usual 'villains.'

"We later learned the horrible fate of those poor souls. Worse than that of stray animals. They were hauled in front of a 'people's tribunal' and condemned for political 'crimes', then subjected to public humiliation and torture, and finally executed. For the women, we can guess what disgusting form the humiliation and torture took." Mme Yvonne paused, swallowing hard.

"Oh, God," I whispered under my breath, dropping my head in my hands. The naked truth about Vivienne's identity must have been exposed during this so-called torture. Despite the midday heat, I broke out in a cold sweat.

Probably reading my mind, Mme Yvonne skipped to the inevitable conclusion. And so I learned, dazed and incredulous and heartsick beyond words, that Vivienne's body had been discovered a couple of days after her abduction, stripped and mutilated, tossed in a back alley with the others like used rags. All the victims were found gagged and bound, coiled up in the fetal position, some blindfolded, many bludgeoned to death with rifle butts. Long after their brutal demises, their faces remained contorted in silent screams of horror.

There were no tears left in Mme Yvonne. Her droning voice drained and muffled, like a distorted echo in some dark, twisted tunnel, growing fainter by the second. Then nothing.

I was all alone, lost in darkness.

I jumped when she touched my arm, her hand tiny and cold, almost icy—much like the numbness inside me. She leaned closer, her eyes full of empathy and concern.

"Are you okay, dear?" she said.

I squeezed her hand in response.

After a while, she turned to Dean. "I wish the two of you had time to come back to my place. It helps to be with friends at times like this. Grief is such a lonely burden."

Dean tossed me a gauging look. "If we go now, we can get back before the curfew."

"Please, Roger." Mme Yvonne sounded hopeful. "Lee Anne wanted to come today, but we thought it might be too crowded for a hospital visit. She's waiting at my house. She needs to see both of you alive and well. There has been too much sad news lately."

At the mention of her name, my heart surged with such longing it ached. Flushed with all kinds of emotions, I nodded in silence, and we stood. As we headed back to the terminal, I fumbled in my shirt pocket for the black shades and slipped them on over my eyes.

It had been nearly two months since I'd last set foot in Mme Yvonne's villa, but it felt like ages. The place seemed different—subdued, almost somber. The young girl in black silk trousers and white shirt who used to open the gate for us was no longer around.

"She and her mother went to visit relatives in Cần-Thơ over Tết. They've been detained by all the fighting," Mme Yvonne explained as she unlocked the tall wrought-iron gate. "We pray nothing bad happened to them, but we have no way to find out."

We followed her along the familiar stone-and-grass walkway between the high walls of flowering tropical vines. Inside, the garden lay asleep under the afternoon sun, unrecognizably quiet without the happy sound of music and laughter. The overgrown shrubs appeared in bad need of a trim, and an air of desolation hovered over this former scene of merriment.

From our favorite table under the bougainvillea arbor, Lee Anne rose when she saw us, and she practically ran to greet us. The very sight of her set my heart pounding. It was all I could do to keep from bolting at her. She was dressed in a modest white *áo dài* over silk pants of the same color, with a conical straw hat looped over her arm—the uniform of high school girls in Sài-Gòn, who could be seen fluttering on the capital's streets after school like swarms of white butterflies in bright sunlight. Despite a brief awkward moment during which we weren't sure whether to hug or shake hands and did a little of both, we were choked up to see one another again after the events of recent weeks. Then we all started to speak at once, caught ourselves and stopped, and broke out laughing, ecstatic to be alive among friends.

"I am so thankful you are both well," Lee Anne finally got it out, still breathless with excitement. "Did you visit with Dick? How is he recovering?"

"Physically, he's doing better," Dean answered. "But he's devastated by the news of Vivienne's death, as we all are." He realized his blunder and stopped as Lee Anne's eyes welled up at the mere mention of Vivienne's name.

"How are you and your family, Lee Anne?" I hastened to change topics.

"We have been very fortunate, thank you." She dabbed her eyes with a white handkerchief, managing a wan smile. "My husband did not make it home for Tết but at least we know he is safe, thank heavens. But let me bring everyone some refreshment."

When she and Mme Yvonne excused themselves to fetch us some lemonade, I followed them inside the house to wash my hands. Continuing through the front lounge to the hallway at the end, I noticed the office door left ajar across from the bathroom. Without thinking, I stepped over, poked my head inside, and recognized the same cluttered setting where Vivienne had first poured out her heart to me. From the doorway, I could still see her sitting behind the desk, staring out the glass door at the sunlit patio beyond, her face turned away in shame as she told of her secret burden. It was like yesterday.

I hastily retreated into the bathroom, locked the door behind me, then turned the water full on. Leaning over the sink, I succumbed to the bridled emotions of the day, my body racked with grief as I thought of Vivienne and Dick, their tragedy, and her brutal death.

When I returned to our table under the arch of bougainvillea, Lee Anne seemed to see right through to my distress despite my attempt to cover it up. Without a word, when nobody was looking, she slipped me a fresh handkerchief from her purse.

"You mentioned Elise is out of town?" Dean must have been biting his tongue all day long for the proper moment to address his burning concern.

"Yes, indeed," Mme Yvonne replied after a long draft of iced lemonade. "It's too bad you all just missed her by a day. But Lee Anne can catch you up on her situation."

Lee Anne set the conical straw hat on the grass next to her chair, swept her long black hair back over her shoulders, then leaned forward. "You probably heard by now that Huế was the hardest hit of all the cities in the South," she began as Dean and I hung on to her every word. "It was also Elise's hometown. Her family was there when it all happened.

"The whole thing started when the communists took advantage of the holiday cease-fire to attack Huế on the First Day of Tết. They captured the city by surprise and occupied all or part of it for twenty-six days straight. The South Vietnamese Army and US Marines had to fight from door to door and reclaim one street at a time. The bloody battle left our ancient capital in ruins. The Old Citadel and Imperial Palace were destroyed with the rest of the residences. People say dead bodies littered the streets, and soldiers had to shoot and kill rabid dogs that fed on them . . ."

Lee Anne paused, her chest heaving with emotion, her eyes downcast, blinking.

I braced my arm against the back of her chair, behind her shoulders.

She folded her hands in her lap, drew a long breath before continuing. "During their occupation, the Việt-Cộng rounded up thousands of people around the city who they accused to be traitors to the Revolution. Those folks were marched off to 'reform camps,' and nobody saw or heard from them again. First gone were civil servants of the South and military personnel on Tết leave, along with captured Westerners, like the three doctors from the West German Cultural Mission who taught at the Huế Faculty of Medicine. Next went the community leaders: religious figures, prominent citizens, intellectuals, and others like them. Then in the final hours, even teachers and high school students were taken prisoner by the communists during their retreat from the city."

Lee Anne shifted in her chair, drawing her shoulders closer together. Beside me, Dean sat so still I wasn't sure he was breathing.

"The worst fears have come true since the first day Huế was set free, two weeks ago now. Almost every day, all over the city people have uncovered mass graves that hid the bodies of those missing: in many schoolyards in town, under the sand dunes along the Perfume River, or among the salt marshes just outside the city limits. The victims had been tied up with bamboo strips or wires, chained together in groups of ten or more. Many were struck and killed by rifle butts, some cut down by machetes or stabbed with bayonets, still others with no visible wounds, most likely buried alive; the 'luckier' ones received a bullet in the head. It was a barbaric mass execution, like the ones in the North in the 1950s. Our whole country is in mourning for Huế. From our most beautiful city, it has become our sorriest . . ."

Mme Yvonne and Lee Anne were weeping quietly now, shoulder touching shoulder as if for mutual support. Sweat was beading on Dean's forehead.

It was a while before Lee Anne picked up her tearful account. "Elise's father had always been somebody important and wealthy. He was among the first people the Việt-Cộng sent away after they took over. Then last week on a playground in the Gia-Hội district, a young boy was digging in the sand for crickets when he discovered human remains not fully decomposed. Close to two hundred bodies were found buried in layers of three or four in that shallow mass grave. Their remains were dug up and laid out on long tables in a school nearby. People from all around flocked to the site to sift through clothing items and personal effects in search of their missing relatives, even as they prayed they would not find them there. Elise's family was among that mourning crowd. Their last hope was crushed when they identified a tattered shirt that had belonged to her father, his sandals, and a small medallion of Buddha he used to carry on him for good luck.

"Her mother had always kept contact with Elise, so she got the news right away. She was devastated because she had hoped for a chance to make up with her father and ask him for forgiveness. The family held off the funeral to wait for her, and kind Mr. Bill helped get her a seat on the first American flight to Phú-Bài Airport at Huế.

"She just left yesterday morning. Her first trip home in over two years."

Lee Anne and Mme Yvonne held hands, struggling in vain to stem back the flow of tears. It struck me that even at their young age they couldn't cry enough tears for themselves, for their friends and families, and their people.

So much tragedy, so much sorrow—on such a beautiful land.

"I wish we'd known and been there for her," Dean muttered, his head hanging low. "Any idea how long she'll be gone?"

"She did not know." Mme Yvonne took over for Lee Anne, who appeared exhausted. "She needs her family now, and they certainly need her. She may stay up north awhile." She touched Dean's arm. "It all happened too fast, *mon ami.*"

We lapsed into silence. It was such a far cry from all those innocent, happy times I so fondly remembered, and it pained me to look at my friends now. There was so little I could do for them.

"I am really sorry for all you've been through," I heard myself blurt out, rather pointlessly, addressing no one, and everyone—those here present, and the ones missing, too.

Nobody spoke for a while. There was nothing more to add.

And then, as in a dream, I heard Lee Anne's voice, calmer now.

"It is the time we live in. Our elders would call it a time of Mulberry Sea."

"Mulberry Sea?" I repeated.

"Mulberry Sea—*Bể Dâu*. It's a legend from the Ancient Chinese. In the old days, people grew mulberry fields and harvested young leaves from the plants to feed to silkworms. According to popular belief back then, the world underwent cycles of great changes every few thousand years or so. At the start of each new cycle, blue oceans would turn into mulberry fields, and mulberry fields into blue oceans. The world as known would be gone, completely erased."

"A sea change," Dean said.

Lee Anne turned to us, and I recognized that smile of resignation on her pretty face.

"But in our stormy history, those upheaval cycles always returned much sooner than in the legend. And lately, it feels like we are entering a new cycle again. Another time of Mulberry Sea."

In the afternoon sunlight, she looked more beautiful than I'd remembered, a simple vision in white underneath an overhang of glorious red bougainvillea. So young and pure. So vulnerable. I felt my chest tighten, making it harder to breathe, but not for one second did my eyes wander from her face, as though any moment's distraction might see this lovely sight swept out to sea—swallowed into oblivion like the old mulberry field.

Dean and I hardly exchanged a word during our chopper ride to Biên-Hoà from Tân-Sơn-Nhất, each lost in our own musings. It had been an extraordinary day, which culminated in an emotional, albeit hasty farewell at Mme Yvonne's due to the impending curfew. The women were in tears as we hugged each other good-bye, with the promise to meet again in four weeks' time. We'd probably all thought then, although nobody had said it out loud, that four weeks seemed an imponderable eternity under the current circumstances.

I glanced over at Dean, immobile as a rock next to me. It must have troubled him greatly that he'd just missed Elise and hadn't been there for her in her grief. Ever so private, he had never discussed their friendship, though we all noticed how relaxed and happy he always looked around her. But now with the open-ended separation, once again both their lives had been put on hold. Nevertheless, it should be of some comfort to him that no door had slammed shut on them—not yet—unlike for Dick and Vivienne.

I closed my eyes, chased the last thought from my mind.

In my shirt pocket, against my chest lay the soothing softness of Lee Anne's handkerchief. I had "forgotten" on purpose to return it to her, having always wanted something of hers to hold on to. It was a square of white cotton embroidered in one corner with a small floral pattern, and in another with her Vietnamese name, Liên, in fancy cursive. Without pulling it out of my pocket, I could still smell her fragrance on it. In a way I didn't fully comprehend, it brought me closer to her and gave me a sense of security—a peaceful kind of joy.

In these times of madness and despair, that was all I needed.

Chapter Seventeen

On the surface, the status quo prevailed in country during March and April of 1968, even as the winds of change began to gather gale force stateside.

Under military pressure from the Allies, the Việt-Cộng continued to lose what footing they'd gained at the outset of the Tết Offensive, and they were forced to order a general retreat. Back at home, however, this crucial fact remained buried under nightly avalanches of TV news fixated on the gory facets of war. Lost amid all the gruesome details was the original sense of purpose, the lofty ideal of freedom and democracy that had brought us to Việt-Nam in the first place. Instead, there grew serious doubt about a successful military solution that could prove timely and cost-effective, and this in turn fanned an already widespread feeling of frustration. Beneath this swelling tide of pessimism swirled an undercurrent of dismay at MACV's inability to anticipate and preempt Tết, no matter that it had resulted in failure for the enemy.

By mid-March, the national debate on the war reached a new climax when Robert Kennedy announced his presidential bid as an antiwar candidate. It confirmed to the public that the foundations of the Lyndon Johnson administration's foreign policy, as related to Việt-Nam, were being openly questioned and challenged, even inside the President's own party. This only added fuel and fury to the already vociferous discourse. Soon, this growing rancor would come to a head in the form of violent protests in the streets and organized sit-ins on college campuses all across the US.

Out of their desire to shield me from unnecessary distractions, my family seldom mentioned the escalating antiwar sentiment stateside. Nor did I wish to discuss what information I managed to glean from newcomers freshly arrived in country or from printed material sent from home. We shared a tacit understanding to avoid this increasingly controversial and divisive subject that none of us could control. From everyone's perspective, I only had three months left on my tour, so the one thing I should focus on now was to get out in one piece.

One April afternoon, after the first thundershower of the returned monsoon season, I heard a hesitant knock on my office door and looked up at a familiar face peeking in.

"Tweety. I was just wondering about you. Did you get a confirmed date?" I recalled having been told earlier about his upcoming DEROS. The young medic had arrived at Biên-Hoà a year ago on the same C-141 Starlifter as Bob Olsen, which meant Bob would have been heading home as well. I waved Tweety to an empty chair by my desk.

He stepped inside the office, field cap in hand, but remained standing. "Yes, sir. Things have settled down enough that they've lifted the freeze, and I'm allowed to keep my original date. I've just now picked up my boarding pass for Friday a.m., sir." He scratched his head, blushing as he continued. "I just want to say, sir—it's been a real honor to serve with you this past year."

Surprised and touched, I got up and went over to him with my hand outstretched. "Likewise, Tweety. Likewise. Only wish I could keep my favorite medic until the end of my tour. You'll be sorely missed, young man."

He squirmed, looking guilty as he accepted my handshake. "I promised Captain Olsen I would extend if he did, sir. But with him now gone . . ."

I smiled. "Say no more. I'd never hold you to that."

"I heard you're going short, Lieutenant, and I was fixing to get you the same calendar I got Captain Olsen." He shot me a sheepish look.

"But on second thought, I didn't want to jinx your last hundred days the way I did his." His voice quavered at the memory of our departed friend.

I grasped him by the shoulders. "Nonsense. That wasn't your fault. Listen. You're one hell of a good soldier, and a first-rate medic to boot. You've done our team proud. Captain Olsen would've told you himself."

I glimpsed a flash of frustration in his eyes and sensed some hesitation even as he weighed whether to speak his mind. Then the questions came tumbling out in a breathless rush.

"Did you catch the President's speech yesterday, sir? I couldn't believe what I heard him say. How on earth can we defeat the enemy if we stop bombing them? Especially when they've made it real clear they ain't playing by nobody's rules. Please set me straight if I'm wrong, Lieutenant. It's not like we're losing the war and need to sit down and negotiate with them commies—are we, sir?" He caught himself, turned red in the face. "Excuse me, sir, for mouthing off like an idiot. But so many good men like Captain Olsen have given their lives for the cause. It'll be a dang dirty shame if the politicians just let it all go to waste now."

He was referring to the bombshell news that had just dropped on all of us, LBJ's March 31st televised speech to the American people. In it, the President announced the US would unconditionally suspend all bombing of North Việt-Nam despite their flagrant violation of the Tết cease-fire, in hope of nudging them to the peace negotiations table. He also declared he would not seek or accept his party's nomination for another presidential term.

Overnight, the political wind had shifted.

"We can only hope our leaders know what's best for the country, Tweety," I said, without as much conviction as I'd wanted to project. "But tell me. What's in store for you now?"

He stood silent for a moment, staring at the floor, then scratched his head again. "I've got thirty days off to go home before I report to Nellis AFB, sir. North Las Vegas, Nevada."

"Isn't that where you're from? Nevada?"

"Carson City, Nevada, sir. So Nellis will work out just fine. My parents couldn't have been happier with the news. My mom wants me to get out of the Air Force when my four years are up. But I haven't decided yet."

I offered the young medic a final handshake, gripping him tight by the shoulder with my other hand. Drawn-out good-byes never were my strong suit. "You've served your country well. Be proud. Now go home to your family. And whatever you choose to do, have a great life."

I watched until he disappeared out the front door. Try as I did, I couldn't stop my thoughts from drifting to Nancy Olsen and baby Ricky, all alone in the Land of Ten Thousand Lakes with no war hero coming home to them.

On April 4, 1968, the news struck like a rocket from the sky, stunning a nation already in turmoil and deeply divided over the war efforts: Martin Luther King Jr. had been shot and killed in Memphis, Tennessee. The shock was even more staggering as the public hadn't recovered from President John F. Kennedy's assassination five years earlier.

The country reacted with a convulsion of violent riots in the cities as mourners took to the streets to vent their grief and anger. Racial tension, already heightened, erupted like wildfire all across America. A new season of discontent was in full swing.

Watching in awe those scenes of civil unrest replayed day after day on the TV screen at the club, I realized an age of Mulberry Sea was indeed dawning—even in our sweet homeland clear across the ocean.

A week before we were expected back at Mme Yvonne's, Dean showed up at my office door accompanied by someone in a tiger-stripe floppy field hat. Ever since he'd moved back on base with his buddies in the 145th CAB for better security, we'd been getting together regularly, at least once a week when he wasn't called away.

"Look who I brought over to see you," Dean announced as he strode in.

"Hey, Roge. How goes it, old man?" said a familiar voice behind him.

I jumped and dashed out to greet Dick Hayashi, who had stepped forward. He appeared thinner, a bit pale from having been laid up in bed the past month, but otherwise his same old easy-going self except for the striped boonie hat that had thrown me off initially.

"You a new member of Special Forces now?" I asked Dick, pointing at the hat. "Give me a minute to finish this last report, then we'll go get some chow next door. Best cheeseburger in III Corps. Ask Dean here."

Fifteen minutes later, we all sat at a table in a corner of the officers' club, bottles of beer and plates of cheeseburgers and french fries in front of us, while the Monkees crooned "Daydream Believer" from the jukebox. Dick leaned back and started to chain-smoke from a half-empty pack of Red Pall Mall at his fingertips, ignoring his food and drink.

"Can't make it to the city this weekend with you, kiddo, much as I want to," Dean began, in between mouthfuls. "I'm filling in for a colleague on R&R and running deliveries to Mount Sam in Châu-Đốc, on the Cambodian border." Then with a chuckle, "First time I get to play postman, paymaster, and medicine man, all at once."

Seeming to feel my gaze on him, Dick turned to me. "I'll be tagging along with Dean. I want to do an in-depth piece on the villagers in that neck of the woods. Find out how precarious their lives were under Charlie's oppression, and how much has changed after the SF guys arrived and trained them to fend for themselves." He forestalled my questions by raising his bottle. "Don't worry. The doc gave me a clean bill of health—about time, for damn sure. I've been itching to get back on the road since my first day at 3rd Field."

"What's the big hurry?" I suggested. "Hang around town awhile longer, until you get your full strength back. Why don't you come with me this weekend to Mme Yvonne's?"

I must have touched a raw nerve, for he glared at me.

"What's the big hurry? Innocent victims are being tortured to death by fucking Việt-Cộng every day—good, decent people like Vivienne and Elise's father. Yet nobody back home ever hears of them, let alone gives a shit. When was the last time you came across a news report that shed light on these barbaric crimes? Or have they been largely overlooked in favor of sexier stories? Stories that put in doubt our ability to win this war outright, or bring into question our moral standing vis-à-vis the conduct of war. It boggles my mind that my fellow journalists have focused their scrutiny almost exclusively on the US and its Allies, hardly ever on the other side and what nasty stuff *they've* been up to. The coverage is so freaking lopsided you'd think we're rooting against the home team. That just ain't right, man."

He paused and downed his first swig of beer, slopping some over his shirtfront as his hand still shook from the outburst.

Dean and I exchanged glances in startled silence.

After a while, Dick removed his fogged-up glasses then covered his face with his hands in utter weariness. "I wish to lend my voice to all those hapless victims so the world can hear their stories, you know?" he said, barely stirring from his slumped posture. "All the injustice and cruelty they suffered at the hands of the Việt-Cộng must be exposed, so people don't lose sight of the main reason we're here in the first place."

He looked up at Dean and me with bloodshot eyes and a twisted, forlorn smile.

"It's easy to get caught up in the politics and passions of the moment, but simple-minded me continues to believe it's our American values and duty to assist the downtrodden whenever we can. If we don't, who the hell will? So damn few in this crazed world have the backbone to stand up against evil anymore."

I felt hot in my face and neck, shamed but deeply moved by Dick's sincere passion. Such philanthropic idealism, from a kid who'd spent the first years of his life under the scorching sun of Manzanar. Perhaps, as pointed out by none other than Vivienne, those very circumstances had endowed him with a keen sense of empathy for the underdog, and the tragic events of recent months had only sharpened it. As the music died down at the old jukebox, it crossed my mind that the daydream believers among us were those with the heaviest crosses to bear.

"What's in the plan for you, after Châu-Đốc?" I asked quietly.

Dick lit up another cigarette before answering. "I'm still working on my boss to let me head north to Huế next. The city is one giant tomb in the Tết aftermath, from what I hear. So many horrendous stories screaming to be told, yet nobody in the press pays attention. I suppose they're too commonplace to be considered worth writing about." He shook his head and sighed. "Mme Yvonne gave me Elise's contact info, so I'll be sure and look her up once I get there."

"You've been to see Mme Yvonne?"

"We spoke on the phone." He looked away, blinking back a new tide of emotions. "Don't know if I can set foot there again . . ."

Reaching for his beer, he turned back to Dean. "Any message for Elise?"

There was no immediate reaction from Dean, who was contemplating his empty bottle.

"What's the point?" he finally said, with a shrug. "She's back with her family in Huế, and I'll be shipping out by year-end anyway. It was probably best things worked out the way they did. No messy good-bye. No surprise breakup to brace for."

Then scoffing, he added, "At least we'll always have Sài-Gòn, as Bogie might say."

I could feel Dick hesitating, and then he spoke, his voice measured, yet earnest and full of anguish. "I can't tell you how often I've wished for one last good-bye with Vivienne, even if only in a dream. But second chances are just that, mere wishful thinking. So take this for what it's worth: you've got to seize the moment before it passes you by forever, or like me, you'll live to regret it every single day." He gave a long exhale and slammed his bottle down. "Enough said already. I'm the last authority on such matters. Is it time we get going, Captain?"

Dean had stood. Dick and I rose in turn, and we proceeded to the door. Outside, the air felt warm and muggy from an earlier thundershower that had coalesced the swirling red dirt into steamy mud puddles. Dick fished something from his pocket, handed it to me.

"Here, Roge, your own key to my apartment," he said. "So you don't have to bother my Corsican buddy each time. Do me a favor. Look in on it when you're in the city. I've no idea how long I'll be gone this time. But I'll be in touch."

We shook hands. I waved at Dean, who winked back with a tip of his invisible hat. As they trudged off, I had the feeling a gate had just come down behind us, sealing off a happier phase in our lives, relegating it to the graveyard of memories. Just as randomly as war had thrown us together, an unlikely group of friends from such disparate backgrounds, so had it begun to wreak its wrath and pull us apart, crushing hopes and dreams, breaking hearts in the process. First Bob, then Vivienne, and then Elise; now Dick, and even Dean in all likelihood, would be missing from future gatherings at Mme Yvonne's, should those pleasant affairs ever make a comeback. Like monsoon clouds on a sultry afternoon, they had come, my good friends, bringing sweet rain into my life—and then gone, much too soon, before I realized what special blessings their friendships had been.

As I made my way back to the dispensary, the slanting sunlight glinted off the water in a ditch nearby, blinding me for a second. My mind flashed back to that instant a year ago, last July, when I'd first stepped off the plane onto the red soil of Biên-Hoà—dazed from the seventeen-hour flight over from the West Coast and blinded by the tropical sun. Somehow this evening, much to my consternation, I felt like a newbie all over, lost and confused, my heart again full of apprehension and loneliness.

The snowmelt waters ran swift, sprayed and splashed their way between steep boulders on the banks, and propelled our small canoe in a perilous lurch forward. Through the glacial mist, I glimpsed ever-greens fly by on both sides and heard rumblings downriver swell to a roar. With a joyous start, I recognized the familiar scenery: Yosemite Creek awakening in the spring and barreling across Eagle Creek Meadow to its rendezvous with the Merced River on the valley floor below—a timeless rite of spring in the High Sierra. The noise and furor grew deafening as the raging waters lifted our canoe like a dead tree trunk and hurled it over the granite cliff down the abyss of Yosemite Falls. Voices shrieked in terror as we tumbled pell-mell in the dense white fog, their shrill edge trailing into a blaring siren that jarred me awake.

My eyes opened instantly.

"Roger. Wake up," Paul was shouting in my ear. "Incomings. We got to get out of here."

I was up like a shot. We threw on some clothes, grabbed our flak jackets and helmets, and bolted out the door. My hazy brain managed to register the time on my alarm clock—1:15 early Sunday morning, hours before I was supposed to meet Mme Yvonne and Lee Anne in Sài-Gòn. So conditioned were our bodies to this nightly routine that we could go through the motions even roused from the heaviest sleep. In the dark, survival instincts were our sole guiding angels.

A big surprise awaited us outside: our usual bunker was burning bright, the sandbags on top of its steel planks having caught fire from the hooches next to it. Those had taken a direct hit and gone up in flames, which explained the loud explosions and fearful screams I'd heard earlier in my nightmare. Sand poured out from the burned bags like blood from open wounds, rendering the bunker useless. In the flickering light, men darted in panic to the next bunker some fifty yards away. We hastened to follow.

Meanwhile, the siren blared on.

Out of breath, we reached the bunker only to find it crammed full.

"Squeeze in, we'll make room," yelled a good soul among the huddling crowd. In a split second, I decided the place was much too packed to be safe.

I tapped Paul's shoulder, shouted in his ear, "Let's check out one more."

We backed out, then sprinted at top speed toward the next shelter. We had covered no more than thirty yards, about half the way, when a bright orange flash from behind us lit up the entire scene. I turned for a quick glance.

A tremendous blast knocked me off my feet, slammed me forward to the ground, punching all the air from my lungs. A hailstorm of debris rained down on me.

Stunned and choking with dirt, my ears ringing like a thousand church bells, I strained to suck in a breath. Then a projectile struck me on the side of my head.

It felt like my brain had exploded. I keeled over.

A last glimmer of thought shot through my mind—"Oh, shit"— before total blackness swallowed me whole.

Chapter Eighteen

Gradually the surroundings came into focus: the whitewashed walls, a small louvered window cranked open to let in air and sunlight, the tin-roof ceiling. Then, from my outer field of vision, a familiar face looming closer, watching me anxiously.

"You're back," declared Paul from a chair by my bed, his blue eyes bright with relief. "You're in the dispensary. How are you feeling?"

"A little buzzed." I reached up and felt around my head—no bandages—then proceeded down my arms and legs. Everything was where it should be and appeared in working order, wiggling awake upon command, albeit slothfully. "What happened?"

Paul smiled, patted my arm. "It's 0700 hours. You've been conked out for most of the night." He gave my shoulder a firm squeeze. "It's wonderful to share this sunrise with you, roomie. We darned near missed it."

According to my hooch mate, we'd both escaped death by a hair. Only moments after we'd dashed from the overcrowded bunker, a 122-mm rocket hit and blew it to smithereens, killing all inside but a handful of survivors.

Life and death—separated by one split-second decision.

Right this minute, our mangled bodies could have been lying in the morgue—cold and stiff, zipped up in tagged body bags, ready to be shipped home. The notion was staggering and made my head spin. My thoughts flashed to the kind-hearted stranger who'd offered to make room for us in that doomed shelter. Did he make it out alive?

"We'd both gotten thrown to the ground by the concussion," Paul explained. "But you lucky son-of-a-gun cheated death a *second* time."

He reached down and picked up a steel pot from the floor next to the bed. It was mine.

Holding it up, he pointed to a marked indentation on the side. "Looky here: you got hit by a nasty chunk of shrap after we went down. It knocked you for a loop. If not for this here helmet, I wouldn't be talking with you now, my friend. Not even a scratch. Just a beaut of a goose egg on the side of your head. I packed ice on it as soon as we brought you in. It should go away in a day or two."

I took the helmet from him and slowly traced my fingers over the dent. It felt deep, like a gouging scar. I closed my eyes.

"Seize every moment. You never know when it might be your last," Dick had warned us, only hours earlier.

"How many?" I wondered out loud.

"What?"

"How many survived in that bunker?"

"Three," Paul replied, his eyes cast toward the window. "Out of fifteen, mostly kids on TDY from up country. The shelter was pulverized. Nothing left but a giant hole." He exhaled heavily, with a hint of a shiver. "Twenty-five rockets in all, a couple of direct hits. But almost all the casualties came from the bunker."

"I'm getting up right now to give you guys a hand." We simply had to push forward and take care of business. Anything to keep from dwelling on the tragedy. It was our only hope.

Paul held up a hand to stop me. "The weekend staff has got it all under control. You get to play patient today. My patient. I'll check back in a while, after I catch some shut-eye."

"I still have to get ready," I said. "I've got a ride to Tân-Sơn-Nhất this morning at ten."

I attempted to sit up, but my head felt like a nightmare of a hangover and sent me sinking back on the pillow with a grimace.

"It's out of the question," Paul said firmly. "You've got to nurse that little head bump. That means plenty of bed rest and fluids. You know the drill. Anything else can wait. Doctor's order."

"Nonsense, with all due respect, Doctor." I tried to smile. "A couple of APC tablets and some dirty-socks coffee, I'm good to go." I sat up, more gingerly this time. "Come on. We almost died. What can be worse?"

Paul stared at me in silence. I'd said the D-word.

"This appointment better be important," he finally grumbled, shaking his head. "At least allow me to look you over, for my own peace of mind."

He lent me a hand to get out of bed, then proceeded to run me through a battery of tests to evaluate my balance and coordination and check off a list of possible symptoms. Aside from a nagging headache and some residual tiredness, everything looked in the clear.

"Well, Doctor, just humor me," Paul said when he was through. "Do what you got to do, but remember. No strenuous activity, and drink plenty of fluids, especially in this heat."

As we were leaving, I thanked him for taking good care of me. He stopped at the front door and from its sunny threshold took in the bright new day.

"Seeing as how you saved my hide once again, it was the least I could do," he said. "If it weren't for you, I would've stayed put in that first bunker."

There was something besides gratitude in his voice. Something I felt in my own heart. A sense of awe and wonder at this unfathomable mystery we call Fate.

_____

The wrought-iron gate creaked open and Mme Yvonne's face peered out. Her eyes opened wide when they recognized me. "*Merci, mon Dieu.* I was hoping it was you. Come in, please." She sounded relieved, but weary all the same.

I stepped into the calm surroundings that had been my occasional refuge from the world for the past year. The helicopter ride to Tân-Sơn-Nhất had proved rougher than expected, with every little jostle aggravating the dull pain in my head and making my stomach queasier. Through the whole trip, my jumbled thoughts kept wandering back to that first visit at Mme Yvonne's with Bob, Dean, and Dick—all absent today for various reasons.

As the gate clanked shut behind us, I caught sounds of music and voices wafting from the inner garden. Mme Yvonne turned to me with an apologetic expression. "A business associate, a friend of my husband, is going back to the States," she said. "So Bill and I are having a get-together in his honor. It's a last-minute surprise. I did not even know until a few days ago."

Taking my hand, she added gravely, "But you and I, we need to talk."

In silence, we hurried past a merry crowd in the garden directly inside to the lounge. I recognized the bartenders mixing drinks at the counter in the far corner and the two hostesses in *áo dài* waiting with their empty trays. We waved at one another.

Mme Yvonne pulled me down next to her on the couch by the Baldwin piano, the same upright console Elise had played with such dazzling artistry.

"A dreadful thing just happened, *mon chéri*. I need your counsel on it," she began in a shaky voice. Her eyes looked somber and puffy, as if she'd been crying for some time. "It was all so sudden. I have yet to figure out what best to do. Oh, *Sainte Mère de Dieu*. Why does horrible news always come in bunches?"

I patted her hand. It felt cold and rigid. "Tell me, please. What's the problem?"

She finally pulled herself together. "Lee Anne is here. She arrived an hour ago. I took her to my office so she could have some quiet. I kept telling the poor girl to go lie down in my room and rest, but she refused."

My heart skipped at the mention of her name, and a chill of foreboding crawled up my back. I must have been crushing Mme Yvonne's hand inadvertently for she cringed, and I loosened my grip. Not wishing to cause her additional stress, I fought hard to refrain from rushing her.

In bits and pieces, Mme Yvonne struggled to recount the latest events. It was all I could do to hold still and listen to her strained voice while not ten steps away from us, behind that silent door, sat Lee Anne. All by herself.

"They showed up at her house this morning as she was getting ready to leave. Her mother had run out for a quick errand, and Lee Anne had just helped her dad back to bed for his morning rest. Somebody knocked on the door. She said the minute she answered it, she knew. Two of her husband's fellow officers stood at the door with hats in hands and grim faces. They asked to come inside, helped her to a chair, then broke the news to her—with their condolences."

Dumbstruck with disbelief, I dropped my head. Lee Anne's worst fear had come true. What agony she must have gone through, caught totally off guard and all alone—like Nancy Olsen on the day Bob died. I'd have given anything to have been there for her.

As if sharing my thoughts, Mme Yvonne fought back new tears. The past few months had been horrendous. Only weeks beyond the ides of March, this year had already wrought a store of death and sorrow upon our small circle of friends, as it had over the whole country.

On one occasion before Tết, Lee Anne had told me that nearly everyone in Việt-Nam had suffered the loss of a friend or a family member due to the war. "It is sad but it seems our fate in life," she'd remarked at the time. "You see, we have always had to fight for survival because we share a border with China. For thousands of years, the Chinese kept trying to conquer us. They only gave up in the last century after the French arrived with modern weapons and colonized Indochina by force. Then for eighty years the French ruled and exploited us, until the Japanese invaded and took over from them during World War II. And can you believe it? In just five years under Japanese occupation, two million of our people were either killed or starved to death."

She had paused momentarily, shaking her head at the ghastly memory.

"Unfortunately, the killing and suffering continued for us even after 1945. The communists immediately launched their 'liberation campaign,' and since then our country has been torn apart by civil war. Now it is my generation's turn to defend our freedom. We are ready to do our part. What is the choice? Nothing worthwhile comes for free, do you agree?"

Little had she suspected that day that her family would soon be destined to pay the ultimate price once again, having already lost her younger brother during the 1954 evacuation.

My heart broke for them.

Presently, Mme Yvonne regained enough composure to resume her account.

"Vĩnh, her husband, was due for a forty-eight-hour leave this next weekend, his first since Tết. It was to be a special time for them. Their three-year anniversary is the same weekend. Then last night out on patrol, his jeep ran over a mine. Four men were killed on the spot, including Vĩnh. Not one gunshot was fired. It was the most quiet night they had had in a while." She rocked back and forth in her seat. "Oh, *Sainte Mère Marie*. What we are supposed to learn from this? Vĩnh was barely twenty-seven. And Liên, all of twenty-one, already a widow."

According to Mme Yvonne, the news had so stunned Lee Anne she probably didn't shed a tear during the officers' visit. "When it was over, the poor child saw the dispatchers to the door and waited until they were gone, then she locked up the house and left, as she had been all set to do before the interruption. As if nothing had happened. How in heavens she managed to get in a taxi and arrive here, I will never know.

"But I could see she was in a total daze, that something was terribly amiss. So I brought her back here to my office, away from the crowd. Even then it took some doing to get the complete story out of her, for she was not coherent, as you can imagine."

Mme Yvonne stared into my eyes as she clutched my hand in earnest. "Oh, Roger, *chéri*. I am really worried about her. I broke down when she gave me the news, yet she herself remained so calm—so detached, like there were no feelings at all. This is not healthy. You know it is not. She has got to find a way to let it out.

"Anyway, this is not the best place for her to be, with all the carrying on and such. Unfortunately, I cannot cancel the party and send everyone away. It is clear the poor kid should not be left alone, but I doubt she is ready to go home to her parents. They will be devastated by the news, for sure, and she is in no shape to deal with all that right now. What can we do for her, dear? Please, help me think of something."

My head was spinning, unable to focus. But I knew I had to be with Lee Anne. "I'll go in and see her now," I said. "You get back with Bill and the guests. Let me handle it from here."

"Please take good care of *ma petite soeur*, Roger. You know she's like a sister to me."

I got up and gave Mme Yvonne a warm hug. "I may try and get her out of here if I can."

She nodded, drew a long breath, then crossed the French door into the garden.

I immediately scurried across the lounge toward the closed door at the end of the hallway.

———⌒◦

I knocked and listened. Not a sound.

Never would I have imagined such an ordinary door could look so forbidding. Softly so as not to startle her, I turned the knob, stuck my head in.

The hair on the back of my neck rose as a hot-and-cold sensation slithered down my spine. The lights were out in the office and the floor-length curtain was halfway drawn across the sliding glass door, but my eyes could still make out an all too familiar scene.

Somehow, somewhere, I'd taken a wrong turn and stepped back in time.

Immobile as a stone statue behind the desk, her face turned away toward the serene setting on the outdoor patio, she sat lost in sorrow— a portrait of loneliness. She gave no indication she had heard me intrude on her solitude.

I stumbled a few steps into the room and was about to call her name—Vivienne—when she slowly turned around. I stood transfixed, mouth open and dry, heart pounding.

Lee Anne. My eyes blinked.

"Oh, sweetie," I murmured in the shadow as I approached the desk.

Half her face was still drowned in the shade, her eyes peering out at me. There was a flash of recognition in them, but they conveyed such weariness, and as Mme Yvonne herself had noted, something akin to aloofness. She was wearing her beautiful Tết *áo dài*, the yellow silk decorated with sequined chrysanthemum flowers—*áo hoàng-hậu*, her "queen's attire," as we had called it. I had a suspicion she might have chosen it for my benefit, remembering how much I had admired it, perhaps only minutes before the dispatchers knocked on her door.

I sat down at the desk, facing her. We looked at each other. Then I reached across the desktop and took her hand. It felt cold and lifeless in mine. I got up, stepped to her side, and put my arm around her shoulders.

"Come on, sweetheart," I whispered, bending close to her ear. "We need to get you out of this dark cave. Let me take you some place where we can talk."

I had no idea where we could escape to for some privacy.

The capital was bursting at the seams, jam-packed with people everywhere. Downtown was out of the question, being the hub of all activities for locals and foreigners alike. The Botanical Garden crossed my mind, but it was more of a fun place for young couples on dates, thus hardly appropriate for our purpose. Then the answer came to me as I was helping Lee Anne into a blue-and-yellow cab outside the National Music Conservatory, a short block from Mme Yvonne's.

"Passage Eden, please," I told the driver after we'd settled in.

He stared at me with a quizzical smile. I repeated our destination, adding, "By the Rex Hotel." The man finally flashed a broad grin and nodded with enthusiasm. "Okay. Okay. You good. You number one."

It didn't take long before we arrived at the bustling curbside in front of Passage Eden. From there, it was a brief walk to Dick's apartment on the ground floor. I had brought his key with me, thinking I might later look in on the place as promised. But as it turned out, it seemed the perfect sanctuary for Lee Anne right now: private and peaceful, out of the scorching midday sun, with a bed to lie down in and rest if she so desired.

I unlocked the door and ushered her in.

It smelled closed-up inside. Some loose mail was strewn on the tiles by the door. The only window was shut, a drape pulled over it, blocking out street noises from the sidewalk. The place looked neat and tidy even in the dim light, like a well-scrubbed hotel room   more like heaven, in comparison to my hooch at Biên-Hoà.

I guided Lee Anne to sit down on the edge of the bed, then stepped to the window and flung open the drape to let in daylight. A compact phonograph in sunflower yellow sat on the desk below the window, a 45 single on its turntable. I clicked it on for background noise and pulled on a long chain dangling from an old ceiling fan to start the air circulating.

As soft music rose and filled the room, I returned to Lee Anne's side. She hadn't spoken all this time and had simply followed my lead without reaction. Though increasingly nervous about this apathy, I had respected her silence, thinking it best to let her come out of it on her own, when she felt ready to talk.

"It's warm in here," I said. "I'll run down to the street corner and pick us up something to drink. Make yourself at home. Dick would really want you to. Lie down and rest, why don't you. I'll try and be quiet when I get back."

"Thank you. I will be fine," she replied, her voice hollow and emotionless.

Hesitating a moment, I closed the door behind me and left her to her thoughts.

To my surprise, the Corsican shop owner instantly recognized me. It had been three months since Lee Anne and I had stopped in. "*Ah, bonjour, vous revoilà*—here you are again. You want key to Richard's *appartement*?" he greeted me in his booming voice.

I waved back at him. "Not this time, thank you. I just need a couple of things."

I grabbed a few goodies from the shelves, enough for a simple snack for two in case we got hungry later: a French baguette, a box of Laughing Cow cheese, a couple of bananas, and a six-pack of Coke bottles from the fridge. I set everything down at the cash register and dug in my pocket for my wallet, but the old man waved me off.

"Don't worry, *monsieur*," he said. "I will put it on Richard's *addition*. That's what he told me to do." He then gathered all the items in a brown bag and handed it to me.

I thanked him and left, clutching the bag in my arm and hastening—no, running—back to Dick's studio, suddenly seized with panic. I shouldn't have left Lee Anne, even for a few minutes, alone in an unfamiliar environment in her current state of mind. What the hell had I been thinking?

The final dash robbed me of my last breath as I staggered into the room, nearly dropping the grocery bag and still seeing white from the glaring sun outside. But I already knew.

Lee Anne was no longer sitting on the bed where I'd left her.

My eyes blinked repeatedly trying to adjust to the shadows inside. The curtain had been drawn back over the window, filtering out the harsh daylight once again. The darkness cast a soothing atmosphere, further enhanced by the breeze from the ceiling fan.

Then I made out her frail silhouette leaning against the desk, head bowed. Music swirled around her, pouring forth from the record player, rapturous and tender like a lover's embrace. To my dismay, I recognized Eddy Arnold's rich baritone crooning "Make the World Go Away," a song about broken hearts and second chances, the vagaries of life and redemptive love. Precisely not what Lee Anne needed in her hour of loss. I kicked myself for not having checked before playing the record.

Quietly, I shut the door and set the groceries on the kitchen counter. With trepidation, I approached her, not sure what to do.

She heard me and turned. I stopped, face-to-face with her mere steps away.

Her eyes glistened in the dark. They reminded me of Vivienne's the last time I'd seen her alive, at Mme Yvonne's before Têt—struggling to project poise and dignity while tottering on the brink of tears and emotional collapse.

"Three years we had been married . . . I had not once been to the Botanical Garden with him—" she started, her voice hoarse, then choked up.

I rushed over and reached for her hand.

I wanted to tell her I understood, maybe better than she thought I might—how the war had robbed her of adolescence and its playful rites of passage; how she'd grown up from schoolgirl to responsible housewife to co-provider for the family in virtually no time; and how she and Vĩnh had been forced to put their lives on indefinite hold, settling for one forty-eight-hour leave at a time. So much deprivation and sacrifice, so much hunger and yearning on their part—all coming to a crashing end. All for naught.

Yet no words came. Just a swelling in my chest that cut short my breath and stung my eyes.

I felt her hand fluttering in mine, its small grip closing tighter around my fingers.

"So much we had not shared. Even simple little things," she murmured. "Never time, never a chance . . ."

Then came the tears, at long last. Without warning, they silently rolled down her cheeks and dripped on my hands, one drop following another, warm and gentle like fresh rain.

I took her in my arms, drew her close to me. That's it, sweetheart, that's it, I whispered to her in my thoughts. Just let it out, let it all out. All the pain and grief and rage. You don't need to be strong and brave. This is your time to weep. This is your time to mourn.

My arms wrapped around her, I felt the warmth of her small body nestled against mine. Her cheeks rested on my chest, dampening my shirtfront with tears, while her shoulders shook in silence. The phonograph must have been set on automatic replay, for the music kept playing on and on as I held her close and rocked her gently in my arms.

Immersed in song and shadow, we were locked in place in a slow dance of sorrow.

How much time had elapsed, I didn't know, until I felt her stirring in my arms. Looking down, I saw her face veiled in tearful grief, though her eyes were closed. Her warm breath grazed across my neck—soft as a sigh, and reminiscent of the scent of lotus from that afternoon over the pond not so long ago. I shifted around to support her from the back, then slowly coaxed her toward the bed. Perhaps after the release of emotions, she might now be able to catch some much-needed rest.

Bending down until my knees almost touched the floor, I eased her languid body onto the mattress, then leaned over to straighten the pillow. For one fleeting moment, my lips brushed against her cheek and our breaths mingled together. In shock, I registered the salty taste of tears on her sweet skin. Here, in the crook of my arms, by tragic twists and turns of fate, I was holding everything my heart had secretly yearned for.

Appalled by such an inopportune thought, I drew back. But her hand clung to mine, refusing to let go. I remained kneeling by the bed.

Against the white pillow, shrouded in the silk of her long, black hair, her unadorned face appeared even paler than usual, except for her lips burning bright red with inner fire. Hesitantly, I reached to brush the hair from her face and wipe tears from her closed eyes. My hand lingered just long enough for a stolen caress.

Overcome with awe and tenderness, my throat tightened and my own eyes welled up. The next thing I knew, my whole body tensed up under the distinct pressure on the back of my neck, gentle yet insistent, of her hands pulling me closer to her.

Until, startling us both, our lips touched.

A lifetime later, I still recall the taste of hunger and despair on her lips that day, which seared my own like a burning cut and filled my soul with indescribable agony. It was a kiss of reckless abandon, of rebellious rage from years of suppressed yearnings and denied happiness   and for me, the blinding storm that snuffed out any last glimmer of reason.

Swallowing hard, I cast all caution to the devil and surrendered to her beckoning.

In a fog of bewilderment, I cupped her face in my hands and covered it with kisses until my lips settled in the soft nook of her neck. I shut my eyes, inhaled the scent of her. In a flash, I was back in an alpine meadow in the High Sierra on a hot summer day, drunk from the heady scents of wild flowers and pine forests and the rush of life all around me. My skin was on fire, sending tingling sensations through my body to the very tips of my fingers and toes.

During all the movement, the snap buttons around the collar of her *áo dài* had come undone, exposing a bare shoulder and the top of her slip. I buried my burning face in her shoulder, and the balmy skin reminded me of moss by a mountain stream: damp and velvety, as refreshing as the cool mist it grows in. She writhed in my embrace, and as my lips clung on to her ivory softness with greater urgency, her arched body melted in a wave of shudders.

She bit her lower lip to stifle a moan. Her rapid breathing matched my own as she drew me tighter against her until my head came to rest on her bosom. I could hear her heart pounding as furiously as mine and feel the same pulsating heat course through our limbs like untamed fever. In a haze of dreams, I found myself on the bed alongside her, face to tear-stained face, bodies entwined in a tender, desperate embrace.

Taking refuge in the warm solace of each other's body, we were lost to the world and all its madness. And for once, nothing more mattered.

My eyes blinked open to the sight of the ceiling fan drawing soundless circles above me.

Strains of music floated in the air from somewhere far off, maybe in my imagination.

I lay sprawled out on my back, bathed in sweat and half light, my brain straining to emerge from the depths of torpor. As images came flooding back of the frenzy and passion of early afternoon, my fumbling hand detected the emptiness next to me.

I jolted awake.

It had been no fantasy after all. I was still in Dick's bed in his apartment. But Lee Anne had vanished from my arms, where she had curled up earlier when together we drifted off to sleep, her slender body perfectly molded to mine.

I sprang upright, but blinding pain shot through my skull, sending me crashing back on the pillow with a groan—a vivid reminder of the concussion, until now conveniently ignored if not forgotten. My eyes watered, and I gulped deep breaths through my mouth to ease the pain. Then, gingerly, I tried again and sat up against the headboard.

Lee Anne had indeed slipped away without a good-bye. I must have dozed off, exhausted from the day's physical and emotional whirlwind on top of the head blow from last night. She probably hadn't wanted to wake me and had just let herself out, no doubt to return to her grim situation and begin dealing with it. The thought of her shouldering her crisis all alone gave me fresh pangs of anguish and filled me with sadness. I decided I'd contact Mme Yvonne later to discuss how we could assist Lee Anne and her parents through this trying time.

The only proof of her earlier presence was a faint imprint next to me on the mattress, where she had snuggled up against me. Calling her name under my breath, I rolled over on my stomach and buried my face in the sheets, trying to breathe her lost scent, my arms wrapped around the contour of her remembered shape, unwilling yet to part with this only vestige of her.

Already I missed her with all my being.

Frame by glorious frame, the movie replayed in my feverish mind with a clarity that made me shiver again. Eyes closed, I could still feel her body—pristine and flawless, skin like satin—pressed up against mine in total despair and abandon. Never before had my heart experienced such agony and ecstasy, and the memory was almost unbearable. Right or wrong, I was thankful I had stayed by her side—no matter that both our lives would change irrevocably after today. One thing was for certain: in the months to come, as Lee Anne and her parents made the difficult transition to life without Vĩnh, I vowed to be there to assist them in every possible way.

But I'd have to sort all this out later, as I needed to hustle to get back to Tân-Sơn-Nhất before the curfew. Moving deliberately so as not to trigger another pain attack, I gathered my clothes from the floor, dressed, then straightened the bed. Something yellow shook loose from the rumpled sheets. Lee Anne's headband, made from the same silk cloth as her *áo dài*. It must have slipped from her hair during our moments of passion and had been forgotten in her haste to get away.

As I stooped to retrieve the piece of material, the past twenty-four hours struck me as a dream. A blurred line between death, sorrow, and stolen happiness. But in a snap, the dream had dissolved. She had vanished like some creature of fantasy, and I was left holding the only thing real—a thin strip of yellow silk.

Carefully tucking the headband in my pocket, I locked up the place, then headed out.

Chapter Nineteen

"Hate to break it to you, Doctor, but you ain't going nowhere anytime soon," Paul announced matter-of-factly after checking my vitals. Then, after a brief pause, "Unless we need to move you to 3rd Field, if your condition doesn't improve soon."

He was referring to my slow-recovering concussion, further complicated by a dreaded case of FUO (Fever of Unknown Origin), a potent combo that had sent me straight to bed upon my return from Sài-Gòn. To preempt any attitude from me, Paul had enlisted Captain Morgan's help in imposing a week's bed rest on me. Annoyed though I was by his clever move, I tried not to show it lest The Kid grew a big head from his newfound power.

Deep down, however, I had to agree with their call. For the past several months, physically and emotionally, I'd sensed myself drifting ever closer to the edge, so it was indeed time for me to take a break and regroup—or risk more serious consequences down the road.

These long hours of forced leisure also allowed me a chance to mull over the recent events. My mind had been preoccupied since the weekend with all kinds of thoughts of Lee Anne: how she'd been bearing up under the stress of her new situation; what practical help I could offer her during these difficult times; but above all, whether she'd felt put upon or dishonored by what had transpired between us. I wished she could just see into my heart and understand that for me the beautiful dream we'd experienced together had been sincere and spontaneous outpouring of love—in no way disrespect, despite the dreadful circumstances. And even though this surprise development would turn my life

234 C. L. Hoàng

upside down, with painful decisions and repercussions I hadn't yet dared to contemplate, I longed to be back by her side. But at the pace my recovery was crawling along, that wasn't likely to happen soon.

Paul made sure the message came across loud and clear. "No work, no alcohol, no *travel*—no nothing, for a week." Then with a smug grin, he struck down any protest. "Captain Morgan's order." I rolled my eyes in silence and let The Kid savor his moment.

The week went by fast. I spent much of that time sleeping, allowing my body a chance to catch up. Even Charlie must have felt burned out and required a breather, since for the first time since Tết we got to enjoy an extended quiet period with no rockets at night. "The calm before the storm," warned the more cynical—and experienced— among us. Nonetheless, everyone was thankful for a little reprieve.

By weekend, my condition had improved, though still not to my doctor's total satisfaction. But as we were confronted with a temporary shortage in our staff—a red-tape snafu had delayed the arrival of two new GMOs—I was deemed recovered enough to go back to work. With the return of the monsoon season, the temperatures had escalated and a large portion of the base personnel had succumbed to the hot and soggy weather, keeping the medical staff busy around the clock. Until more help arrived and were broken in, which might take several weeks, there was no possibility of me getting away on the weekends. As the days wore on, the prospect of seeing Lee Anne anytime soon all but faded, and I became restless, then downright despondent.

Along came Dean Hunter to my rescue. Fresh back from "temporary duty yonder," he swung by one late afternoon to see how I was doing, having heard about my close call.

"Everything's fine. I'm good as new," I assured him. "You got a minute?"

I pulled him aside, gave him a quick update on Lee Anne's situation— excluding the grand secret that had unfolded at Dick's place.

He shook his head when I'd finished. "There's no end to it, is there?" he said, running a hand over his face. "Poor kid. What's going to happen with her and her family?"

"Can you call Mme Yvonne and find out? She must have some idea what's going on. I've been really worried about how Lee Anne's holding up through all this."

Dean shot me a look. "Sorry, kiddo. I should've left Yvonne's number with you."

"Just call her, will you? Let me know if you learn anything." The truth was I felt nervous about talking to Mme Yvonne for fear I might accidentally betray Lee Anne's confidence and our secret.

It took him less than twenty-four hours to get back to me.

"Nobody has heard from Lee Anne since she was last seen with you," he said. "Yvonne prefers to wait a couple more days before trying to get hold of her." There was a pause, then a long exhale. "There's the business about the true nature of her job: her parents think she works for USAID. Yvonne will have to be careful when she goes to see them. Nothing's ever simple."

I shifted in my chair. *You don't know the half of it.*

Thus there was nothing we could do but wait to hear back from our friend, who had promised Dean she'd call the minute she found out something. This waiting frazzled my nerves, but I dared not breathe a word to a living soul.

Another week dragged by before we got some news.

"Lee Anne has been running ragged making funeral arrangements and taking care of her parents," Dean brought me up to date after receiving his long-awaited phone call. "Vĩnh had always been like a son to them, so they took the news very hard, especially her dad who wasn't well to start with. Thank God Yvonne was able to help out."

My stomach twisted in sympathy for Lee Anne and her family, and in total frustration at my situation. Less than twenty miles from Sài-Gòn, yet here I was, stuck on base, unable to even talk to her, let alone to lend her a hand in confronting the greatest challenge of her life.

"I want to pay for the funeral," I told Dean. "Please ask Mme Yvonne to advance it for me. I'll settle up on my next trip to Sài-Gòn, which hopefully won't be much longer."

Dean squeezed my shoulder in response.

As I counted the days, April 1968 drew to an innocuous end—when, from nowhere, a new tidal wave came crashing down on us.

It started with an eruption of fresh hostilities across the demilitarized zone separating North and South Việt-Nam. Seizing on the political turmoil stateside and LBJ's announcements that the US would unilaterally stop bombing and not invade North Việt-Nam, the communists launched a full-scale campaign along the DMZ to establish their own invasion corridor into the South. The enemy, so close to their last gasp after the Tết debacle, had suddenly found a second wind. In recent months they must have sensed, as we all had, a weakening of the American public's resolve and felt emboldened. Against wishful thinking on our part that they'd come to the Paris peace talks to negotiate a conditional surrender, they opted instead to go for broke, yet again, on the scorching battlefield of South Việt-Nam.

Around 0300 hours on the morning of May 5th, "incoming" sirens startled us anew from sleep. After three wonderful weeks without incident, our nightmare returned with a vengeance. For forty-five interminable minutes, thirty-one rockets and twice as many mortars rained down on Biên-Hoà AFB and kept everyone flattened to the dirt inside the bunkers. When the all-clear finally went off, we crawled out from the dark and stood speechless at the havoc wreaked on our base. It looked as if a tornado had just ripped through, carving out a swath of deadly devastation amid the rows of hooches. Paul gave me a haggard look that summed it all up: bad news.

With blind luck, our dogged enemy had scored direct hits on the temporary housing for personnel in transit: greenhorns just arriving in country for their first tour, and one-year veterans awaiting to board their Freedom Bird flight home. Their barracks had been reduced to rubble, spilled sand from burning bunkers partially covering the bloody mess underneath. Search-and-rescue medics clambered over the debris to unearth the injured and the dead, while others scrambled to put out the fires.

Complete chaos reigned at the dispensary as we struggled to cope with the gory aftermath. The few beds in the back were filled in no time, so new casualties had to wait on their stretchers in the cluttered hallway alongside body bags. Their cries and moans echoed through the cramped building, which reeked of blood, sweat, and bodily excretions. Non-medical personnel helped out in whatever capacity they could, from bagging up dismembered bodies to comforting the shell-shocked wounded waiting to be treated or med-evac'ed. Our shorthanded staff worked frenetically from one row of stretchers to the next, doing triage and calling life-and-death decisions as fast as humanly possible.

After many hours, bleary-eyed and drenched in sweat, we finally got through tending our last casualty. Relative quiet had returned to the dispensary since most of the patients had now drifted to sleep under sedation or from extreme fatigue. Those with serious injuries had been transported to the field hospitals in Long-Bình up the road, as we'd gotten wind earlier that Tân-Sơn-Nhất and 3rd Field Hospital were once again under attack from heavy guns and ground forces. A *second* wave of the General Offensive, *à la Tết*? We had exchanged incredulous glances but had been too busy and tired to dwell on the news.

At 0545 hours, the situation having stabilized, we decided to take turns and grab some early chow at the club. It had been a long, hard night, and we all needed a boost of energy. Paul and I and our small group had just headed out when the shrill sound of air-raid sirens pierced the early-morning air, freezing us in our tracks. We stared at one another. Someone rolled his eyes, mouthed the dreaded word, "Incoming." *Again.* The bunkers were a short sprint away, but we couldn't just abandon the patients. I pointed over my shoulder and we turned, making a mad dash back inside and throwing ourselves to the ground. Some rolled under desks or beds for protection, but most of us simply sprawled out across the bare floor, arms and hands over heads, bracing for the worst. It took energy to even get scared, and we hardly had any left.

For the next fifteen minutes, it was more of the same pandemonium as Charlie lobbed ten new rockets and a smattering of mortars at the base, tweaking our ragged nerves one last time for good measure before dissipating like ghosts at sunrise. The earth shook, the building groaned for what seemed an eternity, then suddenly—eerie silence. When the all-clear signaled the danger had blown over, we crawled up on our hands and knees, staggered back on our feet, even more dazed than after the previous round and no longer in any mood for breakfast. Weary beyond emotion, we nonetheless steeled ourselves for a new onslaught of emergencies, which, to our great relief, didn't materialize. It appeared the odds had swung back our way and we had dodged the big bullets this time, with no direct hits or serious casualties. But hanging in midair with the smoke and red dirt was a distinct feeling that something sinister was again afoot.

By mid-morning, the full extent of the nocturnal aggression became known. Biên-Hoà AFB had been but one of the hundred-plus targets under assault from the Việt-Cộng during the night, with Sài-Gòn and its airport Tân-Sơn-Nhất taking the brunt of the firestorm. Under the cover of darkness and a salvo of rockets and mortars, thirteen NVA battalions had slipped past the security cordon to launch a new attack on the capital. In the process, they overran a portion of the Tân-Sơn-Nhất airfield and shut down its runway for some time before being repelled by US forces.

In various parts of the city, brutal house-to-house combat raged on all morning between the infiltrators and the ARVN with no sign of abating. It turned out the latest campaign of death and violence by the communists against innocent civilians in the capital had only just started. In the annals of the Việt-Nam War, this bloody chapter would come to be known as mini-Tết.

"You realize, of course, it's all posturing ahead of the Paris peace talks, which open a week from today," Dean pointed out that evening when we dragged ourselves out to grab a late bite. "Their goal is to create an image of Sài-Gòn under siege for the consumption of the free world, mostly America. That's much easier to pull off than a real military victory."

"And yet it has the exact same desired effect," I concurred, my appetite suddenly gone. "The more carnage and mayhem they spread, even among women and children, the stronger they think they'll come off to the world, and the better their bargaining position." My thoughts drifted to all the tragedies befallen my South Vietnamese friends and their families, going back to 1954. "It's always the little folks who end up paying the price, but Charlie doesn't give a shit. Anything for the Party and its cause. How's that for the end justifying the means—little people be damned."

More upsetting news awaited me at the hooch on my return.

"Did you hear?" Paul sprang up from his cot the minute I trudged in. "Four foreign correspondents were ambushed and killed in Chợ-Lớn this morning. It's all over the news." Chợ-Lớn was the over-sized and bustling Chinese district of the capital, essentially a city unto its own. My heart started pounding as I sank to my bed. Dear God, please. Let it not be Dick. Not another friend of mine.

"Actually, five of them went to cover the fighting there and got caught in a VC ambush," Paul continued, still visibly shaken. "According to the one survivor, they waved their IDs and shouted '*Báo Chí*' to let it known they were journalists. But the VC commander in charge just scoffed at them. Then he strutted up to their Mini-Moke, pulled out a pistol, and shot them. Just plain shot them. One by one. Point blank. Even worse, two of them had been wounded during the ambush and were on the ground next to the jeep. The lone survivor escaped by playing dead."

I saw the dismay in Paul's eyes, but my taxed brain was fixated on one thought only. "Any names or affiliations of the victims?" I finally managed, almost too scared to find out.

Paul droned on as if he hadn't heard me. "A fellow correspondent found the four bodies in the afternoon after the ARVN reclaimed the area. He took them to the morgue at Tân-Sơn-Nhất for identification, but no names have been released so far. It was confirmed, though, the victims were with Reuters and AAP. One British national and three Australians, I think."

I covered my face in my hands, let out a groan as I fell backward, overcome with relief. A sense of shame washed over me for having such a selfish reaction to the tragic event, and it struck me how utterly pragmatic and self-preserving I'd become in just a short time. Rolling over on my stomach, I hid my head under my pillow, suddenly seized with an urge to dump everything and escape from this hellhole, as far as my legs would carry me.

Exhausted, I could no longer make out the rest of Paul's ramblings, and sleep came swiftly, albeit fitfully. In my dream, I watched myself atop a pile of rubble digging out buried victims. Everywhere I turned, arms and legs were sticking up through the sand, grasping desperately for help. But to my horror, when I pulled on them they yanked loose without an attached body.

Then the scene abruptly switched to the idyllic setting of the Zoo and Botanical Garden, where I saw Lee Anne in her magnificent yellow-silk *áo hoàng-hậu* ambling away from me and up the mossy stone steps outside the Temple of Remembrance. I called her name and frantically waved her matching headband. Stopping on the highest step, with the sun and the wind in her hair, she looked in my direction and waved her last farewell, then turned and disappeared inside the temple. Before I could start after her, the monument burst into flames.

With a muffled scream, I shot up in bed, heart hammering and body dripping with sweat. The hooch was mired in darkness, the air dank and sour. Then I heard Paul turn over in his cot.

"Bad dream, eh?" he muttered. "What time is it?"

I glanced at the alarm clock. "Go back to sleep. It's only 3:15."

"What's the use? The devil Charlie will come knocking anytime now," he grumbled.

Good point. Might as well stay awake and be ready to scamper for your life.

I lay back down, still disturbed by the vivid images in my nightmare. It all felt so real—from the heartbreak of watching Lee Anne run away, to the utter despair of losing her in a sea of fire. A terror like I'd never experienced before. Was this a premonition of what was to come? Would I see her again? Soon? Ever? Most troubling of all, how might she be interpreting my prolonged absence after our time together? As callous abandonment or further proof of disrespect? All boiling questions; none with an answer.

Paul was tossing and turning in his cot, unable to go back to sleep as well, yet neither of us seemed to want to start a conversation. For the rest of the night we lay there, silent in the dark, wrapped in our own thoughts and counting the minutes until sunrise, half expecting the blasted siren to go off any moment, which it mercifully refused to do this night.

The fighting dragged on for another week, right up until the eve of the Paris peace talks. Having made their point for the time being, the Việt-Cộng withdrew back into the jungle, leaving behind thousands dead. In terms of American casualties, mini-Tết had proved the costliest fortnight of the entire war. But nothing even came close to the mayhem and suffering inflicted anew upon innocent civilians, mostly those living in the capital. Horrific door-to-door combat had again invaded their streets and destroyed their neighborhoods, while rockets slammed down death and terror night after night. Hundreds lost their lives and thousands more were wounded, with upward of one hundred thousand rendered homeless.

Although in the end Charlie didn't score a single victory on the battlefield with this wave of urban attacks, he nonetheless dealt another blow to the psyche of Americans at home. Clearly, he appeared immune to combat losses and proved capable of rebounding fast, even from a military disaster on the scale of Tết.

A couple of days after things went quiet, I was dispatched to 3rd Field to follow up on some patients recuperating there—in all likelihood, a thoughtful gesture from Captain Morgan. Without so much as an inquiry into my private affairs, he'd inferred from all my prior excursions and from my state of high anxiety regarding the fighting in Sài-Gòn that I would welcome a run there as soon as the situation permitted. Indeed, a number of us on base had Vietnamese friends in the capital, and we'd been greatly concerned for their safety during mini-Tết. This little-mentioned fact wasn't lost on the captain. Hence, I guessed, my surprise assignment, which was much appreciated, and the first travel allowed in weeks.

"It's my job to remind you to stay alert and use good judgment around the city," he simply cautioned me the evening before the trip. "Also, don't lose sight of the curfew. Give yourself plenty of time to get back."

It was impossible for Dean to extricate himself from the understaffed hospital in Biên-Hoà, so I left alone on an early chopper to

Tân-Sơn-Nhất. At 3rd Field, the official business was carried out promptly and without a hitch, and by noontime I was in a taxi on the way to Mme Yvonne's. As I watched the street scene drift by outside the open windows, it crossed my mind how these field trips to Sài-Gòn had become much lonelier in recent months. Of the original Three Musketeers plus Bob, only I had had opportunities to return lately, and even then I never knew which remaining friends I'd get to see again. Sad but true, continual change had become the only invariable in our lives, a reality made clear by how fast our own close-knit circle had shrunk.

I breathed with relief when Mme Yvonne's familiar face peered out from behind the wrought-iron gate moments after I rang the bell. With Dean really swamped of late, I hadn't wanted to impose on him to telephone her ahead of my arrival.

"Hello, Yvonne. I hope it's not a problem to drop in on you like this," I said with a smile. "Last-minute arrangements, but I figured I'd take my chances."

Without a word, she stepped out in front of the gate and gave me a hug. Then, taking my hand, she pulled me inside and closed the gate behind us.

"Roger, *chéri*. It's so good to see you," she said in her singsong voice as she led me between the vine-covered walls into the lush garden. "I was just about to call Dr. Dean. Come, darling. Have a seat here, in your favorite spot in the shade. Let me run get you some cold lemonade. *Mon pauvre*—poor guy. You must be dying of thirst in this heat."

I dropped down on the garden chair at our regular table under the bougainvillea. Stretching my legs, I leaned back, rested my eyes behind my sunglasses. The air was fragrant with jasmine and enlivened by an unusual sound, the only sound in this serene tranquility, so lovely yet so foreign these days: the happy chirping of birds in the trees.

My memory flashed back to our first time here with Dick. What a delightful surprise to stumble on this incredible oasis right in the

244 C. L. Hoàng

heart of Sài-Gòn—not merely a safe haven from the horrors of war, but an outright happy place where guests were encouraged to check all worries and burdens at the gate. I could still hear the music of Henry Mancini, mingled with gay voices and laughter and the merry clinking of glasses. But most of all, I remembered the raspy voice of Vivienne welcoming us as she leaned against the back of Dick's chair, her hands resting on his shoulders. A lifetime ago.

"You look relaxed, dear. I'm so glad," said Mme Yvonne, returning with a small tray with two glasses on it. She didn't see my eyes closed behind the dark shades.

I sat up. "What was it you were going to call Dean about?"

"Here, darling. Let me know if you need more sugar. À votre santé—to your health."

We clinked glasses. She sat back, her eyes averted from mine while she took a slow sip from her perspiring glass, then another, before setting her glass down.

"I wanted to bid adieu to you all, but his is the only number I have," she blurted out.

I froze, my glass to my lips, not trusting that I'd heard right.

She turned to me with a wan smile. "It's a shock, n'est-ce-pas? I know. I cannot believe it myself. Bill has just finished his contract last week, and he wants to move back to the States. No more extension this time. He has lived here five years now and he has been feeling homesick for some time. Besides, he's nervous that Sài-Gòn isn't safe anymore." She looked down at her hands now folded in her lap. "I told him, it's decided then. As his wife, I want to do what makes him happy. And wherever he goes, I shall go with him."

I swallowed hard. "How soon are you moving? Jesus, Yvonne. And where to?"

"In two weeks, before the end of May. We have given notice to the landlord." There was a hint of anxiousness in her voice. "Bill was from Atlanta, Georgia, so that's where we're headed. The Peach State, I was told it's called. Sounds very pretty. How far is it from your home state? Maybe you can come visit us, *oui*?"

"Clear across the continent from me, but it's only a few hours' flight," I said, trying to smile. "It's a big move for you, Yvonne. Are you ready for it?"

She looked at me pensively before answering. "I *am* a little bit scared, to be honest with you. All my life I have never set foot outside Sài-Gòn, you know, and now I am moving halfway around the world to a foreign country. How crazy is that?" She laughed softly, shaking her head in disbelief. "So yes, I got butterflies in my stomach. But the way I see it, Roger, my home is by my husband's side. It doesn't matter where we live, as long as we are together. At least over there we won't have to fear the rockets."

"To great adventure, and a wonderful new life in America." I lifted my glass to her while doing my best to keep my mixed feelings in check. "I'm sure everything will work out just fine. The best to you and Bill. No one deserves it more."

She smiled gratefully, but her eyes were red. "You probably heard about my papa. I have never given up hope that some day he will come back for me. It's the one thing that has sustained me through the years. But once I leave the country now, that dream is dead. There will be no way for my daddy to track me down. It will be like saying good-bye to my past. You know, burying it forever. It's hard . . ."

I reached across the table, took her hand in mine. Together we shared her sadness in silence. In the rising afternoon heat, even the carefree birds had quieted.

After a while, she went on. "It's not easy to leave all my friends either. Many have worked here with me a long time, now they must find a new job somewhere else. That is one more thing weighing on my mind. Oh Roger, I really dread the next two weeks. There will be a lot of crying. You know how we girls are."

"You haven't told anyone?"

"Nobody knows yet, except—" She caught herself and looked away.

I waited, then decided to press her. "Except—Lee Anne?"

There was a soft sigh. "Yes, Lee Anne." Mme Yvonne turned back to me, her eyes full of apologies. "I have been waiting for just the right moment to tell you, *mon ami*."

I felt the breath knocked out of me. *What now?*

Mme Yvonne rotated her chair to face me. Filtered sunlight through the arbor dappled her hair and features. Despite the shade, the mugginess was oppressive. A summer storm must be blowing in, as announced by rumblings of thunder in the distance. Or was it a B-52?

"She and her family have left the city. She asked me to say good-bye to all of you for her."

That was all I heard. Mme Yvonne's lips were still moving, but my brain had seized up.

I sat dumbfounded, staring ahead without seeing.

"Why?" I mumbled after some time.

"Sorry you had to hear about it this way, my friend," Mme Yvonne ventured. She waited a minute before continuing. "They had to sell the house after the funeral. Just could not afford to keep it anymore. I offered to help, but it would only delay the inevitable. So they have gone to stay with relatives outside the capital."

"Where? Is it far from here? I can help them, Yvonne."

There was no answer for a while. And then she locked eyes with me, and I saw hopelessness in hers. "They are in mourning, Roger," she said slowly, agony in her voice. "Her parents still don't know she worked here before, and she wants to shield them from any more stress so they can all cope with their grief. Only then can she hope to start over and try to build a new life for herself—for all of them. It is best to leave them be. *C'est la vérité*—it's the truth."

I stared blankly at her, not understanding what she was saying. "Surely you must have a new address for her. I just want to keep in touch. Maybe send them something."

Her eyes welled up. "*Mon pauvre ami*—my poor friend . . . Lee Anne knew you might ask, so she made me promise not to divulge it. You have done so much to help her already, and she said she cannot thank you enough. There's simply no way for her to return your kindness except to wish you and your family the best of everything when you go back home." Then she repeated in a shaky voice that sounded almost pleading, "Just leave them be, *chéri*. It is for the best."

Darts of pain stabbed me all along my spine.

So. This was it. The sudden end for us. It was all over when here I'd thought we were just getting started. The bewildered look on my face must have been painful to watch, for Mme Yvonne turned away. I struggled to pull myself together.

After a long silence while I strained to gather my thoughts, I took off my watch and pushed it across the table toward her. "Do me this favor, Yvonne, as a friend. This is my gift to Lee Anne and her family. Please accept it for them since you won't give me their address to send it to. It isn't much, but it's the only thing of value I've got. I want them to have it."

It was a Rolex Oyster my parents had bought me as a special gift on my graduation from medical school. It must have cost them a pretty penny, but they'd wanted to mark the occasion with me. "To celebrate your leaving the ranks of starving students," my father had said with a laugh, watching my mom strap it on my wrist. "And becoming a starving intern instead?" I'd retorted, deeply touched to see them so proud and happy for me. And the watch hadn't left my wrist since.

Mme Yvonne gasped when she saw it. "*Oh, non, non. Absolument pas.* I cannot possibly accept this. Lee Anne will be mad at me if I do. It is way too much gift, darling."

"It's not for you, so you can't refuse it. Please. It's a little something to help them out. You of all people should know they need all the help they can get."

And I'm sure you guys would understand, Mom and Dad.

Before Mme Yvonne could protest further, I excused myself to go wash my hands.

———⌒⌒———

Truth was, I wanted a few minutes in private to revisit the indoor lounge where I'd first met Lee Anne, but the place looked in a state of disarray. All the furniture had been pushed back against the walls to make room for moving boxes, and the floor was littered with miscellaneous items in various stages of getting packed. It was hopeless to try to see past this clutter and imagine again the happy scene of earlier days. Change, irrevocable change, had already set in, well underway to erase all traces of our Shangri-La.

I didn't so much as glance at the closed office door across from the bathroom, for fear of reopening wounds and compounding the hurt. Splashing cold water on my face, I fought to hold on to my last shred of self-composure. It would be most inappropriate to get emotional on Mme Yvonne when she herself was already in turmoil about her big move. Besides, seeing how she seemed unaware of the secret between Lee Anne and me, it might be wise for me to show restraint and not to reveal any more than I could help. Looking in the mirror, I told myself to buck up and put on my best face so we could enjoy our last moments together.

She must have thought likewise, for there was music in the air when I returned to the garden, a piece I'd never heard before.

Guessing my question, she smiled and explained. "We always listened to American music when we had guests here before. Today I want to share with you some music of my youth. This is a French song that was all the rage when I was still at the Lycée. 'Le Temps de l'Amour' by Françoise Hardy, my favorite singer. I love her voice, so tender and melancholy."

She started singing along in a hushed voice, but soon choked up and had to quit. "The song is about that special time in our lives, 'the time of love,' when our hearts were young and alive, and filled with dreams. As you can see, it gets me very emotional every time."

With a sweet smile, she got up from her chair and glided over to mine. "If I'm not mistaken, I have never had the honor of dancing with you, Dr. Connors. Could this be my lucky day?"

I stood and offered her my hand. "The honor's all mine, dear lady. Watch out for my two left feet, though."

And so we slow-danced, there on the soft green grass under the arbor, for the remainder of the song and the album. Neither of us said a word as the music worked its magic and transported us back to happier days. Together, in our thoughts, we were bidding farewell to the past.

When the music stopped, Mme Yvonne stood on the tips of her shoes and planted a peck on my cheek. Her face was damp with tears. "For the good times, dear friend. May God bless you," she whispered in my ear before we separated and made our way back to the table.

In silence, we sat and drank the last of the lemonade.

"Next time we meet again, it'll be in the Big Peach, I suppose," I finally said with a forced smile, hurrying to add when I saw the quizzical look on her face, "That's Atlanta's nickname."

"Ah, so much I need to learn about Atlanta." She pulled her shoulders up in frustration. "Lee Anne loaned me her copy of *Gone with the Wind*, but I haven't had time to read it yet."

It must be the same book I'd given to Lee Anne as a gift last Christmas. It dawned on me right then just how futile it would be to try to escape from all the memories of her.

I scribbled down my APO address for Mme Yvonne. "I'm here for a couple more months, but they'll forward my mail in any case. Drop me a line when you're all settled into your new home. Let me know how you're doing. I want pictures, too. Okay?"

We rose. She took my hands, gave them a squeeze. "Be safe, Roger. Thanks for everything. Send Dean and Richard my love." Her final hug said all that hadn't been said.

She stood at the gate and watched as I crossed the street on my way to the Conservatory to catch a cab. When I heard the wrought-iron gate clank shut behind me, I slowed to a stop and turned. For one last time, my eyes lingered over the arbor of orange hibiscus that hung above the gate like a big welcome sign, the sight of which from the street had always hastened my step and filled my heart with excitement. Already hidden from view behind this rustic entrance was my one sanctuary from a world gone berserk—now forever sealed off and entombed with the past.

As I resumed my course, my eyes went blurry and my face felt wet. The rain had started to fall.

Chapter Twenty

As reality began to sink in, I slipped into a blue funk.

With two months to go until my DEROS and a heavy load weighing on my mind, I decided to forgo my last chance for R&R while also toying with the idea of extending for another half-year. Besides the lure of an early exit from the USAF upon my return to the States, it would give me time to track down my friend Dick and enlist his help in locating Lee Anne and her family. Or so my thinking went, until I awoke in the night with Mme Yvonne's plea ringing loud and clear in my ear: "Please leave them be, dear. It is for the best." Whatever Lee Anne's reasons— family obligations, or concern for social stigmas and biases in her traditional culture—there was no ambiguity as to her wishes. She had requested to be left alone with her parents.

Much as it pained me, it seemed the only right thing to do: to respect her decision and not pile on to the extraordinary burden already on her shoulders. I wanted desperately to help make life more tolerable for her and her parents, but not to the point of intruding on their privacy and causing them more stress or trouble. Do no harm, first and foremost, was the golden rule here. Overriding my own desire to see her again was my sincere concern for their well-being, and in particular, their safety. Now that they'd moved out of the capital to the less secure suburbs or countryside, any contact with Americans would surely attract unwanted attention.

As if to highlight this very point, Charlie returned to launch another wave of attacks on Sài-Gòn during the closing days of May, no doubt in the hope of scoring more cheap points against civilian targets. Once again death and terror ruled parts of the city, and I could only imagine how much more perilous it was for those living outside the capital. Totally in the dark concerning the safety of Lee Anne and her family, I buried myself in work in an attempt to keep the worries at bay. But like the stealthy enemy, they crawled out at night and haunted my dreams, waking me in sweat-drenched terror in the small hours of the morning. Paul never made a fuss over it, though I'd be surprised if he didn't think Three-o-clock Charlie had gotten the best of me.

In the midst of this ongoing madness, the news of Robert Kennedy's assassination in early June dropped like a bombshell on a nation already in turmoil, a scant two months after Martin Luther King Jr.'s own violent death. The sweltering summer appeared to careen out of control, and even the coolest of heads began to wonder.

Dean and I, with The Kid tagging along sometimes, still met at the club after work for an occasional drink or smoke. But long since gone were the ready laughter and excitement that used to precede our past weekend jaunts. Though we never discussed it, we both realized the curtain had fallen on that happy phase in our lives. For good.

One night before lights-out, Paul brought up the subject for the first time. The news had all been about General Abrams replacing General Westmoreland as US Commander in Việt-Nam come July 1st, and we'd been discussing it when Paul dropped the question. "You really haven't said much, but aren't you on the home stretch yourself? Will I get a new hooch mate soon?"

"Can't wait, can you?" I teased him. "I considered extending, but in the end decided not to. I'm following Westy home in a month's time. The final paperwork arrived just days ago."

"With your orders stateside, too? Where are you serving out the rest of your two years?"

"Mather AFB, outside Sacramento," I said. "It's a few hours' drive from my folks. Then another ten months and I'll be out of the Air

Force. Hopefully forever. Can't remember what life was like as a civvie."

There was a touch of envy in his voice. "Any plans for your thirty-day leave?"

"Haven't given it a thought. It hasn't really hit me yet." That was the truth, my mind having been consumed by yearning for Lee Anne. "But I'll start boxing up my junk and have it shipped home ahead of me. Any books, magazines or what-not you want me to leave with you?"

Paul shook his head. "How about we exchange helmets? I want your lucky steel pot."

I picked up my dented helmet, set it squarely in his lap. "Done. It's yours. May it ward off bad luck and keep you out of harm's way, as it did me."

He flashed his boyish grin in response.

One afternoon about two weeks out from the day, Dean poked his face inside my office door and signaled me to take five. He had on his tiger-striped jungle fatigues and floppy hat, which meant he either had just returned from the boonies or was on his way out.

"I don't recall when's your big day, so I wanted to stop by and see you before we head out to camp," he said as we plopped down at our regular table in the corner at the club. "A Falstaff for you as usual? Drinks on me, kiddo."

For a while we carried on small talk over the beers, both of us careful not to bring up any names of our Vietnamese friends. No point going there and getting mired in nostalgia. I dropped a dime in the jukebox and hit a random select button, and by pure chance the sparkling sound of Paul Mauriat's "Love Is Blue" came pouring out. This had been one of Elise's most requested piano pieces when it was still a little-known French hit called "L'Amour Est Bleu." For fleeting minutes, the familiar music swooped us up and carried us, despite ourselves, back to those innocent days.

When the final note evaporated in the dusty air, Dean let out a long exhale and pulled himself up, breaking loose from the short-lived spell.

"You been following the news on the home front lately?" he asked.

I nodded, not sure what he was driving at.

"Then you know how strong the antiwar movement has grown all across the country, especially in your home state. I hope you're not expecting a welcoming band at the airport. You're landing at Travis near San Francisco, right?"

Another nod. It began to dawn on me where all this was going.

"You might want to forewarn your family then. In case they're meeting you off the plane. Beware of protesters picketing outside the main gate. Most likely they'll try to harass you about your service in country. Ignore them, man. Just get the hell out of there as fast as you can." He pinched between his eyebrows. "The passion's boiling over out there. People have gone crazy with anger and frustration."

"Has it gotten that ugly?" I asked. "Are we the bad guys now? Perhaps I should tell my family to just wait at home, let me catch the bus back. No way I want them subjected to that spectacle. It'll be very upsetting to them, not to mention unsafe."

Dean tapped out a cigarette and offered it to me. It was a Ruby Queen, the favorite smoke among his native CIDG buddies. When I declined, he lit it himself and took a long drag.

"I heard incredible stories from guys just gone back recently," he said. "Many were booed and hissed and called 'baby killers.' Some were spat on, if you can believe it. Others had their AWOL bags ripped out of their hands. In some instances, the mob even hurled rocks and red paint at their cars as they pulled out of the gate. Great fucking way to welcome home your war veterans, eh?"

I stared at him, incredulous. How in the hell—how had we come to this?

"Maybe I'll change my mind and extend for a while," I mumbled at last, half serious. "Not sure how anxious I am to go home now and face that music."

"Sorry, bud. Just thought I'd prepare you so it won't hit you between the eyes when you step off the plane. The times they are a-changing. But it'll do no good to rearrange your life because of it."

My thoughts flashed back to Bob and the ultimate sacrifice he and his family had made. How would they have felt in the current toxic atmosphere? I cringed and hastily pulled back from this train wreck of thought.

"Got to ask you a favor," I said, removing Dick's key from my wallet. "Can you return this to Hayashi? I doubt I'll see him before I leave. It's a damned shame. Would've been nice to have the latest news of him for his folks in Lone Pine."

Dean stuck the key in his back pocket. "There's a man with a mission—more like a death wish—ever since the tragedy with Vivienne." He drew a sharp breath, apparently unaware he'd just broken our tacit agreement not to mention our Vietnamese friends. "I heard he's been trying to sneak into remote hamlets to document Charlie's war crimes against civilians. Even SF guys don't venture in those places. Not without serious backup. The kid's out of his mind."

It struck me again how things had changed for all of us in one short year. One by one, we had become swallowed up in our own maelstrom of tragedies, yanked apart from one another in different directions, each tumbling headlong toward his unknown destiny while the others watched helplessly. An anecdote Lee Anne had told me that afternoon long ago as we were strolling in the shade of poinciana trees suddenly popped back in my mind.

We'd been discussing the difficult lot befallen her people throughout their long history and how they'd always seemed to find the resilience to cope with it.

"There is no secret there," she'd tried to explain. "We just do our best then let the—chips fall? How do you say—wherever they fall? In the end, it is all about destiny. Nobody can foresee or explain it." She had then smiled at me. "We have a nickname for 'Fate' in Vietnamese. *Con Tạo*. Can you guess what it means?"

"The Crazy One?" I said.

She raised her eyebrows in surprise. "You are close. Word for word, *Con Tạo* means 'Child Providence.' You see, through the ages our elders have always compared Fate to a fickle child at play, with us mortals its playthings. There is something to that, don't you think?"

Her words had struck a chord with me back then, but they took on an even more prophetic and personal meaning on this somber night.

I turned to Dean. "Guess I won't mention any of Dick's daredevilry to his family at home. It would just make them worry sick. And you, too, Captain. Take care of yourself. Stop pressing your luck all the time. It's bound to give at some point."

As we stood, Dean reminded me, "If I'm not back before you go, leave me a note at Woodson Compound with your contact info. I'd like to keep in touch."

On our way to the door, I noticed with concern the catch in his step. "That ankle still bothering you after all these months?" I asked.

"Nothing a little therapy can't fix," he said. "Just a matter of taking the time for it."

We stopped outside the club in the deepening twilight. He squeezed my hand in an iron clasp. "I get it's been no camping trip for you in Việt-Nam. But you came, and you done good. I'm proud of you, guy." Before I could react, he clutched me closer and gave me the briefest of bear hugs. "We'll see each other again, I hope. One way or another."

Dean had never been one to demonstrate his emotions, so his thoughtful words and action caught me by surprise and touched me deeply. At the same time they also brought home the sobering realization that the end was indeed upon me. I was going home. For real.

As I stood there—dumbstruck, my breath caught in my throat— he pivoted on his heels and limped off, his hand still raised in a farewell salute.

That was the last I saw of Dean "the Lonely" Hunter.

⌒

In my final days at Biên-Hoà, Paul kept me close company as if to save me from spending too much time alone, and we hung out together even more than we already had. It was a comfortable routine I gladly settled into since it helped to keep my mind off the coming big change. Starting with a dinner of cheeseburgers at the club right after work, we'd hang around long enough for Paul to watch Bobbie "the Weather Girl" Keith perform her nightly gags on Channel 11. Along with all the fellows in the club, he'd stay glued to the tube until the end of the show when she purred her signature signoff, "Until tomorrow, have a pleasant evening, weatherwise and, you know, of course, otherwise." On that cue her fans erupted in uproarious laughter, whooping and hollering their approval as the blond, mini-skirted weather girl grooved to the music from the Box Tops' hit single "The Letter."

"She's hysterical, isn't she? And easy on the eye, too," Paul once remarked, immediately blushing at his own effusion. "Sometimes I forget I can still laugh like this."

Amen, I thought.

From the club, we'd step next door to the movie theater that doubled as a house of worship on the weekend and catch whatever was being shown that evening, usually a rerun of a John Wayne western or some old Bob Hope comedy. Most of the time we could not even hear the audio, which was muffled by jets taking off from the nearby runway or trucks rumbling past out in front. But that didn't bother us in the slightest since we already knew the stories by heart. It was more about just letting the visuals lull our brains into temporary respite.

After the movie, we'd return to the club for a nightcap beer before lights-out. Paul would make me listen to his new jukebox favorite,

Steppenwolf's "Born to Be Wild," over and again until I could no longer stand it and had to insist we leave. It was a surprising departure from his bedtime standard, "Green, Green Grass of Home," and seemed out of character with the squeaky-clean image that had earned him his nickname. But then it might simply have been a manifestation, in his case, of that pervasive change we all underwent in Việt-Nam.

As mundane as this nightly routine appeared in retrospect, it served its useful purpose at the time, filling the hours and the void in my heart. Until bedtime, that was. Alone in the dark, I faced my past and my future as I pondered the consequences of my actions while sounding my own motives and innermost feelings. With Lee Anne gone, the future stretched empty and unclear before me. One thing was certain, however: I could no longer return to the way it used to be with Debbie after all that had happened. Only days from being reunited with loved ones whom I hadn't seen in a year, I was racked with secret guilt for finding so little comfort in the occasion. Instead, a sense of doom sprung over me as I knew I was about to fly straight into a storm—the biggest crisis of my life.

Adding to the building tension, my final days didn't go without a hitch.

Forty-eight hours before my scheduled flight, I finished out-processing and went to pick up my boarding pass only to discover I had been bumped.

"Sorry, Lieutenant. Last-minute reassignment," the old sergeant at the desk said. "It'll be another couple days. Or you can hitch a ride on a Graves Registration flight to Bangkok any day of the week, then switch planes over there. Many folks go that route if they can't wait."

I assured him I could.

On my last day, I was granted time off to tend to loose ends. Around noontime, all packed and with nothing left to do, I checked out an Air Force-blue cracker box to go for a drive. One final spin around this windswept dirt bowl I'd called home for the past year—and then, adios.

Without a thought in mind, I drove to the open area on the north side where Bob had taken me before. A shower had cleansed the air and dispersed the clouds, revealing the bluest of skies. In bright daylight, the remote site did not appear nearly as forbidding as I'd remembered. There was even a feeling of peace and serenity about it, reminiscent of the mountain meadows at home in late summer. I pulled off the road and hopped out. Squinting to the northwest, I located the hillock with the small pagoda, or what was left of it, perched on top. During Tết, the Việt-Cộng had used the temple as a surveillance post to coordinate their attacks on the base. Army gunships had retaliated with heavy firepower and demolished the old structure, causing an outcry among some in the press. From where I now stood, the charred ruins showed like the carcass of a downed bird of prey.

Judging from the surroundings, I must have been near the spot where Bob and I had parked and talked that evening—a lifetime ago, it seemed, when death and tragedy hadn't yet tainted our personal world. In a flood, memories burst forth that had been carefully stowed away all these months, as vivid and poignant as if from yesterday.

Wide open fields of reed and elephant grass extended on both sides of the road, stretching well beyond the barbed-wire fences along the north border to the encroaching jungle on the outskirts. I wandered off from the road and waded into the tall grass, which came up to my chest. The setting resembled countless landing zones all over South Việt-Nam. I imagined myself jumping from the skid of a hovering slick, then scrambling through the grass for cover as intense enemy fire zinged past my head. Would I be among the slow-footed kids who never reached safety behind the trees, immediately mowed down on their first time out? The last images they'd glimpse of this earth as their stunned faces hit the mud would be of these long, thin blades of elephant grass swaying gently in the sun.

So much death. Brutal, obscene death—with no rhyme, reason, or justice. My brain reeled off the list of its recent victims and their loved ones within my small circle of friends and acquaintances: Lee Anne's husband; Elise's father; Vivienne; Bob; the MEDCAP team; Joey. Most of them cut down in the prime of youth. All with so much yet to live for.

I thought of Bob. How he'd be missing out on all the milestones in Ricky's life. His first baby step, first spoken word, first day in school, first Little League game . . . Fuck. The man had never even had a chance to rock his newborn son and sing him to sleep with "Puff, the Magic Dragon." It had all been stripped from him when it was still just a fantasy of happiness.

I slumped to the ground on one knee amid the tall grass—face buried in hands, my body crumpled under the strain of emotions. Ignoring the tropical sun beating down on my neck and the palpable heat rising in waves from the red swamp, I said a prayer in my heart for my departed friends and comrades. Then, at long last, I bade good-bye to this mysterious and tortured land whose destiny had been entwined with mine over the past twelve months.

Next morning, at 0600 hours, Paul drove me to the passenger "terminal," a makeshift structure under a tin roof right off the parking apron by the runway. It was still dark, with streaks of pink and orange barely piercing the eastern skies. The temperature was almost pleasant.

"Hallelujah. You made it, champ." Paul gave me a hearty slap on the back. "Remember the time the debarkation barracks got hit by a pair of 122s?" Indeed I did. How could I forget the kids bunking there that night, who had just completed their tours and were waiting to fly home the next day? Many of them had been killed or maimed in their sleep, mere hours away from safety and freedom. It was a tragedy of the most perverse nature. I heard relief in Paul's voice. "I was so nervous Charlie might pull a dirty trick like that on your last night here."

"Would've been my time then, wouldn't it. Might as well go out with a bang, I've always said." The bravado fell flat, but in truth, there was nothing anyone could have done to prevent such a disaster anyway, and we both knew it.

Paul pulled up in front of the building. I jumped out, grabbed my travel bag.

"If you ever find yourself in my neck of the woods, look me up, will you?" he said, for the umpteenth time. "I'll even drive a couple of hours to come see you, if necessary."

I felt bad, having not made a commitment of any sort with him although we'd exchanged contact information earlier. It had nothing to do with him personally. Just a reflection of my own suspicion of what the future might hold. After all, hadn't Bob and I tempted fate before when we'd jumped the gun and made similar plans for the future? So why risk jinxing it for Paul by repeating the same mistake?

"You betcha," I mumbled while avoiding his eyes.

Paul scurried around to my side to sneak a peek inside the terminal. The place was already teeming with guys in fresh uniforms, all waiting to board the same flight at 0650 hours.

"I recognize some gunship pilots in there," he announced excitedly. "You'll get a proper send-off for sure. Keep your eyes on the windows."

I smiled. In farewell to their comrades flying home, the Assault Helicopter guys sometimes flew escort for the outbound jetliner along the taxiway, in flights of two on either side of the aircraft. It was good to see Paul so taken with these traditions of military camaraderie rather than being obsessed with death and danger.

I pumped his hand. "You'll do just fine, I'm sure. Your day will come before you know it. Hang tough, buddy."

As Paul took off in his jeep, waving back at me in the rear-view mirror, a small convoy of empty buses pulled in. Minutes later, the gate at the terminal's far end swung open. New arrivals filed into the building and were directed to the idling buses. As the nervous newbies passed through the terminal, all the waiting passengers stood and clapped with loud cheers. Their Freedom Bird had arrived with their replacements, and any moment now they'd be allowed to board and begin that long journey home they'd been dreaming about since day one.

I gazed at these new kids in their brand-new uniforms and recognized my own ghost from a year ago. Jetlagged, lost, scared witless of the hostile unknown, and still brimming with innocence, not yet having stared death in the eye. The one striking difference was their remarkable youth, for most of them appeared fresh out of high school. They had a lot of growing up to do in a hurry, if only for a decent chance at survival. My stomach knotted as I couldn't help but wonder how many would make it back here in one piece a year from now, and then, if those lucky ones could pick up their old lives where they'd left off.

After the newbies were gone, our boarding began in earnest. We lined up by numbers and filed through the gate onto the tarmac, making a beeline for the Bird with the Golden Tail, a sleek Continental Airlines Boeing 707 that shimmered in early sunlight. Around me, men were all grins. Clambering up the ramp, somebody ahead of me pumped his fist and shouted at full throat, "Fini, Việt-Nam!" to more cheers and whistles.

It took a few minutes for all to settle and buckle up. Then the door closed and the plane rolled away from the apron. It taxied past rows of concrete revetments where the war birds were parked before turning onto the runway. I peered out the windows. No signs of helicopter escort off either wing as Paul had anticipated. The chopper pilots must have gone out on company sorties and not made it back in time to see their comrades off.

After a momentary pause, our pilot poured on the power. An electric silence descended over the passengers as the jetliner accelerated down the bumpy runway. It dipped and bounced a few times, then with a sudden lift swept into the air. Outside the windows, the earth tumbled away in a dizzying flash of colors: the deep-red soil of Biên-Hoà; the luxuriant shades of green in the triple-canopy jungle surrounding the base; the mirror ponds from a checkerboard of rice paddies; and, slithering eastward toward the blue Pacific, the silver snake of the Đồng-Nai River.

Way down there, beneath the monsoon clouds, somewhere on that cursed land that I had grown strangely attached to, Lee Anne and her parents struggled all on their own.

My mouth was pasty. I felt depleted and hollow inside, almost nauseous.

In that surreal moment thousands of feet above ground, with the morning sun slanting in my eyes, the plain truth hit me square in the chest and sent me spiraling down a pit of despair.

I was going home, but my heart remained behind—with my lost true love.

Just then the cheerful pilot came on the PA to announce that we had reached altitude and were now free to get up and move about as we wished. The cabin erupted in huge cheers and applause. We had officially made it, safe and secure beyond the range of anti-aircraft artillery, once and for all extricated from the claws of war. The boys were coming home. For certain.

And so it was—finally, and truly—good-bye, Việt-Nam.

The end of the road. For better or worse.

I turned to the window for quiet and privacy.

Grown men don't cry, least of all on a grand occasion like today.

PART III

"All Passion Spent"*

California
July 1968 – September 1999

*John Milton (1608-1674)

Chapter Twenty-One

Coming home was a bittersweet experience.

In a twisted kind of way, it reminded me of a famous Vietnamese legend, the legend of Từ-Thức Lee Anne told me one Sunday afternoon in Mme Yvonne's garden. According to this ancient folktale, the mandarin Từ-Thức one day resigned his post and went hiking into the mountains. While trekking the wilderness, he stumbled upon Thiên-Thai, the mythical Land of Bliss, and was invited by the gentle folks who lived there to stay for as long as he wished. After an extended visit, however, Từ-Thức grew homesick and took leave of his hosts to make his way down the mountains. A great surprise awaited him back in town: the people and scenery had changed to the point of being unrecognizable, as if he had wandered into a different world. Upon inquiring around, he was astounded to discover he had actually been gone for a very long time. More than a hundred years, in the earthly calendar.

Although I'd be hard pressed to call a war-ravaged Việt-Nam the Land of Bliss, I nevertheless could relate to that feeling of being ill adjusted, even lost, after my return. Like a wanderer just back from a hundred years in the wilderness.

In my case, the external landscape had remained as immutable as the majestic mountains in whose shadows I had been born. But there was no doubt I had come home a changed man, and right into the boiling atmosphere of a nation in full-blown crisis.

Just as Dean had warned me, we ran smack into a crowd of agitated war protesters when my father drove his 1963 Impala station wagon out the front gate of Travis AFB. Fortunately for us, they were chasing and shouting after a big bus ahead of our car and hardly took notice of us. The bus was transporting a load of freshly repatriated servicemen to the San Francisco Airport, where they'd continue on the final legs of their flights home.

Save for that tense, awkward moment at the gate, which everybody in my family did their best to put behind us, my homecoming brought great excitement and joy to all, in particular, my mother and Debbie. While my parents and older brother spoke over one another during the trip home, Debbie seemed content just to sit next to me in the back seat, quiet and serene, her hand nestled in mine. Between all the questions and answers, I peeked over at her and caught her glancing my way with a smile. *It's so good to have you home again*, her sparkling eyes seemed to whisper to me.

Looking back on this confusing period of my life, I couldn't be more grateful to my mom for noticing straight away how out of sorts I really was. In her subtle, thoughtful way, she made sure I was allowed breathing room from well-meaning friends and neighbors who stopped by to welcome me back. With infinite care and patience, through countless homey details around the house, she worked hard to get things back to normal quickly for me.

As the tourist season reached its peak in late summer, my parents and Jerry had their hands full running our family's bed-and-breakfast. Yet they wouldn't hear of my sticking around to lend them an extra hand.

"Take Debbie camping with you," Jerry urged me one evening during dinner at the kitchen table. "In case you forgot already, it's springtime up in Tuolumne Meadows. But you better hurry. The wildflower show only lasts a couple more weeks at most."

"You kids can borrow Mom's Polaroid camera, if you want," my dad chimed in. "It really takes great pictures. You saw the ones we sent you."

My mother waited until they left the table to make her own suggestion. "Why don't you take my car and drive up to Bishop and spend time with Debbie?" she mentioned casually. "I'm sure she's made arrangements at the hospital to take time off to be with you. Your home leave will be over before long, and she's been real sweet to let us have our time with you first."

I promised Mom to heed her advice just as soon as I made it over to the Hayashis and said hello to them, the least I could do for Dick and his family.

It was a relief when Suzy Hayashi answered the door. She'd always been my favorite in Dick's family since she was closest in age to us—only two years older, or the same age as Jer—but mainly because she had always seemed congenial and easy-going, despite the ever-looming specter of Manzanar in the family's history.

Her almond-shaped eyes opened wide when she recognized me. "Roger Connors. What a nice surprise. I heard you were back from Việt-Nam." She stepped aside and invited me in.

We visited in the dim-lighted living room that looked out on a small inner courtyard. After Suzy inquired about my service time at Biên-Hoà, our conversation turned to Dick.

"My parents always complain he doesn't write home often enough," she said.

As a result, Dick's family had remained largely in the dark as to his activities. In fact, I wasn't sure if they even knew about his sojourn at 3rd Field, so I avoided the topic altogether.

"He's not the only guilty party," I admitted with a smile. "I've been accused of such an offense myself. Not to make an excuse for us, but there's always so much happening over there. It's pointless to burden you folks at home with all the details and cause you more concern. Rest easy, though. Last time I saw him, back in April, he was doing just fine."

"We all worry about Dick, but it's worst for my parents," Suzy spoke softly, a touch of melancholy in her voice. "You really can't blame them. He's their only boy and the baby in the family. You know how he always pushes to get out in front, to prove himself, no matter what danger. So anytime we don't hear from him for more than two weeks, which is more often than not, my parents get all stressed out."

Her face, partially hidden behind a cascade of long black hair, angled away from me, toward the sun-dappled courtyard. We fell silent, staring out at a garden of dwarf Japanese pine trees and maples accentuated with miniature bamboos.

And then, it happened.

I was suddenly back in the office at Mme Yvonne's, looking out the sliding glass door at the small patio beyond. Sitting across the desk, with her back to me, was Vivienne—poor, dear Vivienne, in the throes of agony over her long-guarded secret and her breakup with Dick. Then, in a replay of a scene from recent past, she slowly turned around, and it was Lee Anne, instead, staring back at me with mournful eyes, exactly as I'd seen her the last time. I sat transfixed, my forehead damp with cold sweat.

"Roger. Are you okay?" Suzy's anxious voice pulled me back from my trance.

I blinked—rattled by what had just come over me.

Wiping my forehead with the back of my hand, I forced a chuckle. "It's been tough to shake off the jetlag on my return. I nod off at the dining table sometimes. It's embarrassing." Then I changed the subject and proceeded to tell her about Sài-Gòn, focusing mostly on Dick's bachelor studio in the heart of the capital. We chatted a while longer before I got up to leave.

"Don't be a stranger, now," I reminded Suzy as we exchanged hugs. "Keep me posted on what's going on with our guy, will you? We didn't get to say good-bye before I left."

Done with all the excuses, I dragged myself to face my moment of truth.

My mother, as usual, was correct. Debbie had requested two weeks' vacation from the county hospital where she worked, in anticipation of our spending time together. Considerate as always, she never asked about my unexplained silence during my final months at Biên-Hoà, concentrating instead on making me feel welcome home and allowing me time to ease back into "normal life." For that, I was indebted to her.

A new routine was quickly established between us. I'd drive up to Bishop in the morning and we'd spend a nice, easy day around town, the highlight of which would be a picnic lunch in the city park. Sometimes, on the spur of the moment, we'd grab a backpack and take the scenic drive to Bishop Creek Canyon for a daylong hike amid the magnificent Sierra scenery. Back to her apartment in the evening, Debbie usually insisted on preparing my favorite home-cooked meals, but we also often dined out at a cozy eatery downtown in case we wanted to take in a movie after dinner, before I drove home for the night.

On the surface, it seemed just like the good old days. We talked about everything under the sun, as we always had, except for the one topic that mattered most—our relationship. Though she was much too nice to press the issue, Debbie must have sensed, no doubt with some bafflement, the undercurrent of my discomfort. I tensed up each time we touched, and increasingly avoided looking her in the eye. It pained me to watch her try so hard to bring me back.

As life inched back to "normal," the distance inside me grew wider.

About ten days before my home leave was to expire, I casually mentioned to Debbie that I was ready to go camping in the Sierra backcountry. We were having our picnic in the park.

"Fantastic," she exclaimed, excited as a child. "It's been a long while since we last went together. Maybe we'll be lucky and catch the wildflowers still in bloom. Is Jer joining us, too?"

272 C. L. Hoàng

I jumped on the opening.

"I'm going alone this time, Debbie." It wasn't so much the words as the tone in which they tumbled out. Even to my ear they sounded harsh, impersonal. Like a cold shoulder.

She looked at me in silence, but her brown eyes couldn't disguise the surprise and the hurt. Yet she voiced no protest or questions. Our pleasant luncheon came to an abrupt end.

"I just need some time to myself," I explained, no less clumsily, though in a softer tone.

She turned away, let her gaze escape to the lovely gazebo in the middle of the lake. And then I knew I couldn't just stop there. This was the dreadful moment I'd been bracing for, the moment of reckoning when at last I must come clean and own up to the truth.

If I was ever to go through with it, for both our sakes, it had to be now.

I cleared my throat, dry as dirt. "Deb . . . there's something I must tell you."

She slowly turned back to me, and we held each other's gaze for a long minute. As her eyes welled up, it suddenly dawned on me that she already knew. That she had known for some time now. I'd forgotten how acute her instincts had always been, how very perceptive she was. With the possible exception of my mother, nobody could read me better than Debbie.

In the end, as always with her, Debbie made it easier for me.

"You . . . haven't been the same since you got back." Her voice, barely above a sigh, was nearly drowned out by the birds' chirping. I almost missed her next question, so softly was it uttered, as if addressed to herself. "Did you meet someone over there?"

I'd often imagined there would be so much I'd want to say to her in this excruciating moment, to try to explain, to apologize. As though a torrent of words might help wash away some of the pain. But my taxed brain deserted me, and not a single word escaped from my lips.

All I could do was stare at her. Breathless. Then I nodded.

Even with my eyes now trained at the grass, I knew her heart was breaking. As was mine. There was no outburst. No hurtful confrontation. Only bone-numbing sadness. And silence.

Something died inside of us.

I lost track of time, until Debbie began to gather up the picnic stuff. "I'm going back now," she finally managed.

"I'll drive you."

I heard a stifled sob. "Please . . . don't. I'd rather walk."

In a daze I watched her go, my lifelong best friend, and wondered how I could ever forgive myself for causing her all this pain. Yet, to my dismay, I still couldn't summon the right words to say to her even as my last chance was slipping away. As she rounded the corner and disappeared from sight, I felt a gate close behind her.

Like Từ-Thức of olden days, I could no longer go home.

Ten days later, I left Lone Pine without saying good-bye to Debbie and reported to Mather AFB for my next assignment.

Chapter Twenty-Two

Had I really wished to put Biên-Hoà as far behind me as possible, I couldn't have done much better than Mather AFB outside Sacramento, California. Besides the geographical distance between them, the two bases offered striking contrasts in most every aspect, from their primary military functions to the corresponding pace of life.

As the sole aerial navigation school for the USAF, Mather was home to the 3535th Flying Training Wing, Air Training Command, and its fleet of Convair T-29 "flying classrooms." Such an environment would normally have been immune to stress and tension, if not for the base also hosting the 320th Bombardment Wing, Strategic Air Command.

On fifteen-minute nuclear alert against a sneak attack by the Soviet Union, the 320th operated a squadron of B-52 Stratofortresses and a squadron of KC-135 Stratotankers, half of which had to be kept fueled, armed, and ready for instant takeoff at all times. Many of its crews and aircraft had seen combat action in Việt-Nam during Operation Arc Light in 1965–1966, but the wing's current focus was on training and standing alert, with a rigorous regimen that nonetheless could not rival the breakneck pace of Biên-Hoà AFB.

Mather was not a war zone, and that alone made a huge difference to which my body needed time to adjust. Even after months on base, I still woke with a start throughout the night, covered in sweat and disoriented by the startling silence of my new surroundings. In the peaceful wee hours of the morning, the noise inside my head grew louder, driving me to distraction. So I began sleeping with a fan on in the background, a habit that has stuck with me to this day.

A nice surprise awaited me at Mather in the person of Captain Morgan, who'd arrived from Biên-Hoà a month earlier upon his return to the States. It was comforting to see a familiar face at my new post, someone who could relate to what I'd been through in country without the need for words. We simply picked up where we'd left off, with me still reporting to him. Never before had I felt more grateful for some continuity in my life.

Our workload at the base hospital, a cluster of old-fashioned wooden structures, was comfortable. Well staffed and equipped, we were seldom overwhelmed with emergencies the way we'd always seemed to be at 3rd Tac. With plenty of daylight left in the summer evening after work and few options for fun activities, I borrowed a page from my old hooch mate, Bob Olsen. I set a goal to learn all I could about Mather AFB, from the colorful history to its present-day strategic operation.

An often-told anecdote dated back to the final days of WWII. In June 1945, four B-29s on a top-secret mission from Wendover Field, Utah, touched down at Mather. For two days while their crews stayed on base to process paperwork for overseas duty, rumors swirled about the mysterious aircraft, then the world's largest bombers. These appeared to have been specially modified and stripped of their gun turrets, perhaps, as was whispered, to accommodate some highly sensitive cargo. The base's commanding general drove out to the birds to see for himself. He was about to climb aboard one of them when the guard on duty asked him, politely yet firmly— at gunpoint—to stop. The airman was under strict orders to shoot any unauthorized person, meaning anyone outside the 509th Composite Group in charge of the airplanes, who attempted to gain access to them. After a tense standoff, the general backed down and left—or the incident might have escalated into a major crisis with unpredictable consequences.

Months later, it came out that those bombers belonged in a fleet of fifteen special B-29s known as the Silverplates. Their crews had been stationed for over a year at Wendover Field, where they had trained in utmost secrecy to carry out the atomic bombings of Hiroshima and Nagasaki. When they made a stop at Mather Field on those summer days in 1945, the four birds in question were on their way to Tinian Island in the Pacific, from where the ultimate mission was to be launched. One of them, best known by its code name, The Great Artiste, went on to play a significant role in both bombings. Along with The Artiste, "the incident" lived on in Mather's war lore.

Even these days, the place still retained an air of mystery, particularly regarding its top-clearance Strategic Air Command operation.

Like most people who had served in Việt-Nam, I'd learned to recognize the earth-shaking rumbles of B-52 carpet bombings. But the giant aircraft, which took off from Guam or Thailand, had always remained elusive to us as they cruised at very high altitude to escape detection by the enemy. Only now at Mather did I manage a rare peek at these legendary BUFFs ("big ugly fat fellows"). Even on the ground and from a distance imposed by security, these flying wonders inspired great awe. With their long, slim fuselages, massive wingspans and proud, tall tails, they glimmered in the sunset like golden beasts at rest.

Eight out of the squadron of fifteen were on nuclear alert at all times—to conduct doomsday missions if it ever came to that. They were parked on concrete stubs at 45-degree angles to the dedicated runway, in a herringbone, or Christmas-tree, configuration. Crews and pilots stayed in alert quarters built partially below the ground surrounding each apron. A number of similar SAC bases existed across the country. Their purpose was to disperse and safeguard our arsenal of heavy bombers so as to prevent the Soviet Union from wiping out the entire fleet with a surprise first strike. After all, our very existence hinged on the outcome of this ever-looming Cold War.

As intrigued as I truly was with the tradition and tight security at Mather, I couldn't keep up my initial good intention of immersing myself in the environment, the way Bob certainly would have. After a month of giving it my best, I concluded I could never become an Air Force guy in his mold. Time and again, my mind wandered off from all things military to return to dwell on the wreckage of my private life. By no coincidence and much to my irritation, sleep had all but deserted me at night. The cumulative lack of rest began to affect my daytime functioning and job performance, as both my energy and my ability to focus sank to their lowest levels in years.

As time wore on and autumn descended on the Sierra foothills outside the base, my sleep problem only became exacerbated, and a sphere of darkness began to weigh down on me. Try as I might to dismiss it as ongoing adjustment to new conditions, deep down I couldn't quell a sense that I was about to hit bottom, physically and mentally. The realization frightened me. But like a passenger on a sinking ship with no rescue boat in sight, I could do nothing more than watch, in mute despair, as disaster unfolded.

Shortly after my arrival on base, my mail followed me there, among it a forwarded letter from Mme Yvonne addressed to my old P.O. Box at Biên-Hoà AFB. She and her husband Bill had settled down in a suburb of Atlanta called Morningside. She spoke lovingly of the house they had purchased there, her first true home—a dream she'd never hoped to see fulfilled in her lifetime. "Come visit us soon when you get back, *cher ami*," she wrote. "We will be thrilled to welcome our first guest of honor." This wonderful excitement aside, Mme Yvonne admitted to being a bit overwhelmed by her recent uprooting. The enormous change that accompanied it was a culture shock she was still learning to cope with. I also picked up, between the lines, a sense of resigned loneliness and a longing for the old country. Not once, however, did she mention any of our Vietnamese friends, maybe for fear it might open old wounds for me, or maybe to spare me dreadful news she knew I couldn't handle. To my bitter disappointment, I gleaned nothing from her letter about the welfare of Lee Anne and her parents. Like millions of nameless, faceless refugees of war over the years, they'd been engulfed in the all-consuming firestorm, most likely never to be seen or heard from again—mere entries to some meaningless statistics.

The mail also included a one-page note from Paul Nilsen, The Kid. No doubt scribbled in the last minutes before lights-out while he listened to "Green, Green Grass of Home," it brought me some latest news of Biên-Hoà. "Fewer rockets here on base," it simply stated, "but fierce fighting in War Zone C along the border. Dr. Dean has been very busy."

I'd heard about this so-called Phase 3 of Tết, launched over the second half of August 1968. The Việt-Cộng had struck several towns along the Cambodian border in addition to their favorite target, Sài-Gòn. As before, their objective had been to inflict more losses on US troops to score a political and psychological victory rather than a military one. With many Special Forces camps along the border, it was no surprise that Dean Hunter had his hands full again. I wondered how much longer his hard-pressed luck would continue to hold up.

But there was one bright spot in Paul's letter. "Do I remember right you had to cancel your trip to Penang, Malaysia, because of Tết? Well, guess what? I'm going there next week on my R&R. Beautiful place, from what I've heard. Will send you a photo of the hundred-foot-long reclining Buddha when I get back."

At least one of us gets his priorities straight, I thought wistfully.

Which was more than I could say for myself, an assessment my mother would have agreed with. She hadn't said a word about my falling out with Debbie, probably hoping that in time we could still work things out. But it was impossible to miss the sadness in her eyes the few times she and my dad drove up to see me. Debbie had always been the daughter they never had, included in all our family occasions even during my absence. In fact, the special bond between them had grown stronger this past year through their shared concern for my safety in Việt-Nam. Seeing me now without Debbie by my side had proved more difficult for my mother to handle than she could disguise.

On one of my parents' visits, a beautiful Sunday in October, I could tell something was amiss. My dad was unusually subdued, while my mom looked pale and agitated.

"What's the matter, Mom? Are you feeling all right?" I asked with apprehension.

"Suzy Hayashi stopped by yesterday," she said, reaching for my hand and squeezing it gently. "They had just received news of Dick from his bureau in Sài-Gòn. She asked us to let you know . . ."

My stomach did a flip. I sank back in the chair.

I felt my mom's arm around my shoulders as my dad's voice picked up the report. "He went to cover some big fighting and never returned. No one knows what happened to him, because there was no body found. He just went missing. But it's been weeks already, and they now suspect the worst. We're so sorry, son."

Another of my friends gone. Vanished into thin air. Swept up in the never-ending cycle of war and death. Yet somehow I'd been spared from the carnage. So that I might stay behind and mourn for them all, one by one? Numbly, I stared at my parents, unable to even ask a question. All I felt inside was sheer exhaustion. And emptiness, like nausea. I wished to just crawl in bed and go to sleep for a long, long time.

For the remainder of my parents' visit, by unspoken consent, we said nothing more of the news. Even the slightest hint of it might unhinge everybody, most of all me.

With November came the presidential election, the culmination to a tumultuous year in US politics during which antiwar sentiments rose to unprecedented level. A few days after Richard Nixon emerged victorious from a historic and contentious three-way race, a letter arrived from Dean Hunter.

Biên-Hoà AFB, 7 Nov 1968

Hello Roger,

How you doing there, kiddo? Hope you've had an easy letdown back to "The World."

You probably heard by now what happened to Dick Hayashi. You must have questions, so I'll try and fill in the gaps for you to the best of my knowledge.

You may have caught the news that we recently quashed another VC offensive, their third this year. Among their targets this round was the city of Tây-Ninh near the Cambodian border, also the seat of the Holy See of the Cao-Đài sect. During peak monsoon season in Aug/Sept, two NVA divisions attacked the city and captured a few city blocks and a Cao-Đài temple complex. They were later repelled by ARVN guys and our troops, but only after some fierce battles that dragged well into October.

Unknown to me at the time, both Dick and I were on site during that bloody stretch. Him to cover the hostage situation of the hundreds of monks and worshippers held prisoner at the temple, and me to provide medical support to SF/CIDG camps on the outskirts of town. I only found out about it long after the smoke had cleared. By then he had vanished without a trace, and has been listed as missing ever since. For all we know, he was captured during the fighting then taken across the border when Charlie retreated to Parrot's Beak inside Cambodia.

You know how hostile the Việt-Cộng feel toward investigative journalists like Dick. What they fear most is to have the cold-blooded tactics they use against their own people exposed to the free world. The same reason they executed those Reuters and AAP correspondents in Chợ-Lớn back in May, during mini-Tết. Human lives mean diddlysquat to those killers. I hate to even think it, but I fear the worst for our friend. Any hope for his survival is fast eroding with each passing day, and it's been two months since he disappeared. Searches and underground inquiries have turned up no lead so far. You know damn well I can never give up on him, yet my brain tells me we need to brace ourselves for the worst.

Sorry to be the bearer of sad news, kiddo, but I assume you'd rather hear it from me. Take good care of yourself. Be well, and be strong. You and me, we're the only two remaining in our little group from a year ago, so let's don't lose touch, okay? I'll update you immediately on any new development.

Your buddy, D.H.

Catching me at my lowest point, Dean's letter with its sober conclusion was the final blow that sent me crashing into the wall. Worse yet, it opened the floodgate to painful memories of my other losses, all carefully suppressed up until then. After reading the letter, I skipped dinner and went straight to bed. The next sunrise found me curled up under the cover in virtually the same position, with no energy or motivation to get up and going, having not caught a wink of sleep all night.

A low-grade fever, out of nowhere, further complicated the matter and kept me from work for a second straight day. At the end of it, Captain Morgan stopped by for an impromptu visit. One look at me and he decided on the spot to check me into the base hospital, which had a few open beds at the time.

"Total exhaustion, plus severe dehydration," he pronounced with a certitude that allowed no argument. "About time someone gets things under control here, since you obviously haven't."

Thus I spent the second half of November in the hospital, secluded in a room for four where I was the only occupant. I remained in bed for most of the day, dozing heavily, without dreams, under the influence of mild sedatives prescribed to combat my insomnia. Of this period of lumbering torpor, which lasted about a week, my memory was scarce and fuzzy—snatches of waking moments here and there, when I took my meals or medicine or mumbled hi to the nurse who came in to change the IV. Then slowly, as my body got caught up on much-needed rest, the fog began to lift and my waking hours grew longer.

Captain Morgan informed me he had set up a schedule for me to speak with the chief of psychiatry, a buddy of his. "Real down-to-earth fellow," he assured me. "It's nothing formal, and strictly off the record. As soon as you're back on your feet, you guys can meet and chat a couple of times a week. Doesn't have to be in his office. You can join him after hours for a walk and talk things out along the way. Get them off your chest. It can't hurt."

Reading the reluctance on my face, he put an end to the discussion. "The way I see it, it sure beats a referral to David Grant Medical Center down the highway. But they do have a number of specialty-trained psychiatrists there, if you prefer." He stood and concluded his visit. "Your choice, of course, Lieutenant. As it now stands, I'm short of one GMO. We need to get you back to work one way or another. And soon."

Having little say in the matter, but nevertheless recognizing how close I had come to a total breakdown, I acquiesced begrudgingly to my therapy sessions with the chief psychiatrist, if only to keep from getting transferred to DGMC at Travis AFB. At least at Mather, I wouldn't have to witness the twenty-four-hour frenzy of debarkation and medical airlift from Southeast Asia. Meanwhile, diligent Captain Morgan had notified my parents of my stay at the hospital, probably to make sure I received enough moral support to get me through this rough patch.

My mom and dad left Jer in charge of Moon Meadows and rushed up to see me. It was the week before Thanksgiving, just days after my hospital check-in. When they arrived, my brain was still murky from all the make-up sleep, which only added to their worries. Seeing that I needed more rest, however, they kept their visit short but promised to return the next week to celebrate the holiday with me—in grand style, courtesy of Mom's home cooking. She chatted and smiled at me the whole time, but the concern in my mother's eyes revealed what sad state I was in.

The intervening days of complete bed rest were helpful. I felt more alert, even a bit hungry, when I greeted my parents Thursday morning the following week. They trudged through the door with armfuls of big brown bags containing what I assumed to be our Thanksgiving dinner.

"You guys beat me to it," I said in the most jovial tone I could muster. "I was hoping to be up and dressed before you all got here."

They set the bags down on the side table then hurried over to give me a hug, obviously relieved to find me in a more lively state than the last time.

"There's a picnic area in the back of the building," I continued. "If you don't mind waiting while I get ready, we can move outside for some fresh air."

"Beautiful day to be outdoors," my dad concurred. "But you sure you're up to it, son?"

"I'm starting to get out, a little more each day. It feels too cooped up in here."

My parents exchanged a quick glance before Mom said, "How about Dad and I carry all the food out now, and you come join us when you're done? Take your time, though, honey." Then she had second thoughts. "Or maybe we'll wait right here. In case you need help."

I waved them away with a reassuring smile, then waited until they were gone before I began getting dressed. With my body rusty and stiff from the long slumber, it ended up more of a chore than usual. I struggled through and was all set to head out when a tentative knock on the door turned me around.

There she was, a shadow in blue just outside the doorway. Looking unsure, a small vase of flowers in her hand, she seemed like a lost child who had wandered to the wrong door.

"Deb . . ." I exhaled her name, taken aback by her unexpected appearance.

"How are you, Roger?" She emerged from the hallway's dimness into the brightly lit room, coming to a stop just beyond the entrance. "I heard you weren't feeling well . . . I—I brought you some flowers." She moved forward, set the vase on the table, then stepped back. "You must be exhausted, so I'll just wish you a speedy recovery and let you rest."

"Debbie. Please . . . won't you sit down?" I motioned to the empty bed next to mine.

She hesitated, then sat down at the foot of the bed, a short distance from where I stood.

We made eye contact.

My heart ached at how thin and weary she looked although she'd tried to conceal it with a touch of makeup and a discreet blue dress. There was no discernible resentment or bitterness in her large brown eyes. Only sadness, and genuine concern.

"You've lost a lot of weight," she whispered.

"I'm getting better, slowly but surely." I tried to smile through my parched lips. "Thank you for the flowers. It's very sweet of you."

Awkward at first but more comfortable as we went on, we attempted small talk. I found out she'd asked to come with my parents, having heard of my illness from my mother. I was deeply touched, considering what nightmare I had put her through this summer.

"You waited outside until now?" I asked.

She looked down at the floor, took a moment before answering. "I wasn't sure if it was a good idea to drop in like this. It's important now that you rest and relax. I didn't want to cause you any upset."

"You're my best friend, Deb. No matter what happens. I'm always happy to see you."

Her eyes blinked rapidly. She dropped her gaze lower.

Pulse racing, I sat down on the edge of my bed and faced her. "I'm so sorry, Debbie—"

"You don't need to go there, Roge," she interrupted, her voice quavering. "Let's not talk about that. It doesn't help your recovery."

I felt an impulse to take her hands in mine but didn't want to startle her. The thought crossed my mind that had I done so at our last picnic together, maybe I would've been able to avert some heartbreak for both of us.

Taking a deep breath, I decided to seize my second chance for atonement.

"Please let me say what I need to say, just this once. I did wrong by you, Deb. There was no excuse for it, and I don't expect you to forgive me. But take it for what it's worth. I never meant to hurt you. It wasn't anything I planned, it just . . . happened. I can't explain it. Anyway, it's over now. In fact, it ended as soon as it started. But that's neither here nor there. My biggest regret through all this craziness is that I've dragged you into it and hurt you terribly. I can't begin to tell you how sorry I am."

The words tumbled out over my ragged breathing, in my mad dash to unload the truth lest I had a change of heart. Waves of frustration and anger rose in my chest against the hopeless, absurd situation, squeezing my lungs tight and stinging my eyes. Somehow, through ironic twists and turns, it mattered none what we did or didn't do, what choices we made or failed to make. We always wound up hurting ourselves and those we cared about. Toys. We were, all of us, but toys. Nothing more than playthings in the hands of a capricious young child. All damaged and scarred, if not destroyed, sooner or later.

I got up, strode over to the window and stared out on the most glorious Thanksgiving Day one could hope for, struggling to regain my composure.

Neither of us spoke for a while, until I heard her gentle voice behind me.

"You went through an awful lot in Việt-Nam this past year, Roger. None of us at home can presume to understand. But we're here for you. To help in any way we can to make the transition easier, so you can put all the bad stuff behind you once and for all. If you're comfortable with it, I'd like to come visit you more regularly. We can talk about your experience over there—or not. It's entirely up to you. We'll always be friends no matter what, as you said. That's all we need to know right now. Let's concentrate on getting you well again. What do you say?"

At once humbled and moved by her kindness, I turned back to her with a grateful nod, barely able to get the words out. "Thanks. I'd like that very much."

"It's settled, then," she said, rising to her feet. "But I've taken up too much of your time. Your parents are waiting for you."

"You're certainly staying for dinner, aren't you?"

She hesitated. "My auntie lives near Davis. I've made arrangements to visit her—"

"Please stay," I said. "Just a little while. It's Thanksgiving."

She gave it some thought, then said, "All right. Just a quick bite. But we mustn't keep your parents waiting any longer."

As we strolled out the door, Debbie turned to me, her eyes suddenly grown misty. "I'm sorry about Dick and all your losses and pains, Roger. I wish there was a way we could bear some of the load for you."

Squinting at the bright daylight outside, I kept quiet. There had been enough explaining for one day. But for the first time since coming back from Biên-Hoà, I felt like I'd finally made it home.

Thus began my "rehab," an informal process that stretched through the holiday season of 1968. As my condition improved, I gradually resumed my responsibility as base GMO, all under the watchful eye of kind Captain Morgan.

Debbie made good on her promise. Using her remaining week of vacation, she came up to stay with her aunt and commuted every day to see me at Mather Hospital. Between her low-key visits and my daily walks with the chief of psychiatry, I started to open up about my experience in Việt-Nam and to slowly work through my feelings. But no more was said of what had taken place between Lee Anne and me, as I believed no further healing could be gained from that. For reasons unknown, Lee Anne had chosen to disappear from my life. Part of me still clung to the bittersweet memory, like one would to a beautiful dream rudely awakened, but I had come to realize it belonged to the past. And I had to move on, as best I could.

Determined to keep her word even after she'd used up her vacation, Debbie drove from Bishop to Mather AFB every other weekend to spend half a day with me. Occasionally she came with my mom and dad, but most of the time by herself. During the winter months, she took the longer southern detour to circumvent the snowy mountains. The trip was several hours each way, but come she did, just as promised.

It was a special time. A time of renewal for us. As part of rebuilding our friendship, we had to get reacquainted and learn to be comfortable with each other again. Through it all, Debbie showed amazing patience and understanding, and her steadfast support gave me a good start on my recovery road.

We went on regular walks through the greenery behind the hospital. Basked in the warm afternoon sunlight, we often felt no need to talk. It occurred to me that this must be as good as it got. This was real life, as temperate and dependable as the California weather itself. This was what I'd been born into, and destined to live. Not the pursuit of passion, or some illusion thereof, in the land of monsoon storms and bloody warfare clear on the other side of the earth. This, when all was said and done, remained my reality. My here and now. My peace. I'd better embrace it—before it was too late.

Toward this newfound purpose, I thought it simpler to let all correspondence from my Việt-Nam acquaintances go unanswered. Their innocuous-looking letters always brought me such angst since

I never knew what horrific news might be concealed in them. Had tragedy struck at Lee Anne's family again, or Elise's? Would Paul make his DEROS without a hitch? Had new leads surfaced to dash all hopes for Dick's safe return? Would Dean sign up for yet another tour? All possible disasters out of my control. Any bad news along those lines could push me back into the deep hole I'd been struggling to climb out of. Weary to the bone of living in constant fear and suspense, beset with survivor's guilt and wishful thinking that nudged me ever closer to the edge, I resolved to turn my back on yesterday and focus exclusively on the future, with blinders on. A clean break with the past was my only chance.

Thus, with great sadness and regret I let them go, my good friends from the Việt-Nam days. As their repeated attempts to stay in touch were met with total silence from me, they eventually gave up and dropped away—one by one, out of my life. The last note I opened and read was a Christmas card from Mme Yvonne and her husband Bill, which, ironically, brought good tidings. It turned out the excited couple was busy preparing for the summer arrival of their first child. Yet even this joyous announcement plunged me into melancholy as it brought back the tragic memory of Bob Olsen, killed before he'd had a chance to hold his newborn son. This was the last straw that cinched my decision to close that chapter in my life, and not a moment too soon.

Christmas 1968 came and went, and so did Debbie and my family, who drove up to Mather to celebrate the holiday with me, since I hadn't recovered enough to tackle the long drive home. As the new year rolled around, I continued to improve, not just in health but with Debbie as well. With no more entanglement from my past, coupled with her willingness to leave bygones behind us, we bridged the gap between us and grew close again, much to my parents' delight.

Knowing how treacherous the mountain roads could be in winter, I was concerned for Debbie's safety on those long weekend commutes and suggested that we visit over the phone until warmer weather. She agreed, mainly to set my mind at peace. In an odd, mysterious way, this new arrangement brought us even closer. We ended up talking on the phone almost every night, more than we ever used to.

But January was a month of grim anniversaries—of Bob's untimely death and the infamous Tết Offensive. With dread, I felt a dark pall settling over me again. To make matters worse, news reports predicted an upcoming repeat of Tết. It was widely expected that the communists would celebrate its one-year anniversary with a new cycle of violence. This brewing tension abruptly came to a head for me one morning while I was out on my daily walk during lunch break.

On that day, I followed a path that took me around to the SAC side of the airbase just as an alert exercise was taking place there, the first one I'd ever witnessed. Even when observed from a safe distance, through a chain link fence draped over with concertina wire and patrolled by M-16-toting security police, it was a spectacle to behold. Frozen in place, I watched with awe as the eight B-52 BUFFs on alert pulled out in perfect sequence from their "Christmas tree" pads and thundered down the main runway, two at a time in a flawless Minimum Interval Takeoff. As the roar of jet engines drowned out the klaxon horn, the giant birds swept into the air. Outside the fence, I could smell their acrid fumes and feel the blast of hot air from their powerful wake.

Suddenly, to my horror, the sky turned black and burst into flames. I found myself engulfed in a tidal wave of Vietnamese refugees stampeding away from a fiery war zone. Drowned in this sea of forlorn humanity, completely disoriented from the horrible din of bombs and artillery fire and people howling in pain and terror, I suddenly heard my name called out in such anguish—a sobbing voice I recognized as Lee Anne's. But before I could turn and search for her among the crowd, the vision dissolved as fast as it had appeared, leaving me weak in the knees, gulping for breath. I staggered toward a nearby oak tree and crumbled to the ground, head in hands and body shaking from the experience. When peace and quiet finally returned following the departure of the last BUFF, I caught myself still whispering her name.

In that moment, I knew this aching emptiness would always be there in my heart, a constant reminder of the destiny that could never be. The same way that her lovely ghost, alongside those of my other friends, would follow me for the rest of my days. It would be a never-ending battle for me to keep the past at bay and to prevent it from intruding into, even taking over, my present. Terrified at the possibility of a relapse, I told myself the time had come to seize back control of my life and to start implementing concrete plans for the future.

In February 1969, I obtained a short leave from Captain Morgan and set out on my first trip home since the summer, arriving unannounced in Lone Pine the night before Valentine's Day, to my parents' pleasant surprise. And while they wished I could have spent more time at home, they understood when I left the next morning to drive to Bishop to see Debbie.

As Mom walked me to my car, she looked happier than I'd seen her in a while.

"Good luck, sweetie," she whispered in my ear, and gave me a hug and a kiss on the cheek. "You kids have a wonderful day. Call me later if you can."

Debbie had sounded astonished over the phone when I called earlier to let her know I was on my way. So as not to rush her, I made a couple of shopping stops along the way, and surprised her even more when I showed up around noon with two dozen red roses and a box of chocolates. She seemed flustered, genuinely touched by the gesture. It was clear she hadn't expected us to be celebrating Valentine's Day together.

"Oh, my gosh. I can't believe you really made it," she said, holding the door open for me, her face flushed with excitement. "Such lovely flowers, thank you so much. Make yourself at home. I'm going to put these in a vase and give them some water."

From the small, tidy living room, I heard her moving around in the kitchen, a cabinet door opening then closing, and water pouring into the vase.

"How bad were the roads driving down?" she asked through the cutout window between the kitchen and living room, rustling paper as she unwrapped the bouquet. "Another foot of snow is expected on Mammoth this weekend . . ."

She stopped short with a sharp intake of breath. I rounded the corner into the kitchen and saw her leaning against the counter, staring down at a little velvet box among the thorny roses, a stunned look on her face. Water was overflowing the crystal vase in the sink.

"What's . . . this?" She glanced up, all but speechless.

Without warning, my mind flashed back to a morbid scene from a lifetime ago—of Dick proposing to Vivienne, catching her totally off guard. A big, fatal mistake.

My heart dropped. Would I now face the same ill fate as my doomed buddy?

"This," I said, grappling nervously to open the box, "is what my mom received from her mom a long time ago. She gave it to me, and I'd like very much for you to have it now." I looked in her eyes. "If you'll still have me."

It was a simple diamond ring set in white gold, which my mom had removed from her trove of personal treasures and handed me last night after I'd confided to her the real reason for my trip. I had no ring, but was planning to propose to Debbie in the morning anyway, not wanting to wait and squander any more time than I already had. Mom insisted I use her mother's ring for the big occasion, especially since Debbie had always been like a daughter to her. At the last minute, I'd slipped the little box inside the bouquet, as a Valentine's surprise. Judging from Debbie's reaction, it must have done the trick. For better or for worse.

292 C. L. Hoàng

"I know it hasn't been easy—" I began anew, but Debbie stopped me by placing her hand over mine, which still rested on the box. Her eyes were veiled in tears.

It struck me then just how much pain and distress I had caused her, and how deeply my personal struggle had affected her life, as mine had been impacted by my friends' misfortunes, only worse. Yet she had remained right beside me, lending me strength and support to find my way back, never for a moment losing faith or ceasing to care. My true best friend, through and through.

Filled with tenderness, I reached and pulled her close to me.

"Welcome home, sweetheart," she finally said, smiling through her tears.

It was all the answer I needed.

Chapter Twenty-Three

Four months later, the week I completed my two-year stint in the USAF and returned to civilian life, Debbie and I had our June wedding in Lone Pine.

Having waited through college, medical school, and the doctor draft, we'd had enough of putting our lives on hold and had decided on a simple ceremony with just families and some close friends in attendance. Captain Morgan and his lovely wife were gracious enough to accept our invitation. He was the only guest who shared the war connection with me, and I suspected he'd traveled this long way to say good-bye and to help me celebrate my exit from the Air Force. It was the last time I got to see an old friend from Việt-Nam before Debbie and I embarked on our new life together.

The low-key wedding was prelude to a simple life we both had always set our hearts on. Not only did we recover from the war's disruption, which had come dangerously close to derailing every-thing for us, but in time, with hard work and a lot of luck, we were able to realize many of our modest dreams. I opened a private practice in Lone Pine, where we worked side by side day in and day out, and we lived in our quaint little place not far from Moon Meadows and Debbie's parents. Ours was an uncomplicated lifestyle in the shadow of our beloved mountains, surrounded by nature and wilderness as we'd always dreamed about. Thus tucked away in what Debbie called "our little corner of paradise," we watched those early years of marriage roll by uneventfully, a sweet summer dream—if one were to ignore the clamor of war.

Which, at the time, was darned near impossible to do.

Television had introduced the war into America's living rooms, and there it stayed, night after night, an unwelcome guest who refused to leave. No matter what the top news du jour—be it the first moon landing, the Yom Kippur War and the oil embargo, or even Watergate—the Việt-Nam Conflict remained in the headlines, solidly entrenched in our national consciousness, like a wound that could not heal. Seeing how confrontational and divisive the issue had become, I learned to shirk all contact and situations that might bring up uncomfortable exchanges about my service overseas. And Debbie, in her sweet, understanding way, would simply chuckle over accusatory grumbling within some circles that I had all but turned into a social recluse.

Meanwhile, the country was again plunged into disarray as events escalated out of control. News of the secret bombings of Cambodia sparked widespread antiwar protests that culminated with the tragic Kent State shootings and a massive student strike nationwide. Soon after, North Việt-Nam launched its 1972 Easter Offensive in blatant mockery of the ongoing peace talks, wreaking even more bloodshed and devastation than during Tết 1968.

On the heels of all this turmoil, the Paris Peace Accords were signed to great fanfare in January 1973. The treaty allowed invading armies of the North to retain their gained positions in the South, and dictated that the elected government in Sài-Gòn recognize and share power with the Việt-Cộng guerillas in the jungle.

It all became clear when in June 1973, only three months after our last troops had withdrawn safely from Việt-Nam, Congress voted to forbid further US military activity in Southeast Asia. For all practical purposes, we had reached the end of our collective rope and were simply giving up. With this peace agreement, we had bought ourselves enough time to pull our service men and women out of harm's way before we completely washed our hands of South Việt-Nam. Without the warranty of US retaliation against future violations, the so-called peace treaty was not even worth the paper it was printed on, let alone the Nobel Peace Prize awarded that year to the architects of the deal.

It was embarrassing how little time it took for the inevitable to play out. In December 1974, fully re-armed and modernized with the latest weaponry from the Soviet Union and Red China, North Việt-Nam renewed its aggression against the South, in effect tearing up the Paris Accords in bold defiance. Still reeling in the Watergate aftermath, the US merely registered a diplomatic protest while President Ford assured the weary public we would under no circumstances reenter the war. Congress took it one step further, refusing to appropriate emergency funds to assist and resupply South Việt-Nam in its self-defense.

Thus given free rein, North Việt-Nam made its move in early spring 1975. Twenty divisions with tanks and heavy artillery crossed the seventeenth parallel and joined the 150,000 troops already in place in an all-out invasion of our former ally in the South.

The end came fast and furious. Shocked and demoralized by its abrupt abandonment by America and the free world, quickly running out of supplies without further military aid, South Việt-Nam lost hope as well as its will to fight, and just plain quit. An astounded world stood by and watched as the fledgling democracy collapsed like a house of cards in a matter of short months. Once again, the airwaves flooded our living rooms with vivid images of war, this time of the panicked retreat of the South Vietnamese army and civilian population from up country and the Central Highlands ahead of the communist advance. Despite myself, I remained glued to the TV screen night after night watching the horrific scenes unfold before my incredulous eyes: desperate soldiers hanging over the railings of evacuation ships off the central coast; throngs of terrified refugees fleeing their ancestral homes and flocking south to safety by any means; miles and miles of roadsides littered with abandoned military stockpile, dropped belongings, and the many injured and disabled left behind. It was mass hysteria and chaos on an apocalyptic scale, like nothing I'd ever seen.

The imperial city of Huế fell to the communists in the final days of March 1975. The news stirred up a swell of emotions in me, as I remembered our "little princess" Elise and her family and the tragedy they had suffered during Tết 1968. Every time the TV camera panned over the sea of haggard escapees scampering south from the ancient capital, I leaned forward in my seat and strained my eyes at the small screen, scouring the distraught-looking rabble in the improbable case I might spot her. And every time my heart sank with disappointment.

By late April 1975, the northern half of South Việt-Nam had fallen under communist control and the advancing Red Army began to close in on Sài-Gòn. As if to underscore the hopelessness of this final episode, a C-5A Galaxy aircraft used in Operation Babylift to evacuate war orphans out of the country crashed at Tân-Sơn-Nhất Airport, killing 138 passengers, most of them children. Here at home, the news reached fever pitch even as President Ford reaffirmed that the war in Việt-Nam "is finished as far as America is concerned."

With the end looming closer and my frazzled nerves about to over-load, I felt the urgency to get away from all the madness and withdraw to my nature sanctuary in the Sierra.

Before the walls caved in on me—again.

"Isn't it a bit early for backpacking?" Debbie reminded me with a gentle smile when I told her my plans. But she immediately added, with typical thoughtfulness, "But if you want to go, I'll stick around here and keep the office open for emergencies. That way you can stay out as long as you like."

So off I wandered, in search of peace and quiet away from the crazy world. But my hopes were soon dashed as the trail solitude only amplified the rumble in my head and the rage in my belly. From dark recesses of my mind where they'd been locked away these past years, memories gushed forth amid the majestic wilderness and swept me back to those early days at Biên-Hoà AFB. It had barely been eight years, yet it seemed forever ago. How could we, as a nation, have done an about-face in that short a span and gone from championing freedom and democracy to deserting an ally in time of danger? How was it that a cause previously deemed noble and worthy of our staunchest support had somehow become a burden we couldn't wait to unload? Had we been fighting for the wrong reasons all along, or had we simply lost heart and quit in the end?

My thoughts drifted to my comrades in Việt-Nam, who had given their youths, if not their limbs and lives, in answer to the call of duty, and to their supportive families who had shared in those tremendous sacrifices. What must they be feeling now, in view of all that was happening? Were their hearts raging, like mine was, against the utter senselessness of it all? Or the unfairness of having been sent to fight a war that, in hindsight, we'd never seemed prepared to win? How could one justify the steep price we had all paid—for naught, when all was said and done? We now must live with the fact that this well-intentioned enterprise had ended up a colossal waste of lives and resources, a costly experiment gone deadly awry. The heartbreaking part of it was: the outcome could have turned out much differently. And bad luck, for once, wasn't to blame.

Gazing at the magnificent scenery around me, I remembered my old hooch mate Bob Olsen and the promise I'd made to take him camping on Mount Whitney. Just one of many memories we had shared in the six months bunking together. But on this lonely hike in April 1975, what stood out most in my mind were our late-night chats when Bob had told me of his hopes and dreams for his wife and newborn son. My heart filled with sorrow, I allowed myself for the first time to wonder how mother and child had been doing without him. The extraordinary circumstances surrounding his death had made the memory unbearable to me, but out here on this snowy trail atop the mountains, under a big open sky with nary a soul around, there was no hiding from the past. Seven years after my hooch mate had departed, old and new realities converged and caught up with me. My unwitting role in his demise—and the ultimate waste of his sacrifice. As I pushed on across the white desolation with no destination in mind, I caught myself humming that old tune Bob used to love, "Puff, the Magic Dragon," the same one he'd often imagined himself singing Ricky to sleep with. The sky blurred with nostalgia.

It turned out one week was enough to convince me I wasn't going to outrun events simply by staying out on the trail this early in the season. So I cut the trip short and headed home.

Debbie welcomed me back with open arms and some staggering news.

"Sài-Gòn fell while you were gone," she dropped the bombshell after helping me unload my backpack, her voice tinged with despair. "Oh Roger, what a horrible mess that was. Our embassy was evacuated in the nick of time, just before the communist tanks rolled in. But those poor local folks. They were beside themselves with panic. Many tried to scale the embassy's walls to reach the last helicopters out. There was great fear of a bloodbath once the communists took over, so people scrambled like mad to get out while they still could . . ."

I leaned against the counter in our cozy, sun-filled kitchen. So the end had come, hard and swift. Like sudden death from a rocket shelling. All those years, nearly fifty-six thousand lives, and unlimited resources. All down the drain. And a season in hell had begun for a small nation that had placed its faith in us, its superpower ally. It wasn't exactly a surprise ending, with all indications pointing in this direction for some time already. But to me, it still felt like a sucker punch in the stomach.

Debbie saw the look on my face and hurried to my side. "Oh, honey," she whispered.

I sought refuge in her arms, my body wracked with emotions as we held each other tight in tearful silence. The occasion was beyond words. For better or for worse, an era had now ended, and with it, a familiar way of life. The old world we'd grown up in, with its ideals and principles, its bright promise and noble intentions, had made way for the new age of pragmatism.

Hugging me close to her, Debbie must have sensed it, too.

A part of me died that day when Sài-Gòn fell, the latest casualty in a doomed war.

By the time the repercussions of the events of Black April caught up with the world in the late 1970s, most Americans had more or less put Việt-Nam behind them and moved on. It was thus a jolt when suddenly we found ourselves forced to confront, belatedly and without the consuming passions of the war years, the consequences of our past actions—and the latest crises engulfing Southeast Asia.

After the communist takeover in 1975, an estimated one million South Vietnamese with ties to the previous regime were imprisoned without charges or trials. Banished to "re-education camps" or "new economic zones" in remote locations all across the country, they were abused, tortured, and executed, away from the world's watchful eye.

Facing this political persecution on one hand, and abject poverty or even starvation on the other, countless Vietnamese made the agonizing choice to flee their homeland. On makeshift rafts, fishing junks, trawlers, and other such floating devices unsuited for navigating open waters, they escaped from the mainland and headed out to the international shipping lanes 160 miles offshore. The lucky ones were rescued by passing freighters while the rest went adrift on the open sea, eventually falling prey to pirates or monsoon typhoons, if not to thirst, hunger, and diseases first. Of the two million "boat people" seeking escape from communist Việt-Nam, one fourth perished on the South China Sea during their perilous journey to freedom. When the story of their desperate quest surfaced around 1978 and continued unabated through the next decade, it stunned the free world and rocked our conscience.

Meanwhile, in Cambodia, the communist Khmer Rouge also conducted their own political purge. Employees of the former regime, professionals and intellectuals, members of religious orders and foreign ethnic groups—all were identified, arrested, and summarily executed without due process. Virtually overnight, the entire country was turned into a sprawling mass grave, the infamous "killing fields" of Cambodia. From 1975 to 1979, in what was condemned the world over as one of the most heinous genocides in modern history, the Khmer Rouge carried out the systematic extermination of 1.7 million of their own people, out of a population of eight million.

Yet sadly, despite the professed outrage, there were no widespread demonstrations around the globe to demand action against such egregious violations of human rights. The silence from former activists and war protesters was conspicuous and deeply unsettling.

Like all who were appalled by these new tragedies, Debbie and I donated to organizations that handled the relief effort for the refugees. But on a personal level, even ten years removed from the war, I remained wary of the emotional hazard involved and didn't allow myself to dwell on the matter. Still, that failed to keep the nightmares from haunting my early-morning hours, when I sometimes dreamed of Lee Anne or Elise adrift in a dinghy on the stormy ocean, or of Dick languishing in a lonely, torturous death on a killing field inside Cambodia. From this period of great despair, I retained a lifelong dependency on sleeping aids, which worked to knock me out for the entire night without a dream.

Around that same time, Debbie and I were experiencing our own share of challenges and disappointments. After years of unsuccessful attempts to start a family, we finally accepted that parenthood wasn't in the cards for us. The revelation prompted a sudden desire for change that compelled us to cast our sights, for the first time, outside of Lone Pine for a new place we could call home. On the threshold of midlife, with children no longer figured in our future, we felt the need for a fresh beginning.

Having done my internship in San Diego years ago, I was familiar with the area and liked it. I persuaded Debbie we should give it a look. In 1980, soon after our marriage entered its second decade, we packed up and moved to the balmy climate of San Diego, exchanging the Snowy Range for the beautiful city by the ocean—and we never left.

While totally embracing the new life in our adopted hometown, we still answered the call of the mountains and returned every year for summer vacation and to spend the holidays with our families. Then in winter 1983, tragedy blindsided us. My brother Jerry was killed in a car accident on a mountain road. The trips back to Lone Pine were never joyful occasions again, though by necessity they became even more frequent than before. My own grief notwithstanding, I wanted to be there as often as I could for my parents, who struggled to cope with the loss. Older now, and heartbroken by this "unnatural order of things"— their words—they nevertheless resisted my suggestion that they dispose of Moon Meadows and relocate closer to us.

"This is our home, honey," my mom would insist every time, a patient but resolute smile on her face. "We've lived here most of our lives, and many of our friends are still here. Truth be told, we wouldn't know what to do with ourselves in the city, much as we'd love to be close to you kids and get to see you often."

So I let them be, not wanting to rob what little peace of mind they had left. Debbie and I just redoubled our effort to visit them and Debbie's parents every chance we got, making the most of our time left with them.

It was time well spent, for which we were thankful. Our parents passed away over the next ten years, one by one like autumn leaves following each other to the ground, but fortunately all in relative peace, without much suffering. The few living relatives we had were scattered across the country, but most of them had long since dropped out of touch. Thus in early 1994, a few months away from our silver anniversary, Debbie and I woke up one morning with the startling realization that we were practically alone in the world, just the two of us.

For the first time in our lives we were completely on our own, with no family support to fall back on, but without responsibilities either. This new circumstance, so foreign and somewhat confounding to us, made us pause and ponder the future.

"You know, we could set sail around the globe and nobody would even miss us," I remarked one weekend to Debbie at the breakfast table. "Maybe it's a good time to do some travel planning, you suppose? If memory serves, someone I know has always dreamed of an extended honeymoon trip around the world."

Years earlier, in the spirit of keeping things simple, we'd been content with a camping trip in the John Muir Wilderness after our small wedding, thinking there'd be plenty of time later for the "real" honeymoon. But that time, of course, had never come. Over the years, the elusive trip had evolved into something of an inside joke for us, if not a lifelong fantasy.

"Seems to me someone else has conveniently forgotten about work," Debbie replied with a soft laugh. "It's not like we're retired, free to come and go as we please . . ." She caught herself, and her jaw dropped. "Oh my gosh. You don't really mean it."

I winked at her, nodding with a conspiratorial smile.

Following our impulsive decision, we both turned in notices at the hospital where we worked, on the very day of our anniversary. Two months later we were officially retired, in time to celebrate my fifty-fifth birthday. Having worked hard and lived modestly all our lives, with no children to support or worry about, we had concluded we'd earned the privilege to start living from now on for ourselves.

The belated honeymoon trip, however, suffered yet another setback, this time postponed by our moving to a retirement community on the outskirts of the city. The resort-like setting of this "active adult" neighborhood, built around a championship golf course and a clubhouse with fine amenities, had always appealed to us. We'd long been waiting for the day, finally arrived, when I became "adult" enough at fifty-five to qualify for residency at Whispering Palms.

"Let's just take the rest of the year to settle into our new home and enjoy it," Debbie proposed after we moved in at summer's end, so thrilled that we'd found our dream retirement place. "It already feels like we're on vacation here. I don't need to travel anywhere right now. We'll have all the time in the world for our big trip later, won't we, dear?"

It turned out the answer wasn't mine to give. Fate, once again, was up to its old tricks.

No sooner had we unpacked and begun to settle in the new place than Debbie came down with what appeared to be a summer cold. Having been a lifelong health enthusiast, she seldom got sick, and then never for very long. So it didn't surprise me that she was at first dismissive of the petty indisposition—until it proved petty no more. By the time she had an inkling something was amiss and checked in with her doctor, the 1994 holiday season was upon us. Her condition had deteriorated significantly, with constant fatigue and discomfort added to a growing list of symptoms. Needless to say, we couldn't get into the season's spirit that year. I managed to put up a Christmas tree, our first in many years, and to do a bit of decorating around our dream home, but we spent the holiday in a state of suspended anxiety, awaiting results from all the lab works ordered by her doctor. It was by far the longest Christmas of our lives.

The news finally came in the waning days of the year and confirmed our worst suspicions. The diagnosis was breast cancer, Stage IV. This belated discovery struck us dumb with its irony since we were both health professionals and Debbie had always been diligent and self-aware concerning her personal health. The fatal slip must have occurred over the previous two years while she struggled, first to take care of her ailing parents from a distance before they passed on one after the other, and then to cope with the grief of mourning in the aftermath.

"I'm sorry, honey. I'm so sorry," she kept whispering to me after we returned home from the doctor's office. I held her tight in my arms, and we cried together, wrapped in the nostalgic sound of "Auld Lang Syne" from the radio in the background.

My memory of the next twelve months remains spotty at best, a blurred stretch of heartache and exhaustion, with some bittersweet moments forever etched in my mind. Undoubtedly for my sake rather than her own, though she'd never admitted it, Debbie decided to fight the disease to the bitter end with an aggressive course of treatment, a nasty combination of surgery followed up with a new chemo trial and radiation therapy.

It was a brave and gut-wrenching battle—all the more since it was ultimately a lost cause, which everyone recognized from the outset.

It did, however, buy us a little extra time, the first two months of which were surprisingly good thanks to her positive response to the treatment. We celebrated Valentine's Day 1995 at home while she recovered from surgery. I got her balloons and chocolates, and this time around, her very own engagement ring—long overdue, and hidden in a bouquet of red roses just like years before. She was in for another shocker when I gave her a special Valentine card, which concealed within its folds a pair of open flight tickets.

"The doctor cautioned us to wait just a bit longer until you get your strength back," I said with enough conviction for both of us, hugging her close to me. "The moment you do, hon, 'Bonjour, Gay Paree,' here we come. The City of Light and Romance, just you and me, baby." Her face lit up with the brightest smile in months, and we went on to plan all the wonderful things we'd love to do and see in Paris.

We never went. Debbie never gained back enough strength to risk a long trip. Eventually, we settled for one last weekend jaunt to the Sierra Mountains in late spring, but even then she had trouble breathing and moving about at the high altitude.

From then on, it was a long, torturous downhill slide, so heartrending to watch that I've since tried to erase it from memory. By midsummer, the therapies had all but lost their initial efficacy while Debbie had also grown too weak to sustain any more treatment. All efforts then switched to keeping her as comfortable as medically possible.

Grief-stricken though I was, I felt tremendous relief for her when at last she slipped away in early fall, barely one year after we'd moved into our dream retirement home.

Over the following weeks, I dragged myself, one agonizing day at a time, through the motions of taking care of Debbie's funeral and cremation. It wasn't until I stood alone in a Sierra alpine meadow where I had spread her ashes that grim reality grasped me by the throat. In the golden light of the dying day, surrounded by magnificent mountain vistas, I shuddered awake from the daze only to feel the excruciating pain of loss and loneliness.

She was gone, and with her, everything that had been life to me—my whole world.

Then came the tears, free-flowing after being dammed up all these months just so we could go on facing each day together. And even though I was thankful she was no longer suffering, my heart broke for her life cut short with so many dreams still unfulfilled. I would have given her my own remaining time in a heartbeat, if only I could.

In the haze that rose with darkness from the meadow floor like a dancing curtain, I caught glimpses of our life together over the decades—from high school to college and on to medical school, followed by the Việt-Nam years then the quarter-century marriage; from the highest peaks of happiness to the valleys of trials and heartaches, with priceless moments of intimacy sprinkled in between; from the minutiae of day-to-day routines to the most memorable events and milestones of our shared lifetime. All flitting by before my eyes like familiar scenes from an old movie or recollections of a wakened dream.

It then came back to me, out of the fog, an old Vietnamese folktale I had heard many years ago then forgotten until that moment. It was the story of a destitute student in bygone days who left his village to try his luck in the imperial capital. After spending his young life immersed in the study of ancient Chinese scriptures, he was eager to sit for the national exam that was held every four years in the capital to select new government officials. The young man gathered what paltry savings he had and set out by foot on the months-long journey, determined to find fame and fortune in the city even if he had to endure the roughest travel conditions. He walked all day every day until nightfall, when he stopped at deserted roadsides to fix and eat his supper before falling asleep on the ground.

On one such night, he was so exhausted that he dozed off while the brown rice was cooking on an open fire and didn't awake until dawn. Resuming his long march, he soon reached the capital where he sat for the exam, which he passed with such flying colors that he caught the emperor's attention as well as his daughter's eye. Recognizing his talent and potential, the emperor granted him the princess's hand in marriage and assigned him to important posts at the court. For his part, the young man did his best to validate this trust, garnering success and praise in all his undertakings. Over time, he rose to become the premier mandarin at the court.

When war broke out again and enemies invaded the border, the emperor commanded the former student to lead an army to its defense as he had so capably done on many occasions before. This time, however, his fabulous luck ran out on the battlefield. The mandarin was defeated and captured by enemy troops, who dragged him by a rope in front of their leader for execution. Down on his knees, his hands tied behind his back, out of the corner of his eye he saw the executioner raise the big sword.

At the instant the gleaming blade dropped and his life flashed before him, the poor student sprang awake with screams and sobs of terror.

Next to him, over the dwindling fire, the yellow millet was still cooking.

He had dreamed a whole lifespan in less time than it took to prepare a skimpy meal.

My last thirty-odd years had also flown by like a dream, from which I now awoke all alone and brokenhearted, without the faintest idea of how to move forward on my own. But even amid the shock and agony of separation, there was one reality I remained certain about. I wouldn't have traded a single day with Debbie for the world.

She had given me my dream of life. Not so much in terms of fame or fortune as a tangible and rare chance at happiness, even more rare as I'd believed it lost forever after Việt-Nam. For every precious moment of this wonderful dream, I wished I'd known some adequate way to express to her my love and gratitude.

In the deepening twilight over the meadow, surrounded with past memories come alive, I said a prayer for my wife and a final good-bye, and blew a kiss to the wind.

Over the years, with Debbie's love and support, I had learned to make peace with my Việt-Nam past, at least not to let it interfere with our life together. Little by little, those old memories seemed to have been crowded out or covered under the moss of time. I felt relief at the thought that maybe, just maybe, that chapter of my life had drawn to some kind of closure on its own, however unsatisfactory. Then, with Debbie's passing, I became convinced that with the last link now broken, the past had finally been laid to rest . . .

⌐

Until tonight.

From a bygone world of fire and bloodshed, the arrival of Dean Hunter's cryptic message has smashed the bottle and set the genie free. The past comes roaring back to life, as fresh and vibrant as if time had stood still.

After three decades on the run, I'm out of places to hide.

In the cool quiet of the night, I close my eyes—and surrender to the ghosts of Việt-Nam.

PART IV

Mulberry Sea

San Diego, California
September 1999

Chapter Twenty-Four

The night has gone.

Pale daylight leaks in around the blinds and curtains on the windows, and I can hear early birds chatter blithely outside. It's the morning after.

I've been up all night reading and rereading Dean Hunter's note, slip-sliding into the past I worked so hard to put behind me. It's amazing how a few scribbled lines can fling open the floodgate and undo the effort of all these years, and how the mind, even with age, is so adept at bridging time and space at the slightest beckoning. As it turns out, the rust of past decades has hardly tarnished the memories, which have lain dormant but intact and have now awoken to assert control once more.

1967 and Biên-Hoà, South Việt-Nam, suddenly feel like yesterday.

I lean back in the chair, close my eyes. This past week has been a whirlwind of big surprises and emotional chaos, starting with my diagnosis of lung cancer, followed by the hasty escape to the Sierra Mountains—my first trip back since I went there to disperse Debbie's ashes four years ago—and topped off with a mysterious message from an old buddy I haven't seen in thirty years.

"Acquaintance from Việt-Nam would like to speak with you."

A tornado has touched down and ripped through the desolate landscape of my later years, turning my whole world upside down, laying bare painful secrets. The Child Providence, once again at play. No use fighting the situation or running from it. It is what it is, as always. On the other hand, fantasy though it may seem, perhaps all this coincidence is a sign, a last chance for me to wrap up unfinished business and set things right.

I clamber off the reclining chair and trudge into my bedroom. Fighting a stiff back, I reach with both hands for a small chest sitting on the floor inside the closet and carry it out to the living room, next to my chair. It's unlocked. I snap the front latches open and raise the lid.

A faint odor wafts up from the chest, the peculiar smell of time captured. The smell of nostalgia.

Inside lies a hodgepodge of keepsakes put away from sight for decades, forgotten on purpose at the bottom of my closet, yet things I couldn't bring myself to part with: old letters I wrote home from Biên-Hoà, which my mom kept in bundles tied with rubber bands; random 1967–68 issues of *Air Force Times* and *Stripes and Stars*; a faded Polaroid photo of me lying on my cot inside our hooch, snapped by Paul Nilsen on a rainy afternoon; various colorful bills of military payment certificates that I forgot to convert back into real money on my last day in country; the short-timer's calendar, with all one hundred squares checked, that used to hang on Bob Olsen's wall and was overlooked by Graves Registration when they came by the hooch to collect his stuff. This particular item makes me pause and take a long, deep breath. I've reached the bottom layer of mementos, where my most personal memories of Việt-Nam lie buried.

As I fish out these special relics, turning them in my hand one by one, they retell their stories in such vivid details it makes my heart ache. There's Puff, the stuffed toy dragon Dean picked up for me on his R&R in Hong Kong, which I planned to give Bob for his newborn son Ricky but never had a chance to; and here's the red *lì-xì* envelope with a mint bill of Lucky Money tucked in it, a Happy New Year gift from Lee Anne the weekend before Tết 1968, the same weekend Bob and the MEDCAP team went down in the helicopter crash. Next to it, neatly folded in a square, is the white handkerchief with her Vietnamese name, Liên, embroidered on it, which she'd lent me that Sunday afternoon at Mme Yvonne's when she saw how upset I still was from our earlier visit with Dick at 3rd Field. Finally, hidden under the jumble is the single item I treasure the most, whose mere sight has always whipped up a storm of longings in me. The yellow-silk ribbon from her hair, accidentally dropped at Dick's place amid all the turmoil that fateful day we last were together.

Sitting on the carpeted floor by the chest, the silk ribbon in my hand and the other contents scattered around me, I feel the years peel away and long-stifled emotions bubble up. So much pain and grief. So much left unresolved, simply swept under the rug of time, smoldering there for three decades. Like a fool, I've worked diligently all these years to suppress the memories and convince myself I had outrun the past. It has been nothing more than self-delusion.

But given the new circumstances in my life, with Debbie gone and me diagnosed with cancer, there's no longer any point in running from the past. I must face it once and for all as I begin to get my personal affairs in order. It's time I come to terms with my life. The whole of it.

I pick up the phone and dial the number on the hotel stationery. Asking for Dean's room, I wait anxiously while the line rings. The sound of my thumping heart grows louder with each ring, then my breathing stops when I hear the click.

It's the automated message center. Nobody is in.

For a few seconds my brain just freezes, as much from relief as surprise, until the beep at the end of the recorded greeting breaks my trance. I exhale sharply.

"Hello Dean. This is a voice from your past. Roger Connors here."

My voice sounds hoarse and unnatural. I pause, clear my throat. "I'd been out of town and just got your message last night. I'd love to see you again, old man. Why don't we make a date for tomorrow a.m. Just come over anytime in the morning. If that doesn't work for you, call me back at—" I give my number, even though his note said he had it. "We'll figure out something."

Then I quickly hang up, my hand shaking from the adrenaline rush.

I did it—chattered on as if no thirty-year gulf existed between us. What else could I have done? There wasn't a simple excuse I could have offered for our loss of contact, so it was best not to try. And although anxious to inquire about the "acquaintance from Việt-Nam," I didn't feel comfortable to bring up the subject in a message left on some answering machine.

So, no matter how urgent, all the questions will have to wait. Just one more day.

Which is just as well, for suddenly the full impact of the past twenty-four hours hits me like a bolt. I feel utterly drained. Without bothering to stop and gather the bits and pieces of my past still strewn all over the floor, I drag myself to bed and crash.

⸻

I sleep through the entire day and a good portion of the night, and wake when it's still dark outside. Not once did the phone ring during that time, so I assume there's no change in the plan. We are getting together this morning, Dean and I—and *she*, too, perhaps.

By the first light of day, I'm all scrubbed and dressed. Standing in front of the bathroom mirror, I stare at my reflection and try to see myself through the eyes of my arriving visitors. Will they be able to look past the years and still recognize the shadow of the young doctor they once knew, or will I be just an old stranger to them? Can we somehow bridge the chasm of three decades and rediscover one another, the way we used to be? Are we ready to visit the past together, even if it reopens old wounds? Suddenly this whole reunion idea doesn't seem so great anymore. The only thing that keeps me from calling Dean back and canceling is that I'd have to come up with a half-decent excuse. It's too late to back out now.

I clear the clutter off the living room floor, then make myself some coffee. No guests to be seen, I begin to pace around the house, now and then stopping by the picture window to watch the front walkway gradually exposed to morning sun. My mind starts to paint the image of a young Lee Anne in a white *áo dài* over silk pants of the same color, with a conical straw hat looped over her forearm, gracefully gliding up to my front door. A soft breeze teases her long black hair. She smiles and raises her hand to sweep it back over her shoulder, the white gown fluttering around her like ribbons of sunlight. The ethereal vision is so vivid it steals my breath and fills my heart with yearnings.

As I pull myself away from the window and resume pacing, the doorbell rings. In the mid-morning quiet, its brassy chime startles and stops me dead in my tracks.

I approach the door in dreamlike motion. Resting my hand on the knob, I inhale deeply, pull the door open—and come face-to-face with my Việt-Nam past.

For seconds, Dean and I stand staring at each other in stunned silence. Then simultaneously we burst forward and grip each other in a mutual hug.

"Welcome home, kiddo," he says in a voice gruff with emotion.

I'm aware that Việt-Nam veterans often greet one another with that symbolic phrase, as a way to make up for the rude welcome many of us encountered when we came home. But this is the first time some-one has ever said it to me, and that keeps me speechless a moment longer.

Fighting to regain my composure, I step aside to invite him in. Nobody else is with him. So roiled up are my emotions I don't even know how I feel.

One thing is obvious. Time has been easy on the Lonely Hunter. He appears little changed after all these years. Still that ramrod posture, the slight catch I noticed in his step when we first met at Biên-Hoà AFB. The same powerful build on a six-foot-plus frame, even with the extra ten or fifteen pounds packed on by age. And of course the boyish buzz cut, now sprinkled with more salt than pepper.

We've barely come inside when he pivots and grasps me by the shoulders, shaking his head in disbelief. "So good to see you again, old buddy. How the heck have you been? I'd just about given up on you."

Still at a loss for words, I simply nod and smile as I motion him to the sofa facing my chair. Dean seems to sense the trouble I'm having and proceeds to fill me in on the particulars. He happens to be on the last day of a weeklong reunion in town with his former comrades in the 5th Special Forces Group, and is going home in the morning. Which explains his excitement when he received my message upon returning to his room last night.

"Great to see you, too, big guy," I finally manage. "I can't believe this is happening. How did you find me in the first place?"

"You kidding me? In this day and age, anything's possible." Dean laughs. "Besides, an old buddy of mine works at the hospital where you were. Same guy who organized this week's reunion." He pauses before adding, "I've known for some time that you live here in the city, but I wasn't sure you wanted to be bothered. You know—you lying low all these years. Just figured I'd take my chances this time. And here we are."

I avert my eyes from his stare. This isn't a subject to discuss right from the outset. There'll be plenty of time later. "How rude of me," I say. "First things first. What would you like to drink? I have water, coffee, or diet soda. Or maybe an early beer?"

Dean jumps up from the couch, a big grin on his face. "Hold that thought. Right now a couple other people are dying to see you, kiddo.

They're waiting out in the car so I could have the first few minutes with you. May I bring them in?"

"Oh sure . . . of course," I stammer, caught by yet another surprise. *So she did make it, after all.*

While Dean dashes out, I again pace the living room straining to pull myself together. But the moment I hear the sound of hurried footsteps followed by a loud rap on the door, my composure flies out the window and my heart skips to a standstill.

Frozen to the spot, I glance up at the open doorway.

In a whirl of excitement, she sweeps in and wraps me in a big, heartfelt hug. Her shoulders heave with unleashed emotion, and my own eyes get damp as we cling to each other while we both grapple for words. "Roger, Roger. How many years has it been?" she speaks first, but immediately chokes up.

I smile through the blurriness and grab hold of her hands. "Elise. What a wonderful surprise. How've you been?" That's all I can muster, even as my gaze stays glued to her face.

Our "little princess." In the flesh. Right in front of me, with her heart on her sleeve, the way she always was. And still as beautiful as ever. It appears she has carried her striking resemblance to Audrey Hepburn into her mature years.

The decades evaporate. All I see is the lovely silhouette of a romantic young woman leaning over Mme Yvonne's Baldwin console, pouring her broken heart onto the keys. My chest swells with such nostalgia it hurts.

Dean steps up behind us. "Roger. There's somebody here I'd like you to meet."

Only then do I realize the presence of another visitor, blocked from my view by Dean's broad back. She takes a few timid steps forward as he turns to introduce her, a young Vietnamese woman with shoulder-length hair and a shy but pretty smile, dressed in pants and summer blouse, as is Elise.

"This is Lan," Dean says as Elise moves to her side and takes her by the elbow, as if to lend support. "She and her husband are young friends of ours. Elise is visiting at their home in Orange County while I'm attending the reunion. When I called last night and told her I was meeting you today, she wanted to come, so Lan offered to drive her down this morning. Lan, this is Dr. Roger Connors. Our long-lost friend."

I shake hands and exchange greetings with my unknown guest. She blushes as we touch, reminding me somewhat of a very young and painfully shy, almost terrified, Lee Anne, when I first met her the day she started at Mme Yvonne's. Already my head is spinning from the merry-go-round of ups and downs, of rising anticipations and dashed hopes, current reality and flashes of déjà vu. It feels like teetering on a high wire in a balancing act between past and present.

And we've only just begun.

I bring out an extra chair from my study, place it next to the sofa, and invite everybody to take a seat. Then, after making sure we all have a beverage, I raise my glass to make a toast.

"We've got a lot of catching up to get on with, I know. Let me just say how fantastic it is to see you all again." I hasten to add while still in full control of my voice, "Thank you for remembering, and for keeping faith through the years. Here's to old friends," then turning to Lan, "and to new ones."

We clink glasses with bright smiles, and after that I settle into my La-Z-Boy since Dean has grabbed the smaller chair from the study, reserving the more comfortable couch for the ladies. We then take turns catching one another up on our lives since the time we lost contact. As the host, I insist on going last.

Thus I learn that Dean had in fact volunteered for an impressive third tour in Việt-Nam, as I had suspected, and had stayed on at the same critical post at Biên-Hoà Provincial Hospital until late 1969. "It changed my life forever," he remarks succinctly, though with a meaningful wink at Elise, who responds with a tender smile.

"What he meant was, it gave us a rare chance to reconnect," she explains, picking up the account from there. "You probably knew my father was killed during Tết 1968 and I had to race home to Huế to be with my family. Without my father, though, we soon ran into some really hard times, so I returned to Sài-Gòn the next year in hope of finding some work. But I had no idea things had changed so much in just a year. Everyone I'd known had disappeared without a trace, except Mme Yvonne, who had stayed in touch from the States via airmail. God bless that gold-hearted woman. When she learned of my trouble, she asked her husband to write me a letter of introduction to an old friend of his who worked at Bank of America in the city. The gentleman was able to help get me a job as a bank teller. Oh Roger, you can't imagine what a lifesaver that was for me and my family. We really owe Mme Yvonne and Mr. Bill a great debt of gratitude."

My thoughts flash to Lee Anne. Where is she? What happened to her and her parents? Did she also get help from Mme Yvonne and her husband? A thousand burning questions, but I tell myself to be patient and to give Elise my full attention as she continues.

"After my job situation stabilized, I went checking around on our old friends again. There was nobody left in Sài-Gòn except Dean here. He must have had a hunch I was coming back and decided to hang around and wait for me. Didn't you, dear?" It's her turn to give him a playful wink, to which he replies with a smiling nod. "Long story short, I got in touch with him and we started seeing each other again every weekend he wasn't away. When he left for home later that year, we both knew he would be back for me after I had a chance to get my family resituated. And return he did, one year later, and we traveled to Huế together so he could meet all my folks. We got married there on Christmas Day 1970. Just a small, simple wedding attended by my family and some close friends. I moved to the States with him soon after that." Her voice filled with happy wonder, she adds, "Next year we'll celebrate our thirtieth anniversary with the new millennium. Can you believe it?"

I rush over to hug Elise and shake hands with Dean. What a fabulous, heartwarming story. I couldn't have wished a more perfect ending for my friends.

"I've always known you two belonged together since I first saw you dance with each other in Mme Yvonne's garden," I remind them with a smile. "It was clearly meant to be. And from the look of it now, I'd say you've got at least another thirty years of bliss to look forward to. I'm so happy for you both. Just wish I could have shared in the toast on your wedding day."

"Thank you, Roger. We feel very fortunate," Dean says, looking tenderly at his wife. "Elise came home with me to Washington, DC, because I was working at Walter Reed Army Hospital at the time. They needed doctors with experience in combat medical service. I stayed there until 1976, then a couple of buddies talked me into joining them in private practice." He shrugs his shoulders, an edge creeping in his voice. "The war had ended, and I figured I'd seen enough of it to last me a lifetime. All the more since we mucked things up so bad in the end. It was time I moved on. To something different."

I'm with you, brother, is my thought. We all lapse into a brief silence.

Then I switch topics. "How about you, Elise? Did you get back to your music study? We all thought you had so much talent. It was always a special treat to listen to you play."

"You know, it was my dream growing up, and my parents' also, that I would one day be a concert pianist," she says, her soft eyes staring past me. "But after I came to the US, I got so involved in building the new life with Dean that I never took the time to pursue a career in music. Then came our beautiful baby girl, and suddenly it dawned on me I had been living my dream all along. A healthy, happy life in the land of freedom, shared with the ones I loved." Her eyes glow with serene contentment, and a light blush colors her cheeks. "Honestly, Roger, I must not have had an ounce of ambition in me. My heart felt so full already there wasn't anything more I could have wished for. And nothing has changed since."

I feel the warmth of her contagious happiness coursing through me. "A girl. How wonderful," I exclaim. "She must be a young woman by now. Please tell me all about her."

"Oh, no," laments Dean, holding his head in mock despair. "You shouldn't encourage her."

"Dean is right. She's the apple of our eyes—what can I say?" Elise's grin lights up her face. "Her name is Clara, after Dean's grandmother and also Clara Schumann, the composer's wife. She seems to have inherited my love of music, but always showed much more aptitude than I ever had at the same age." Noticing my eyebrows raise in disbelief, she laughs. "Don't forget you're listening to a doting mother, okay? But it's true. Music has been Clara's life from very early on, though we never planned to steer her down that path. We weren't even aware how or when she first got the idea in her head that some day she was going to apply to Juilliard Music School. But she did. And lo and behold, they accepted her."

"*Juilliard.* Seriously?" I whistle at the delightful news, cracking my friends up. "Impressive. It's extremely competitive to get in, I understand. Congratulations to all of you. That's quite an achievement. She plays the piano, like you, I suppose?"

Dean and Elise both nod, beaming with undeniable pride. "She's got another two years of graduate studies," Elise says, radiant and bubbling over with excitement. "Honest to goodness, we don't push her. But Clara is always pushing herself. She just won a school competition to perform with the Juilliard Orchestra at Carnegie Hall this coming holiday season."

I shake my head in amazement. "This is getting better and better. Your talent, and Dean's determination. What a winning combination. Our girl is going to go very far, I can tell."

"I only wish she paid just a fraction of that attention to her social life." Elise sighs. "Mme Yvonne agrees with me a hundred percent there. She's her godmother, you know."

"We've stayed in close touch with Yvonne and her husband," Dean explains. "We used to try to get together a couple of times a year, alternating between DC and Atlanta. But it hasn't been that frequent lately, due to Bill's declining health. He's a bit older than all of us, if you remember. Well into his seventies now, and doesn't travel very easily anymore."

"They have one son, Bill Junior, or just Billy Boy to us," continues Elise. "Real sweet boy, older than our Clara by three years and a budding novelist with a lot of promise. He also lives and works in New York City. Just a few blocks from our girl, actually." She glances at Dean and smiles in resignation. "Mme Yvonne and I were hoping they would find time to visit and hang out together, like the close friends they used to be when they were kids. But what's a pair of old moms to do, you know, with such independent and stubborn children?

"By the way, I was thrilled when I learned we were meeting you this morning. So I called Mme Yvonne, and she asked me to tell you hello. She can't wait to see or at least talk with you real soon. She would have come on this trip with us in a heartbeat, if not for Mr. Bill still recovering from his knee surgery last month."

It strikes me rather strange to hear our "little princess" refer to herself and Mme Yvonne as "a pair of old moms." At the same time, it reveals just how fleeting the years have been, with the next generation already coming into full bloom. In a different twist, I'm also filled with a sense of loss, having missed growing older alongside my friends and sharing with them the joys and tribulations that come with the territory.

"So you've stayed in touch with all the friends from Việt-Nam?" I ask.

"With as many as we can," Dean answers, running his hand through his salt-and-pepper buzz cut. "It's therapy for me, if you know what I mean. It helps me come to terms with things, hopefully wrap up any unfinished business along the way."

I nod in wistful silence. It's interesting how he and I made such different choices in coping with the war's aftermath. I wonder now who has chosen the more healing path.

Dean's gaze shifts away from me. "I went to look up Nancy Olsen shortly after I came home, in summer 1970."

"In Minnesota?" My voice suddenly sounds shaky as my body tenses up.

"Little Falls, a tiny town two hours north of the Twin Cities. Even got to take her and Ricky out to the Lindbergh's house that morning after our visit." He chuckles at the memory. "What a rambunctious little carrot top, if I'd ever seen one. Between Nancy and me, we couldn't keep up with him scampering all over the back porch."

He pauses, breathing softly. "Remember that crazy weekend when Bob was supposed to rendezvous with her in Hawaii, and we all wondered what happened to her after his chopper went down? Turned out Biên-Hoà managed to get hold of her after all. Just before she left for the airport, thank God." Another pause, longer this time, then he clears his throat and resumes in a controlled monotone. "After the funeral, she and Ricky moved in with her parents. They helped look after him while she went back to school to get a nursing degree. Bob's father also lived in town, so the boy got to see him regularly as well. I'm sure Ricky was surrounded with love and affection, growing up. As far as I know, Nancy never remarried . . ."

Elise reaches over and takes her husband's hand before continuing the story in his place. "I never met Bob, but I knew he was very good friends with both of you. Dean wanted to look in on his family every so often, and I went with him on a few occasions. Most recently, to attend Ricky's—Eric's—wedding, in June of last year."

She turns to Dean with her gentle smile. "It was a lovely traditional church wedding, right out of a storybook. The bride and groom made such a handsome couple, didn't they, sweetie? You also thought Eric looked the spitting image of his dad."

Dean's face brightens at the happy recollection. "He's grown into quite a young man. Very mature and caring. Nancy mentioned he wanted to stay close to her and his grandparents. So he started his own venture in Little Falls, doing computer consulting for businesses in the area. Very bright kid by all accounts, but money has never been his priority. His family is. His young wife teaches school, I believe. They were high school sweethearts, just like his parents before. Good old Bob would have been proud of his boy."

For a second, my mind fleets back to "Puff the Magic Dragon" and the picture of newborn Ricky that Bob used to carry in his wallet everywhere he went. My throat tightens. Thirty years already our friend has been gone. A good half of our lives, in a blink of an eye.

Yet here we are, still missing and reminiscing about him. That's the measure of the man.

Dean goes on. "I'd drive up and visit the Olsens every time I attended a seminar at the University of Minnesota or the Mayo Clinic in Rochester. Elise would come along once in a while. Sometimes we'd also take a mini vacation after the conference to swing down to Decorah, Iowa, and visit your other hooch mate, Paul Nilsen. You remember The Kid, don't you? After you were gone, he became my regular drinking buddy at the Officers' Club—by default." Dean and I both laugh at this ironic twist, since Paul was no more of a drinker than a Sunday choirboy. "He asked about you all the time, Roger. Still reminded me each time we got together how you saved his life twice in Việt-Nam."

"No, no, no. He exaggerated. I did no such thing," I reply, blushing. "All I did was get him some first-aid care the one time he went into shock. And the other time, it was sheer dumb luck we couldn't squeeze in the doomed bunker. That's how we gave the Grim Reaper the slip, not because of heroics on my part. But that aside, how's life been treating him all these years?"

"Very kindly. He'll be the first to tell you. He runs his own practice in town, is married to a wonderful lady who's given him four beautiful children, and, get this, is about to become a first-time grandfather any day now. Can you imagine? The Kid—*Gramps*? Hell. I keep forgetting how old we are."

We all laugh. I'm relieved and happy to hear that Paul survived his time in Southeast Asia, physically and otherwise, and came home to build the life he'd always dreamed about, in his own corner of paradise tucked away in Iowa's "Little Switzerland."

Dean continues. "He debated coming to California with Elise and me, in the chance we might be able to get in touch with you. But with the baby arriving any day, he couldn't risk it. When I called him with your news last night, he insisted we all get together soon. After the grandkid's here, that is. San Diego, Decorah, or Washington, doesn't matter where, he said. But we've got to plan it ASAP. He can't wait to see you."

Dean's eyes drill into me, his voice softening. "We've all missed you, kiddo. What's been happening with you all these years?"

I gaze down at the floor. "I know . . . I'll tell you all about my boring life in a minute. But first. I've been afraid to ask you. Did they—did they ever find out anything about Dick?"

One by one, the rusty gates to the past have been kicked open. There's no stopping now.

Dean exhales, leans over with his elbows on his knees.

"Nope," he utters. "Not a trace. Even to this day. It's been a terrible ordeal for his family, to not know what happened to him or where his remains might be. His parents passed away a few years back, without closure." I can hear Dean catch his breath.

"There were other journalists who died or disappeared in Cambodia around the same time," he goes on, slowly rising again. "Sean, the son of actor Errol Flynn, and Dick's own buddy, Kyoichi Sawada of UPI, the Pulitzer Prize winner, to name just a couple. But unless their bodies were recovered on the spot, the probability of going back and finding them later was slim to nil. The 'killing fields' were about to destroy all tracks beyond hope."

He heaves a weary sigh. "Sorry, guy. No cheerful news there."

Such is life, I know. The same way the internment camp of Manzanar, an isolated and lonely childhood, the curse of falling in love with an impossible illusion, and the heartbreak of losing that love to war had all been part of life for my friend Dick Hayashi. Up until now, I've made no effort to find out what happened to him, fearing the worst, but deep down I've always held out a glimmer of hope. That there might be justice left in this world after all, and the star-crossed pattern might be broken for once to allow for a different, happier ending to his story.

But that, as Dean has just confirmed, was not to be.

"I couldn't bear to face his folks when I was still living in Lone Pine," I mumble, feeling the burn of guilt on my neck. "I had one hell of a time coping with his news myself. It would've been too easy to let the wrong words slip in their presence, which would have hurt them even more."

Dean nods in sympathy. "I gathered as much. His sister Suzy clued me in on how you had become the town's recluse after your return. Pretty much shunning the whole social scene to stay holed up in your home or office, was what I understood."

"You spoke with Suzy?"

"I met with her, and the family," Dean replies, his voice weighed down with sad memories. "It had always been my intention to pay a visit to the Olsens and the Hayashis first thing after I came back. But you know how quickly time got away from us. It wasn't until spring 1970 that I had the first chance to come out west, on short TDY at David Grant Medical Center at Travis. So one weekend I got out the maps and the old address book, hopped in the car and drove down to Lone Pine, figuring I should be able to catch either you or the Hayashis at home. I did get to meet Dick's family to pay my respects and tell them what a true friend their son and brother had been to me in Việt-Nam. But you're right. The situation was still too fresh and too painful for all of us. Their sorrow was beyond any comfort simple words could bring." Dean stops and raises the glass to his lips to take a sip, long enough for everyone to blink back emotions.

Eventually he continues, his eyes staring off into the past. "Suzy was really nice. She didn't want to get her parents more upset than they already were, so she waited until I took leave and followed me to the door. We stood outside under the pine tree in the front yard and spoke at length about her brother, and you. She was grieving for Dick, of course, but seemed realistic and resigned about his fate. But she also expressed concern for you, Roger. How you had withdrawn into your own world and not seemed interested in the least in reemerging."

Shooting a glance in my direction, Dean hurries on to save me from having to explain. "I'd had an inkling about you already, since my last few letters to you went unanswered. What Suzy told me that day only reinforced my thinking that it might be best to leave you be and allow things to run their course. Time heals all, so they say, but there's no speeding it up, as you well know. Sometimes a little solitude can help quiet down the mind.

"Elise and I have maintained contact with the Hayashis over the years. Once in a while, when memories stir us, Suzy and I would call each other on the phone and we'd reminisce about Dick. In fact, it was through her that we learned you'd moved to San Diego."

I drop my head in guilty silence, at a loss for what to say. Looking back on that dark period, I would have done a number of things differently, starting with the fact that I should have stopped in to say good-bye to Suzy and her family before Debbie and I moved away from Lone Pine. But it was a stressful and emotional time for us back then. We both wanted to get through the move as quickly and painlessly as possible, even as we tried to downplay the significance of it to friends and relatives flabbergasted by our decision. In the end, amid all the hubbub, Debbie and I slipped out of town without bidding farewell to everyone.

"How have you been doing, Roger?" Elise's voice is soothing, though full of concern.

I square my shoulders and proceed to fill them in on the big happenings in my life over the past decades. My marriage to Debbie, and our life together in Lone Pine then in San Diego; our disappointment and sadness over the absence of children; our decision to retire early, followed by Debbie's illness and her passing. I choose to leave out my recent diagnosis so as not to add more gravity to the conversation.

"And now you're all caught up—the good, the bad, and the ugly," I say in conclusion.

"Oh, sweetheart. We're so sorry about Debbie," says Elise in earnest, while her husband nods in concurrence. "I just wish we had been there for you."

I shake my head. "Thank you for your kind thought. I should've done a better job keeping in touch, no question about it. But what's done is done, and the important thing is you're both here now. I can't tell you how much it means to me."

We've been going nonstop since they arrived, and the clock shows it's long past lunchtime. I suggest we take a break and invite my guests to lunch at my favorite local eatery. "It's a hole in the wall, a little Vietnamese restaurant run by a family of former Boat People," I explain. "I like their food a lot. But I'm curious to get your opinion on it, Elise."

She seems to hesitate, casting a glance at Dean, who speaks up for the group. "We'd love to, kiddo, but we need to hit the road pretty soon to get a jump on rush-hour traffic. Our flight leaves early in the morning, and there are some last-minute errands we need to run when we get back to Orange County. How about we settle for a rain check?"

All morning I've been on pins and needles waiting for her name to crop up, but with time quickly running out, I can no longer hold back the one question burning on my mind.

"Have you heard anything about Lee Anne?"

It might as well have been a grenade dropped in the middle of the room.

Everyone freezes, suddenly clamming up. Nervous, meaningful glances dart back and forth between my three visitors, whose expressions have turned solemn. And then, over the growing drumbeat of my heart, I hear Elise's voice, fragile and quavering,

"Roger, dear. We didn't know how to tell you."

Chapter Twenty-Five

My temples throbbing, I look up at Elise.

The color has drained from her face. Her eyes open wide in telltale panic.

"Oh, sweetheart . . . I'm so sorry. I didn't know how to tell you."

She breaks down, unable to continue. Dean slides onto the sofa next to her and wraps one arm around her shoulders, his free hand patting hers in comfort.

Out of the fog of confusion, I hear Lan's voice for the first time since we were introduced earlier—hesitant, trembling with emotion.

"Dr. Connors. I'm . . . I'm really sorry. Auntie Liên is no longer with us . . ."

I stare at Lan with my mouth open. No sound escapes.

Tears roll down her cheeks. She dabs them with a handkerchief but can't seem to stem their flow. There's no mistaking what I've just heard, since everybody is crying now. Even Dean has discreetly turned his face away.

From a distance, I hear Lan's voice again, tripping over her words.

"She . . . *Cô* Liên—Auntie Liên—passed away a year ago."

I'm suddenly freefalling through a dense fog. My body cold and numb.

And then, in the dark void of my mind, I see it again. The same vision that came to me this morning, of an ageless Lee Anne in her white *áo dài* strolling up the front walkway amid ribbons of sunlight.

Then, just as fast as it appeared, the scene bursts into a storm of light so bright it blinds my eyes, about the same time my lips register the warm, salty taste of tears.

Dean is standing next to my chair, his hand resting on my shoulder, Elise by his side.

"I'm awfully sorry, buddy," he says in a pained voice. "We just couldn't . . . we didn't know how to break the news to you."

I wave my hand wearily. "How . . . what happened?"

"Congestive heart failure, due to idiopathic DCM. It could have been hereditary or from an earlier infection of some kind. Just no way to tell. It was diagnosed a few years back, but there wasn't a whole lot they could do for it. We were all devastated."

I search their eyes for an explanation. *You cannot be serious. Dilated Cardiomyopathy?* All these years I lived in fear of receiving news that Lee Anne and her family had fallen victim to the war. Never would I have guessed she'd mustered enough resilience and gumption to survive the damned scourge, only to succumb in the end to an obscure heart disease.

"Roger," says Elise in a nasal voice, "Lan here is a close relative of Lee Anne's. She can tell you more about what happened."

Dean brings the small chair over next to mine and motions Lan to sit down. I turn, reaching for her hand in heartfelt sympathy. The words tumble out, pathetically inadequate. "I am so sorry for your loss. For *our* loss. Lee Anne was a very dear friend to all of us."

Lan nods, her mouth covered in her handkerchief, and takes a minute before speaking.

332 C. L. Hoàng

"Please forgive me for getting all emotional. I lost both my parents when I was very young, and Auntie Liên had always been like a mother to me.

"She worked hard all her life, poor Auntie. So it wasn't a big surprise when she first told us she was getting tired and out of breath more frequently. But when the symptoms got worse, even after she had taken a break from work and had plenty of rest, we became worried and took her to see the doctors. That's when they diagnosed her heart condition, four years ago this summer. As Uncle Dean mentioned, the doctors advised us at the time they could try to treat the symptoms to some extent, but they couldn't reverse or even slow down the condition. From then on her health went downhill pretty fast, to where she needed to rest most of the day and was no longer able to go about her daily chores. I begged her to come stay with us, me and my husband, so we could look after her during the final two years—"

The plain fact finally struck me. "You mean, up there in Orange County?"

"Yes. We'd always lived near each other even before *Cô* Liên moved in with us, in the neighborhood known as Little Sài-Gòn, in Westminster. There's a big Vietnamese community in the area, with all kinds of shops, restaurants, and business offices. Before she became too weak to get out and about, Auntie used to go there on the weekend to do all her shopping. It felt almost like home, she always said."

I can't believe what I'm hearing. Lee Anne—living barely a hundred miles up the road from me, perhaps for years, without my knowing it. It's not inconceivable we might even have passed each other a time or two on the busy highways. Yet all this time I thought we were an ocean, if not a world apart, with no remote chances of ever crossing paths again. Never once have I had an inkling I could have easily been there for her, if only to hold her hand and whisper one last good-bye. A mere hundred miles removed, and the chance of a lifetime squandered, right through my fingers. In a matter of minutes, against all odds, I have found her and then lost her all over again, this time forever.

I sit stunned with the cruel realization, grappling helplessly with fresh loss and regrets.

Elise's voice reaches me from beyond the grayness. "If it's any consolation, Roger, she passed away peacefully in her sleep, at Lan's home."

I shake my head, the bitter taste of sorrow on my tongue. "No one even let me know."

As soon as that slips out, however, I recognize how immature and unfair it must sound, and regret it. But the damage is done, and Elise turns to me with agonized pleading in her eyes. "Oh, sweetheart. Lee Anne wouldn't let us. She made us promise not to bother you."

Then Lan speaks up again. "Dr. Connors, I brought you a package Cô Liên had left for you. I believe there's a letter inside. Maybe it will help explain some things. Sorry it has taken me this long. I should have asked Uncle Dean and Auntie Elise to help me get in touch with you sooner."

Something is pushed in my hand. It's a small package wrapped in brown paper, with my full name drawn on it in flowing cursives in black ink. A shiver runs up my back as I realize I'm looking at Lee Anne's handwriting just a short time before her death. It's beautiful and attentive, though somewhat unsteady. Next to my name, printed in a different, smaller handwriting, is a phone number.

"I wrote down my number," says Lan, "in case you have questions for me after you get a chance to open the package. I'll be glad to hear from you any time at all. But please don't feel you have to call. That's not the intention."

I get up and give her a warm hug. "Thank you so much, Lan. I can't tell you how much all this means to me. But we'll talk again, soon. I promise."

Dean approaches with his hand extended. "Looks like you could use some time to yourself now. We'll get out of your hair and let you be. But we ain't saying good-bye. Elise and I will be in touch in the coming week, and we'll need your help to plan a get-together with the old gang, okay?" Then, with a wink, "With any luck, we won't have to wait another thirty years for it."

I shake his hand. We reach and grasp each other by the shoulder. Then I walk over to Elise, who is standing off to the side with a brave smile despite all the tears. She steps forward to meet me. We share a long hug.

"I'm sorry," I whisper in her ear. "I had no right to take it out on anyone. It was my own damned fault for not staying in touch. I know you miss her and you're hurting just as much as I am." She nods, hugs me tighter before we part.

I walk them to the door, and within minutes they're gone, vanishing around the corner.

As soon as the door closes, I drag myself to the big chair, all my pain and grief finally let loose. It's a good thing my visitors have left, for I can't hold back a moment longer.

Eventually the furor subsides. For the first time in my life, I recognize with undeniable clarity the true depth of my feelings for Lee Anne. After three decades of trying to forget, my heart still breaks at the mere mention of her.

I slowly sit up and reach for the wrapped package on the table by my chair. Again, a slight tremor crawls up my back at the sight of her shaky handwriting. With a lump in my throat, I drag my fingers back and forth over this last vestige of hers, hoping somehow to feel her touch, her presence. Even in her final struggle, she didn't forget me.

With great care so as to preserve all the writings on it, including Lan's contact number, I remove the brown paper to reveal a cardboard container the size of a shoebox. My curiosity piqued, I ease it open and pull out a couple of books and a sealed envelope.

I recognize the books, a hardcover edition of *For Whom the Bell Tolls*, and a paperback imprint of *Gone With the Wind*. My brother Jerry shipped them to me at Biên-Hoà AFB at my request, and I gave them to Lee Anne to help with her study of American literature. They both look in exceptional shape with hardly a stain or a wrinkle to them, except for some yellowing due to aging. I flip open the covers and find inscriptions in her lovely handwriting in purple ink that has faded somewhat over time: "From Dr. Roger Connors, Sài-Gòn, Christmas 1967." And right below them, in faint pencil, a brief annotation that said it all: "Excellent reading!"

A new wave of nostalgia washes over me. I distinctly remember how thrilled she was with these simple gifts, and what fun and spirited discussions we subsequently had about them. They no doubt provided her an escape from the brutal world she was living in, along with the comfort, however dubious, of knowing that war is a universal part of the human condition. I close my eyes and clutch the books to my chest, lost in the memory.

As the past gradually releases its hold, I set the books down on the table and pick up the sealed envelope. It feels pretty thick, with my name on the front in her now familiar handwriting in blue ballpoint. For a minute I sit staring at it, turning it in my hands, half eager and half nervous, almost afraid even, to find out what's in it. Having disappeared from my life all these years, had she suddenly remembered an old friend in her final days? Or had some pointed reason prompted her to reach back into the past one last time?

My hands twitching with apprehension, I slip on my glasses, fumble inside the drawer for the letter opener, and in one swift, clumsy motion rip open the envelope and pull out a sheaf of neatly folded papers, what appears to be a long letter to me—from beyond the grave.

With every beat of my heart, the words tremble and dance in front of my eyes. I finally grip the pages with both hands to make out their contents.

Little Sài-Gòn, Tết (January 28) 1998,

Dear Roger,

As I was writing your name, my heart began to pound so hard I could barely breathe, and I almost quit. But I have procrastinated too long already, and time is running out. I must do this now, ready or not. So please bear with me over the next few pages. I just hope you can read my wobbly handwriting and follow my rambling thoughts.

First of all, how have you been, Roger? Has life been kind to you? Every time I think of you, I feel so much gratitude and affection when I recall all the things you did to help me and my family, and the patience and understanding you had always shown me from the first day we met. That's not even mentioning the sacrifices you and your family had to make during your time of service in our homeland. For all your kindness and generosity, Roger, we can never thank you enough. You deserve only the best that life has to offer, and I hope that has been the case.

All kinds of questions will probably pop in your head when you receive this letter. I don't know if I can answer all of them, but I will do my best. After all, I'm writing you on this First Day of Tết 1998 (Year of the Tiger), exactly thirty years after the bloody events of the Tết Offensive. That's a lot of water under the bridge, as you would say. A lot of life to cover. But I feel I owe it to you to give it a try.

What happened after the last time we saw each other, you must have wondered. The same question but asked in a different way has kept me awake many long nights, back then and throughout the rest of my life: What indeed should be happening now?

Oh, Roger. I just wish we were having this conversation face-to-face. It might be easier for you to understand what I'll have to say, if only you could read it in my eyes, too.

I sit back in the chair, arms dropped alongside my body, one hand still clutching Lee Anne's letter. The words have really sprung to life, and they ring out in my ear as if spoken in her own sweet voice. Eyes closed, I can almost feel her presence, even her soft breath grazing my cheek, mingled with the sweet scent of jasmine from her hair, as she leans in closer and whispers in my ear. Having pondered it all these years, I'm now about to find out from Lee Anne herself the answer to the biggest mystery of my life.

I wait until the wild thumping in my chest eases before reading on.

But given the circumstances, the only thing I can do is to try to set all reservations aside and be as thorough and open with you as I possibly can. I want to make sure this letter covers everything you need to know. And that's my final promise to you, Roger.

I've never shared this with anyone before, but even now, many years later, whenever I look back on the extraordinary events of that April day, 1968, I'm still overwhelmed with emotions: the initial shock and horror of my husband's death, the pain, the anger, the great panic and despair. It's still all here, locked up inside me, as fresh as if it was only yesterday. I was twenty-one, married three years, still full of hope for life and love despite the war. Then suddenly my world came crashing down around me. Overnight I became a young widow of war, brokenhearted and all alone except for two elderly parents who depended on me.

I was caught in my worst nightmare come true.

Then just when I felt I had no hope or strength left to carry on, there you were, right by my side. You reached out to rescue and comfort me. And like someone drowning, I clung on for dear life and wouldn't let go.

What happened next . . . just happened.

Over the years, I've gone back and revisited that day in my mind time and again. It might surprise you to know this: even though I had, and still have, conflicted feelings about it because of our circumstances, not once did I wish that what actually took place between us never had. In my loneliest hour you had given me much needed comfort, and that human bond was what pulled me through, up and out of the dark hole I had fallen in. It gave me just enough clarity in those bleak moments to help me realize that somehow, some way, I must find the resolve to live on, if not for my own sake then at least for my parents'. And for that, Roger, I thank you with all my heart.

I hope you know how special you've always been to me, right from day one when I first met the kindhearted and handsome American doctor who reminded me of my childhood hero, Dr. Thomas Dooley of Operation Passage-to-Freedom in Hải-Phòng, 1954. I had no idea that my new job at Mme Yvonne's would allow me a unique and wonderful opportunity to get to know you, even to play tour guide to you around Sài-Gòn on the weekends. We had such fun times exploring the capital together, didn't we, Roger? The downtown district, the Municipal Zoo and Botanical Garden, the flower market on Nguyễn-Huệ Boulevard in the final weeks before Tết. Do you still remember?

It was so sad and ironic, though, that with you I got to do the little things Vĩnh and I could only dream of doing but never had a chance to, even as a young married couple. Between the war and family responsibilities, we never seemed to find the time to catch a breather, just the two of us alone. That was my biggest regret after he was gone. Even so, it would dawn on me years later that those innocent fun times you and I shared were the only occasions I got to escape reality and be a young woman again— temporarily without a care in the world, free to enjoy some of life's simple pleasures. I guess that's just one more reason why those happy memories with you have always held a special place in my heart.

Although it makes me blush to admit this even now, I would be lying if I told you the "what if" question had never crossed my mind. Having had to live from day to day most of my life, I'd learned not to give in to fanciful thoughts. And yet sometimes after a nice afternoon spent with you, I would catch myself wondering, in the lonely hours of night, what would have happened if we had met under different circumstances, you and I. But such idle thought, the moment it snuck up on me, would fill me with shame and guilt, and I'd try to block it from my mind immediately.

The fact remained that our situations were what they were and could not be changed. My fate had been linked to Vinh's, and he had been nothing less than a caring and devoted husband who risked his life to protect our families and me. You, on the other hand, belonged with Debbie to whom you were engaged to be married on your return home. The truth could not have been more black and white. And all along I'd convinced myself that as responsible adults, we both understood our obligations and our boundaries.

So imagine my horror when I awoke in Dick's studio that Sunday afternoon, next to you, and it struck me what had just happened, and the chain of events leading up to it. In a second I realized the impossible bind I had put us in. All because of one moment of weakness, of all days on the same day my husband died. I panicked, and in tears I fled without waking you, because I couldn't face anyone right then, least of all you.

Oh Roger, it never occurred to me as I rushed out the door that it might be the last time we'd see each other. I'd never imagined that we would part ways so abruptly. But it did turn out to be farewell for us. Forever. It would become clear to me months later that on the same day I lost my husband, I lost you too, dear Roger.

Her handwriting betrays the turmoil she must have been going through while reliving those painful memories, as it starts to wobble more and even veer off a straight line. Gently, I run my fingers over the scribbled words as if wishing to steady her trembling hand and guide it.

It appears at this point Lee Anne took a break from the long letter, perhaps adjourning for the day and giving herself time to regroup. When she picked up again, it was with a new pen with darker ink. Her handwriting looked stronger and more stable as she moved forward with her story.

The next few weeks were just a blur to me. I struggled to make arrangements for Vĩnh's funeral while trying to stay strong for my parents. His death had hit them like a rocket because they'd been very close to him. My father, who was recovering from his stroke a year earlier, suffered a setback. But thank heavens for Mme Yvonne and the girls. They pulled together and helped us out in every big and small way, or I don't know how we could have made it through that time. After the funeral, I fell sick and couldn't seem to get better. Mme Yvonne became concerned and she finally insisted on taking me herself to see my doctor.

I can't think of a better way to do this than to break the news to you straight, Roger, as the doctor did with me during that visit.

After giving me a thorough exam and inquiring about my recent health history, he told me in a calm, reassuring voice that the unpleasant symptoms I'd been experiencing lately were nothing serious to worry about.

"*Congratulations,*" *he said with a kind smile and a twinkle in his eyes, apparently unaware of Vīnh's death. "This morning sickness shall pass. You're going to be a mother.*"

Chapter Twenty-Six

I bolt upright in the chair.

Adjusting my eyeglasses, I reread the last paragraph word by word to remove any ambiguity or possible misinterpretation. Still, my astounded mind can't seem to grasp the full meaning of it, skipping and skirting around the edges like a frightened bird.

Breath held in suspense, I gather my wits and dive back into Lee Anne's letter.

You can imagine how dumbfounded I was. The doctor became alarmed and fetched Mme Yvonne from the waiting room to come in and help me. One look at me and she knew I couldn't go straight home in my condition, so we went back to her place instead. I remember crying in the back of the taxi the entire trip. I was heartsick and scared, feeling more lost and lonely than ever. What would normally be joyful news to a young married woman just felt like the end of the world to me.

How could I have not known, given all the symptoms? But then again, between the funeral and trying to adjust to new life circumstances, I must have blocked out everything and prayed for the best. I guess deep down I'd been terrified of the obvious implication. The last time Vĩnh had come home had been before Tết, in January. So if I was only now having bouts of morning sickness, then the baby I was carrying inside me would have had to be yours, Roger, from what happened in Dick's apartment on that day in April.

I freeze, unable to even utter a sound, as if the back of my chair had suddenly turned into a block of ice. My head swims—that dreamlike state one experiences when hiking in the rarified air on mountaintops.

Struggling for breath, I stare out the window. It must be sunset because the natural light on the patio is fading fast, yielding to another balmy evening. The outdoors looks tranquil and idyllic, as always this time of day. But under that familiar veneer, nothing feels remotely the same as it did just a while ago. The stunning revelation has wreaked a profound change, and my private world, until now well defined and compartmentalized, suddenly comes unhinged.

Lee Anne *pregnant*? With *our* child? The notion is so staggering it's impossible to wrap my head around it, even as I repeat it to myself over and over in a silent mantra. Meanwhile a new, indescribable sensation—a confounding mix of excitement and sheer terror, of drunken elation and gut-wrenching sorrow—has found its way into my heart, stirring and lifting it, and setting it racing like a wild horse. I rest my weary eyes to let it all sink in while I try to compose myself. Failing to achieve that, and burning to get all the details, I suspend my disbelief and press on with the letter.

With nowhere to turn, I panicked and confided my situation to Mme Yvonne, as ashamed as I felt to burden her with such a personal matter. But that woman has a true heart of gold. Once again, she came through for me with total support and none of the judgment. Her immediate reaction was to offer to contact you on my behalf and let you know. But even though I was still shaken and had not been able to work out any answers, I felt certain I didn't want to do that. This was all my fault, and I wasn't about to let it turn Debbie's and your world upside down. She was engaged to you and was counting the days until you came home from the war. I knew what that felt like, and I couldn't allow myself to do anything to keep you from her.

Oh Roger, how I wished we'd met under different circumstances! But as things stood, in all good conscience I had to decline Mme Yvonne's offer. I made her promise to respect my wishes and not breathe a word to you. It broke my heart to have to make that decision, which was unfair to all of us but, as I believe until this day, the only possible one. And so we had suddenly reached the end of our road, you and me. It was farewell without saying good-bye. Because it would be so easy to change my mind, I knew I must avoid seeing you again.

Mme Yvonne asked me to promise in return I wouldn't resort to any desperate measures. She didn't need to worry. As helpless as I was feeling then, I sensed with every fiber in my body that I wanted this baby. It didn't matter that I had absolutely no idea how I was going to break the news to my parents or carry the baby to term without bringing shame on the family, or how later I would manage to raise it on my own while caring for two elderly parents at the same time. No. I had no ready solutions. Only problems, each more daunting than the last. But my instincts told me I was going to love this baby with all my heart and cherish it more than life itself. For in the end, it was all I had left.

In the following weeks, while I remained lost in an aimless daze, poor Mme Yvonne found herself in full panic mode as she approached her moving date to America. She was scrambling to leave me with some kind of arrangements and suggested that I postpone telling my parents until she could finalize all the loose ends.

A few days before she left Việt-Nam, we got together at her place on Nguyễn-Du Street for the last time. It was just the two of us under the trellis of red bougainvillea where we all used to gather, in a previous lifetime it seemed. We dared not reminisce about the old days for fear neither of us could stop crying. Our hearts were crushed.

"Roger stopped by last week. He insisted I accept this for you," she said and produced the Rolex watch you had left with her. *"He wished to do more to help you and your parents. I had to lie to him that you had moved away, as you'd asked me to do. Oh, poor darling. Have you any idea how hard it was? I just fell to pieces inside."*

We cried and held each other, but we both knew it couldn't have been any other way. Thank you, Roger, for having thought of me. It meant more to me than you could ever guess, especially in those times of hardship and loneliness. And although money would always be a struggle for us, I would hang on to your watch as an heirloom for our baby."

"Our baby." The words jolt me to my core with their simple truth.

I hadn't a clue that afternoon when I scurried away from Mme Yvonne's villa that I was unwittingly turning my back on my unborn child. Had I pressed her just a little harder, perhaps she would have broken down and divulged what she knew. But as fate would have it, I gave up too soon and as a consequence walked away from my baby. One blind, hapless decision and father and child ended up separated from each other all these years, perfect strangers in isolated worlds, with my old watch the only physical link between us.

Overcome by a crushing sense of loss and wastefulness, my heart aching with sadness and bitter regret, I bury my face in my hands and surrender to the emotions.

It's a while before I pick the letter back up and read on.

Mme Yvonne went over the arrangements she'd made for me. It turned out she had contacted our friend Elise, and together they had worked out a plan to come to my rescue.

You might recall Elise had flown home to her family in Huế after learning her father had been killed during Tết. Now, through

Mme Yvonne, she invited me to come and stay with her and her family, at least until the baby was born.

"You wouldn't be imposing on them in the least. Elise asked me to be sure and tell you that," said Mme Yvonne. "You two were best friends. She wants to do whatever she can to see you through these tough times. Think about it, Liên. This way, nobody around here would need to know about your condition."

Torn with guilt and doubt, I broke down in tears.

"What about my parents, Yvonne? I can't just run away and abandon them. They really need someone to look after them, after all that just happened."

She took my hands in hers. "Here's what I'm proposing, chérie," she said. "Remember the help I have, a widowed mother and her young daughter, refugees of war from the Central Highlands? I was going to have to let them go when Bill and I leave, but they have no place to go back to. Now, instead, we can send them to stay with your parents and take care of them while you're gone away to Huế. I think it will work out for everyone."

She raised a hand to stop the question on the tip of my tongue. "You needn't worry about expenses. I have some savings set aside from the business the past two years, and I'll make all necessary arrangements to handle payments and such. You won't have to do a thing."

Her eyes teared up as she sought to quell any protest from me. "When I was still Little Black Girl in our old neighborhood, you and your parents were the only folks who accepted me for who I was. You all treated me with real kindness, so much so I had often thought of you as my family. I'll never forget that as long as I live. I just thank my lucky stars I'm now in a position to be able to help you. So please. Let's don't make a fuss about this."

After their tremendous effort to pull things together for me, how could I possibly refuse the thoughtful generosity of my friends? I still choke up every time I think about it.

But next, I had to come clean to my parents about my disgraceful secret.

Let me just say it was one of the most difficult things I ever had to do. I had let my parents down in a big way, at the worst possible time. To this day, I still cringe with shame and anguish at the memory. But in the end I was still their flesh and blood, and despite their understandable disappointment, Bố Mẹ never stopped loving me. If anything, they felt sorry for me and worried themselves sick over my well-being. Together, we tried to weather the storm the best we could, and they supported my decision to get away from Sài-Gòn for a decent period of time. And so, in August 1968, at the start of my second trimester of pregnancy, I hugged my parents good-bye and boarded a plane to Huế for my first trip ever away from home, fighting not to cry in front of them.

I can visualize Lee Anne on that summer day, a brand-new war widow of twenty-one, three months pregnant yet none the wiser in the ways of the world, as she climbed the stepladder onto the plane, leaving behind her parents and her home in order to escape from the past. Meanwhile, eight thousand miles away, I'd been struggling to put my own life back together, totally oblivious of the crisis unfolding across the ocean, thereby wasting any last chances to come to her assistance. It must have been a horrendous ordeal for all of them, Lee Anne in particular. The unstated trauma, revisited thirty years later, is still evident through her trembling writing hand. It appears at this point she had to take another break from the letter, most likely adjourning for the day once again. Her next writing looks more steady, as if after a decent night's rest.

The last months of 1968 went by uneventfully. I settled into my temporary life in Huế as a guest of Elise's family. It was only after arriving that I discovered they had fallen on hard times following her father's death. Yet they wouldn't let me contribute, even modestly, to the daily expenses. "It's just an extra bowl and pair of chopsticks for you, Liên," Elise would tease, before suggesting, "Save the money and buy your mom a plane ticket to come visit when the baby gets here. She's welcome to stay with us as long as she wants."

In late January 1969, two weeks before the new Tết and a little earlier than expected, I started getting labor pains. Luckily my mom arrived the next day, in time to join Elise and her mother in rushing me to the hospital. It ended up a fifteen-hour affair. I don't remember much about it except the ripping pain and one special incident, which I will now share with you.

It was around 3:00 a.m. on the last day of January. I had been in labor since noon the previous day, bathed in sweat, and out of my mind with pain. In that final instant when I felt I was going to pass out, my thoughts turned to you for comfort, and I cried out your name. Then something remarkable happened. I could have sworn I heard your voice answer me over all the commotion, calling my name as if you were trying to find your way back to me. It was such a welcome sound. It lifted my spirit and filled my heart with joy and relief. The next moment, the drawn-out struggle came to a sudden, merciful end. The pain lifted off my wrecked body and a calm exhaustion took over me, seconds before I was startled by that most miraculous sound—the shrill cry of a baby just arrived in this world. My mother, who had stayed by my side the whole time, leaned over with a fresh cloth and wiped the sweat from my face. She smiled and whispered in my ear, "Well done, sweetheart. You've got yourself a beautiful baby boy."

I crash back against the chair and blow out through my dry mouth, my body depleted but all prickly from excitement.

"A boy. It's a boy," I scream in silence, so ecstatic to make the first discovery about my newborn child, as a proud new father would probably feel when he accepts the precious bundle into his arms and makes eye contact for the first time. Despite arriving some thirty years late, the news still boggles the mind and defies full comprehension. I keep repeating every nugget of information to myself, trying to get accustomed to the extraordinary fact. Lee Anne and I have a son together, born in the imperial capital of Huế at 3:00 a.m. on January 31, 1969.

Gradually, I'm filled with a sense of wonder and gratitude to have been, even if unknowingly until now, part of this greatest miracle of life. In the warm glow of revelation, a long-forgotten memory floats up from some dark crevice in my mind, awakened by Lee Anne's mention of her unusual experience.

It was 1969, a fortnight before Valentine's Day. I was stationed at Mather AFB, recovering from my recent bout with depression. On a walk during lunch break that day, I stumbled across a SAC Alert exercise conducted by the resident 320th Bombardment Wing. The awesome spectacle threw me into a panic attack. Knees buckled, I found myself trapped in a nightmarish vision, engulfed in a sea of refugees fleeing from a combat zone. Over the chaos, I suddenly heard Lee Anne's voice, helpless and sobbing, calling to me. As I fought against the human tide to search for her, the hellish scene dissolved into thin air following the departure of the last B-52 on alert. I staggered to a nearby oak tree and collapsed to the ground, still whispering her name.

Looking back in amazement on this forgotten episode, I realize in a flash of insight that my experience coincided exactly with Lee Anne's—noontime in California being 3:00 a.m. the next day in Việt-Nam. Incredible though it may sound, it appears that at the moment of our son's birth she and I were somehow able to reach through to each other, albeit for just seconds. In a small way, through some wondrous phenomenon, I was present for the arrival of our child into this world. Clutching the letter to my chest, I wish I could have shared this belief with her.

Oh Roger, the minute I laid eyes on that bundle of miracle nestled in my arms, I knew I had fallen in love for life! All the pain and heartache of previous months were instantly wiped away, and my heart overflowed with love and blissful joy. He was a beautiful baby, so perfect in every detail, from the cute wrinkled nose to his tiny fingers and toes. All I could do was hold him snug in my arms and cry big tears of happiness. Weighing 3.5 kilograms (or roughly 7.7 pounds, I think, a good-sized baby by our norms), he turned out to be mostly you and very little me: light complexion, with threads of gold for hair and sleepy blue eyes that peeked up at me with gentle curiosity when he managed to open them. But none of that mattered much to me. I was just thankful he was healthy, first and foremost, and then, from all early indications, as sweetly disposed as his father.

My mom asked if I had picked out a name for the baby.

"Yes," I said. "I think I shall call him Sơn." It's a popular Vietnamese name for boys, and it means "mountain." I chose that name in your honor, Roger, because I remember how much you loved and missed your Sierra Nevada when you were away from home that year.

Out of respect for Debbie's and your privacy, I put down "Unknown" for father on the birth certificate and gave our baby my last name—Trần.

I feel a stab in my chest at these sobering last words, which clearly capture the sorry status of our newborn son and presage the social stigma that would likely dog him his whole life. Even though I appreciate Lee Anne's noble intention to keep me out of trouble and thus free to pursue my planned destiny, I can't help but wish she had involved me for our boy's sake, consequences be damned. Nothing more was written on the subject, but I know as a mother she must have agonized over it, and now I share her heartache.

With the pregnancy behind me and greater responsibilities lying ahead, I sat down and began the serious task of planning our future. Sài-Gòn was my hometown where my roots were, as well as the land of opportunity and the safest place in the country. So it became clear that my best chance would be to move back there, even if it meant having to confront my past. Around that time, Elise herself concluded that she, too, would need to return to Sài-Gòn to find a job to support her family. We discussed between us, then two months after Sơn's birth, we packed up and left Huế together to return to the capital, with the baby in tow.

The first thing I did after getting back was to find a new neighborhood to move my family to, in the hope we could start over where no one knew my past. I also invited Elise to come live with us so she wouldn't be all alone like the year before. It worked out great for all of us.

We struggled in the beginning, but our guardian angel once again intervened on our behalf, this time from her new home in the States. Mme Yvonne asked her kind husband to write us a recommendation letter to a friend of his who worked at Bank of America in Sài-Gòn. Thanks to him, Elise and I got jobs as bank tellers and things improved for us from then on.

With my parents helping out with Sơn, I signed up for night classes at the university to resume working toward my bachelor's degree in English. Meanwhile, Elise managed to get back in touch with Dean Hunter and they began seeing each other again on the weekends when he was in town. After all the tragedies and tears of the past two years, it was wonderful to see them back together and so much in love, a true miracle of happiness in those dark times. It couldn't have happened to a more deserving couple.

Our little boy in the meantime grew like a weed, or as we say in Vietnamese, as if he were being inflated before our eyes. Go ahead and laugh at me if you must, Roger, but I swear he also grew more adorable with each passing day, looking just like the little angels featured on the Similac calendars. And sweet-tempered he was, too, for he seldom disrupted my sleep at night or caused his grandparents much trouble during the day. In no time, this newcomer had become the bright center of all our lives, and he even had Uncle Dean and Auntie Elise wrapped around his little finger. He certainly was the reason I lived for, why I strived hard every day to build a decent life for us. Every time I cuddled his plump little body in my arms and listened to him coo softly at me, I thanked the heavens, and you, Roger, for this most precious gift.

During Christmas 1970, I traveled to Huế again, this time to be a bridesmaid to Elise at her and Dean's wedding. It was a small ceremony attended by her family and some close friends, but also a farewell party since the couple was moving to the States after the wedding. I was thrilled to see that together they had made it safely through the war and reached their happy ending, but it was really hard for me to say good-bye to my remaining best friends. With everyone in our little group either dead or gone away, it was final closure to that special past we had all shared, those few glorious weekends in 1967 when life wasn't all about war and death, but also about exciting new friendships and the sweet promise of love. As I bade the newlyweds farewell, I sensed my last thread of connection to you unravel, too. From this point on, all I had left was memories.

But life kept rolling on. In June 1971 I completed my bachelor's degree in English, then qualified for my teacher's credentials. Following a dream I'd had since before my university days, I quit my job at the bank and became an English teacher at a public high school in the neighborhood. Between my baby at home and my kids in school, my hands were pretty full. Life, while not great, could have been much worse.

Which was exactly what happened to all of us in the South when the thirty-year war abruptly ended on the last day of Black April, 1975. After the US pulled out of South Việt-Nam and cut off all aid to us, our defenseless country crumbled overnight against advancing communists from the North, fully backed by the Soviet Union and Red China. When Sài-Gòn fell on April 30, 1975, a long, dark night descended over our homeland.

Roger, there isn't enough ink to write about all the misery and suffering the South experienced during our most recent "mulberry time." Countless people were sent to "re-education camps" or "new economic zones" in the jungles and mountains, where they died from deprivation or maltreatment. The "luckier" ones among us were allowed to remain in the cities but now faced a collapsed economy and a police regime like we'd never known before. Because of my former association with Americans, "the people's enemies," I was stripped of my teaching job and my family got pushed to the bottom of the food-rationing list. We had become the fringe elements in this new "workers' paradise" and were treated as such.

If not for Elise and Mme Yvonne continuing to send me money through Elise's family in Huế (so it wouldn't get intercepted by the government, who had me on their watch list), we likely would have risked starvation. As it was, we managed to survive one day at a time, but not my father, who suffered another stroke and passed away in 1977. The grief of his loss took a toll on my mother, and she soon followed him. By 1980, five years after the country's unification under communist rule, our once-happy family had dwindled to just the two of us. Me and my boy against the world.

Sweat trickles down my back. I feel Lee Anne's loneliness and despair, as palpable as if I were holding her in my arms, and my heart bursts with bitter anguish. Had I stayed in touch with my friends, I would have learned about all this and done everything possible to come to her and Sơn's help. So much pain, so much time wasted that could have been prevented. I drop my head, the weight of thirty years crushing my shoulders.

The post-1975 years were really tough on Sơn, not just because of our personal losses and severe deprivation, but also because of the fostered hostility against Amerasian kids. There were a significant number of mixed-blood children in Hồ-Chí-Minh City (old Sài-Gòn) alone, most of them left behind by unknown GI fathers from the war years, now treated with scorn as reminders of a shameful past. Many were abandoned by their mothers, who could no longer support them. They ended up roaming the streets begging for food. Called Bụi Đời, or "Dust of Life," these homeless kids were among the youngest victims in our broken-down society. Sadly, their plight was drowned out by the greater collective misery and went ignored.

Even Sơn, still fortunate enough to have a family and a home, could sense the growing bias against his American heritage from kids in his school and around the neighborhood. It only complicated matters that with each passing year, the boy grew to look more and more like you, Roger. All blue eyes and wavy brown hair with a cute, dimpled smile, which made it impossible for him not to stand out as an easy target for other children's taunting. It pained me to watch him turn from a happy, outgoing young boy to one who was withdrawn and cautious beyond his age. Yet I was powerless to stop it from happening. Above all else, though, it was his innocent questions that tore me up inside.

One night when he was five or six years old and I was putting him to bed, he looked up at me with those eyes like marbles and asked, out of the blue, "Is he real big, Mommy?"

"Is who real big, baby?" I answered distractedly while tucking him in.

"Daddy," he exclaimed, taking me completely off guard, the first time he ever asked about you. "Is he even taller than you? Does he have colored eyes like me?"

All I could do then was pull him close to me and rock him gently in my arms. "Yes, dear boy. Your daddy is taller than me by this much," I managed, smiling through the tears and showing him with my hands. "And his eyes are sky blue just like yours. I dare say you look exactly like him, only a lot smaller. You know why? It's so you can fit snuggly in my arms. Like this, see?"

Another day, when he was a bit older and we were walking home from school, he tugged at my hand and declared, "I want to learn to speak American. Will you teach me, Mommy?"

"Why in the world do you want to do that?" I played dumb, though with a sudden fluttering in my stomach.

His answer was ready, as if he had figured it all out in his little head, even without us ever discussing it. "Daddy is American, so he doesn't speak Vietnamese like you and me, right? But I want to be able to speak to him when he comes to get us."

My insides went cold. Those innocent words carried me back to my childhood days when young Mme Yvonne, then a poor little black girl without a father, had confided similar dreams and hopes to me. Like Sơn at the same age now, she had bugged her mother to teach her a few greetings in broken French so she could welcome her beloved papa, whom she had never seen except in her sleep, should he show up one day at their doorstep.

Averting my eyes from Sơn's, I ruffled his soft hair and tried to sound as jovial as I could. "It will just make for more study and less playtime for you, you know. But I'll be glad to teach you, honey, if you promise not to complain about that later."

For a while he had a close friend in a little girl about his age who lived down the street, a war orphan recently brought to stay with her uncle and his family. Both kids until then had found themselves more or less isolated from their peers, one by her burden of grief, and the other by his Amerasian blood. Maybe they shared a sense that they didn't fit in, and it brought them together to find comfort in each other's company.

Then one day the whole family just disappeared. It was widely speculated they had made their way to the seaboard and from there escaped by boat out of the country, fleeing from this "workers' paradise" with nothing but their lives. This sudden loss of his best friend affected Sơn more deeply than I had suspected at first, for he grew even more quiet and withdrawn. It all boiled up one afternoon when he rushed home from his sixth-grade class, visibly upset.

"Mom, I'm not a bad boy, am I?" he demanded, on the verge of tears.

Before I could react, he went on, his voice shaking with hurt and anger. "My teacher said I was. She did. She said Americans are mean people and that's why they were all kicked out. Then all the kids pointed at me and laughed."

As I pulled him into my arms, he began to sob. "It must be true. I must be really bad . . . nobody wants to be friends with me. Even Daddy doesn't want me . . . he never came back for us, Mommy . . ."

Oh Roger, the pain I felt right then was worse than any knife cuts, but I knew I must stay strong for our son. So I held him tight and covered his head with kisses and let him cry his little heart out on my shoulder. When I thought the worst had passed, I wiped his tears dry then squatted in front of him and looked him in the eye.

"Hey, baby," I said, "you're the most wonderful boy any parents could ever wish for. I am so thankful to have you. And I assure you Daddy would be, too, if he could be here with us and see you with his own eyes. He would be so proud of you. I just know it. But he can't come back to us now, honey. They won't let him."

Son started to cry again, so I held his face in my hands and shushed him softly. "I promise you some day when you're all grown up, big and strong, I'll explain everything to you so you know exactly what happened, and you can decide for yourself then. But no matter what, darling, I guarantee you Daddy would want to make sure that I love you plenty enough for the both of us. And I do."

I couldn't sleep a wink that night, hurting and crying for our son into the morning, wondering if there wasn't a better way I could have handled the crisis. Until this day, I have no idea how much he believed what I said to him, but he never brought up the subject again.

My sight blurred with tears, I can hardly make out these last few lines. Lee Anne was right. The pain I'm feeling for her and our boy is almost physical, pulsing and stabbing along my back. It's such heart-breaking irony, as I think back on those years, that while Debbie and I were trying to conceive a child of our own, this beautiful young boy yearned so painfully for me from halfway around the world. What a shame, and what a terrible injustice to him. All that time lost, all that love and hope squandered. There's no possible way I can ever make it up to him, and that's a tragic burden my heart will always have to bear.

This last incident convinced me once and for all there was no viable future for Son in this homeland that rejected him. And so, like countless other folks without hope all over Việt-Nam, I began to explore the only option available to us. Thousands of people had escaped to freedom on makeshift boats rescued by international freighters off the coastline. But then, on the other hand, thousands more not so fortunate had perished on the high seas or at the hands of pirates, never to be heard from again. It was a desperate and dangerous gamble, an all-or-nothing last resort, even setting aside the heavy penalty meted out to those caught attempting it. As much as I wanted a better life for Sơn, I was paralyzed with fear of the extreme consequences.

Luckily in the end I didn't have to make that agonizing choice thanks to the intervention, once again, from my devoted friends and benefactors, Elise and Mme Yvonne. In 1980, a long letter from Elise advised me that she and Mme Yvonne had hired a lawyer in Washington, DC, where she now lived, to look into the Orderly Departure Program and to file a petition on Sơn's and my behalf. This humanitarian program had just been authorized by the US government to allow Vietnamese citizens meeting certain criteria to immigrate to America as political refugees. Under this charter, it appeared we would both qualify. I, as the widow of an ARVN officer who used to work alongside American advisers, also as a former employee of Bank of America, and Sơn, as a child of half-American descent, even judging by looks alone.

It took two long years and a mountain of red tape to convince the communist government to let us leave. Finally, in 1982, after Sơn's thirteenth birthday, he and I boarded what you might call our own "freedom flight" to America. As we looked out the windows at the rice paddies and jungles below, we cried and said good-bye to the beautiful but tragic homeland we'd loved our whole lives, knowing we might never see it again. Meanwhile, the future, even with the promise of long-sought freedom, remained as mysterious as the bright white clouds we were flying straight into.

It turned out we were sponsored by a church group in Orange County, California, who had volunteered to assist us rebuild our life in this land of sunshine. Their welcome committee came to greet us at the airport, and with them were Dean, Elise, Mme Yvonne, and Mr. Bill, who had all flown out from back east for the occasion. You can imagine what an emotional reunion it was. It had been less than fifteen years since we had all come together, but it felt like a whole lifetime of upheaval. Until it actually happened, none of us had dared to hope we'd meet again.

Words were inadequate to express the joy and relief we all felt in that unforgettable moment. We three girls clung to each other, crying, until I heard Dean ask Son a question, and I introduced our boy to everybody. From the appreciative looks in their eyes, I could tell they all noticed his striking resemblance to you. Auntie Elise pulled him to her and reminded him how she and Uncle Dean used to cradle him as a baby in their arms. Mme Yvonne remarked what a handsome young man he was growing up to be. For the first time in months, I saw him crack a shy smile, and I knew then things would work out just fine for us in this new adopted homeland.

I'm not going to bore you with details of our new life in America. It's a nice, simple existence, blissfully uneventful, like day and night compared to the living nightmare we had escaped from. After all, in this land of freedom and opportunity, all one needs to do to get a shot at a good life is work hard and respect the law, and that's pretty much what we've strived to do since our first day. Given the urgency of our situation, it wasn't practical for me to go back to college to study for my teaching credentials. So I chose a new career path and became a Licensed Vocational Nurse. It was hard work, but it provided me with a satisfying job that earned a decent living for Son and myself.

To my amazement and relief, it didn't take our boy long to adapt to his new environment. He took to it like a fish to water and just seemed to blossom in this free and open atmosphere. After spending the first year assimilating the language and culture, he caught up with school and was admitted into the appropriate grade. From then on, there was no stopping him. It was as if he understood, even at his tender age, that he'd been given a second start in life and it was up to him to make the most of it.

I still remember those early evenings when he sat at the kitchen table doing homework while I prepared dinner over the stove after a long workday. On several occasions, he looked up from the books and said to me in earnest, "You know, Mom, I'm going to get a good job when I get out of school so you don't have to work so hard anymore." His heartfelt words choked me to tears every time, and needless to say, they took away all my burdens.

Oh Roger, you'd be so proud of him. He's everything a parent could wish for in a son, and I'm not saying that just out of love. Although not the most outgoing kid, no doubt because of his childhood experience, nor the most fun, since he leaned more to the serious side, he was popular with his peers who appreciated his sweet temper and thoughtfulness. Likewise, Dean and Elise, as well as Mme Yvonne and Mr. Bill, have always had a soft spot in their hearts for our son, initially because of their connection to you and me, and then as they got to know him over the years, for the nice young man he had grown into.

You'll be pleased to know that Sơn had inherited more than just your good looks, but also your scientific bent. He has always shown a natural knack for the sciences and has consistently excelled in those classes. I'm sure he didn't get that from me, but eventually it earned him a full scholarship to the University of California, here in Irvine.

Four years later, in 1991, he graduated at the top of his engineering department. My dearest Roger, it was without doubt the happiest and proudest day of my life when I got to see our baby in cap and gown, triumphant over all the odds against him. Nobody knew, but in my grateful heart I was sharing every glorious moment of it with you.

"Now it's my turn to take good care of you, Mama," he said as he put his arms around me while I tried to wipe away the tears. "You've been working hard all your life. It's only fair you get some

rest now and do fun stuff for a change. Go travel and visit your friends back east, why don't you, Mom? It seems they've always come out here to see us."

I thanked him for the offer but hung on to my job. I was too young yet to retire, I reminded him, and besides I still found fulfillment in my work. As a mother, I could also foresee the day coming when he'd need to take care of his own family, and I wouldn't want to burden him with extra responsibility.

As it so happened, that day wasn't too far off.

Remember I wrote about Sơn's best friend in Sài-Gòn, the orphan girl who had come to stay with her uncle's family a few doors down from us? And how devastated our boy was when they all disappeared one night? At the time, it was rumored they had attempted to escape by boat to freedom, but nobody could confirm it. We never learned what had happened to them.

But fate works in mysterious and confounding ways. It turned out the whole family had somehow made it safely to America and had settled in nearby Long Beach. It would be a few years yet before Sơn and his long-lost friend crossed paths again, purely by chance and this time as young adults attending college at UCI. When they finally reconnected, Sơn told me, it was like they had never lost touch. In time, their renewed friendship would only grow stronger.

I couldn't have been happier for our son. She was the perfect girl for him. Smart, pretty, and so sweet, but most important, they shared a unique bond with each other, having come from similar disadvantaged backgrounds. On a level that even a parent could seldom get to, they had always understood each other's deepest yearnings from a young age. Whenever he was with her, there was a peace about him, a quiet happiness, as if he was finally home. What more could I want for my boy?

And so, after she graduated from college one year behind him, they got married with everyone's blessings. All our friends flew out for the happy occasion. Dean and Elise's beautiful and talented daughter, Clara, played the piano at the wedding.

Since the apartment Sơn and I had occupied wasn't large enough for all of us, I suggested the young couple get their own place. They planned to rent a house and have me come live with them, but I gently declined their thoughtful offer. This wasn't Việt-Nam, where it was customary for two or more generations to stay together under the same roof, and I thought it would be nice for the newlyweds to enjoy their privacy.

It wasn't like they were moving across the country or anything. In fact, they lived just blocks from me and frequently stopped over after work for dinner or to invite me to their place on the weekend. I had always liked Sơn's wife from the first time we'd met, but I soon took to loving her like my own daughter. I'm happy to say our affection is genuine and mutual. She's soft-spoken and considerate, intelligent without pretension. Inside and out, she's as beautiful as the flower whose name she bears. Can you tell, Roger? I'm crazy about our daughter-in-law.

Her name is Lan, which means "Orchid" in Vietnamese.

Lan. The name reverberates through my head like a shockwave. She was right here, only hours ago, sitting just steps away from me.

My daughter-in-law.

Sơn's wife—and the future mother of my grandchildren.

I can still hear Dean's voice introducing her to me. "There's somebody here I'd like you to meet . . . This is Lan." And then her hand so soft in mine. I didn't even have a good look at her, so flustered was I to see Dean and Elise again after thirty years. The whole time the three of us were busy catching up, she just sat, quiet and self-effaced, next to Elise on the couch. But in the end she did come and sit by me. It was she who gave me an account of what had happened with "Auntie Liên," along with the package.

But why pass herself for Lee Anne's niece instead of her—our—daughter-in-law? Why didn't she tell me everything right then, after making the effort to drive down with Elise and deliver the package to me in person? Why didn't anybody else, for that matter? Do they all know the complete story? And what about Sơn? He didn't come with his wife.

My head spinning, I stare at the sheaf of papers in my hand. Perhaps there's still more to be revealed in the conclusion to this marathon letter, which must have taken a great deal out of Lee Anne. The current page had abruptly ended where I stopped, and to my surprise, I discover she had started a second letter instead.

Little Sài-Gòn, March 15th 1998,

My dear Roger,

By the time you receive these letters, you'll probably have heard about my heart condition. It isn't good, and it's deteriorating faster than the doctors have expected. That's why I didn't get around to finishing my other letter. But there are a couple more things I need to mention to you while I still have a chance. So please bear with me again.

My greatest regret, Roger, is that I didn't let you know about our son. I did what I thought was best for you, given the circumstances. But even now as my time draws near, there's still that lingering doubt whether I did the right thing for all of us. It's what prompted me to write you at length, so you may learn the whole truth some day. And when you do, I hope you'll find it in your heart to forgive me.

I have also told everything to Sơn and Lan, and explained it was my decision and mine alone that kept you out of Sơn's life. The last thing I would want to leave him with is the mistaken assumption that you had abandoned him, that he wasn't wanted. I also made it clear that after I'm gone, it will be entirely up to them if they wish to get in touch with you. It will be their turn to make the call. The only request I have is that they exercise discretion and good judgment if and when they do approach you, to minimize any upheaval in your life. To that end, they may enlist Dean's assistance for any helpful information he can gather through his network of friends. I told them I have a letter for you that would explain everything in detail, which they are to deliver into your hands if they ever decide to meet with you. Along with it are some old, treasured keepsakes I'd like you to have.

It's my sad suspicion it might be a long time before Sơn comes looking for you, Roger. It wouldn't be any long-standing resentment against you that will keep him away, for he's really not one to hold a grudge, but rather his deep-rooted fear of rejection from those early childhood years. Maybe some day when he has a child of his own, he will understand how great a father's love can be, then realize what he's missing in his life and start searching for it.

My sweetheart—may I call you that, just this once—this may well be the last time I write you. Though my heart is full of tears of this impending farewell, I'm grateful for the chance we had in this lifetime, no matter how fleeting it was. There's so much more inside me than I can express in words, but I do want to say to you, my dear, sweet Roger, "Thank you for everything." It is my fervent wish that in time fate will turn kinder to "our family" (how I love those simple words!) and allow you and Sơn to one day connect, without causing you difficulties. When that wonderful day arrives, just know in your heart I'll be there with both of you, sharing in your happiness.

God bless, and my love always,
Liên (Lee Anne)

My head in my hands, I can hardly breathe or move a muscle.

Images flash by on an endless reel before my mind's eye, of a time and place long since gone, buried deep under the Mulberry Sea. The table on the green lawn under the arbor of bougainvillea, the juice stand on a busy street corner downtown Sài-Gòn, the lotus pond in the Botanical Garden, the spring flower market on Nguyễn-Huệ Boulevard. Superimposed over all these scenes are luminous memories of Lee Anne with her radiant smile and her long, silky hair the color of tropical night, in a beautiful *áo dài* that lifts and swirls with each graceful step.

This—this is my Việt-Nam, the one I loved and always will.

I finally stir. The room feels cold and deadly quiet, weighed down by heavy loneliness.

Lee Anne is gone.

It was as if she had come to say good-bye before setting out on a long journey, and we had spent the whole day and night catching up and she had just now walked out the door. I can still feel her presence almost, hear her soothing voice and smell her breath like lotus flowers, and my empty arms ache for her. She has brought me an unexpected and most incredible parting gift, one that binds us together, in life as in death. Even as my heart is pained by her physical absence, it overflows with love and gratitude for her.

I glance at the clock on the fireplace mantel. Another night has slipped away, and soon it'll be sunrise again. As overwhelmed as I am by this latest whirl of events, I don't feel the slightest need to go to bed. There's a long list of things that demand immediate attention, and my feverish mind is racing a mile a minute, planning and prioritizing.

After all, I have three missing decades to make up for—and precious little time to waste.

Chapter Twenty-Seven

It's all I can do to force myself to stick to my regular routine—coffee, newspaper, shower—then to while away a couple more hours before calling Lan, so as not to disturb her too early.

As her phone starts ringing, I suddenly realize it may be Sơn who answers, and my heart leaps into a sprint. And so it's a relief, tempered with a measure of disappointment, when I recognize Lan's voice on the other end.

"Hello," she says—as I freeze. "Hello? Who is this?"

I swallow hard. "Lan. It's Roger Connors. How are you?"

There's a momentary pause, quickly followed by a cheerful "Good morning, Dr. Connors."

"Roger, please. I hope I didn't pick a bad time to call."

"Not at all. Your timing is perfect. I just got home from my doctor's appointment."

It's my turn to pause.

"Is . . . everything all right?" I catch myself. "Sorry, I don't mean to—"

"No, no. Everything's fine. How about you?"

I take a deep breath, then plunge ahead. "I've read Lee Anne's letters. The ones in the package you brought me. I wish you had said something to me, you know, when you were here yesterday. I would've loved to have spent more time with you and gotten to know you better."

Big silence. I cringe. "I'm sorry. Maybe I can call back another time when it's more convenient to talk?"

"No, no. It's okay. I'm home alone. I—I just need a minute, please."

A shuffling sound, like she's sitting down. I hear her exhale softly.

"Sorry about that. I just didn't expect to hear from you so soon." Her voice sounds breathy as she hastens to add, "I mean, I didn't know what to expect, truthfully. But I'm so excited you called." She chuckles nervously, clears her throat before continuing. "I apologize I didn't tell you everything yesterday. There was so much to explain. I thought you might want to hear the story straight from *Mom*—as told in her letter, that is."

My heart skips a beat. It's no longer "Auntie Liên." Just plain, sweet "Mom" now.

"You mentioned she passed away last year. I didn't even ask when."

"A year ago, in July." There's an added tremor to Lan's voice. "It was a Sunday afternoon. She passed very peacefully in our home. Both Sơn and I were by her side."

She pauses, as if realizing she has just brought *him* into the conversation. Then, hesitantly, she resumes. "Nobody knew at the time what your situation was. So Mom had asked us and all her friends not to disturb you with her news. Then after the funeral, my husband and I just had no mind to do anything, least of all reopen the past. It was only recently I decided to start looking into all this. Dr. Connors—Roger, may I—may I be completely open with you?"

"I wouldn't have it any other way. What's on your mind?"

"I hope you forgive my clumsy handling of things. Sơn doesn't really know I've come to see you. I kind of did it on my own, with Uncle Dean and Auntie Elise's help."

My heart sinks. I draw a blank, not knowing how to respond to the new disclosure.

Her voice grows softer, almost pleading. "I love my husband very much. There's nothing I want more than to see him fulfilled and happy. As an orphan growing up, I missed my parents terribly, so I've always felt it would be a shame if Sơn went through life without getting to know you. I do believe deep down he would welcome a chance to connect with you. He's just terrified of—what your reaction might be."

"So you wanted to protect him."

"I—I only wished to make sure he wouldn't get hurt. When Uncle Dean and Auntie Elise told me you now lived alone a hundred miles south of us and they were trying to meet with you, I begged to tag along. It seemed like a perfect chance to honor my promise to Mom and deliver her package to you in person. And should nothing come of it afterward, well then, Sơn wouldn't even have to know about it."

Her voice drops to an apologetic whisper. "I'm sorry I wasn't straightforward with you. It was never my intention to be deceitful, or disrespectful—"

"No, Lan, I don't blame you a bit. It makes perfect sense why you did what you did." In a low voice, I ask, "If you're not busy now, can you tell me a little about Sơn?"

There's an instantaneous smile in her voice. "Where do I start? When I first saw you, I was struck by how much you two look alike. His hair and complexion are darker than yours, but the resemblance is unmistakable. I know now what he'll look like in thirty years! Mom maintained he also has your temperament and your brains, though she thought he's quieter than you. Most people wouldn't have guessed this about Sơn, seeing how he's always been a city person and all, but he loves the outdoors, the mountains in particular, and he takes me backpacking in the Sierra every chance we get. And at the risk of sounding ridiculously partial, I've got to tell you also that he's the most wonderful husband, but most important, a good, decent man with a big heart. I can go on and on about him all day long, if you have the time."

My heart thumping with excitement, I seize on the opening. "Better yet, how about we all get together soon. This weekend maybe? I'd love to invite the two of you to my place. Or I can drive up to Orange County, whatever's more convenient for you."

I sense her hesitation, ever so slight, and immediately reproach myself for moving too fast.

"I haven't had a chance to discuss any of this with Son," says Lan with a hint of a sigh. "He hasn't broached the subject since Mom brought it up before she passed away. But I'll talk to him tonight after he gets home from work. I promise." Thoughtfully, she adds, "And Roger, I'll be sure to let him know you really want to see him."

Before I can thank her, she has spontaneously arrived at the next decision. "Let's go ahead and tentatively plan on Saturday for Son and I to come visit you, if you're free that morning. But I'll jot down your number . . . in case it doesn't work out."

Without being asked a second time, I hurry to give her my phone number. "Thank you, Lan," I mumble in a daze, still not believing it's really happening. "I can't wait to see you and Son this weekend."

Never before have I meant anything more sincerely.

And never have I wanted something so badly yet dreaded it at the same time.

I get up before sunrise on the big day.

The early morning stillness feels wonderful. To my relief, the phone never rang once all day and all evening Friday, and that's an auspicious sign that nothing has changed. Our planned get-together is still on for later.

By the time my coffee is ready, the birds are raising a ruckus in the pepper trees by the patio, but I'm much too excited to sit back and enjoy the scene at leisure. Already wide awake, I barrel through my morning routine so that by seven o'clock I'm all scrubbed and dressed, ready and anxious to welcome my expected guests.

Slowly, the hours tick on by, with no sign of visitors.

I can hear occasional passing cars on the street out front, but not a sound of one pulling up to curbside. Doubtful thoughts race through my mind, and I fight in vain to turn them away. As I check the clock for the umpteenth time, the shrill ring of the telephone shatters the silence, making me jump from my chair.

I pause for a deep breath before reaching for the receiver. "Hello," I say, struggling to keep my voice calm even as I'm telling myself, That's it. He's not coming.

"Roger. Did I wake you?"

I drop my head and force a polite smile. "Hi, Lan. You guys can't make it today?"

There's a brief silence on the other end, and then, "Roger, it's your neighbor, Margaret. I'm calling to invite you over for a lunch barbecue later this morning. My boyfriend Buster is handling the grill." She goes on sweetly in that little-girl voice of hers, which I have mistaken for Lan's. "Nothing fancy. Chicken, hot dogs, and corn on the cob. It'll be just you, Dottie, Buster, and me. You don't want to miss Dottie's delicious lemon meringue pie."

I shut my eyes, suppressing a big exhale. "Thank you, Margaret, but I'm expecting company any minute now. In fact, I thought this was her calling from the road."

A pause, then she recovers with aplomb. "You're welcome to bring your lady friend with you. The more the merrier. And we'll all get to meet her, too."

I shake my head wearily. *Oh, dear. Not now, please.* But I manage to control my voice. "It's a couple I'm waiting for, actually. And we've made plans already, I'm sorry. But thanks again, Margaret. It's very nice of you all for thinking of me."

Replacing the receiver, I'm about to go sneak a peek out the front window when I hear a hesitant knock on the door, like a question hanging in the air.

They're here. This time there can't be any confusion.

My feet are glued to the floor, even as my heart sets off on a gallop. The big moment I've been anxiously awaiting—it's here. Upon me.

And then panic sets in. I mustn't keep them waiting, or they might give up and leave. Mouth dry and jaws tightened, breathing harder and faster by the second, I fight off the jitters and scurry to the door. My clammy hand fumbles for the knob. It finally turns, and the door creaks open.

⁓

It's been impossible for me to imagine what a moment such as this would feel like. But nothing could have prepared me for the eerie feeling of staring into the mirror of time and gazing at my own ghost from years past.

Standing erect on the patio before my unblinking eyes is a younger version of myself. Thirty years of age, dark-complexioned, with a solemn expression, much as I must have appeared to my family upon returning from Việt-Nam in summer 1968.

For endless seconds we stand awestruck, face-to-face, peering in disbelief at the flesh-and-blood incarnation of our respective past and future. Then a flash of recognition lights up his handsome young face. In that moment, our hearts know with final certainty.

We are bound together for all time by inseverable ties.

"Hello," he utters in a hoarse voice, his upper lip dappled with perspiration. "I am—"

"Yes, I know." I smile and rush across the threshold, my hand extended.

Everything I've practiced in my mind for this precise moment— it's all gone by the wayside. Nothing I can say or do seems appropriate enough.

He reaches out and accepts my offered hand. This first physical contact between us sends a jolt through my body. I take another clumsy step toward him, gently pull him closer to me, and wrap my arm around his shoulders.

He tenses up but doesn't resist. And then, ever so lightly, his free hand comes to rest on my back. All at once the fences come crashing down.

Shedding all inhibitions, I throw both arms around my boy and hug him—for the first time in our lives. As his arms in turn close around me, swells of emotions ripple through me like never before. A sense of joyful pride and loving tenderness, infused with the most acute feelings of nostalgia and regret. In my mind's eye, I'm holding the lonely young boy who so yearned for his unknown father. And yet, even as I clutch his shivering body in my arms, it strikes me with immense sadness that they aren't nearly big enough to soothe away all the despair and heartache of his solitary youth.

"I'm sorry, son. I really am . . ." I whisper in his ear, unable to continue.

His grip tightens around me, his shoulders heaving in silent struggle. Swept together by unleashed emotions from three decades, in danger of losing our last shred of control, we hang on to each other. An old man and his grown son.

It is a while before we break apart.

I step back, take another good look at my boy, then grasp him by the shoulders again.

"Welcome . . . welcome home, son," I say.

Simple, magical words that fill my heart with wonder and gratitude.

They are the traditional greeting among Việt-Nam veterans, but somehow they seem natural and appropriate in this instance. As much as any of us who served over there, if not more in some aspects, Sơn has been a victim of this wicked war, a "veteran" witness of all its horrors and bloodshed as well as its devastating aftermath.

The fact that he made it through and has found his way to me is nothing short of a miracle.

It suddenly dawns on me. "Where's Lan? Didn't she come with you?"

He scratches his head and gives me a shy, crooked smile reminiscent of Lee Anne's. "She wanted to give me a few minutes with you first. I'll run get her now."

His voice is warm and measured, with a faint trace of Lee Anne's Vietnamese accent. My eyes also catch the familiar-looking Rolex Oyster on his wrist. The watch I'd left behind.

He turns to go, then stops, looks back at me with gleaming eyes. "I'm really sorry I didn't come sooner," he blurts out, blushing in the ears like a guilty kid. Before I can react, he has slipped out of sight around the corner.

My head is still buzzing from his words when I hear their footsteps hurrying back.

What appears next before me takes my breath away. Slowing down as they approach the patio, with her arm looped around his like a happy new bride hanging on to her prince, is Lan. Beautiful, smiling Lan, dressed in that dazzling yellow-silk *áo dài* that captured my heart years ago. Instantly, I'm back at the Tết flower market on Nguyễn-Huệ Boulevard with Lee Anne.

Her soft hand touches mine. "Are you all right . . . *Dad*? May I call you that?"

I reach out, wrap her in my arms, which she reciprocates warmly.

Eventually, we regain our composure. Lan sidles back next to her husband, and my heart brims with joy at the lovely sight of the two together.

"This gown belonged to Mom, but she said she only wore it a couple of times many years ago," says Lan as she smoothes down the front flap with the exquisite chrysanthemum design embroidered on it. "I admired it so much Mom wanted me to have it. I had it refitted to wear at our wedding." Clutching Sơn's hand and lowering her gaze, she adds, with color rising on her cheeks, "You weren't at the wedding, so I thought I'd put it on for today's special occasion. Before I grow too big for it."

There are no words. All I can do is smile.

"You look wonderful in it, sweetheart," I say, recovering at last. "It fits you to a tee."

She glances up at Sơn with a cryptic smile, and together they step closer to me.

"We've got something to share with you, Dad. We want you to be the first to know," she announces sheepishly, though beaming with uncontainable excitement. "We . . . Sơn and I . . . we are expecting our first baby."

I can only imagine the stunned look on my face because Lan has to repeat the news again, this time more slowly to allow it to sink in. "You're going to be a *grandfather*, Dad."

Sơn follows up in earnest, his face bright with expectation, an excited tremor in his voice, "We're so thrilled for the baby, that it will get to meet *Ông Nội*—Grandpa—when it arrives."

Without warning, from some deep cracks in the hardened soil of my soul, tears spring up and roll down my cheeks before I can blink them back.

All these years . . . the emptiness . . . the incessant longing for that mysterious something.

And then, like the mulberry field of old that emerged from the bottom of the sea, this huge missing part of my life has miraculously surfaced, with surprises beyond my wildest dreams.

I stagger forward, my arms wide open. We all come together in a tight hug circle.

"When . . .?" I finally manage. "How long have you known?"

"The other day when you called, I had just gotten confirmation from my doctor." Lan can't stop smiling even as she's dabbing her eyes with a handkerchief. "I was still in shock and hadn't had a chance to tell Sơn yet."

"How far along are you? When's the big date?" The questions roll off my tongue before I stop short and tap myself on the forehead. "Forgive your old man's manners, letting you stand out here all this time. Come on in, both of you. We've got a lot of catching up to do. I don't want to miss a single detail."

Tenderly, I put my arms around their shoulders and guide them toward the door.

As we're heading in, I catch something out of the corner of my eye.

The morning sun is just coming around to bathe the walkway in a pool of golden light, and for one split second, I glimpse a ribbon of sunlight flitting around the corner—like the front flap of a white *áo dài* fluttering in the breeze.

A wonderful peace descends over me. A lightness I haven't known ever before.

Epilogue

San Diego, Labor Day Weekend, 1999

To my (yet unborn) grandchild,

My dear little one, I'm not sure what sweet nickname to call you since we don't yet know if you're a boy or a girl and your ecstatic parents seem determined to keep it a surprise until you actually arrive. Not that it makes any difference one way or the other. You're going to be as cute as a bunny all the same, and we already love you more than you'll probably be able to stand it. It's just that Grandpa can't wait to cradle you in his arms, and short of that, I only wish I could visualize you better while sitting here writing to you.

Let me start this letter by saying I'd love nothing more than to stick around a while longer to welcome you into this world and watch you grow up. But that decision, my sweet child, is not entirely up to me. To be clear, I'm doing everything in my power to tilt the outcome in our favor. The Monday after I learned the fabulous news of you, I called my doctor and asked him to set me up at once for whatever course of treatment he deemed necessary to combat my lung cancer and make me well again. Kind Dr. Graham reassured me the chances of success are excellent in my current condition, but I've learned long ago that on these matters only time will tell.

So just in case I might be gone before you come to us, I want to make sure I say hello to the newest and cutest member of our clan and tell you how much Ông Nội loves you—how much I am going to miss being here with you. It's what prompted me to start this note. If on the other hand, luck is on my side and I do get to hold you at your moment of birth, this can still serve as a reminder of Grandpa's love for you, when I'm no longer around.

It will be a while before you're old enough and can read the letter for yourself, even longer still before you start pondering the great mysteries of life. Who are you? Where did you come from? How did you get here? What was it like before you? By the time such natural questions sprout up in your awakening young mind, it's most likely I will have been long gone. But it is my wish to leave you with enough information about our family history so that in your own time, if you so desire, you can piece together some of the answers for yourself. Toward this goal, my dear child, I shall make every effort to set down on paper, apart from this letter, my memory of the circumstances that brought all our destinies together and defined us as a family. For better or for worse, it is our shared story, the common thread that links and shapes all our lives. It's only appropriate that it be preserved and passed on to your parents and you.

There's one last thought I'd like to share with you before we part, something I haven't told a living soul. Let it now be our secret, between Grandpa and you.

For the longest time after my return from Việt-Nam in 1968, I struggled to make sense of my experience over there, to glean some hidden meaning from its burden of sorrows and regrets. But all that did was raise new questions and create more doubt and frustration in my mind. In the end, I simply gave up and shut the door on that part of my life.

Until you all came along.

Meeting your parents for the first time was a tremendous godsend for which I couldn't be more grateful. At my age and *with my health, it was more than just a second chance. It was my final and only chance to connect with the family I never knew I had, and to enjoy this happiest blessing so often taken for granted. And then, on top of that, imagine my astonishment and immense joy when your parents announced the wonderful surprise of you. In that amazing moment, the answer I'd been searching for all along struck me.*

Are you ready now for our secret, my little one? The answer, sweet and simple, was—you. All three of you. In the mysterious grand scheme of life, you were the real purpose, the ultimate reason why I got sent to Việt-Nam all those years ago. For it was in that land of monsoon and tragedy, the home country of your dear grandma, that our common destiny was to begin. It just takes a lifetime for the higher design to unfold, I now realize.

But I've rambled on long enough and you need a break from all this serious talk, I know.

I hope we'll get to chat face-to-face some day, and you can ask me all the questions you want then. But no matter what the future holds for us, my sweet child, I am thankful to even have this opportunity to write to you. I welcome you to our family and wish you the best of luck in pursuing and fulfilling your personal destiny. Soon, it will be your turn to write your own story.

Just know in your heart: to Ông Nội always, you're my true miracle.

Acknowledgments

Having finally reached *The End*, I thought I'd allow myself to use a cliché to describe this six-year enterprise as a labor of love, with emphasis on "labor." Many people have helped me see it to fruition, and I'm indebted to all of them. I'd like to especially thank:

Kathryn Jordan and Arlene Prunkl for their expert guidance in the craft of writing and for their fine editing; Nick Zelinger for the professional book design; Derek Murphy for the beautiful book cover.

Bob Grimes, whose unwavering support and encouragement inspired me to start, and to finish, the book; Becky Pirkle for proofreading the manuscript and making suggestions for improvement; Christy Wright, Dave and Sandy Carey, Dr. and Mrs. Peter Caldwell, Burcin and Jennie Ergun, Tom Overbaugh and Sirawat Matecrawat, and Kim Haddock for plowing through the early drafts and giving me constructive feedback.

Last but far from least, I'd like to thank my sisters Lan-Hương, Tường-Vân and my brothers Phong, Dzũng for their loving support and unabated enthusiasm throughout the project. This book is for you guys and your families.

Appendix
Glossary of military terms

AAA – Anti-aircraft artillery.

ARVN – Army of the Republic of (South) Việt-Nam, under the government of Sài-Gòn. Its soldiers fought alongside Americans.

BOQ – Bachelor Officer Quarters.

CAV – U.S. Armored Cavalry (armored personnel carriers, light or medium tanks).

Charlie – or Victor Charlie, aka VC, short for Việt-Cộng. Communist guerillas who fought against Americans. They were trained and supplied by North Việt-Nam, with the full backing of the Soviet Union and Red China.

CIDG – Civilian Irregular Defense Group. A program sponsored by the U.S. government to develop South Vietnamese irregular military units from minority populations.

CONUS – The contiguous United States.

DEROS – Date eligible for return from overseas. During the Việt-Nam War, it was the date when a serviceperson was to complete his or her one-year tour of duty.

Điện-Biên-Phủ – Site of the climactic battle between the French and the Việt-Minh communist-nationalist revolutionaries.

It culminated in a comprehensive French defeat and the signing of the 1954 Geneva Accords that divided Việt-Nam into a communist North and a democratic South.

DMZ – A demilitarized zone on the seventeenth parallel that came to form the border between North and South Việt-Nam. It was established by the Geneva Accords.

frags – Shrapnel from fragmentation grenades or other explosive devices.

fragged sortie – A sortie (combat mission) scheduled by a "frag (day-to-day operation) order".

GMO – General Medical Officer.

hooch – A rugged hut/shelter for U.S. military personnel in Việt-Nam, made of plywood and screen and shared by two or more people.

LBR – Local Base Rescue and Firefighting Team. Handling emergencies around or near the base.

MACV – U.S. Military Assistance Command, Việt-Nam. Overseeing all of the various military units in Việt-Nam.

MEDCAP – Medical Civic Action Program. Providing limited medical treatment to the local population.

NVA – North Vietnamese Army under the communist government of Hà-Nội.

SAR – Search-and-Rescue.

SOP – Standard Operating Procedure.

TDY – Temporary Duty Yonder (or Temporary Duty Assignment, TDA).

USAID – United States Agency for International Development. Administering civilian foreign aid.

Việt-Cộng – Guerilla army based in South Việt-Nam and trained and supplied by the communist North Vietnamese. Also known as VC, Victor Charlie, or just Charlie.

Made in the USA
Charleston, SC
20 April 2016